Praise for D.B. Reynolds's
STONE WARRIORS . . .

Of Damian . . .

"I have to admit, I really didn't think I would like this new series as much as I LOVE the VIA series . . . boy, was I WRONG! I loved the storyline, the camaraderie, the bantering, the humor, and most especially, Damian!!!! He is a Warrior God, as he continually and hilariously likes to remind Casey."

—*Dorsey-Swept Away by Romance*

"Witty banter, tons of action and sizzling chemistry are woven into an engaging and compelling plot that sets the tone for what promises to be a fantastic new series by this talented and very clever author."

—*Karla—Swept Away by Romance*

Of Kato . . .

"Here's a riddle for you; what's hotter than a summer heat wave? I thought you would be way ahead of me on this one. Correct, this absolutely mind bending, mind boggling, vicious, sexy down right dirty, delightful novel from Ms. Reynolds."

—*La Deetda Reads*

Of Gabriel . . .

"I definitely recommend this fabulous addition to the series. It's a great read and I can't wait for more!! 5 Vampire Warrior Stars!!!"

—*Wrath Lover Reviews*

Of Dragan . . .

"As usual DBR gives her readers a compelling, fast paced, sexy, and exciting storyline with fantastically intriguing beautiful characters. I can't wait for more!!!!!"

—*Wrath Lover Reviews*

Other Books by D. B. Reynolds

VAMPIRES IN AMERICA

Raphael * Jabril * Rajmund * Sophia
Duncan * Lucas * Aden * Vincent

Vampires in America: The Vampire Wars

Deception * Christian * Lucifer

The Cyn and Raphael Novellas

Betrayed * Hunted * Unforgiven
Compelled * Relentless * Detour

Vampires in Europe

Quinn * Lachlan * Xavier

The Stone Warriors

The Stone Warriors: Damian

The Stone Warriors: Kato

The Stone Warriors: Gabriel

The Stone Warriors: Dragan

The Stone Warriors: Nicodemus

Nicodemus

by

D. B. Reynolds

ImaJinn Books

IMAJINN

ImaJinn Books
PO BOX 300921
Memphis, TN 38130
Print ISBN: 978-1-61194-999-5

ImaJinn Books is an Imprint of BelleBooks, Inc.

ImaJinn Books was founded by Linda Kichline.

We at ImaJinn Books enjoy hearing from readers. Visit our websites
ImaJinnBooks.com
BelleBooks.com
BellBridgeBooks.com

10 9 8 7 6 5 4 3 2 1

Cover design: Debra Dixon
Interior design: Hank Smith
Photo/Art credits:
Background (manipulated) - © Mikhail Dudarev | Dreamstime.com
Man (manipulated) - © Svitlana Ponurkina | Dreamstime.com

:Lnjh:01:

Dedication

To all the readers who were with me for this Stone Warriors saga, thank you with all my heart.

I hope you enjoyed the ride.

PART ONE

Chapter One

Somewhere in the mists of time . . .

EXCITEMENT WAS like a drug in his veins as Nicodemus Katsaros stormed onto the battlefront, his stallion dancing with anticipation, the beast a weapon on four legs, trained for war from the day he'd been born. Just as Nicodemus had been. The second son of a great ruler, he'd been slated to serve as the general of the king's armies, with his older brother becoming king upon their father's death. But magic had intervened. Nico, as he was called by the four warriors who were his best friends, had been born not only with royal blood in his veins, but more importantly, he'd been born with the gift of magic.

There were others in this day and age with some level of magic, from hedge witches to great sorcerers. It was the size of the gift that mattered, the potency of the magic.

Nico's magic was initially seen as one more skill he would bring to the service of his father, the king, but that perception didn't last long. Nicodemus Katsaros wasn't just any magic user, he was the greatest sorcerer alive. By the time he was sixteen, Nico had surpassed his father and brother, and every other sovereign of his time, as both conqueror and ruler. Other sorcerers, big and small, came to challenge him, to claim the lands and people he'd already conquered. And one by one, they'd failed.

This morning's battle, with banners flying and horns blaring, would be the greatest of Nico's life, possibly the greatest in history. For this morning, he would face Sotiris Dellakos, the only sorcerer who still dared oppose him for the right to rule the known world. This day would bring the final confrontation in what had become years of fighting between them. From the first time the teenaged Nico had defeated the much older Sotiris, the two had been waging war with each other, clashing over bits of land and the men to farm it, marching back and forth across their world until there wasn't a yard's worth of dirt that hadn't been trod upon by armies and left sown with the bones of the dead.

But this day, this battle, would be different. Nico felt it in the blood surging in his veins, in the power burning in every muscle and sinew as his body responded, eager to do battle with the despised Sotiris. When the first horns sounded, he glanced left and right, sharing fierce grins with the four fighters who joined him on the line, their horses dancing with excitement, held in check by the strength of the men who rode them. These were Nico's brothers in arms, the four greatest warriors alive, drawn to his side from the four corners of the earth, pulled by his magic to this fight for the very survival of their world.

Damian, a golden blond god of war, sat perfectly still as he surveyed the enemy's forces, their placement, and arms. His military mind took in and countered every detail with the same exquisite precision that had made him an object of worship by those who fought by his side, and those whom he'd defeated, too. He'd been with Nico the longest—from childhood—and was closer than any brother by birth. Beyond Damian sat Kato, his exotic looks and black, ensorcelled blade defining him as the child of a distant land, and to those who understood such things, as the son of a powerful witch. To Nico's other side was Gabriel, perhaps the greatest fighter of the four. Tall and heavy with muscle, his arm flexed easily under a huge, double-edged blade that even Damian would have been hard-pressed to wield. His black hair was pulled into a ruthlessly tight queue and his dark eyes flashed with an eerie glow in the misty gray light of morning. And finally, beyond Gabriel, solemn and watchful, sat Dragan, goddess-blessed and unique even in a world where magic filled the very air they breathed. Muscles bunched in powerful shoulders as he kicked his feet loose of stirrups bare seconds before wings sprouted from his back to rise high over his head, wings that were leathery and taloned like those of the dragons he'd been named after. In a few seconds, the horns would call the advance. Dragan's great wings would beat the air and he would take to the skies, one of Nico's greatest weapons, and very nearly undefeatable.

The first horns sounded in unison when Nico's banner rose high. He lifted his hand, prepared to write his challenge to Sotiris on the skies above the battlefield for all to see . . . but his senses screamed a warning in the very seconds before he cast the spell. His hand dropped and his gaze sharpened when he scanned the enemy's position, looking for whatever it was that had struck his magical awareness like a blacksmith's hammer on forged steel.

He saw it then, a spell flowing over the battlefield in a massive wave of sorcerous energy, a sickly glow crawling unheeded and with no effect over Sotiris's troops, only to pick up speed when it hit the empty field between their forces. Alarms sounded in Nico's mind when he tried and failed to discern the purpose or possible effects of the spell, growing louder when the wave dipped to the ground and narrowed as it drew closer to his own forces.

Spurring his mount forward, he rode out to confront the attack—for there was no doubt as to what this was—and sent a roiling blast of his own magic to meet the sickly wave. *"Beware!"* He sent the mental warning to his four warriors, when the weapon's target became clear to him, and cast a defensive shield in the wave's path, all the while struggling to discern the nature of Sotiris's spell. The two of them had fought multiple times over the years, but nothing the bastard had cast before had *tasted* precisely like this. There was something different . . . something that wasn't *Sotiris*. It didn't make sense, but everything Nico knew of magic and sorcery, everything he'd read or learned from others, was telling him someone else had either designed or powered this weapon.

But how? There were no sorcerers left in this world who could compare to Nico and Sotiris. They'd all been defeated or killed in years past, and not only by Sotiris. Nico's thoughts were speeding like fingers flicking pages, searching for an answer. But it was already too late. The wave was nearly upon them and he couldn't destroy it, not with what he knew. His only chance was to block it, to hold the damnable thing at bay until its power drained away, used up by its own struggles to break through Nico's shield.

Abandoning his horse, he stepped back until he stood before the line of mounted warriors, then grabbed hold of his sorcery and cast the strongest, most powerful shield he'd ever devised, raising it to the same height that the encroaching energy wave had achieved in skating over Sotiris's forces. Nico had cast this shield spell enough times that even with the extra protections specific to this attack, he would still have enough power left to sustain a renewed attack of sorcery against Sotiris, and come out victorious.

Nico widened his stance when the destructive wave was only feet away, bracing body and mind for the collision. He still didn't know what this weapon was, or what it would do. He only knew he had to kill it, had to stop this unknown threat from striking his brothers.

He was the only one who could.

The energy wave stuttered when it hit his shield, and a surge of triumph had Nico throwing back his head, a shout of victory poised to roar from his throat. But his shout became a horrified cry when Sotiris's spell passed through his own as if they belonged together, as if they'd been designed by the same sorcerer. But that was impossible. Wasn't it?

Nico spun, his mind racing as he fought to comprehend what had happened, to decide what to do next, how to save his brothers. But he'd no sooner had the thought than Dragan disappeared, going from physical, to ephemeral, to wisps on the wind in the space of a breath. Nico shouted in denial and prepared to defend Gabriel, who sat next to him with rage roaring from his throat and darkening his face while he searched for an enemy that no one could see.

A moment later, Gabriel too was gone, his furious cries still filling the air as if unaware that the man who'd voiced them was gone.

"Nico." Kato's call had him turning from Gabriel's fate and racing to defend the last two of his brothers before they too were gone. Kato's dark power had risen to meet the destructive wave, and for a moment, it seemed as if the enemy's attack would falter, but then, with a final regretful glance at his leader, Kato too was gone, dissipating like fog in sunlight.

Impossible, Nico thought again, and gathered every last ounce of sorcery he possessed to defend Damian, his lifelong companion, the brother he'd wished into existence when his magic had been a fraction of what it was now. He couldn't lose Damian. Who would help him search for the others, give him strength when he faltered, and share his joy when their brothers were found and they were all together once more?

Damian jumped from his saddle with the ease of a lifelong horseman, his exceptional strategic awareness telling him his only chance was to stand shoulder to shoulder with Nico, to fuse their strengths into one against this enemy. They would face this together as they had so many other challenges, and they would defeat it. The bilious wave would have no chance against the joined power of a god of war and the world's greatest sorcerer. Nico reached out a hand to Damian, wanting the physical connection, knowing it would make their joining easier, their merged power stronger.

But all he felt was Damian's absence. He turned to stare in shock where his oldest friend had always been, and he knew fear for the first time in many years. Not since he'd been a small child at the mercy of his older brute of a brother had he felt the kind of despair that now flooded his lungs as if he was drowning. He was alone. All alone. The weight of it had his head falling forward, his chin hitting his chest. Silence surrounded him, as unnatural as the attack had been, as eerie as the disappearance of the warriors who'd been solid and *real* only minutes earlier. Were they dead? If not, where had they gone?

A laugh arched over the silent battlefield, demanding his attention.

"You stand alone, Nicodemus Katsaros. You cannot win. But come, there's no reason for these many good men to die for nothing. Release your people, and I vow they will return to their farms and towns unharmed . . . if you surrender to me."

Nico considered the offer for a moment. But no longer than that. He'd been unable to stop whatever spell Sotiris had somehow created to throw at his brother warriors, with such devastating results. But there were thousands of human lives still at stake. Not only his soldiers, but their families—women and children, and the many grandparents who were the life's blood of the towns and villages, teaching the others what they needed to know, how to survive every disaster. Including this one.

"You'll need more than one spell to defeat me and mine, you bastard," Nico gritted out. "Surrender yourself, or prepare to die." He spun and strode to his horse with more energy than he would have believed possible only minutes before, but there was a battle to fight—a battle he'd have to win if he was ever to recreate Sotiris's spell and discover what hell the bastard had condemned his brothers to.

Sotiris laughed, then flicked his fingers in a mocking salute before turning his horse and racing back to where his own troops waited.

Nico didn't linger to watch his enemy's retreat. He had mere moments to recalculate a battlefield strategy that had been worked out weeks before, as soon as this valley had been chosen, with its low, surrounding hills and flat central plain. That strategy had been refined multiple times as his scouts brought fresh intel on their enemy's preparations, and then finally this morning, once he and his brothers had seen Sotiris's final deployments for themselves.

But as with every such assessment in the years since he'd confronted Sotiris directly, the core of his strategy assumed not only *his* presence—which was a given—but the active participation of the greatest warriors alive, his brothers-in-arms. And now in the space of seconds, he somehow had to make it work without them.

His mind raced as his generals joined him to consult on the best possible strategy in the face of such an unprecedented loss. They were all experienced and battle-hardened, mostly from his own wars, and yet when he scanned the faces of the men surrounding him, he saw the dread they couldn't hide. To a man, they thought the battle was already lost. That with the four great warriors gone, defeat could be the only outcome. And they were looking to him for a miracle that would make victory possible. Seeing their surrender to whatever hope he could offer, to whatever magical weapons he could pull out of his ass to save the day . . . it exhausted him before the battle had even started.

But he wasn't fighting this battle for the generals, wasn't going to win it to ease their fears. He was fighting it for the farmers and shopkeepers who stood in ranks behind him. He was winning it for his brothers, who had to be alive somewhere in this world or another, this time or another, and waiting for him to find them.

It never occurred to him that they could already be dead. Sotiris would never have been that kind.

Too short a time later, he strode once more to his battle stallion, mounted with a single, fluid leap, and to the cheers of his men, cast the image of his banner onto the sky, where it hung over the battlefield as if rippling in the heavens. It was an easy feat for one of his power, just as it would have been for Sotiris . . . if he'd thought of it first. If the bastard did it now, everyone would know he was simply copying Nicodemus—who'd won every battle they'd ever fought before.

Today was to have been the end of conflict between them, the ultimate victory leading to peace. But that wasn't going to happen now. Nico acknowledged the truth to himself, if not to anyone else. He still intended to win. But it would be a costly victory, one paid with greater bloodshed and death than he'd thought possible. The loss of his brothers had made peace between him and Sotiris forever impossible.

Steeling himself for what was to come, determined to keep any doubts to himself, he brought his big stallion onto its hind legs, waved his sword over his head with a flourish, and led his army into battle . . . alone.

SOTIRIS SHOVED aside fighters—slamming his own men into the churned-up mud with the same disregard he showed his enemy—and strode forward to meet the only combatant who mattered. No matter how many others died during a battle, it always came down to this. One sorcerer against another, brutal magic sparking deadly and unforgiving, until one of them was dead. Or so close to it, that pride permitted a forfeit. Surrender would have been logical, and more likely to end in peace. But there'd never been any reasoning between them.

Nicodemus was covered with as much blood and dirt as his peasant soldiers. For all that the blood of a king ran in his veins alongside his magic, he'd never bothered to maintain the appearance of a great leader to match his heritage or his victories. If asked, he would have spouted some drivel about being no better than those who marched into war at his back.

What a load of shit. He didn't live in a shack, did he? Didn't eat food cooked in the same room where he slept, or marry some poor woman to birth child after child until she was worn out and died. No, Nicodemus and his four precious warriors lived like princes between wars, with the best food in their bellies, and the prettiest whores and noblewomen alike in their beds. And yet, Nicodemus's people loved him and his damn warriors, too. That fed Sotiris's temper even more than the asshole's irreverent arrogance for social custom, or his foolish disregard for how their world had worked for eons . . . how it had to *continue* working, if they were to thrive as a society. Anything else would be chaos, and would drag men of nobility and accomplishment down into the filth and disease of the common man.

Commoners served their purpose, not least that they filled the armies of powerful sorcerers like himself. Of course, there *were* no others like him in this world. That was one truth that Sotiris would prove once and for all when he finally killed Nicodemus.

It vexed him, however, that despite the success of his preemptive attack against Nicodemus's warriors, the battle had gone on longer and been much less decisive than he'd expected. He wondered if Nicodemus had yet figured out the key to the spell's success. A chuckle at his own cleverness was cut off as an eerie silence settled over the battlefield. His steps faltered when he realized that everywhere he looked, soldiers were freezing in mid-thrust, only to sink to the ground in a virtual embrace with the enemy they'd been fighting seconds earlier.

He scanned the strange tableau, seeking the source of what his senses told him was a spell of some sort. But from whom? He tilted his head to listen, searching for a sound, any sound that would give away the spellcaster. Though he already knew who it had to be. Only Nicodemus had the power to halt a full-scale battle.

Drawn by inborn magical instinct, Sotiris's gaze shot skyward to see a huge wave of magic sliding over the battlefield. It was multicolored, drifting and twisting like smoke, dipping down to skate over the ground, wrapping itself around the frozen fighters, slipping down throats and writhing around arms and legs as it swept steadily closer to where he stood waiting.

A beastly growl rose from his throat, burning as Sotiris swallowed the irritation he felt at this show of power by his enemy. It wasn't enough that this display of magic surpassed anything he could attempt in response this late in the battle. It was truly egregious that the bastard had enough magical reserves remaining to undertake such a massive spell after hours of battle against Sotiris . . . even *without* his damn warriors.

"Fucker," Sotiris cursed, and bared his teeth in a fierce grin. Let the princeling have his flashy lights in the sky. Pretty or ugly, only raw power mattered. And on this day, on this battlefield, Sotiris faced a Nicodemus who'd been weakened by a hard battle fought without his most powerful warriors, and now further drained by this useless display.

Victory would finally be his. Nicodemus would die, and Sotiris would rule.

NICO FOUGHT WITH everything he had, pouring power into his soldiers and commanders, bolstering their strength and shielding them where he could. Even so, he watched too many of his men die, their blood making the mud appear crimson as the sun rose higher. He fought with no emotion, no feeling, good or bad. His heart, already numbed by the disappearance of his brothers, had grown colder with every bloody wound, every senseless death, until true despair had begun to eat at his confidence, at the certainty that he'd done the right thing in refusing to walk away from Sotiris's challenge, to surrender and end the bloodshed without a true victory. This, all of this—the death, the ruined lives of families left behind—what good was it? What had he gained for himself, for the people he claimed to care about?

He knew the answer. Knew why he'd refused Sotiris's demand, why he'd found the strength to fight on after the loss of his brothers. *Antonia.* If he'd surrendered to Sotiris, the faithless bastard would have taken his head while he knelt in submission. And if he died, Antonia's life would be forfeit. Oh, Nico had left men behind in his tower to guard her, had given those men orders that should he fall, they were to take her and run to her mother's estate before Sotiris had enough time to attempt a takeover of Nico's castle. Not even Sotiris would attempt to seize Antonia from her mother. The political price he'd pay would be too great. And with Nico dead, Antonia was no threat to Sotiris.

His reasoning made sense, but he found himself unable to take even that small chance with her life. In the short time he'd known her, she'd become the most important person in his life. The one person whose life he simply couldn't risk. And so, he'd fought.

But now, he knew only a desperate need to end it, to stop the blood and death. The moment the rightness of that need had set in his heart, his power had spewed forth without thought. Blanketing the violence and hatred, dropping fighters and beasts alike to the muddy ground, he'd brought perfect silence to a morning that had been drenched with howls of terror and death. The quiet had been so sudden, so unexpected, that Nico had fallen to his knees, his soul utterly empty. It had taken a moment for him to understand what he was feeling. It wasn't only his soul that had shriveled to nothing. For the first time in his life, his magic was gone. Not dead, but drained to the tiniest, useless spark. And he didn't know whether to feel despair or relief.

Sinking back on his heels, he glanced up and caught sight of Sotiris still sitting on his horse, teeth gleaming white in the strange light of magic, as he grinned at the carnage all around him. Nico stared, then blinked several times, doubting the truth of his own eyes. Fucking Sotiris, who'd remained on a hill above the field for most of the battle, risking very little injury to himself, now appeared pleased by what he saw all around. Perhaps his pleasure was only that Nico had used up so much of his own strength. But Sotiris wouldn't know that. Nico's shields were so much a part of him that they demanded no additional power, and would block any attempt by Sotiris to read his energy levels.

Did Sotiris simply assume that Nico had no magic left? That he could steer his mount around the bodies, whether dead or unconscious, and eliminate Nico with a wave of his hand? Hell, the bastard didn't need to cross the field at all. Sotiris was powerful enough to kill from a distance much greater than what presently separated them. But as much as the coward might like to kill from safely across the field, his pride would never permit it. If Sotiris was going to kill Nico, he'd want to be close enough to see the realization of defeat in Nico's eyes. The smug satisfaction of that moment would feed his black soul for years.

An idea bloomed in Nico's mind, sparking something hot and visceral to life in his gut. Too many men had suffered and died to serve Sotiris's endless hatred for Nico. A hatred fed by jealousy not only for Nico's greater power and youth, but for his noble birth, as well. Sotiris's father was a landed aristocrat, far better off than the common men who farmed his fields and populated his armies. But Nico . . . ah, he was the son of a king.

And knowing that, Nico realized something he should have known long ago. There could never be a peaceful resolution to their conflict, because the jealousy that drove Sotiris was fixed in stone. But *Nico* could end it. It might well leave him a desiccated husk, without even a spark of power to rebuild, but at least the endless wars would finally be over.

Fiery rage flooded his senses, destroying everything it touched like the lava that flowed from the mountain peaks in the far north. Every muscle and sinew flexed in renewed pain as his fury burned hotter and hotter, melting the icy despair that had driven him to his knees, and igniting the spark of magic that had lived in his soul from the moment of his conception. He was sorcerer-born. His magic would not be quenched. It *could* not be.

He surged to his feet, filled with renewed purpose. Sotiris would never accept a stalemate, would never agree to a peace. He didn't care about the cost in lives and livelihood, the constant fear that gnawed at the shreds of happiness and contentment that were all too many people had left after so many years of fighting. This war was slowly destroying everything left of their world.

If Nico was to save his world, Sotiris had to die.

His power surged, bursting upward in a torrent of magic that rose once more above the battlefield, creating a protective barrier over every fighter on the field—both those waking from their unnatural sleep and the others who were still alive, but too injured to respond. Even the dead were protected by a spell that covered the field like an umbrella used by fine ladies to shelter from the sun. But this was no bit of ladies' frippery. This was the full might and power of a sorcerer in his prime, driven by loss and rage, fueled by hatred for the sorcerer sitting above the fray, his pale hands safe from the blood and guts stinking the battlefield, his grin an obscene comment on the blackness of his soul.

Well . . . no more.

With no warning to his enemy, Nico sent a deadly bolt of power arching over the field to where Sotiris was still reacting to the protective spell, fighting his horse who was bucking at the crackle of energy nipping its legs. Nico didn't know how much time he had before Sotiris realized what was happening. He knew only that his one chance for a death blow was to take Sotiris by surprise.

The bolt was perfectly calculated. Sotiris was such a bright beacon of power that he made for an excellent target. The ploy very nearly succeeded. Nico thought at first that it had, that the weapon had struck true. Ironically, it was the sheer power of the attack that saved Sotiris's life. The concussive might of the blow was so great that it caused his horse to rear. The animal nearly fell backward, knocking Sotiris from the saddle and sending him rolling in the mud.

When he regained his feet, muddied and furious, it was to send a jagged bolt of magical lightning arcing toward Nico. Unlike Sotiris, however, he was expecting the attack and deflected it automatically, while gathering power into himself for the inevitable duel that would follow.

Nico was so eager for this fight that he wanted to howl like a great beast ready for the kill. But he didn't waste the energy. "Challenge accepted, you fucking bastard," he growled, and leaping back onto his stallion, spurred the animal to the only slice of bare ground left between the two armies. All around him, soldiers fell back, dragging their injured companions with them. This was no longer a war for men to fight. It was the battle they'd all known would end the day. The two most powerful sorcerers alive would now fight, one-on-one, to decide who would rule their world.

As the distance closed between them, Nico drew energy from the protective spell and sucked it back into himself. Neither he nor Sotiris could risk a blanket attack at this point. In the heat of battle, they could well damage themselves while aiming at the other. This would be a duel of concentrated power, with close-range attacks of deadly force.

"We meet again, little princeling," Sotiris sneered.

Nico ignored the taunt. He had neither time nor inclination to bandy words. "Defend yourself," he said simply, and attacked.

The ensuing battle was brutal, with each sorcerer arrowing powerful blows that would have reduced a regular human down to the smallest measure of being. The attacks flew back and forth between them, lighting the sky with such intensity that the watching fighters had to shield their eyes or be blinded. With each new attack, deflections filled the air with the sizzling stink of something burning. The occasional blow still managed to break through, striking not only the battling sorcerers, but their horses who, battle-trained though they were, screamed in pain along with their riders.

Nico rode on the wave of his rage, fueled by the memory of his brothers shredded like ghosts and blown to . . . who the hell knew where? Sotiris was as clever as he was powerful, and lacking even the thinnest thread of compassion. What torment had he sent Nico's warriors into? What agony were they suffering even now, as he fought not only to destroy Sotiris, but to free himself to go after them.

Unfortunately, Sotiris was no weakling of an enemy. He'd lost every battle they'd fought thus far, but while his power would never match Nico's, his jealousy and greed burned nearly as hot as Nico's rage. The battle dragged on into the hottest part of the day, while the churned-up mud around them dried to a map of cracked earth, and their horses' hooves raised a fog of dust to surround them.

Nico was sweating blood beneath his leather armor and woolen tunic, his fingers slick inside the glove on his sword hand. He was struggling to keep his thoughts clear, his spells sharp. If he didn't finish the battle soon, he'd be dead . . . or defeated, which was the same thing. And then, there would be no one to search for his warriors, to discover their fates and free them from certain torment. They would be lost, forever trapped in the hell of Sotiris's making.

Driven by love for his brothers and the desperate need to undo what had been done, Nico gathered everything he had left, every ounce of magic in his veins, all the strength remaining in his body. And struck a blow far more terrible than any he'd ever conceived. The spell sped over the space between them like a cannon fired at close range, powered by the weight of Nico's hatred and desperation, and imbued with the magic of the most deadly sorcerer their world had ever known.

It struck Sotiris with the authority of an iron cudgel to the head, searing his flesh like a fire-blade as it knocked him to the ground. He screamed in agony, writhing in the dust, blinded by pain and power both.

Determined to end this, Nico leaped from his horse and strode the final few feet to his enemy's thrashing form, power already building within him for the *coup de grace*, the final blow that would end the plague that was Sotiris's existence once and for all. But his enemy wasn't defeated yet.

With a rush of displaced air, and before Nico could adapt his strike to the changing energies, a gaping tunnel opened behind Sotiris and swallowed him whole. Nico ran to follow, but both sorcerer and time portal—for that's what it was—had disappeared, as if neither had ever existed.

Nico threw back his head and roared at the heavens, furious at losing his prey, wondering what sort of gods would permit a monster like Sotiris to escape the justice he so richly deserved. Or maybe it was that the gods found amusement in the petty squabbles of such minor beings. Perhaps they were looking forward to the battles to come, knowing just as Nico did, that the war would never be over as long as both of them lived. No matter where, no matter when.

HOURS LATER, Nicodemus sat half-naked, exhausted and alone in his victory while all around him stumbled human fighters. Victors—if there was such a thing after the terrible bloodshed of the day—helped the defeated as readily as their own, guiding them to the crowded tents where healers, both magical and mundane, struggled to keep up with the end-less flow.

Victory? Nico wasn't sure it could be called such, not with Sotiris escaping in the end, and not with the price he'd paid—a price that was so much greater than anyone could know. The brothers he loved more than any on this earth were gone. One moment, they'd stood, the four strong-est, bravest, most loyal warriors a man could ask for, confident that *this* battle would finally bring the long sought-after peace to their world. That Sotiris Dellakos, an enemy Nico had been fighting for what seemed like his entire life, would finally be destroyed.

But in the end, it wasn't Sotiris who lost. It was the four warriors who'd traveled from the distant corners of the earth, who'd come at Nico's call, to fight by his side against the evil that would enslave their world. Those courageous men had been lost before the final great battle had even begun. And they would remain lost, unless Nicodemus could somehow find them and free them.

He swore that he would. That he would not rest—

A woman's scream soared over the battlefield, and he raised his head to listen. Had she been calling his name? What woman had the power to—?

"Fuck!" Vaulting onto his horse, he raced across the battlefield, through his own lines, past bloodstained tents where his medics toiled, trying to save the lives and livelihoods of those they could, making heartbreaking judgments when faced with men and women who were too far gone. Medics and wounded alike watched with tired eyes when he tore past, his own gaze on the white peaks in the distance, where his estate rested in the foothills—where he'd left Antonia behind, thinking her safer there than anywhere else.

But he'd been a fool. Sotiris had disposed of four great warriors with a single blow. Destroying one woman would be nothing to him.

It was far too long before Nicodemus slid from the horse's back while it was still loping through the gate. Too agitated to call down a spell that would let him reach her faster, to open a portal and appear by her side, he ran to his tower and climbed the stairs three at a time, shoving past staff and courtiers alike. He had no time for them or their endless questions about the battle. He had to get to her, to . . .

"Antonia!" The door slammed against the wall while he screamed her name. But he knew. He *knew*. He was too late. She was gone, just as his brothers were gone. Everyone he'd ever loved . . . gone in the blink of an eye.

History would record that he won the war. But he knew the truth. He'd lost . . . everything.

Chapter Two

ANTONIA WOKE from a nightmare that became all too real when she sat up and stared around a room where, she knew instinctively, she'd never been before. It wasn't only the room, though. Everything about it was unfamiliar, from the scents coming in through the open window, to the texture of the ceiling, and even the strange décor which appeared to be decorative paper glued to the walls. She reached automatically for her magic and found it waiting for her, but her relief at its presence was tempered not only by its relative weakness, but by its *wrongness*.

Panic threatened when she realized this wasn't her world. How had she gotten here? She didn't have the power to travel among worlds. Hell, she didn't even have the right kind of magic to travel to different places in her *own* world. Not the way Nico had, she thought, remembering when he'd taken her to the waterfall. Which meant if this was another world, another place or time, that . . .

She jumped to her feet in shock, as the nightmare flashed through her mind once more. Sotiris. Goddess, had he killed Nico? Her head spun in realization, and she fell back down to the bed. The nightmare hadn't been a dream, it was a memory. Sotiris had come for her at Nico's. She'd been sitting in the kitchen garden with the healer . . . what was her name? Magda! Yes, she and Magda had been sitting in the sunshine discussing the healing qualities of various herbs, while Antonia had been subtly *encouraging* those same herbs to grow better and stronger, to enhance their healing effects. Everyone had known the battle had already begun, and though there'd been no reports from the field yet, she'd understood that casualties would soon begin to arrive. Men and women grievously injured, some wracked with pain as they slid closer to death. These same herbs that she nudged to better effect now would help when those injured fighters came through the gates. And though Nico had ordered her to remain in his tower, she'd been set on helping in the only way she could . . . with her magic.

That was why she and Magda had been sitting in the sun magicking while Nico and too many others were putting their lives on the line, risking injury and death to stop . . .

Antonia frowned. Something had happened then. At the very moment she'd thought about the war and whom they fought against . . .

She covered her mouth against the cry that rose from her throat. Sotiris had come. One moment she'd been bathing the herbs in warm waves of her magic, and the next . . . oh Goddess. Magda had fallen with a cry, and when Antonia had turned, Sotiris had been standing there. He'd been bloodied and muddy in a way she'd never seen before, his eyes filled with madness. And he'd stared at her with such fury that she'd immediately known he'd come to kill her.

Antonia remembered rising to face him. Determined that if she was about to die, she would do it with pride that she'd finally taken a stand against his cruelty, his endless greed for *more*. More gold, more land, more farmers who starved while he filled his coffers with the fruits of their labor. And above all, more power. Sotiris's only desire was to be the greatest sorcerer in their world, the greatest sorcerer who'd ever lived. But Nicodemus had stood in his way, and though Sotiris had tried many times, through war and treachery both, to rid himself of his fellow sorcerer, he'd never succeeded.

Until Antonia had created the hexagon.

She hadn't meant to, but the fates had been playing their usual games with human lives and Antonia had stupidly followed where the magic took her, taking step after step until she'd looked down one day and truly seen what she'd created.

She'd known instantly that she could never turn the weapon over to Sotiris. She'd also known that she couldn't hide it from him. She'd worked in *his* tower, and he was far too powerful and too paranoid not to sense the development of such a formidable device on his own estate. He'd started coming by more often to check on her work. And though she'd exaggerated the problems she was having, he'd seen the potential in the hexagon and had kept track of her progress.

Her only fail-safe was that the device required priming before it would be effective. The chosen victim's blood was the crucial element in the final spell that brought the weapon to readiness. Unfortunately, Sotiris had figured that out, and once he had the device, he would no longer need her cooperation. Blood wasn't hard to come by in battle. Sotiris would need only to bribe one of Nicodemus's people, to obtain a sample of his blood, and then he'd kill both the traitor and Nico.

And turn the entire world into a nightmare of his making.

So she'd lied, telling Sotiris she was still refining the weapon, when in truth she'd been plotting a way to meet Nicodemus in person. She'd wanted to evaluate the man, beyond what she'd heard from Sotiris's constant rages. If he'd proven to be as corrupt as Sotiris, she'd have destroyed the hexagon altogether, and accepted her fate. What was one woman's life against the future of an entire world?

But Nico hadn't been corrupt. He'd been brilliant and clever, kind and generous, so beautiful, and so gods-damned powerful. Her future had been set within minutes of meeting him. She'd known then that the hexagon would be primed against Sotiris, and would ensure Nico's victory instead.

Just as she knew when she'd stared up at Sotiris in Nico's sunlit garden that something terrible had gone wrong. And she was about to die for it.

Antonia covered her eyes and cried, convinced that her Nico was dead, along with his warriors and too many others to count. And that her world, the one she'd been born to, the one that sang to her magic as if she were rooted as deeply in the soil as the oldest tree, was condemned to a pitiless future.

The door to the room she was in now opened without warning and she looked up, not bothering to hide her tears, not caring who was barging in so unceremoniously.

"Awake at last?" Sotiris's voice grated with disdain, his gaze hard when he glared at her, waiting for a response.

She didn't give him one, other than to glare back at him, and to wish her tears had dried so he wouldn't have the satisfaction of seeing her fear. "Where are we?" she asked. "What have you done?"

"What have *I* done?" he demanded, coming close enough that she could see the murder in his eyes. "I'm not the traitor in this room, you thankless bitch. I gave you magic. I taught you everything you know. *And you tried to destroy me!*" he thundered so loudly that the walls seemed to shudder with the force of it.

Antonia had said everything she needed to. She had no defense that this man would understand, much less accept. And she'd already asked the only question she needed answered. Where was she? And how could she escape the wild-eyed creature that Sotiris had become?

"Your lover is dead," he sneered. "And his damn warriors will soon wish they'd joined him." His laugh was harsh, and so viciously mean that her soul ached at the sound of it.

She didn't know whether to believe anything he said. But even if Nico wasn't dead, he might as well be. This wasn't their world. Her magic had been warning her of that from the moment she'd woken.

"You haven't answered my question," she said, putting as much steel in her voice as possible. "Where am I?"

"You're in France," he said tauntingly. "Not far from Paris."

Antonia mentally scrolled through her geography lessons, but knew she wouldn't find either of those places. "Why?" she asked.

He surprised her with a serious answer. "I grew weary of living in a world where that jester of a sorcerer is worshipped as some kind of god." He shrugged. "So I discovered how to leave. And now, here we are."

"But why am *I* here? You don't need me. And you sure as hell don't care about me."

"You think I would leave you to live happily ever after with your lover, instead?"

So, she thought, *Nico wasn't dead, after all.* She didn't voice her thought, hoping he'd reveal more. "There's very little magic in this world," she said instead. "You must realize that."

"Yes. Little magic, but fewer magic-users, and those who exist are weak. Here, I'm a fucking god."

She swallowed hard, holding back her reaction to his insane proclamation. And yet, if he could harness what magic existed here, and hoard it for himself, he *would* be like a god. And she wanted no part of it. If he thought she would be his willing assistant again, his delusions of godhood had rattled his brain.

"Don't worry," he said, chuckling, as if reading her thoughts. "I no longer require *your* services, and I wouldn't trust you if I did. No, you're here to serve out your punishment for betraying me. Everything you know, everything you are, will be gone. Your life will continue, though everyone you meet, befriend, or even love, will fade and die, leaving you alone, century after century, as your magic keeps you living long past the usual age in this world. But that won't matter, because you won't even know your own name. You'll be nothing and no one . . ." His mouth curved in a cruel smile. "Except what I choose. Your name, where you live, how you spend your days, even your memories, will be only what I decide to give you."

Antonia closed her eyes again, not granting him the sight of her fear . . . and her hatred. She couldn't fight him. Couldn't stop whatever he planned to do with her. Not yet. But her magic was rooted in the earth, and though this wasn't her world, she could feel the life of it. It was weak yet, but it would grow. And when it did, she would grow, too.

Stronger, smarter, more determined. Until he became tired of watching her simply exist. And as he tired, her magic would slowly, quietly eat away at his control over her. Until she was no longer his puppet. And then it would be her time for revenge.

Chapter Three

Five weeks later

IT TOOK NICODEMUS weeks of painstaking work, weeding out the dregs of Sotiris's spell that lingered over the ground where they'd stood before the battle, capturing the last vestiges caught in his own clothes, and on his skin. Endless hours were spent sampling the *taste* of the spell's essence, until he finally knew what had been done to his brothers. Somehow, their enemy had trapped them in the ephemeral sands of time and space, and cast them into the void.

What he still didn't know was whether Antonia had met the same cruel fate. Her scream had come *after* his defeat of Sotiris, which would seem to indicate her punishment had been different somehow. Sotiris was a heartless monster, but she'd been the bastard's closest companion for over a decade, far closer to him than anyone else. Was Sotiris so cruel that he could condemn the one person in the world who might actually have loved him to a hellish existence? Had the bastard *ever* loved her back? Or had she been nothing but a convenient path to influence, one who just happened to possess enough magic to be of use to him? Nico didn't know the answer.

He did know that discovering *what* had been done to his brothers and Antonia wasn't enough. He needed to learn *how* it had been done. If he could replicate the spell, he could find them, one by one, and do whatever it took to free them. But all these weeks later, he was no closer to finding what he needed.

Too tired to scream his frustration, or even to notice the disarray all around him, he shoved books and scrolls off the library table. He'd all but abandoned his own castle, spending day and night searching every nook and cubby of Sotiris's expansive estate, uncovering spell-sealed stillrooms and work spaces, searching libraries full of notes and diagrams, and shelves of scrolls so ancient that even Nico had been unaware of their existence. He stood now in a vast library containing what must be one of the greatest collections of sorcerous material in the world. But where there'd once been long rows of ceiling-high cases filled with neatly catalogued tomes, there now stood empty shelves surrounded by piles of half-open books and torn pages, with all semblance of order gone. It was as if storm winds had blown through the open windows and wreaked havoc with the utter disregard of nature.

Outside the room, servants and others whispered as they tiptoed past, not knowing if their Lord Sotiris was indeed dead, and if this crazed sorcerer was their new master. Or if the rumors were true, and Sotiris had fled for his life, never to return, abandoning his tower and estate, along with all the people who had lived and served him there.

Nico paid no attention to any of them, barely aware they existed, and that only because someone was providing him with regular deliveries of food and drink. The small corner of his brain that was still thinking rationally about something other than magic, was aware that those deliveries were the only reason he was able to keep going. He hadn't slept more than an hour or two at a time in longer than he could remember. His days and most of his nights were filled with the search for clues to the spell Sotiris had used to exact revenge on him. His pain, the loss of everyone he loved, was nothing compared to what those same people must be suffering.

His brothers had been trapped in stone. But what the hell did that mean? Were they dead, with only their souls remaining trapped in some random statue for all eternity? Or were they alive and aware of every minute that passed while they remained imprisoned? He didn't know which was worse. And were they cursed to remain prisoners forever? Or would they be free once the stone wore away with the ages? And how did one measure that? Gods forbid, it could be millennia before they were freed. Could they remain sane after all that time?

And what of Antonia? Everything he'd discovered thus far seemed to indicate she'd been cursed separately, differently. But unlike with his brothers, he had few details about her disappearance. There had been hints of a similar spell used against her, but the smallest variation of the spell's intent could mean so much. The great thinkers of his world insisted there were many worlds, some like theirs, some not. Which meant that while his brothers had all been sent to the same world, since they'd been cursed by the same spell and within minutes of each other, Antonia could have ended up in a completely different world. Someplace Nico might never identify, much less figure out a way to get to.

Other than his own empirical findings, he'd uncovered few clues as to either spell, but Sotiris must have left notes somewhere. He'd clearly expected to be the victor in their final battle, which meant he hadn't counted on the need for such a hasty exit. Besides, not even Sotiris was good enough, intelligent enough, to keep every nuance and component of every spell in his head. Virtually immortal, sorcerers lived a very long time. They required accurate records of their research, of the spells they cast, details of successes and failures alike.

Even if Nico was unable to locate the specific spell his enemy had used, he could compile a close facsimile if he knew which constructs had been used, which specific ingredients were included, or if Sotiris had made use of any sorcerous precedents.

"My lord."

It took Nico a moment to register that someone had spoken to him, and even longer to recognize the voice, and to remember that he'd actually summoned this person. The one thing he knew for certain about this disaster—at least insofar as his warriors were concerned—was that he'd been betrayed. His brothers had been relegated to a living hell because someone they'd all trusted had violated their sworn oaths of loyalty. Nico didn't yet know the specifics, or what service the traitor had performed for Sotiris, but he'd caught a brief *scent* before the spell had completed its task, and that scent had been one he recognized. It was painful to accept that a man Nico had known most of his life, a man he'd counted as a friend, could have forsworn himself so readily.

Schooling his expression, he turned to greet the traitor. "Antioch." He permitted a trace of relief to enter his voice when he said the manservant's name, wanting him to believe that his rightful lord was pleased to see him alive and well. Nico *was* pleased, though Antioch soon wouldn't be.

"Lord Nicodemus." Antioch's voice trailed off as he looked around the wreck of what once had been an orderly library. "You sent for me, my lord?"

A spark of renewed energy had Nico straightening to his full height, mind clear and focused on this one thing, this one man. Had Antioch only known about the rage fueling his master's renewed alertness, he'd have been running for his life. But it was too late for that now. *Far* too late.

Nico smiled. "I've made a bit of a mess here, I'm afraid," he said, raising his hands in a helpless gesture. "I got caught up in my search and well . . . . It's a fine collection, but I'm going to need help putting it back to order. Else it will be useless in the future."

He gave the traitor an inquiring glance, but since there'd been no question, the man responded with only a weak smile.

"Given the specialized knowledge required," Nico continued, "the compensation will be significant. And as it is likely to consume some number of weeks, it will be a job well worth taking on. I was hoping to find someone on Sotiris's staff with knowledge of the collection's previous order, and thought perhaps you could query the servants, and locate at least one person with some familiarity—"

"I would be pleased to undertake the task for you, my lord," Antioch offered eagerly.

Nico eyed him quizzically. "I wasn't aware you had ever worked for Sotiris or his family."

The manservant's face flushed with heat, and for the first time, he appeared uneasy. Blinking repeatedly, he cast his gaze around the room, as if searching for the right words to say. "I never . . . that is, I was not a servant for Lord Sotiris or his family. I was thinking more of my familiarity with your own library and thought perhaps—"

"So you've never been in this room before?"

The man was struggling to breathe, panting as if overcome with some emotion. That would be fear, if he retained an ounce of intellect. "My lord, I—"

"Be very careful of your next words, Antioch. Should you utter a single syllable of justification for what you did, your death will be a thousand times more painful."

"My *death*? My lord, I don't—"

"Feigned ignorance will be similarly painful." Nico's words were deep and commanding, the voice he used on the battlefield to issue commands . . . or cast spells.

Antioch dropped to his knees, sobbing openly. "Forgive me, my lord. I didn't know—" Nico's hand flashed and the manservant screamed.

"I did warn you that pretending ignorance would be punished. There can be no reason, no pretense, as to your knowledge of Sotiris's intent in persuading you to betray not only myself as your sworn lord, but the four honorable warriors who counted you as a friend, who risked their own lives to save you and your family more than once. What did Sotiris pay you, Antioch? How little was your honor worth?"

"My lord, please—"

"How much?" Nicodemus demanded. Not because he cared about the amount . . . or perhaps he did. Maybe he needed to know the price of betrayal for a man who'd been with Nico since he'd been fourteen years old and establishing his own first household. A man who'd been more than trusted by the four warriors who were Nico's brothers. Antioch had celebrated victories with them, had shared drink and meals with them. How much was such a friendship worth?

"Land," Antioch said in a barely heard whisper. "A farm for my family . . . my grans, my parents, a future of freedom for my children."

"Tell me then, did Sotiris pause, as he ran for his pathetic life, to deliver the price he promised you? Did he provide a grant to the farm where your family can live out their days free of the onerous service demanded by myself and my warriors?"

"My lord, no, you were never—"

"Answer the question!" Nico bellowed.

"No," Antioch whispered. "I was to receive the land grant after his victory."

"So you're not simply a traitor. You're a fool."

"Please, my lord, my family—"

"Will receive your death benefit."

The servant shrieked as heat bloomed low on his tunic and grew, consuming the fabric as if fire were eating its way out of his gut. The tunic turned to ash as he screamed, as he rolled on the floor in agony, being slowly consumed by a fire that didn't touch a single piece of the paper or parchment in the room, though the man himself was enveloped head to foot.

Nico watched dispassionately, uncaring of the servants who scurried past outside, of their frightened looks or gasps of fear. He felt nothing while the tower grew silent, while even the horrific screams of the traitor failed to pierce his soul. He simply stood and watched until there was nothing left of a man who no longer existed in this world, a man whose family would soon forget he'd ever been a part of their lives. Nico would make sure of it.

He stood motionless staring at the black stain of ash on the floor, until the light faded outside the window, leaving him in total darkness. He should have been celebrating with his brothers tonight, rejoicing that their long campaign against Sotiris was over. He should have been bidding his warriors a fair night with the women bouncing on their knees, and gone to his own tower, to the woman waiting for him there, the woman he would spend the rest of his life with.

But a lone traitor had taken all of that away from him.

There was no joy left in this world for Nico. He wanted to escape, much as Sotiris had already done. But his research wasn't complete yet. He had to remain long enough to locate Sotiris's most private records.

Five lives depended on it. Six, if he included his own, which would be worthless if he failed to rescue his friends and the woman he loved. The woman he would always love, no matter how long he lived, or how long it took him to find her.

Shoving to his feet, he cast a light spell and glanced around the wrecked library. The answers he sought weren't in this room. It was time to try another part of the estate, another spelled workroom or library. He spied a tray of fresh food on the floor outside the door. It had probably been left by some unfortunate maid, who'd had the bad luck to be delivering his meal on the cusp of Antioch's punishment. He was sorry for the woman, but wished he could bring the treacherous manservant back to life and kill him all over again.

Reaching for the tray, he slapped together some bread and meat, and carrying it in one hand, gripped the flagon of ale in another and started down the hall. There was a lady's tower at the far end of this wing. He'd been told early on, before he began to act sufficiently deranged that the servants had avoided him, that the tower had been used by Sotiris's mother when she visited with her various ladies in waiting, because the topmost room was warm and bright, no matter the season.

Alternating bites of food with gulps of ale, uncaring that he was leaving as much of both in his wake as down his throat, he reached the twisting stairs at almost the same moment he completed his meal. Setting the now-empty flagon on a stone sill, he brushed off his hands, marshalled his considerable intellect into a mindset that suited his abilities and goal, and started up the stairs.

Halfway to the top, he knew he'd been told wrong. This was no ladies' sewing solarium. He hadn't passed a single room or closed door while ascending the winding stairs, and had encountered only the occasional small window which provided the bare minimum of light required to navigate, especially given there were no unlit torches along the walls, or even brackets for such. He thought back to his approach to this estate several weeks before and knew he'd seen not only multiple windows on this tower, but more than one balcony. *A concealment spell?* he wondered. A veil to make the tower appear to be something it wasn't?

Two turns of the stairway later, he caught a familiar scent. It was an herb that many magic-users kept on hand, one that he himself used frequently to stabilize potions. Two more twists of the stairs and his skin prickled at the touch of a spell that stretched across the stairs' passageway, giving the appearance of a stone wall and an end to the stairs' upward progress. It was well-done, but it had never been designed to fool someone whose power surpassed Sotiris's own.

Nico walked through the spell's fabric and stopped to study what he found there. Glyphs filled the twisting walls all around. Defensive wards overwrote what looked like . . . progress notes. It was as if whoever had created the wards had used the walls as a canvas of sorts first. Some of the spells were basic, almost childlike, but as he climbed, they grew more sophisticated and complex. None of them were quite complete, as if the writer had known exactly what he was doing and had left off the final component on purpose. Though whether it was to conceal it from others, or to prevent the spell from going active, he didn't know. What he *did* know was that the magic-user who'd done all of this had been both brilliant and powerful.

Sotiris. The name whispered in his thoughts. And though he was reluctant to acknowledge his enemy's skill, he wasn't so foolish as to deny either Sotiris's ability or intellect.

He wanted to rush up the remaining stairs and discover what lay at the top of this carefully camouflaged and protected tower. But he forced himself to go slowly, to consider the writing on the walls, and what it might mean for an unwelcome intruder. As he studied the glyphs, in particular, he was increasingly concerned over what he found. These were symbols more than words, though they did comprise an alphabet of sorts. One that Nico was familiar with, although not so familiar as Kato. These were the words of a long-forgotten tribe of witches who'd been driven out of this part of the world many generations before Nico had been born. In fact, the Dark Witch, who was so infamous that she had no other name, and who happened to be Kato's mother, was almost certainly a descendant of those same witches.

Nico had seen enough of Kato's spell work to recognize the alphabet. Time and distance had altered the glyphs somewhat, but not so much that there was any question of their origin. A renewed pang of loss stabbed his heart at this reminder of his lost brother. Kato could have deciphered the spells in an instant. But Kato wasn't standing in this stairwell. It was up to Nico.

Sinking to the hard stone floor, he settled into a meditative position and began deciphering the various glyphs and messages, his mind working at a speed few others could match. It was a speed that would exhaust him soon enough, and he'd have to sleep, and eat again. But that wouldn't stop him. He'd sit there however long understanding required.

SOMETIME LATER, he opened his eyes to total darkness. Not even the faint light of the rare few windows lit the space around him. A bare thought later, and a sturdy flame—like that of several thick candles—lit the space. A cold food tray sat on the table nearby—either Sotiris's cook preferred Nico's company and continued to feed him, in hopes that he'd stay, or some of his own staff had arrived to check on the welfare of their master. Picking up a small pitcher, he took a long draught of wine, then stood and brushed off his clothes. He needed a bath. The thought made him pause. This was the first time since he'd arrived in this place that he'd considered the state of his body. A moment later, he understood why.

However long he'd already spent working on translating the walls of this secretive tower, his unconscious mind knew before he made the connection that what he sought was behind the concealed door at the top of the tower. Not only that, but he knew how to safely access that room, and what to look for.

Wasting no time, he climbed the final few stairs and placed his hands on what appeared to be a solid wall, as covered with writing as all the others. Concentrating more than was probably necessary, but unwilling to risk an error that might shut him out forever, Nico pictured the necessary glyphs in his mind, added a careful measure of his power . . . and nearly fell on his face when the wall in front of him disappeared in a cloud of dust that smelled of magic, herbs, and old paper.

This was what he'd been searching for—Sotiris's *sanctum sanctorum*. The place where he'd done his most important work, where he'd crafted his own spells, the one room above all others that he would consider *his* alone. Hope soared for a brief, brilliant moment, before reality doused its spark. He'd found the room, but now he had to find the spell. It could be anywhere, anything—a magicked scroll with the necessary words. A device that waited only for one final ingredient before bursting forth with whatever sorcerous energy would accomplish its goal. Nico's task was complicated by the fact that every sorcerer, especially those as powerful as Sotiris, had their own lexicon, their own method of powering their magic for use.

It took too many more days and sleepless nights, but Nico didn't give up. He'd have remained in that room for years if that's what it took. As it was, he had no idea how much time had passed when he finally rested his head against the wall and closed his eyes, overcome with emotion. He'd done it. He knew what Sotiris had done, and how he'd done it. And knowing that, he wished he'd kept the traitor Antioch alive, so he could make the bastard pay for eternity. His warriors would live a nightmare existence—never dying, aware of the passage of time, of people, and places. But never able to interact with anyone, never able to alert anyone to the horror of their imprisonment. And none of that would have worked without the traitor's help.

Tears flooded Nico's eyes and poured down his cheeks to soak his tunic. He made no effort to stop them, too tired and disheartened to try. He would get up soon, work his own version of Sotiris's spell. He couldn't follow his brothers. He didn't know where they'd gone, because Sotiris hadn't cared. He'd tossed them into the maelstrom with no more concern than the winter winds gave an individual snowflake.

No, he couldn't follow his warriors, but he could follow Sotiris. And knowing what he now did about Sotiris's spell and what had powered it, Nico was confident that the four warriors would at least have landed in the same world as the one Sotiris had escaped to. The bastard was too cruel to permit the warriors to suffer with no witness. He'd want to locate them, wherever they'd landed. Not to free them—Sotiris would never be that kind. No, he would locate Nico's brothers one by one, then collect them like trophies, so he could taunt them in their captivity.

Given the four warriors' physical proximity and the fact they'd all been taken within minutes of each other, Nico believed they would not only land in the same world, but would do so close enough in time as to make no real difference. He couldn't offer any assurances, even to himself, that he was correct in his assumptions. But he believed he was right, and the only sorcerer who could have confirmed his suppositions was the same bastard who'd condemned them to their living prisons.

There was no one else in his world whom he could consult for a second opinion. He was the only one with the skill and knowledge to decipher Sotiris's spell. But even if another sorcerer with the necessary skill had existed, Nico would have been hard-pressed to trust them.

There was only one magic user he would have trusted that much. And she was gone.

His mind conjured up a picture of Antonia. Beautiful Antonia, whose magic contrasted so much with his own that he'd feared at first they could never be close. Where his was a force of raw power, of war and conquest, Antonia's magic had its roots in the earth itself. She nurtured and healed, where he wounded and destroyed. Her inner sanctum, the place she sought out when she needed to restore the balance of her soul, was warm with the scent of fertile earth and growing things, filled with misty air that somehow soothed even his battle-roughened soul.

She was a power unto herself. Not a sorcerer as such, although her magic was amazingly strong. But she was more than the sum of her magic. She was the most courageous woman he'd ever met, something she'd demonstrated over and over again. Had she been with him now, she'd have risked anything, including her own life, to help him find his warriors. And while she wasn't powerful enough to conjure the spell necessary to follow them, she'd have surpassed Nico himself when it came to researching and translating Sotiris's notes.

She'd also have known instinctively what steps Sotiris would have taken to achieve his deadly revenge. Having drawn his attention at a young age, she'd eventually proven to be so apt a student that he'd brought her to his tower to study, and she'd finally ended up collaborating with the bastard.

At least, until she'd met Nicodemus.

Chapter Four

Two months before the battle

NICODEMUS LIFTED his face to the warm sunlight pouring through the open window, before bending his attention once more to the scroll spread open across his desk. He was taking advantage of a rare break in the hostilities with Sotiris to enhance his knowledge of ancient spells that had been forgotten or discarded, but which he might improve for use in the continuing war. He could say honestly that he'd yet to find record of a sorcerer who was his equal, dead or alive. Sotiris believed himself to be Nico's match at worst, and superior at best. But the continuing conflict between them—with Nico steadily winning and expanding the breadth of territory he claimed as his own—told the truth of their relative strength. But Sotiris was persistent, if nothing else, while Nico would have been happy to walk away. He had no grand ambition to rule the world and was content with what he currently held. But Sotiris was a cruel overlord who refused to change, and who, moreover, had repeatedly rebuffed all attempts at a peaceful resolution between them. And so, they fought endlessly, and would probably continue to do so until one of them was dead.

Nico lifted a flagon of ale, intending to wet his throat, when the soft scuff of a footfall on the stone stairs made him set down his drink and turn, a defensive spell on the tips of his fingers. His servants had standing orders never to climb those stairs, and his four warriors would never have stepped so softly.

He was on his feet, eyes focused on the final turn of stair visible through the open door, when the very last person he'd have expected came around the curve and, seeing his martial pose, went perfectly still.

"Lord Nicodemus."

He'd never heard her voice before, and was surprised to find it as melodious as the morning birdsong outside his bedroom window. He lifted his gaze from the automatic perusal of her feminine form and caught the slight twinkle of amusement in her pale gray eyes.

"Lady Antonia." He managed to utter her name without embarrassing himself, and wondered what had overtaken him. He did not become flustered in the presence of even the most beautiful women. But this one, who was lovely enough, but not the equal of some, had him as tongue-tied as a raw youth. More importantly, she belonged to Sotiris, which surely made her an enemy. For all that she never appeared on the battlefield, it was well known that she had significant power, and was particularly skilled at both conjuring and casting spells.

Dark lashes fell demurely over those pale eyes as she stepped into the room, and when she looked up again, all traces of humor were gone, hidden behind a mask of polite perfection. "Forgive me for intruding, my lord. I would not have done so, if the situation were not—" She hesitated before choosing her next word. "—critical."

Intrigued enough that his unusual first reaction to her presence fell away, Nico swept his arm toward the small, sunlit seating area, which was much neater than the rest of the room, solely because he never used it. "Sit, my lady. I have ale, but I can ring for tea, if you'd—"

She laughed, and his heart seemed to pulse harder against his chest for a moment. By all the gods in heaven and hell, how had Sotiris managed to hold on to such a light spirit for so many years? And what was she doing here? Now?

"I am not so delicate that I don't enjoy a fine ale, my lord."

At his charming best—which was damn good—Nico smiled and filled another flagon, giving her the same full measure as he now poured for himself. He delivered hers with a courtly bow, before sitting in the chair across from her and waiting politely until after she'd taken a sip to ask the obvious. "My tower is always open to a lovely woman, my lady. Though it is rare that one has sufficient magic to make it this far without mishap."

"You flatter me, my lord. I am more than aware of your own power and have no doubt that you permitted me to approach you."

It wasn't true, but he wasn't going to admit it. He was intrigued, however, because he was aware of *her* power, too. And she *didn't* have either the strength, or the right kind of magic, to approach him without notice, much less to access his most private tower. Though he doubted she'd have been able to cross the room's threshold without serious injury to herself, had he not invited her inside.

He remained silent, waiting for her to explain her reasons for being there, sipping his ale as if her visit was nothing unusual.

She shot him a quick glance, then another, before a sigh offered her surrender to their unspoken test of wills. "May I speak frankly, Lord

Nicodemus? And with assurances that this conversation will not reach my lord Sotiris's ears?"

Nico cocked his head curiously. "I can assure you for *my* part, Lady Antonia."

"That will do, since I value my life too much to whisper a single word of it myself."

He came alert. "If you are in danger, my lady—"

She waved one delicate hand. "Nothing so drastic. Not yet, and not ever, if you hold to your assurance."

"I give you my word, on my honor."

She met his gaze steadily, as if looking into his soul. "And I have heard that you are that rare being . . . an honorable man of power and title."

Nico dipped his head slightly, acknowledging the compliment, but held to his patience, waiting for her to begin.

"I had *not* heard," she said tartly, "that you were a man of such patience."

It was his turn to laugh. "My mother will be pleased that you think so. What brings you here, my lady?"

"Save your breath and time. Call me Antonia," she said impatiently, though she was nobly born and due the courtly courtesy.

"And I am Nico," he said, too charmed to tease her any further.

"Nico," she repeated, as if tasting the name. "I had wondered if your family shortened the name any. Sotiris never calls you anything but Nicodemus. When he's being polite, that is."

"Which brings us to my surprise at finding you on my doorstep."

"Yes." She sobered instantly, and he regretted the loss. "This war has killed so many, and left so many others broken. Widowed, orphaned, their lands devastated for generations to come, which will only leave more dead from starvation and disease."

He didn't know what to say to that. She surely knew that the war only continued because Sotiris refused to agree to a peace.

"I have something for you," she said, the words tumbling out as if she feared they wouldn't be spoken otherwise.

Alarm spiked, and he did a quick scan of her person, fearing she'd concealed a deadly weapon from him and now planned to set it off, killing both of them in the process. She hadn't struck him as a woman planning her own death, but it wouldn't be the first time that a loyal person suicided to protect their lord.

Her eyes widened when she sensed the scan, which he'd made no effort to conceal. "No," she said urgently. "That is not . . . I would never do such a thing."

He shrugged. "I don't know you, Antonia. I do, however, know Sotiris quite well. He would sacrifice anyone, even you."

She dipped her head almost shamefully, as if Sotiris's evil was her own. "I am not he. Nor do I share his every thought or intent. Which is why I'm here, instead of there."

"Speak plainly."

"Yes, it will be best if I do so. I do have something to show you, but because I knew I would not make it this close to you if I had it with me, I concealed it in the stables along with my horse and carriage."

Nico studied her a long moment. He sensed no deception in her, but no fear either. "Before I agree to approach this . . . *thing*," he insisted, "you will have to speak plainer."

The glance she gave him was full of impatience, but had she thought he'd simply go along meekly to whatever death she had planned for him? And if his death wasn't the goal, then surely she would be gratified rather than irritated by his distrust. He was only trying to keep himself alive.

She sighed deeply. "I will state it as plainly as I can then, my lord. I have in my carriage a weapon so powerful that when deployed, it will weaken its target to such an extent that victory will be yours."

"And why would you give it to me?"

"I told you," she snapped, then closed her eyes to compose herself. "Forgive my impatience. I've taken a huge risk in simply coming here, much less discussing this with you. And that's on top of the months I've spent designing it, testing it to the smallest extent possible, and fearing for my own life with every step. I cannot be away from Sotiris's tower for too long. He will note my absence. And don't think for one moment that he has no spies in your court. If I am seen by one of them, and my visit reported back to him, he will eliminate me without a thought."

Nico wanted to doubt her statement of Sotiris's vengeance, but couldn't. She brought allies to the sorcerer's military efforts through her mother's family, but that same family wasn't so powerful that Sotiris would hesitate to alienate them. Not if Antonia tried to kill him. He stood. "Very well, my lady. Let us visit the stables, then."

STANDING IN A stall, the words of a defensive spell on his lips, Nico watched as Antonia finished unwrapping the *thing*, which still had no other name or description. But the power he sensed as the wrappings fell away was significant enough to have him taking an automatic step back, even as his fingers began to sizzle with power.

She gave him a quick, startled glance before finishing with the leather wrapping, obviously having sensed his power build-up. "Nico?"

"No offense intended, my lady. But that object carries a heavy signature."

"It does indeed, which is why it works. Shall I continue?"

They were standing in the stable's carriage stall, which while heavily used in winter, was presently empty of any except Antonia's small rig. And that was only because she'd requested that it be parked inside. She hadn't needed a reason for her request, because she hadn't been asked. Her appearance and carriage were enough to establish her noble standing, and that, in turn, was enough to have servants going along with whatever she wanted. Short of visible murderous intent, Nico supposed. He hoped that was true anyway.

A quick scan of their surroundings, augmented by his magic, told him no one was within hearing range, inside the stable or out. He held his hand open, palm up, in a gesture for her to continue. "Please."

That didn't mean he assumed it was safe, however. The defensive spell he'd prepared required only a twitch of his finger to become active.

Antonia held the object in one palm while she lifted a final, dark blue silk covering to reveal . . . a rock. It was not what he'd expected, but then magical devices rarely looked like what they were or could do. In fact, it was far more usual for the design to conceal or obfuscate the device's intent by making it resemble something quite ordinary. In this case, the rock was bigger than Antonia's hand. She didn't appear to be expending any particular effort to hold it out for his inspection, however, which meant it probably wasn't heavy. It had a roughly hexagonal shape that appeared to be natural, since he could see no visible signs of it having been chiseled. The surface was also rough and weathered in a way that told him the stone most likely wasn't a particularly dense material.

But for all its ordinary appearance, there was nothing ordinary about it. This was a powerful weapon in the right hands. The question was . . . whose hands? And to what purpose?

Nico opened his senses a fraction wider and immediately felt the device pulling at him. Or more like tasting . . . and rejecting him. He frowned and, glancing up, found Antonia closely observing his reaction.

"You feel it," she stated.

He regarded her a moment longer before saying, "This weapon is targeted, but not at me. Who then?"

She nodded and started to re-wrap it with the silk, but then glanced up in a silent request for permission to do so. Or rather, to ascertain that he had no objection, since he doubted she needed permission from him for anything.

"Its target hasn't been selected yet. It must be primed with a bit of the target's blood first."

"What will it do once primed?" he asked.

"Draw away a magic-user's power very quickly, even a sorcerer's. A trickle at first, but then a flood, until there is nothing left."

Nico stared at her in shock. "Is it permanent?"

"No, the effect will hold as long as the target is in range. And once he, or she, moves out of range, it will take days—or longer, depending on the target—for a full recovery. The more powerful the target, the faster the recovery, obviously.

"Why show this to me? You're Sotiris's—"

"I have my reasons. Perhaps I simply require a test subject."

Unsatisfied, yet unworried, he persisted. "But why me, specifically? Any other sorcerer would have done as well if all you want is a test. Sotiris and I are sworn enemies. How do you know I won't use it to eliminate him and establish an empire of my own?"

"I don't spend every hour in my workroom, crafting spells and counter-spells," she replied tartly. "I wasn't raised to be a porcelain doll sitting on a shelf until she is invited to dance. My mother is a strong woman who rules her own keep. My father petitioned *her* for the marriage, not the other way around."

"And yet, here you stand, so she obviously granted his petition."

She chuckled. "One would hope that's true, for my mother's honor, if nothing else. But such matters are usually judged on the degree to which it benefits the two houses. Alliances can be useful."

"And Sotiris? Did your mother find *him* a useful alliance?"

"She can barely tolerate being in the same room with him, but does so for my sake. Once my magic ability revealed itself, I required training not only to use my gift, but to ensure that in my ignorance, I didn't harm myself or others unintentionally. And there was no one else in my mother's court who had the talent or skill to teach me."

"And yet, though you clearly have learned enough to continue on your own, and have such doubts that you would share this weapon with *me*, you remain with him." The observation demanded a response, but he had a good idea of what she would say.

Antonia shrugged gracefully. "My mother and I are close, and I am a sorcerer, even if not one as powerful as you or Sotiris. Mother and I communicate often, and she finds my reports useful."

He chuckled. "So you're her spy."

Another graceful shrug that offered no apology for the truth.

"Should you decide to turn this very powerful device over to me," he reminded her, "it will no longer be safe for you to remain in his lands, much less in his tower."

"Of course," she agreed. "It had been my plan, in any event, to depart immediately for my mother's keep. Unfortunately—"

"Ha! Now we get to it."

She scowled. "There is no 'get to it.' Sotiris is no fool. He is always aware of what I am working on, and has full access to my workroom, which is in *his* tower. You detected the power of the device immediately. You also sensed that it represented no threat to you and dismissed it. Do you believe Sotiris's reaction would be the same?"

"No."

"No," she repeated sharply. "He already knows of its intent, though he does not yet realize that it is complete and waits only to be primed. He assumes as you did, that I created it for his use, first of all, against you. If he ever discovered that I intended to prime it *against* him, he would seize it, and my life would be forfeit. He is a suspicious and unforgiving man, and would assume that if permitted to live, I would eventually create a second device for you or another of his enemies."

She paused to inhale a calming breath before continuing. "I have no desire to die, my lord," she said softly, her back to him while she re-wrapped the hexagonal stone and placed it in a wooden casket in the carriage. "Unfortunately, he'll realize soon enough that the device is gone and will ask about it." She sighed, then finally turned to face Nico and looked up to meet his eyes. "I have no power compared to his, no defenses against him," she said quietly. "If he becomes suspicious, he will seize the thoughts from my mind, and I will be helpless to stop him. He'll know everything, and I will be dead."

Nico frowned. "I am no murderer of innocents to permit you to sacrifice your life for nothing. I've seen the damn thing and sensed its potential, and I have no reason to doubt you. If it's not yet primed, you should return it to your workroom, if you can do so safely. Is that still possible? Rest assured that I have no intention of donating blood to its completion. I'm fully aware that blood holds power. I employ extensive precautions against mine being used against me."

ANTONIA SIGHED again, but long and slow this time, a sigh of relief that Nicodemus understood her dilemma and didn't plan to sacrifice her to ensure his own victory. "I can return it safely," she replied. "And I will." She hesitated over whether to tell him what was on her mind, but decided he had to know her plans for the device. His reaction might be very telling and affect her decision, and the hexagon's future. "You must understand, Nico, that my intent was never to create such a deadly device. My magic prefers creation, not destruction. But now that the damnable thing exists, its morality and use are mine to determine. Should it be used at all? And if so, who among us is wise enough to use it well? I would not want that responsibility, and yet whatever action I take could place it in the wrong hands."

"Antonia."

She looked up in surprise at his gentle, almost sorrowful tone. "My lord?"

"Nico," he corrected softly, then continued, "If you believe that its destruction is your only answer, then I will do everything in my power to assist you in that. If you want to consult the great thinkers of our world, dead or alive, I will make that possible. The dead ones, obviously, only in their writings, since necromancy has never been a talent of mine," he added with a rakish grin.

Damn the gods, but this man was appealing. Not as a sorcerer, but as a *man*. She was certain she'd never met anyone more charming and likeable. She sighed, and cursed the fate that would bring him to her in this dangerous time and under these impossible circumstances.

"And I would welcome your thoughts. But *you* must understand that today's visit was possible only because Sotiris is traveling. It is rare that he does so, however, and another such trip is unlikely."

A slightly surprised smile tipped his lips, even as his golden-brown gaze studied her with such intensity and for so long that she had to fight against the urge to squirm under his scrutiny. He was no longer a powerful sorcerer evaluating a useful tool. He was a man appraising a woman. And she'd had enough men look at her that way to know the difference. Granted most of those men hadn't been nearly as striking as this one. She'd heard tell of his beauty and assumed it was exaggerated, or a magical seeming he'd created with a tiny sliver of his extraordinary power. But standing this close to him, surrounded by his scent, and pinned under the focus of those eyes, she knew the rumors hadn't done him justice. He was easily the most handsome man she'd ever seen. *And* the most fascinating she'd ever met.

It was his power. To her eyes, it surrounded him with a nimbus of color that seemed to change with his mood. It had sparked like lightning earlier, when he'd been very nearly angry with distrust of her. He must light up the sky when he waged war, she thought, and wondered if his power brought storms over the battlefield, with the heavens themselves responding to the release of his magic. She would have liked to see that. Would have liked to see Sotiris brought low by the same magic, even if it meant using the damn device.

She might yet live to see it, if the damn hexagon didn't cause her death. The moment she'd understood what her magic had created, she'd resigned herself to the possibility of an untimely demise. She'd told Nico she didn't want to die. And, goddess, she did *not*. But if it meant removing Sotiris from the world, using what power she'd been born with—power that some said was, in fact, a *gift* from the goddess herself—did she not have a moral obligation to sacrifice one life—her own—to save so many others? But was she wise enough to make such momentous decisions?

Sotiris wouldn't hesitate to use such power. But unlike this beautiful man before her, Sotiris had not an ounce of humility, nor the desire for knowledge beyond that which furthered his own goals. But she'd scanned what she could see of the rows of books and scrolls in Nico's tower room. The majority had dealt with magic and sorcery, including those written by great sorcerers of the past, which was only natural. But there'd also been histories of their world, stories that went beyond the lives of only the few sorcerers who'd lived there. Another entire section of shelves had been tomes written by the great philosophers and ex-plorers, not only those long dead, but the ones still alive and teaching.

She smiled privately, remembering the few collections of poetry she'd seen on those shelves, and wondered if he read those to improve his appeal to women ... of all stations. She had a feeling Lord Nicodemus didn't limit his charms to proper ladies only. Although honesty had her admitting, to herself at least, that he would hardly require poetry to win over anyone of the female persuasion.

As if he knew what she'd been thinking, he smiled, his eyes crink-ling while they seemed to dance with amusement. "How much freedom do you have to leave Sotiris's tower?" he asked. "How closely does he monitor your comings and goings?"

"I am mostly left alone, free to do as I wish, though I have no doubt that his guards monitor my movements. But it's also true that he could call for me at any moment, and when he does, I must be there to respond. Otherwise, he will become curious, or more likely suspicious, and seek me out by whatever means necessary."

"What of this afternoon, then? Are you certain his travel was genuine, and not a ploy to catch you consorting with his enemy?" He said that last playfully, but his expressive eyes told her he was serious and perhaps even concerned for her safety.

"Sotiris greatly prefers never to travel other than what is required by his various wars. The current journey was long-planned, a consultation with a useful ally who resides at some far-flung distance, and who never leaves his tower. Sotiris trusts the man, or so he claims. I don't believe he trusts anyone. It's more likely he wants to take advantage of some unusual skill the man possesses, nothing else."

"I see. Well, then, do you ride?"

She smiled in surprise. "Yes, of course. Since before I could walk. My mother is a superb horsewoman."

"As am I. Or rather, horseman, which is obvious, one hopes."

As if there was any doubt, she thought wryly, but kept the observation to herself. He hardly needed fresh compliments to boost his ego.

"Your stable," he said, "or rather Sotiris's I suppose, is about to acquire a new trainer. He will bring fresh stock with him, and upon meeting your charming self and learning of your skill as a horsewoman, will suggest a new mount among his stock for your personal use."

"How very gentlemanly of him."

"Indeed. Even more so when he insists on riding out with you to ensure your safety, until you are fully comfortable with the new horse."

"That, good sir, will cause a scandal if this new trainer looks like you."

"You're too kind."

Bullshit, she thought. And yet, she was charmed. There was no conceit in his banter. He simply seemed to like engaging with her. And probably every other woman, too. But still, she could enjoy his company while she had it.

"You may be assured, Lady Antonia, that my appearance will present no threat to your honor. Quite the opposite, in fact. I have no wish to draw attention to myself, especially not within the confines of Sotiris's estate."

"That would be wise," she agreed. "When do you anticipate this new trainer arriving, and how will I ensure that we meet?"

"I will arrive early tomorrow morning," he said, a clear challenge in his gaze. "As for the other, you need only visit the stables as you would normally. Preferably before noon, as I have duties here and my absence will be remarked upon if I'm away for too long."

"And just as my mother has spies in Sotiris's tower, so too does Sotiris have spies in yours."

"It is the way of things," he commented, seeming unworried.

"Yes, it is." She paused, looking up to meet eyes which were no longer laughing or arrogant, but filled with sincerity. As if he understood that she needed to know what kind of man he truly was. Not the great sorcerer, but a serious and ordinary man. The latter of which he would never be. And yet . . . "I am trusting you, Nico. More than I have trusted any other person, except my mother."

"Trust runs both ways, Antonia," he reminded gently.

For some reason, that simple statement of truth reassured her, and suddenly she felt younger than she had in years, possibly since the day she'd first arrived at Sotiris's tower. A laugh tried to bubble up her throat, but she swallowed it. Private feelings were one thing. Sharing them was something else entirely.

"Very well. If you're sure."

"Like you, my lady, I have no desire to die. Be assured that I am in no danger from that device if you return it to Sotiris's tower. I learned to protect myself from enemies near and far at a very young age."

She regarded his serious mien for another heartbeat, then picked up the silk-covered hexagon, wrapped it in folds of leather, and walked to the back of her carriage. Once there, she buried it in a picnic basket that was already half-full with the remains of an extensive feast. Turning from her task, she caught his raised eyebrow and explained, "Sotiris keeps hounds. They are trained to scent any magic coming through the gate, regardless of who or what transports them. Given my magical abilities, it is expected the hounds will react to me, but the food adds an additional barrier to detection, which I find prudent given the hexagon's potential."

"You worry for my safety, but are you certain it's safe for *you* to go back there? You're welcome to remain here. We have more than enough guest quarters suitable for a lady."

She would have liked that. She'd certainly have slept better. But she shook her head. "No, for all the reasons I already explained, this—" She gestured at the basket with its dangerous cargo. "—has to return to

Sotiris's tower with me." She paused, then said, "I am not helpless either, Nico. You may rely on that as well."

"I shall, but don't betray my faith, Antonia. I'm looking forward to my new job as a horse trainer, and would deeply regret losing you as a patroness."

Far too charming for his own good, she thought. And yet, when she guided her carriage through the gates and out onto the road back to Sotiris's estate, she smiled at the thought of seeing him the next day. No matter *what* he looked like.

AS PROMISED, NICO appeared at the gate to Sotiris's estate the next morning riding a black gelding and leading two beautiful mares behind him. What the gate guards saw wasn't the handsome and powerful sorcerer, however. He wore the garb of an ordinary peasant, but with the addition of good riding boots and leather chaps over well-made cotton trousers. A dark brown, flat cap covered his streaked brown hair, which was tied into a neat queue at the back of his neck. His hands were weathered and scarred, and the face that looked out from under the cap was that of a man who'd spent a lifetime in the sun and wind—a lifetime considerably longer than Nico's had been.

His expression was modest when he removed the hat and held it to his chest as he bowed slightly from the waist. "Petros Vasilis, good sir. Newly hired for the stables."

The guard studied him a long moment, gave a short nod, and said, "Beautiful beasts there, horseman. Are they yours?"

Nico smiled proudly. "All three bred and raised from birth by my own hand."

"You'll be welcome, then. Not to speak ill of the dead, but our last stable master had a hard hand with the animals. Looking at those, your hand is a mite gentler."

"You'd be right on that, good sir. I find the beasts respond better to kindness than brutality."

"Go on through, then. Stables are to the right, just past the main building."

"My thanks, and good day to you." Nico wanted to kick the gelding into a faster pace, eager as he was to see Antonia again, but knowing she'd hardly be waiting at the barn doors for his arrival, he kept to a slow walk, making use of the time to study Sotiris's estate from inside the walls. He'd seen it before, studied every detail of it, using his sorcery.

He'd even constructed a model of it for his war room. But seeing it with his own eyes was enlightening. Not only the buildings, but the people coming and going, busy with their work days. His own estate was a mostly cheerful place at this time of day, with children chattering as they ran to morning classes, women calling to each other over laundry and stove fires, and the smell of fresh bread and roasting meats filling the air.

Sotiris's estate was as busy, but quieter and more orderly, though the same tasks could be seen being carried out as he rode past, and the aromas were mostly the same, including the distinctive scent of the stables. He followed that scent past the main building, with its multiple towers, and across a large yard to a well-maintained barn, with several sturdy paddocks. The former stable master might have had a hard hand with animals, but he'd clearly kept the stables in good order.

Nico dismounted at the paddock nearest the barn entrance and tied all three horses to the fence before walking through the wide-open double barn doors. An older man emerged from what was clearly a tack room, just as Nico paused to inhale the sweet, familiar odor of horses and fresh hay.

"Petros Vasilis," he said, by way of introduction. "Newly hired for the stables here."

"Aye, we were told you'd be coming." The man held out a rough, calloused hand, introducing himself as Nico took the hand with his own, which was similarly calloused though mostly from wielding a blade. "Yorgos Karolis," the man introduced himself, "but Yor is good enough. You brought your stock with you?"

"I did, some of them at least. Outside."

"Let's take a look then. Lord Sotiris breeds mostly for war mounts, for himself and his generals, though the Lady Antonia does like to ride for pleasure." He stopped when he saw Nico's three animals. "Well, those are a damn fine recommendation for your breeding skills. How's their training?"

"All three are sweet and fast. The gelding's a big horse and needs a strong hand, but has the temperament for war. As for the mares, they're both fine riding mounts. The chestnut is the younger one, but at three and a half years, she'll be ready to breed soon. The bay's her dam, sired out of a war stallion I bred ten years ago. He's in Lord Nicodemus's stable now."

"Ah." Yor grimaced.

Nico, aka Petros, grinned. "I don't take sides when it comes to my horses. The lord caught sight of the stallion and bought him on the spot.

He's known for keeping a good stable, just like this one, so I sold him."

"All the same, I'd keep that quiet for now."

"Understood."

Yor was examining the chestnut, running a hand over her legs, checking eyes and teeth. "Lady Antonia's favorite mare pulled up lame just yesterday," he said, without looking up. "Nothing too serious, but she won't be rideable for a week or two. She'll be looking for a replacement. This pretty filly would do nicely."

"I'd be honored. Though I'd prefer to go out with her the first few times. The mare is saddle-trained, of course, but she hasn't been ridden much yet, not out in the open. Better to have a strong hand around at first."

"We'll check with the lady. She's usually out here a bit later in the morning. In the meantime, you can stable all three. Let me show you the rest of the barn."

THE NEXT FEW hours were filled with introductions for Nicodemus, to animals and people both. He met and gentled Sotiris's two stallions, both of which he had confronted in previous battles. But Nico had a gift with animals, and though the stallions had been hell on four legs when they'd fought, they whickered like friendly colts when he stroked their necks and spoke softly.

"You have a gift," a feminine voice said from behind him.

Nico turned with a slow smile for Antonia, whom he wasn't supposed to know. Frankly, he was surprised she recognized *him*, even though he'd told her he wouldn't look like himself. He tugged his hat off and held it before him with nervous hands, eyes mostly downcast, with only quick glances up at her. "My lady," he said with proper deference.

"Lady Antonia," she provided. "My cattle foreman tells me you've a fine hand with the animals. High praise, indeed, coming from Yor. He also said you've brought some of your own horses, including one which might do well for me."

"Yes, my lady. She's young and spirited, but takes well to the rein and has a good heart."

Antonia grinned. "A good heart. And what does that mean, Master . . ."

"Petros Vasilis, my lady."

"Master Petros, then."

"She's even-tempered and aware of her rider at all times. She's never been known to spook so badly that her rider loses their seat, and she's easy with the other horses."

"A paragon of horse flesh."

"She is a fine mare, my lady. I would be honored if you would ride her, though as I told Yor, I would prefer to ride out with you until you get to know each other."

"I've been riding since I was a child, Master Petros."

"Indeed, my lady, and I mean no offense or comment on your skill. It is perhaps my own failing that I am protective of the horses I breed. I like to be certain they go to responsible riders."

"I take no offense," she said easily. "I find your care admirable. Do you extend it to the horses you care for, as well? Or only those of your own?"

"I would never harm an animal, Lady Antonia. Nor stand by and watch someone else do so. Some animals are *bred* for the slaughter, but even that can be administered with minimal fear and suffering."

"You have a kind heart to go with your gentle hand. I accept your offer. I will ride out this morning, and you will ride with me."

Hearing her proclamation, the stable boys rushed to get the two horses ready. Antonia would be riding the young mare, while Nico rode the gelding. No one else was ever permitted to mount that one. He'd bottle-fed the horse from birth, after the colt's mother—who'd been bred too young, and *not* by Nico—had rejected him. Nico had slept in the barn for months, becoming the only parent the colt, and now the gelding, ever knew. When they rode together, they became one, moving in perfect harmony, each knowing what the other would do before it happened.

Antonia had disappeared for the time it took the horses to be prepared. Nico hadn't known why, nor did his role permit him to ask. He couldn't help wondering, however, if Sotiris had returned, and if Antonia had gone into the house to share a morning meal with him. The idea grated on his nerves, until his teeth began to grind loud enough to be heard. It made him question his decision to undertake this sub-terfuge, which had no real purpose but to visit the lady.

It was far too late for such doubts, however. If he disappeared now, it would draw unwelcome attention and questions. And if Sotiris happened to become involved, he could very well detect Nico's pre-sence. Neither of them closed their estates to travelers. Such a move would affect the common markets too greatly. They each had specific protective spells cast against the other. Nico was only able to gain this much access to Sotiris's estate because the bastard hadn't been in residence the previous night, when he'd cast a few spells of his own to counteract Sotiris's efforts. That, too, was only possible because Nico knew Sotiris so well, and could counter the magic he detected.

That wasn't to say there wouldn't be any *other* magic floating about that he failed to detect. Sotiris was a world-class ass, but he was also a very powerful sorcerer. Why else would their rivalry have continued for so many years?

"Master Petros." Antonia's sweet soprano sounded like a song when she said his name.

"Lady Antonia. Everything is prepared. We awaited only your return."

Antonia rolled her eyes at his flowery language, while Nico knelt on one knee to offer her a mounting assist. She had changed into leather riding gear, which was an improvement over the morning gown she'd worn previously. But the outfit still included a long, split skirt to conceal her feminine charms. He'd been relieved when the stable boy had produced a fine, leather saddle, not unlike his own. He'd feared at first that she might choose to ride side-saddle, and though he'd met many female riders who did quite well with that arrangement, he desired to ride far enough that Antonia wouldn't fear detection, and that meant moving fast over sometimes uneven ground.

They kept to a decorous pace as they rode around the main residence and through the gates, with Nico maintaining his pose as the older, experienced horse master by her side. It wasn't until they'd dropped behind the rise facing the estate that Nico pulled up and caught her attention.

"Are you ready to ride, Antonia?"

"I thought we were," she countered, with an impish smile that said she knew full well what he intended.

"You claim to be an accomplished rider, my lady."

"I don't claim. I state the truth. And can you please drop the damn disguise. It's uncanny to hear your words coming from another's mouth."

"But this is not my *voice*."

"No, but those are your words, as well as the confidence that coats them."

Nico hadn't considered the possibility that his disguise could be so easily undone by one who knew him. Sotiris would certainly have recognized him. But then, if he'd known his enemy would be meeting him, Nico would have put more effort into the spell.

"Over the next rise," he conceded. "I wouldn't want my deception revealed out of impatience."

"Set the pace then, Master Petros, and be assured I will match you."

Nico grinned, and without further warning, took off across the narrow valley, heading for the next set of hills. The road was well-traveled and free of hazards, but he cast a spell ahead of him anyway. He had no concerns about his own safety, but he had only Antonia's word as to her skill, and found himself unwilling to take any risks.

ANTONIA'S HAT HAD fallen back to lie against her neck, and she knew her cheeks would be bright pink with sunlight and wind both. But she didn't care. She loved riding and had chafed at the restrictions placed on her by Sotiris. At home on her mother's estate, she'd spent most of her childhood dressed as a boy and behaving like one, too. At least during the day. In the evening, she'd bathed and dressed properly, and then sat to dinner with whatever adults were in residence, learning the proper etiquette while trying not to shovel food into a stomach that had used up every bit of sustenance from her midday meal. Fortunately, her antics had been viewed as charming, rather than scandalous, although she knew it was largely because she'd been a pretty child. She was now the same as a woman, which brought certain indulgences, although gobbling food was no longer one of them. She smiled at the thought, and when Nico dropped below the rise through the trees ahead of her, she had to urge the mare to a faster pace, wanting to keep up, if only to prove to him she could.

As a result, her speed was such that she had to pull up hard when she found him stopped in the middle of the road, no more than thirty paces ahead of her. The sweet mare rose on hind legs for a brief instant, but then was back on all four with nothing more than a shuddering blow of protest before remaining calm and still beneath Antonia.

Nico turned when the mare's hooves hit the dirt road, his expression a combination of concern and surprise. But it was Antonia who was truly taken by surprise, when she saw not Petros's pleasant brown gaze, but Nico's hazel-gold eyes looking back at her.

"You dropped the seeming spell," she said unnecessarily, and immediately flushed at the obvious observation.

He grinned, and Nico's usual confident, cocky expression was back. "I feared for a moment that you intended to trample me to death."

"Not yet," she replied breezily. "I prefer to hold back that option until I'm certain of intent."

"And what do you believe to be my intent, Lady Antonia?"

She walked the mare closer, then leaned across the distance between them and said in a low, sultry voice, "Seduction, Lord Nicodemus."

His eyes widened in surprise, and he laughed, but there was something more in those golden eyes. A clear purpose that took her teasing comment as an invitation . . . although she doubted Lord Nicodemus Katsaros ever bothered to wait for an invitation. He was a man who would take what he wanted, and ensure the woman loved every moment of the taking.

Antonia had limited experience of seduction, and no encounters at all that she'd loved. "You look . . . better as yourself," she told him.

He gave her a courtly bow from the waist. "You're too kind, my lady. Shall we ride? I hope to get well away from the estate before we stop for lunch."

"Lead on, my lord."

They rode the length of the narrow valley before winding through a thick forest to emerge on a grassy hillside overlooking a broad river valley below. Houses were clustered around an ancient-seeming fortress, and spilled outward until they occupied every part of the valley that Antonia could see.

"What is this place?" she asked, surprised that she'd never come across it in her own wanderings.

Nico didn't answer immediately, but stared at the distant fortress for a long moment, before turning to study her before he spoke. "Those are the lands of King Jodokus Katsaros. My father."

Well, that explained his familiarity with the location, and probably her own ignorance, too, since her escorts would never have wanted to trespass on another king's lands. "You're close to your family?" she asked, assuming the answer would be yes.

But Nico's disgusted snort told another story. "Hardly. As the younger son, I was expected to lend my talents first to my father's successful rule, and ultimately to my brother's, as well. My own ambitions were meaningless."

"Truly? That's rather shortsighted of him. Surely he would be better served by having such a powerful ally in his own son."

"He never saw it that way. Nor did my lady mother. I left at fourteen years, hungry to put my magic to use and discover my own future. We haven't spoken since, beyond the occasional passing courtesy."

"Have they actively opposed you? Allied with your enemies?"

"My father King Jodokus is far too shrewd to take it that far."

"He's not *too* terribly shrewd if he disowned *you*. You could crush him like a bug."

Nico laughed. "You flatter me yet again, my lady. Come. There's a pleasant picnicking spot not far from here. We can rest the horses while we eat, and discuss . . . seduction."

An unexpected thrill of excitement caught Antonia's breath at his words. She *wanted* to be seduced by this man. But why this one, and not another? And how could she be so attracted to the one person that Sotiris hated with every shred of power he possessed. He would kill her if he ever found out she'd even been *speaking* to his enemy, much less that the speaking had become seduction.

And still, she didn't care.

"I trust you brought lunch," she told Nico archly. "I certainly didn't."

He gave her that warm, knowing smile, as if he was already planning the best way to remove her clothes. "Trust me, my lady. I have it well in hand." He swung his gelding around and proceeded along a game trail through the trees, clearly assuming she'd follow.

Admiring his broad back and strong arms, seeing the dappled light turn the gold in his hair into flashes of the sun's fire, Antonia sighed. She trusted him, but she also feared that what he planned to have well in hand before the day was over . . . was her.

NICO STUDIED Antonia's elegant profile as she lay with eyes closed on the blanket his cook had thoughtfully included with the picnic lunch she'd prepared. There'd been a speculative look in her eye when she'd handed over the leather bag—a look that invited a sharing of confidences. But he hadn't accepted the offer. Antonia's position was too precarious for him to tell anyone that he'd be sharing an intimate picnic in the woods with her. He didn't know if Sotiris loved her, or if she was merely the by-product of a desirable alliance. But the bastard would be furious if he ever discovered they'd been having private conversations . . . or more. Nico knew that pursuing her was a mistake, that the consequences would be far worse for her than him. But he couldn't simply drop it, couldn't let her go about her life before he'd made her laugh again, before her mere presence sent additional streaks of heat arrowing straight to his heart, as they did every time she smiled. Before he'd tasted her plump lips and warm mouth, or held those full breasts in his hands. He closed his eyes, shutting out the sight of her, before he embarrassed them both with his growing reaction. He wanted this woman in a way he'd never wanted another. Wanted her warm and sated in his bed, not just for one night, but for . . . more. He couldn't think beyond that, couldn't name what his heart was telling him. He'd never before had such thoughts, and didn't trust them now. She was lovely and intelligent, warm and enchanting, but with a wicked wit and a bold tongue. But how did he know if she wanted him, or whether she was intentionally seducing him for Sotiris? Or worse, whether the idea of seducing *her* was attractive to him, mostly because of her relationship to his enemy?

"You're staring, my lord," she murmured, without opening her eyes.

"I'd say rather that I'm admiring, Lady Antonia."

She chuckled. "Is this more of your seduction?"

Nico regarded her for a moment longer, while his thoughts fought a battle between desire and reserve. The latter might have won if she hadn't chosen that moment to remove her hat and do something with her hair that let the raven-black curls tumble past her shoulders.

His groin tightened as if she'd stroked him with a delicate hand on his cock. Swallowing a groan of surrender, he stretched out deliberately close and pushed a few stray curls off one soft cheek. "What are we doing here, Antonia?" he whispered, needing to hear her reflect his own confused thoughts.

A thick brush of black lashes lifted to reveal gray eyes staring back at him. She swallowed hard, and it was the first sign of true nerves she'd shown. "Nico?" That was all she said, but he didn't need more. Leaning closer, he touched his mouth gently to hers. A brush of lips, a hint of warmth, while her fingers trembled against his cheek . . . Nico groaned and took her in his arms, feeling her breasts against his chest when he crushed her lips to his and forced his tongue between her teeth, where he swallowed her hungry, little moan.

"Wait, wait!" It was a breathless cry while she gripped his shoulders with both hands.

Nico pulled back, his heart thrumming with desire, his thoughts hazy with need. "Antonia?"

"No. No," she repeated, when he would have lifted completely away from her. Her grip on his shoulders tightened. "I needed . . . I needed to breathe."

Her chest rose and fell against his when she drew several long breaths. "Your kisses are potent, my lord."

"If so, it's the nectar of your lips that feeds them."

She laughed in delight. "Oh, you are far more charming than your

49

reputation would have me believe."

"My reputation?"

"Of course. All the fine ladies—old and young—are filled with lust when you walk into a room. Though I suspect the tales of seduction some have repeated are greatly exaggerated, or the product of restless dreams."

"And what of you, Antonia?" He said it lightly, but his gaze was serious as it bored into hers.

Solemn gray eyes studied him a moment too long, before her lashes fell, and she spoke in a rush, as if unsure she could get the words out any other way. "I would keep any such tales of seduction close to my heart, where my most precious memories are forever stored."

"Antonia." It was a fervent whisper, a plea for release from the terrible passion pulling them together, even as it begged her permission for him to take her right there on the blanket, with the sun glinting blue off her black hair, and the trees murmuring an invitation to use their shadows for concealment.

Her only answer was another quiet moan when her arms tightened around his neck, and she pulled him down until he feared his weight would crush her. But that fear vanished when her lips met his in a bruising demand for more.

Nico forced himself to go slowly, stroking his hand down her clothed body with deliberate care, lingering over the swell of her breasts, bound tightly beneath the crossed leather lapels of her long riding coat, but not so tightly that he couldn't feel the weight of them, or the hard pebble of her nipples pushing for attention against the thick fabric. With a stifled groan, he buried his face in the warm curve of her jaw and inhaled the sweet scent of her skin and hair, enhanced now by the perfume of her arousal. His groan deepened with hunger as he kissed the delicate flesh behind her ear. He wanted to bite her, to mark her so every man would know she was taken. But that would be reckless beyond reason, though reason struggled to prevail when she cried out, not in pain, but desire, arching her back to push her breasts harder against his embrace, and scraping her nails through his hair to hold his mouth against her skin. It was almost as if she *wanted* him to bite her, to leave his claim on her.

"Antonia," he said harshly, forcing himself to lift his mouth from her neck, only to come down hard on her mouth, his tongue shoving between her teeth once more. "We should stop," he murmured against her swollen lips. "We should—"

Her response was immediate as she wrapped her legs around his hips, then pushed him onto his back and straddled him. She leaned down and breathed against his mouth, "I don't want to stop." And then sitting up, she put both hands to the ties on her shirt, swiftly undid the tight bodice, and freed her breasts to spill over the top of the leather in creamy swells of temptation.

Nico had forced himself to stop once, but he didn't have it in him to do it again, not when she arched her back allowing two rosy nipples to peek over the loose bodice. "Damn it, woman." Not a man to ever assume the submissive role, he rolled her beneath him and filled his mouth with one breast, sucking until her nipple was plump against his tongue, and then bit down on the delicious nub until she cried out in such surprised pleasure-pain, that he knew no man had ever pleased her that way. He growled deep in his chest with satisfaction at that, wanting to be the first to bring her many such erotic delights . . . the first and the last. His feelings went beyond simple lust or desire—with every breath, he was more convinced that Antonia was meant to be his. Not for a day or a month, but forever, and damn the consequences. His thoughts were tumbling as his mind tried to remind him of the danger in seeking to make truth of that desire. But his body didn't care. He wanted Antonia, and he was going to have her.

He knew he shouldn't take her like this, on the ground in the forest, where someone could easily happen by and see their indiscretion. But he needed more, needed to touch every inch of her silky skin, to taste her pussy, not just on his fingers, but with his tongue inside her, licking the juices of her opening as her body begged for his cock.

Squeezing one firm thigh, he spread her leather-clad legs and slid his hand between them, pressing hard enough that he could feel the heat of her sex as he rubbed back and forth, until she gave a surprised gasp of pleasure and cried his name, "Nico, please."

"Please what, my lady? What do you want?"

She sobbed a breath and said, "I want it all."

Growling every curse he knew, Nico struggled with the closure of her leather pants. He'd never encountered pants on a woman before, other than undergarments. He'd never had to break any ties except flimsy fabric or ribbons. His own breeches were in danger of ripping open from the pressure of his cock, which was straining to the point of pain in his need to slide into Antonia's body.

Forcing himself to slow down, to control the hunger raging in his blood, he breathed deeply, but only succeeded in driving his need higher when the scent of her filled his nostrils and drifted to settle in his throat.

He went a little crazy then, tearing open the ties on her pants, using both hands to shimmy them down her legs before he was truly aware of what he was doing. He was kissing the smooth skin of her abdomen, nipping impatiently with his teeth at the delicate fabric of her underwear, not caring if they remained whole. He wanted her naked to his eyes, his mouth, his tongue . . . his cock.

He groaned when her pussy was finally bare and the full scent of her assaulted his senses. Unable to stop, he shoved her pants down until he could spread her thighs enough to glide his tongue into her slit and taste the lushness of her arousal. His probing tongue found the tight nub of her sex, and he licked it hard, eliciting a shocked cry from Antonia.

"Yes. Nico, yes!"

Lifting his head once more, Nico tugged her boot from one foot and all but tore her pants leg down and off, giving him room to spread her thighs and delve into her delicious pussy. He used his thumbs to open her sex wide to his every sense. Her folds were swollen with desire, her opening creamy and welcoming when he slid first one finger, and then two inside her. He might have stopped then, if she'd begged him. Might have brought her to climax with his fingers and settled for her hand on his cock, but his thumb scraped the hard pearl of her sex and she climaxed without warning, her inner muscles slamming down hard on the fingers he was sliding in and out, and her thighs clamping viciously around his shoulders while she slapped a hand over her mouth to muffle her screams.

Swamped by a desperate need to have her, he tore his own pants open and freed his cock. Then bending her naked leg at the knee, he shoved it high against his shoulder and slammed his cock deep into her body. Her startled gasp was lost to his senses as he absorbed the sheer heat of her pussy, the satiny slick wetness when her muscles flexed and drew him ever deeper, surrounding him like a scalding silk glove. Wanting more, he pulled out and immediately shoved back in, the friction of his thick penis on her tight sheath increasing the heat of her until he thought their bodies would burn each other up. But still her delicate muscles urged him deeper, caressing the length of him, squeezing his thickness, driving him forward until he could go no farther, until the tip of his cock touched her firm inner border and his balls slapped hard against her perfect ass.

And then he was moving, driven to fuck her harder and harder, desperate to spill his seed inside her, to brand her inside as he dared not mark her breast. And as he thrust deeper and faster, Antonia gripped his shoulders, her soft cries of pleasure warm against his cheek, becoming groans when he shoved into the secret warmth of her body, protesting when he withdrew. With every cry, he grew more frantic, needing to release the heat that was boiling in his groin like a volcano waiting to blow. And when her pussy suddenly clamped around him like a vise, when her screams of pleasure pierced his ears with their intensity, his own climax exploded inside her, so quick and with so much force that his cock bucked and throbbed for what seemed like eternity until it finally lay sated within her trembling sheath.

Nico lay still for several minutes, too stunned to move. He was aware of their hearts pounding in time with each other, the sound so loud that it filled his ears, until Antonia's soft sobs made every other noise disappear. Her face was pressed to his shoulder, her whimpers muffled as she held him tightly. Cursing to himself at the idea that he'd hurt her, maybe crushing her with his weight, Nico rolled to one side and cradled her in his arms. Tears wet her cheeks, and her eyes were swollen and red when she glanced up at him.

"Did I hurt you, my love? I'm sorry." He brushed away the moisture on her face, and when she shook her head, he asked, "What then?"

"I never—" She swallowed another sob. "It's never been like that before. I've never felt . . ." Her words were interrupted by another soft cry.

Nico wanted to deny what she was saying, at least to himself. Wanted to ask what she meant, because while he prided himself on his ability to please his lovers, there was nothing special about what he'd done. But the words wouldn't come. He knew exactly what she meant, because he'd felt it, too.

"What are we going to do?" she asked in a small, desperate voice.

"I don't know, love. The blood's all left my head and I can't think just now," he added in a poor attempt at lightening the mood. He sighed and hugged her more tightly. "I don't know, but we'll figure it out. We'll be all right."

"He'll never let me go."

Nico's expression hardened, though she couldn't see it. "Who says we're going to ask?" he growled.

BY THE TIME NICO escorted Antonia back over the hills to Sotiris's estate, he was Petros Vasilis once more, having recast the seeming spell once they'd started home. With all the emotional turmoil in his head over his feelings for Antonia clouding his thoughts, he'd almost forgotten. She'd been the one to remind him when they'd been about to leave the cover of the forest behind.

But when Yor greeted them as they dismounted outside the barn, it was Lady Antonia who returned his greeting with a gentle, but friendly smile.

"And how was the new mare for you, my lady?" Yor asked, placing a mounting block where she could easily reach it, and offering her a hand in assistance.

"Very pleasant, Master Yor. She has a sweet temper and a remarkably smooth gait. She'll be an excellent addition to our riding stable, if we can persuade Master Petros to part with her."

"It was your gentle hand that brought out the best of the ride, my lady," Nico commented. "I should perhaps be trying to persuade you to grant us another ride, rather than the other way around."

Antonia's brow arched at his obvious double entendre, the color in her cheeks running high. But not so much that it couldn't be attributed to the effects of the lengthy horse ride. "Well," she said gamely. "I would very much enjoy another ride, if you're willing."

"It would be a distinct pleasure, my lady. I'm honored." He raised a brow of his own in a leer, careful that Yor couldn't see. He was about to suggest a time and day, when everyone turned at the sound of shouting from the gate.

"Lord Sotiris has returned," Antonia said, her eyes wide with alarm when she looked at Nico. "Forgive me, Master Petros. I must run if I'm to be ready when my lord calls for me."

Nico watched her leave, the skirts of her riding coat held high as she ran for the kitchen door across the courtyard. It galled him to leave her alone with Sotiris. She clearly had no love for him, and from the worry in her eyes when she realized he'd returned, it might be that she feared the bastard instead. Fuming at his inability to do anything about her situation in that moment, he hardened his protections against the possibility of Sotiris detecting his presence, and began making plans to free Antonia from his clutches, even if it meant finally killing the enemy sorcerer once and for all.

SOTIRIS RODE through the gates with his escort, tired after the long unnecessary journey. If the fool sorcerer he'd ridden to visit hadn't possessed something Sotiris had wanted desperately, he'd never have agreed to the visit. Even so, he could have fetched the damn object using his own much greater power if the other would have agreed. He'd have to reevaluate the man's usefulness after this. If everything went as planned, Sotiris would defeat Nicodemus in the coming war, and there'd be no one left to stop his plans to rule . . . everyone. Perhaps then, the fool's value would diminish sufficiently that he could be disposed of, along with Nicodemus.

He couldn't have said what interrupted his thoughts and had his face lifting like a hound's to scent the air around him. Just for a moment, he thought he'd detected an intruder, someone he couldn't identify. He just knew that whoever it was didn't belong within Sotiris's estate. But a moment later, the scent was gone as servants and stable boys came running, surrounding the riders like ants on a hill, eager to serve their betters in the only way that gave their lives purpose.

He caught sight of his estate manager as he dismounted and gestured the man to come closer. "Where is Lady Antonia?" It irritated him that she wasn't among the small crowd that had come out to greet him.

"The lady is in the kitchens, seeing to the proper preparation of your meal, my lord. Your journey must have gone smoothly."

It was the man's way of noting that they'd had no advance warning of Sotiris's arrival, though he'd never have been so bold to speak it outright. Sotiris never sent word of his imminent return, although he knew the estate manager posted watchers when the lord was expected, in order to prepare an appropriate reception. Sotiris preferred to surprise his people, to ensure they were doing their proper tasks even when he wasn't there to see to it. Antonia had the authority to oversee the staff when he was gone, but for all her skill with magic, and what he had to admit was a fine mind, she was far too gentle when dealing with the servants.

Sotiris didn't bother to acknowledge the manager's response, other than to glance without interest at the bustle of servants and luggage, and say, "See to all this before coming inside." He then strode into his tower without another word.

Chapter Five

THE NEXT MORNING, Nico passed through the gate of Sotiris's estate with a nod of greeting to the guards, who once more saw horse master Petros Vasilis arriving for work.

"No fancy horses this morning, Petros?" one of the guards called with a gap-toothed grin.

"Just this one," he replied, leaning forward to slap the gelding's neck.

"He's a beauty."

Nico tipped his cap in thanks and continued through the yard, around the main buildings, and to the barn, where the mares recognized him and called a loud greeting. He dismounted and stabled the gelding, then began checking other horses in the barn, including his two mares. He'd always enjoyed working with horses, and liked to think he had a special affinity for them. So he didn't mind doing Petros's chores. It gave him something to do while he waited for Antonia to show up at the barn.

He'd spent much of the previous night worrying over her situation. The question of her safety with Sotiris once more in residence had been foremost in his thoughts, though there was little or nothing he could do to change the situation, short of getting rid of Sotiris once and for all. That solution wasn't out of reach, since he and Sotiris both were building toward one more battle before the winter snows locked them in their respective towers until spring.

They'd already waged too many battles, fighting for control of fields and towns and the farmers and tradesmen who worked there. But those battles had been nothing but substitutes for their real competition, which had little to do with land and peasants, and everything to do with magic. Nico would have been content to share his world with Sotiris, just as he did with many other magic users with less power. Sotiris was just one more.

The problem was two-fold. First, Sotiris was a negligent and demanding lord, which had most of those whose land they fought over preferring Nico as their lord. By the same token, he was too much aware of the farmers' plight to walk away from a fight that would improve their lives and livelihoods. But the most stubborn aspect that kept them at war was Sotiris's refusal to concede even a square foot of land without fighting for it. He simply wouldn't accept that Nico was the stronger sorcerer, and was determined to fight war after war in an effort to prove himself the greater power.

And so they fought. Months could go by with no new battle between them, but everyone knew it was a fragile interlude, and that the next conflict was already brewing.

And that brought Nico's thoughts back to Antonia, and the need to ensure her safety by finally getting rid of Sotiris permanently. It brought to light, in a way it hadn't before, the need to *kill* Sotiris. The bastard was an expert at surrendering the field when it became clear he was about to lose, and he seemed to experience neither grief nor guilt at leaving his loyal people continuing to fight while he fled. Maybe he fooled himself into considering his many flights to be strategic retreats, rather than the blatant acts of cowardice that they so clearly were.

Still, Nico had always permitted those retreats, making no attempt to chase down his enemy and eliminate him. He told himself he was saving lives that might have been lost, had he continued the fight. But perhaps the time had come for him to set aside his own brand of cowardice, if not for his world which had suffered too many decades of constant battle, then for Lady Antonia. He was ashamed to admit that it was her safety that finally tilted his position toward the goal of sending Sotiris to his death.

At some point, Nico became aware that he'd been so caught up in his stable work, and the hours it provided for him to get lost in his own thoughts, that most of the morning had already passed. He removed his hat, mopped his brow, and put the hat back on, then set aside his pitchfork, and walked the long length of the barn to the big, open doors. The sun was almost directly overhead, which confirmed his sense of the time. But there'd been no sign of Antonia. He considered it likely that Sotiris would demand most of her time now that he'd returned—for at least the next few days, in any event.

Antonia had said Sotiris had undertaken the long, arduous journey to visit a friend who possessed an item or knowledge that Sotiris required, and that the friend would only do business in person. If Sotiris had been willing to discomfit himself to that extent in order to acquire what he wanted, then he was working on a new spell that might well be near completion. It could even be the case that the spell's finish was lacking only that one component that the distant friend possessed. In which case, Sotiris would expect Antonia to work closely with him to finish the spell, possibly for several days.

Nico considered all this as he stood in the barn's open doorway, enjoying the relatively cooler air, and wondering what his enemy was plotting. It was a certainty that whatever fiendish spell Sotiris was crafting would be used against Nico and his people.

Antonia might know precisely what was involved. Her magic didn't reach the heights of Nico's or Sotiris's, but it was powerful all the same. In some ways, her skill with new spells was greater than theirs, because of her affinity for nature and her brilliance in crafting the right words and components. The hexagon she'd designed and created was the perfect example, though the final product chilled her soul with its deadly nature.

Nico had far greater power, but he didn't possess the patience or spell knowledge to even imagine such a weapon, much less to create it himself. But he could use it, and so could Sotiris. Once it was properly primed, it would be powerful enough to change the very trajectory of their conflict. He'd questioned his own thinking in having Antonia return the damn thing to Sotiris's tower, and had to admit that her safety had been the overriding factor. But in the final analysis, he benefitted from the deception, too. Better for him to know of the hexagon's existence and location, while permitting Sotiris to believe the thing to be safe and secret, than to ignite an immediate confrontation with Sotiris when he discovered the device had been relocated to Nico's tower. Especially when Antonia was the only other person who knew of the hexagon, understood what it could do, and had the necessary access to steal it.

Besides, while she clearly didn't trust the weapon in Sotiris's hands, she hadn't yet made up her mind about Nico either, and still seemed to prefer destroying the thing altogether. The fact that she hadn't could mean the hexagon was too volatile to reliably risk destruction. And that made Nico wonder if Sotiris's recent journey had been to acquire some final component of the device or spell that would stabilize it sufficiently for use. He should have asked Antonia about that, but he'd been too intent on seducing her instead. Idiot. He'd have to remember to ask next time he saw her, which didn't appear likely to happen on this day.

Catching Yor's eye when the man came around the barn, driving a small wagon, Nico walked over. "Good morning, Yor, though the greeting's a tad late, it seems."

Yor tipped his head back to glance up at the sky. "It's an autumn sun, already speeding through the sky. I was by earlier, but you barely noticed. It's a lucky man who enjoys his work that much."

"I like horses," Nico said, with an unapologetic shrug. "Speaking of which, has the Lady Antonia been down this morning? I was hoping she'd give the mare another ride. It's good reinforcement for the horse's training."

"Oh, aye. The lady had nothing but good words for that mare. She came by the barn last night, after dinner. The meal's a more formal affair with the lord returned, so it was late. But I found her in the stall, spoiling the beauty with carrots and nose rubs. She didn't say anything about riding today, though. She can't get out here as often when Lord Sotiris is in residence."

"Ah. I'd almost forgotten he'd returned yesterday. Too concerned with my own chores, I suppose. Well, if you see her again tonight, please tell her I'm available at her convenience. She's a fine rider, and a good match for the mare."

"I'll do that. You still staying down in the town?"

"Aye. It's a nice room I'm renting, with a good stable. And I do enjoy a pint in the tavern of an evening."

"Well, I'd best be getting this feed out to the cattle," Yor said, and with a flick of the reins and a tip of his head, he headed around the barn and down the dirt path to the grassy fields where a goodly number of cattle grazed contentedly.

Frustrated at the situation, which was largely of his own making, Nico went back to work. He needed to finish up and get back to his own estate before dark. He was beginning to suspect Sotiris would declare war much sooner than Nico had originally assumed. He had his own preparations to complete, his own commanders to brief and armies to call up and arm, his own sorcerous weapons to design and test.

He'd see Antonia tomorrow. If she couldn't come to him, then he'd damn well go to her.

ANTONIA SAT hunched over her worktable, fingers cramped and eyes straining as she fought to complete the last, fine details of the hexagon and the spell that would arm it. She worked by simple candlelight, rather than using any of her energy to power the brighter light of a sorcerer's lantern. The urgency to finish was an evil spirit looking over her shoulder, judging her efforts and finding them wanting. She'd known all along that time was short to finish the device, if she hoped to get it to Nico. Although before meeting him, she hadn't been sure that was the best course. She'd had an alternate plan in the event Nico had turned out to be either a brutal autocrat like Sotiris, or at the other extreme, a foolish womanizer who couldn't be trusted with such a powerful device.

Now that she'd met him—and so much more—that concern had been put to rest. Unfortunately, Sotiris's return had brought the unwellcome news that he was accelerating his timetable for declaring war on Nicodemus. He wouldn't tell her why, other than hinting at a spell that would deprive Nico of his best weapon at the very onset of the war, irrevocably shifting the scales of power and ensuring Sotiris's victory.

Antonia had wracked her brain, replaying every conversation she could remember having with Sotiris over the last few months, but could come up with nothing that would equal so powerful a spell. It couldn't be a device, since Sotiris would almost certainly have demanded her assistance, since she was, very simply, more skilled than he was at the fine work involved in crafting magical devices. That left only a spell of some sort, which could be anything. The only hint she'd had was that Sotiris had successfully acquired some critical element during his recent journey. But since he wouldn't tell her anything beyond that, she had no idea what it could be.

She straightened abruptly when her back cramped without warning, a knife blade of pain sliding between overworked muscles. Her desk was higher than usual, positioned to enable her to work standing or sitting in equal comfort . . . or discomfort. She sat on a high stool, feet propped on the bar between the legs. The stool had no backing and so provided no relief for her muscles, even when she straightened to relax. She'd promised herself more than once that she'd appeal to one of the estate's woodworkers for a better design, but it seemed there was always some other demand on her time. And now that time was slipping between her fingers as she raced to finish the hexagon and get it to Nico.

But it wasn't only the hexagon occupying her thoughts. Sotiris's comment regarding Nico's "best weapon," kept replaying in her head while she worked. She knew little of his weapons or spells, and what she did know had come from Sotiris, who was full of disdain for his foremost enemy. Their dinner conversation was often peppered with sneering observations of Nico's irreverent approach to life and living, and scornful comments regarding the four warriors whom Nico had reportedly called to his side from the four corners of the world, with the express purpose of defeating Sotiris. Though she'd never said so aloud, Antonia had considered it quite brilliant on Nico's part to have recruited such warriors, and thought it spoke well of him that the warriors had traveled over long distances to fight a war in which they had no allegiance, only to fight at the side of a sorcerer whom they'd never met. That fact, more than any other, had convinced her to approach Nico with the hexagon.

But now Sotiris was plotting something else, something that he believed would turn the battle to his ultimate victory. He knew about the hexagon, of course, knew what a powerful weapon it was, and still believed it would be his to use. But it wasn't the hexagon he meant when he spoke of a spell that would deprive Nico of his greatest weapon. So what was it? And more importantly, what was Nico's greatest weapon? If she knew that, she might be able to figure out what Sotiris was up to. But she simply didn't know enough, which made her a poor vessel for such a critical piece of information.

She stood and began pacing the room, forced to thread her way around not only furniture, but piles of books and dismantled devices, which, though well organized, still occupied too much floor space. Finding the room unsatisfactory for meaningful pacing, she slipped down the few stairs to the main hallway and resumed her march back and forth.

It was the silence that finally penetrated her spinning thoughts, and made her realize how late the hour was. Feeling as though she was the only person awake in the entire castle, she crossed to a narrow window and saw that even the kitchens below were dark, with only the reddish gleam of a banked stove fire lighting the empty room. She stared for a moment while her thoughts took an entirely unexpected turn, then walked quickly to a crossing hallway and over to a second window which looked down on the barn and paddocks. It too appeared totally dark and unoccupied, though she knew at least one stable hand would be on night duty, most likely dozing in a warm corner.

Racing back up to her room, she changed clothes quickly, donning clothing that would permit her to mount and ride a horse with ease, and yet remain unremarkable to anyone she happened upon before making it off the estate. She would avoid the front gate, since the guards there would certainly note and remark upon her unusual nighttime departure. The evasion would slow her down, but she could take the trail that wound behind the barn and over to the cattle pens, from where she could reach the main road, which was well-maintained at this time of year.

And from there, she would make speed directly to Nico's and

hopefully arrive before dawn. After that . . . she didn't know what she'd do after that. It would depend on what he made of Sotiris's pronouncement, but one way or another, she would have to return to her tower. Because the hexagon was there, and she dared not take it with her. Not yet. Not with Sotiris so close. He would detect the device's absence, and immediately begin searching for it. And for her. When the time was finally right for her to turn the hexagon over to Nico—and she had no doubt that time would come—she would have to leave this place forever. Sotiris would never forgive her when he discovered what she'd done.

NICO WAS SLEEPING when the knock came on his door. His sleep hadn't been restful or sufficient, but he had finally collapsed into his bed, fully dressed, and too exhausted to think, much less undress. He'd managed to kick off his boots, but nothing else.

So when the pounding started, he was inclined to ignore it. Nothing could be so important that it demanded his attention with the sky still dark outside his window. When the pounding not only didn't stop, but intensified, and was accompanied by soft but frantic calls from his manservant, Seneca, he first cursed viciously, but then called out for his man to enter.

"Forgive the intrusion, my lord. I would not have done so, if it were not imperative."

Nico sat up and blinked blearily at the man for three full heartbeats, before the urgency of his words penetrated. His battle-trained mind cleared in an instant, and he began pulling on his boots. "What's happened?"

"It's the lady, my lord. Lady Antonia."

Nico's head snapped up. "Antonia? Is she injured? Where is she?"

"She is not injured, my lord. But she's here, in the kitchen."

He stood and walked to the door, running impatient fingers through his unbound hair. "What the hell is she doing in the kitchen? Never mind," he added, realizing that her current location wasn't the critical question. Rather he should be asking why she was here at all, and in the middle of the night. Assuming Seneca would have no answer to that, since whatever had brought her here had to be both important and secret, he took the stairs two at a time and headed for the kitchen, thinking it wasn't a bad place for a secretive meeting. Antonia would attract far less notice there, especially if she'd had the sense to dress the part of a kitchen maid.

When he made it downstairs, he strode the length of the huge dining hall and shoved his way through the thick wooden door into the still-warm kitchen. He spotted her immediately, despite the boys' clothes she must have borrowed from a stable hand. Going to her side, he drew her into his arms, not caring who saw. "Are you well? Are you hurt?"

She leaned into his chest for a moment, before pulling back to look up at him. "I'm fine, but I have news you need to hear." She glanced at Seneca, who was the only person in the room and currently preparing a pot of hot tea. "You may choose to tell whomever you wish," she told Nico quietly. "But you need to hear what I have to say in private."

"Of course." He raised his voice slightly and said, "The tea is most welcome, Seneca. Thank you. If you would wait in the dining hall, we can serve ourselves. I'd rather hear what the lady has to say, before it passes to other ears."

Seneca walked over to the table and set down a tray holding two cups, the teapot, and the usual accompaniments, then gave a slight bow and left the room.

"He won't be offended?" Antonia asked, watching him leave.

"Not at all. He's been with me long enough to understand that some things are better left unknown. If he needs the information, he knows I'll tell him."

"A good man, then. A trustworthy servant."

"He's that and more. Sit, love, and tell me why you're here." He pulled out a chair for her, then sat next to her and watched, with fading patience, as she poured the tea, then took an immediate sip from her cup without cooling it with the provided cream.

"Antonia."

She looked up and met his gaze.

"You've news for me that was important enough to bring you here in the middle of the night, at no small risk to yourself. Talk to me, my love."

She took a last sip, then cupped the tea in both hands as if needing the heat, despite the warm room and the huge banked oven behind her. "I worked all day on the—" She glanced around, then gave him a meaningful look and said, "The rock."

He nodded, understanding she referred to the stone device she'd called "the hexagon."

"The work got hold of me and it was late before I realized the time. I knew Sotiris would expect me for dinner, and was just leaving my room when he visited me instead."

Nico's gut tightened at the image his mind conjured of that visit, but he said nothing, figuring she'd impart the news that had brought her to him so late, if he let her tell the story her own way.

"He hadn't shared many details of his journey before he left, and so I was surprised when he offered what he clearly believed to be good news about the trip's success. He said he was moving up the timetable for declaring war, because he'd designed a spell that would—and these are his words—'deprive that bastard of his best weapon in the first moments of battle, before the horns have even finished blowing.' He declared it would result in his swift and conclusive victory.

"I wracked my mind for most of today—constantly pulling my attention from the rock's design—trying to determine what kind of weapon he could mean, but came up with nothing. And then, it struck me that *you* would understand what he meant, and that you needed to know what he planned."

Nico lifted the hand she'd placed on the table and held it while he considered what she'd said. His greatest weapon? He had many advantages over Sotiris, not least being the level of his raw power, which was greater than the other sorcerer's. And yet, after all these years, they were still locked in battle, simply because Sotiris was older, trickier, and far more ruthless—willing to sacrifice the lives of his fighters for minimal gain, or to protect his own skin.

Nico contemplated his many spells and magical devices, attempting to rank them in terms of their past success, trying to view them as Sotiris might. But though he sat in silent thought for some minutes, he couldn't identify any one that he would consider his greatest weapon. Was the other sorcerer being apocryphal? Did he suspect Antonia's loyalty and was trying to draw her out?

He shook his head, dismissing both possibilities. Sotiris was not a fanciful or even subtle man. If he had something to say, he'd use the bluntest words possible. As for suspecting Antonia of duplicity, she'd said before that he'd kill her if he knew she was contemplating turning the hexagon against him, and Nico believed her. And if Sotiris thought she was sharing information with *him,* he wouldn't take even a few minutes to ascertain the truth of it. He'd kill her at once.

All the same, if Sotiris thought Nico possessed a "greatest weapon," then he needed to figure out what it was before the bastard had a chance to cast whatever spell he'd conjured up.

"Do you know what he refers to?" Antonia asked.

Nico shook his head. "No. Let me give it some thought, though.

But first, you cannot ride back to Sotiris's estate on your own. It was dangerous enough that you came here tonight. If you tried to return now, dawn would be breaking, and you would be seen."

She smiled slightly. "You give me too little credit, Lord Nicodemus. I thought to arrive with Master Petros this morning."

He scowled. "How would we explain that? It would hardly be proper for you to have met him outside the gates, and at such an hour?"

She tsked. "I assumed that you would cast a seeming on me, as well as yourself. And then once in the barn, I could resume my true identity and enter the castle through the kitchen. Few would see me, and those who did would think nothing of it, especially if I were bearing a basket of fresh eggs."

"Would I be conjuring those as well?" he asked dryly.

She smiled. "I'm not certain I'd trust any eggs you conjured. I expected to borrow some from your hens."

"Cook will be unhappy, but I'll tell her I needed them for a spell. It won't be the first time, much to her dismay."

Antonia gave a quickly muffled laugh, and the sound did something sharp, almost painful, to Nico's chest, even as it made him smile. He stood and held out a hand. "Come, my lady. You can't wait here until we leave. I'll take you to my rooms."

She took his hand and whispered. "We'll cause a scandal."

He squeezed her delicate fingers carefully and leaned down to murmur against her ear, "Not if no one sees us."

Chapter Six

THE SUN WAS barely risen when Petros Vasilis and his "young assistant" were allowed through the gate to Sotiris's estate. Antonia had been nervous since she could see her true self perfectly well, no matter how many times Nico assured her that the magical seeming which provided their camouflage only worked on others' eyes, not her own. It wasn't until they'd successfully navigated the gate and Master Yor, outside the barn, that she'd become a believer and tried to take Nico's advice to relax and enjoy their subterfuge.

"I did tell you no one would think anything amiss," Nico said, when they'd bid Yor a fair day and were leading the two horses into the barn.

"Easy for you to say," Antonia reminded him. "I'm the one who would have been hanging from a rope."

"I would never have permitted that to happen. You should know *that* about me, if nothing else."

"You're using logic on an illogical situation."

"It wasn't the *situation* that was illogical, my lady."

She tsked loudly. "You're supposed to agree with me, and attempt to soothe my anxieties."

"Oh, well. You probably should have told me that earlier." He tied each of the horses outside a different stall and went first to the padded container in his saddle bag, where they'd stowed the eggs that Antonia was going to "collect" and take to the kitchen. Only two of the carefully wrapped eggs were broken, which left more than enough for their subterfuge. Glancing around, however, he saw no suitable basket and so conjured one out of thin air. Or so it seemed. What he'd really done was to fetch the basket from the kitchen counter where it began every day filled with fresh eggs.

Transferring the eggs to the basket, he gave a slight bow and turned the whole thing over to Antonia. She smiled prettily in return, before her eyes went big and serious.

"Will you be able to ride with me later?" she asked.

"Is it safe for you to do so? Sotiris won't object if you spend time away from the tower?"

She waved a dismissive hand and said, "He doesn't approve of my preference for riding out into the countryside, but since he knows that it clears my thoughts when I've hit a logjam in my work, he doesn't object . . . as long as I'm back in the workroom in short order."

"Then we'll ride, and if it's easier for you, I'll conceal your identity as we go through the gates."

Her smile had his chest swelling with a feeling he'd never experienced before. It felt like happiness, but he'd been happy before. Gods, he'd celebrated many victories with his warriors with uncontrolled joy. This was something else. Something he'd have to think on later, when he wasn't blinded by the sense of wholesome joy that seemed to surround her in a way that shared itself with him when he was close.

That sense, and others less wholesome, made him want to pull her into his arms and kiss her, to feel her body soften against his while her arms went round his neck. And when he met her gaze, he saw the same desire there. He took a deliberate step back and stiffened his posture into that of a horse master speaking with respect to a lady of the estate. "I am yours to command, my lady, and available at your convenience."

Her smile took on a teasing edge when she said, "Well said, Master Petros. I will return before noon." She glanced quickly over her shoulder, and seeing they were alone, she blew him a kiss before turning to hurry across the yard and into the kitchen with her basket of eggs.

THE SUN WAS already sliding into a cool afternoon when Antonia finally showed up at the stables. Nico had grown more anxious with every moment that passed, worried that Sotiris had discovered she'd snuck out the previous night, and with whom, or even worse, that he'd somehow learned of her intention to turn over the hexagon to Nico before the upcoming battle. He was ready to adopt the seeming of a random manservant and go looking for her, when she hurried into the stables and stopped, letting her eyes adjust to the light as she searched for him.

When he stepped out of the stall where he'd been checking on one of the horses, her entire countenance relaxed and she hurried toward him. Relief warring with pleasure, he met her halfway and took her in his arms. He knew there was no one else in the barn, no one to see their forbidden embrace, but even if that hadn't been true, he would have hugged her. He'd needed to touch and be touched by her, needed the caress of her loving and generous aura like he needed his next breath.

The strength of his hunger for her, the power of it, was a shock to him. He'd known and greatly enjoyed many women, but had never regretted leaving any of them, much less feeling as if some vital part of him was missing when they were away for a morning. The realization of his need for Antonia shocked him, because he knew what it meant, knew what he was feeling, even though he'd never felt it before. And what he'd seen in her eyes both earlier and in that moment, told him she felt the same.

His heart ached with joy in the knowledge, even as despair threatened. Of all the people in this world, or any other, there could not have been a more complicated or dangerous woman for him to fall in love with. And the danger was even greater for Antonia than for him. He could defend himself against Sotiris—he'd done so more times than he could count. But Antonia . . . she had power, but nowhere near the level she would need to protect herself against the other sorcerer. The bastard might even regret what he'd done eventually, but Antonia would already be grievously injured, or dead.

But how could Nico protect her? Even if he lived day and night in these stables, she shared a home with the evil bastard in his fucking tower. If Antonia was in danger, Nico might sense her fear in time to race inside, but it would take no more than an instant for Sotiris to lash out and kill her, whether intended or not.

Tightening his arms around her, he knew she'd have to come home with him permanently, instead. He could protect her in his own tower, his own castle. He had spells upon spells of protection around his estate. But how to convince Antonia of the necessity? He knew instinctively that she would resist leaving Sotiris until the hexagon was not only complete, but primed with the bastard's blood, so that it would target only him. If not for that last, she might have completed her work in Nico's tower, instead. But he understood why she wouldn't want that, either. Magic wasn't a matter of wishing something to be so, and having it happen. Something as complex as the hexagon would have taken her months of research, followed by more months of testing, failing, and refining the magic that went into the damn thing. He wondered absently if it had been properly tested, and if Sotiris had volunteered his blood for those tests. Or had she tested it on herself? The idea of Antonia making herself that vulnerable, and with Sotiris so very close, sent a chill racing up his spine.

"I'll saddle the horses," he said gruffly. He needed to get her out of this place, needed to touch her without worry, to kiss her until her lips were swollen, and her cheeks flushed with desire.

"I can help," she offered immediately, but he stopped her.

"It would not be proper, my lady."

"Oh please, my mother taught me how to saddle a horse before I could ride one."

"I'm sure that's true, but this is not your lady mother's estate. And *here*, a lady does not endanger her delicate fingers by saddling her own horse."

She rolled her eyes, but then sat on a hay bale out of the sunlight and, with a prissy fluff of her skirts, said only, "Well, get after it, then, Master Petros. I don't have all afternoon to wait."

Nico gave her a look that said she'd pay for that later, but since he wanted nothing more than to get her alone, he moved immediately to saddle their horses.

ANTONIA RODE NEXT to Nico, her cheeks flushed hot with the wind of their passage across thick grasslands she'd never known were there. It was nearing the time the grass would wither and die for winter, but the fall rains had been heavy this year and the slender stalks were still green and bending to the afternoon breeze as they followed a dirt path through the fields. She was amazed to have lived so close to this place for so many years, and not known it existed. The knowledge brought home to her as never before how restricted her life had become since she'd come to live with Sotiris when she'd come of age—the polite way of saying she'd begun her menses and was therefore considered a young woman and no longer a child.

It would have been easy to blame Sotiris for her isolation, with his rules and claims on her time, but truth demanded she recognize her own complicity in permitting it to happen. Her mother was beautiful and loved by every man she met, but she was no fainting maiden who blushed every time a man looked at her. She was strong enough to run her own estate, with no man's interference, and she'd raised her daughter to be the same. And yet somehow, Antonia had fallen into passive compliance with Sotiris's wants and priorities. Had it simply been easier to go along? She didn't want to believe she could have been that weak, but all the evidence pointed in that direction. The realization embarrassed her now, when it was too late.

Or was it? She'd gone to Nico with the hexagon, after all. And she'd . . . done things with him, that she had with no other. "*Done things*," she thought in disgust. They hadn't *done things*, they'd had sex . . . all kinds of sex . . . outside, in the woods, where anyone could have seen them. And the truth was, she was hoping they'd do it again that afternoon. So maybe she possessed at least some measure of her mother's strength and courage, after all.

Antonia was so deep in thought that she nearly missed Nico's sudden sharp turn to the right. He'd drawn a fair distance ahead of her while she'd been pondering her courage, or lack thereof, but now drew almost to a stop when he saw how far behind she was.

"Are you well?" he shouted and reined in his gelding, ready to turn back to her.

She waved a hand and urged her mare into a faster pace, calling, "I'm fine. Just daydreaming."

When she caught up to him, he gave her a wicked grin and asked, "What were you dreaming that so engrossed your thoughts, my lady?"

"None of your business, my lord," she replied primly.

"Just as I thought," he said, laughing. "Keep up, and I'll soon make your dreams come true."

Antonia tried for an outraged gasp at his presumption, but her own laugh joined his. "Where are we going?" she asked instead.

"Stop for a moment, and let your senses tell you what's ahead."

She frowned, puzzled. No one had ever asked her to do such a thing before. But she trusted Nico more than should have been possible, given their short acquaintance, and so she did as he asked and reined her horse to an easy halt.

"Close your eyes, love. Let your ears and nose tell you what they will."

She narrowed her eyes at him briefly, knowing this could all be a trick for him to get closer and do something scandalous. But he sat his gelding with casual ease and raised one eyebrow, as if daring her to do it. So she did.

The breeze, cool and gentle over her skin, was the first sensation she registered. It felt good, and she tilted her face up to get more of it on her overheated cheeks. Smiling, she inhaled deeply, not even thinking about what it might tell her, but simply because she enjoyed drawing the grass-scented air into her lungs, without the constriction of the tight bodice she generally wore around the estate, suitable to her station.

After a few minutes, she began paying attention to what else the air might be telling her. The lingering scent of mud told her the rains had left puddles nearby that had soaked into the earth, and would soon be iced over as the weather turned colder. There was a slight odor of fruit, probably apples, lingering on the breeze, which meant there was an orchard nearby, with ripe fruit that would soon be harvested for winter.

Her head tilted to one side as a sound other than the breeze penetrated her senses. A few seconds later, she identified it as running water. A stream? If so, a fairly big one, she thought. The water she was hearing was running fast and plentiful—more a river than a stream. A picture of the most recent map hanging on Sotiris's workroom wall popped into her thoughts. There was no river on that map, not this close to the estate. But what else could it be? And why was it not on the map?

"Water," she said, opening her eyes to regard Nico quizzically. "Running fast and hard. But . . . where?"

His smile was wide and so full of love that her heart seemed to stop for one, thrilling moment. "Come," he said, reaching out a hand, as if they were walking side-by-side, rather than sitting on two high-spirited animals. She took his hand, unable to refuse him anything. Not when he looked at her like that.

They rode side by side, moving easily and somehow managing to prevent the horses from rebelling, though their hands remained tightly clasped. The fields of grass faded behind them when the path wound through a stand of the tallest trees she'd ever seen. Antonia let her head fall back to gaze upward, but couldn't see the treetops for all the foliage, and a thought struck her suddenly.

"Have you taken us somewhere far away from our lands—from Sotiris's estate and yours? Is this your magic at work? And how did I not sense it happening?"

His laugh was delighted, and he did what she'd suspected he might be planning earlier. Reaching out a powerful arm, he circled her waist and, lifting her easily from the saddle, swept her off the mare and onto his lap.

"Nico!" she protested, to little avail. Though, in all honesty, it didn't bother her at all. She was so charmed by the romantic gesture that she wasn't bothered by the impropriety of it. Nor by the saddle horn that would surely leave a bruise on her thigh. She simply didn't care. Because Nico's arms were around her, holding her against the heat and strength of his chest, his breath warm on her cheek. She couldn't have imagined a more wonderful afternoon, or any other man she'd want to share it with.

Closing her eyes, she rested her head on his shoulder and said, "Tell me."

"It's a waterfall," he whispered against her ear. "Far from anywhere you know."

"How?" she asked quietly, more curious than caring about the fact that he'd somehow whisked them and their mounts some considerable distance, and she hadn't felt a thing.

He dipped his tongue into her ear, making her shiver, then kissed her cheek. "Because I'm the most powerful sorcerer our world has ever seen."

She smiled at the non-answer, content to simply *be* wherever they were, with him. There would be time in the future to discuss sorcerous abilities and strengths, to analyze specific spells and how they worked. Right now, she only wanted the quiet of the forest, the growing rumble of the waterfall, and Nico. Everything else could wait.

ANTONIA HAD ONLY half-believed that Nico had magicked them away from their home and into some faraway place with a noisy waterfall. But any doubts she'd entertained disappeared when Nico, with her still on his lap, guided his gelding out of the trees and onto the cliff's edge above the most magnificent waterfall she'd ever seen. It was too wide, and the volume of water far too great, to belong to any river she'd ever seen. She'd have asked him where in the world they were, but the noise was so loud, he'd never have heard her.

"Beautiful?"

She smiled at his voice in her ear. "Yes."

He laughed softly. "So what do you think, my love? Is this unusual enough for you?"

"You know it is. You're just showing off now."

"I'm trying to impress my lady with gifts worthy of her beauty."

"You've succeeded beyond all measure, my lord. This is truly otherworldly."

They sat for a long, silent interlude, while she soaked up the energy of this place with its riotous growth of rich, green foliage and joyfully tumbling water. Their arrival would probably have frightened away any wildlife, but she saw signs that they'd been here, and knew that long after she and Nico were gone, the animals would return.

The rock face surrounding the waterfall was jagged enough to climb, although she wouldn't have dared it. But she wondered out loud, "Do you think there's a cave behind the water?"

She detected the slight stiffening of Nico's muscles when he leaned forward to study the rock face. "It's possible. This river is old and you can see that the rocks nearest the point where the water hits the base are as smooth as satin." He kissed her cheek. "Like your skin."

She tapped his hand playfully. "I'm already yours. There's no need for exaggerated flattery."

He pulled away enough to see her face. "Are you?"

"Am I what?" she asked, suddenly realizing what she'd said.

"Are you mine, Antonia?"

Heat bloomed on her cheeks, but she couldn't lie to him. "Yes," she said with blunt reluctance.

His eyes lit with wicked glee. "Do you trust me?"

She studied his handsome face long enough that she saw doubt begin to shadow his eyes, before she said, "I trust you."

His grin returned. "Then let's explore a bit, shall we?"

"Explore?" she asked worriedly, remembering her conviction that the rocks were beyond her ability to climb.

But he was already dismounting from the gelding and taking her with him. "We'll leave the horses here." He dropped the reins loosely over a branch, then turned to study her. "You'll have to remove most of that," he said, waving a hand in her general direction.

Antonia looked down at herself, wondering what precisely he thought she should remove. She wore a dress, but it was of a simple design. The bodice was fitted, of course, and tightly laced. And she wore a petticoat under the skirt, which was the minimum required for modesty in addition to an undergarment, which Nico had removed quite easily on their previous ride before he'd—

She was unable to complete that thought for fear the blatant lust the image generated would show on her face.

"Your dress, my love," Nico explained. "And," he waved his hand again, "whatever else you're wearing under there."

"My . . . what are you planning to explore?"

His laugh was as free and delighted as a child's. "Many wonderful things. But first, we're going to answer your question. Is there a cave behind the water?"

Excitement warred with prudence in her chest. She did want to know if there was a cave there, and if so, she also wanted to explore it. But why did every excursion with him end with her half-naked in the woods where anyone could see? She sighed and knew she might as well surrender, because if she didn't, he'd simply seduce her into it. And she was discovering that she quite enjoyed being seduced by Nicodemus Katsaros.

"Turn around," she ordered.

His eyebrows shot up. "Why? I'll be seeing every inch of you before the afternoon is out."

"Nico," she whispered in scandalized disbelief.

His answer was to pull her into his arms and kiss her . . . and kiss her . . . and kiss her. Until she could barely put two thoughts together. And she wasn't surprised at all to look down and find her bodice had been completely untied, while her skirt and petticoat lay puddled around her booted feet, which was such a ridiculous sight that she laughed.

"I look ridiculous," she told him.

"You look beautiful. Your breasts are the gods' own creation."

"I meant my boots," she said dryly. "I'm all but naked, except for my boots."

"True, but you should probably leave those on. The rocks might be sharp."

She shook her head ruefully. "I'm beginning to believe that *you* are the gods' own *temptation*, sent to lure me off the path of righteousness."

"Ah well, it's a boring path." He pushed her bodice and blouse off her shoulders, and let them fall to the ground, before he took her hand. "Come, my love. Let's be bad."

NICO WOULD HAVE been the first to admit that he'd expected Antonia to rebel at stripping almost naked for a romp in the waterfall. Hell, he'd been surprised when they'd made love in the woods on the first ride they took together. For all she'd known, anyone could have come upon them, though he'd actually cast a spell which would have *seriously* dissuaded anyone from venturing too close. He hadn't bothered with a similar spell today, because this place was utterly remote. The first time he'd ever traveled here, he'd ventured far from the waterfall, but had found no sign of human habitation. He wasn't sure if this was a different world, or simply a different time in *their* world, but he was confident that they were well and truly alone.

Delighted at both her courage and her excitement, he guided her to what seemed the most likely spot to venture behind the wild and abundant tumble of water. The rocks to either side were sharp and jutting, which provided any number of good footholds, and was the reason why they were *both* still wearing their boots. He had to agree they probably looked odd, but since there was no one to see, he'd much rather look silly, than have either of them end up with bloody feet. Especially Antonia.

"Just here," he said, pointing out the first step on the rock face, which was underwater at the level where they had to cross. There was nothing for it. They were going to get wet.

She sucked in a breath when the water hit her bare leg for the first time, which was only expected. This river was runoff from a nearby mountain whose peaks remained covered with snow year-round. The water was icy cold, and didn't warm up at all until well downstream. For all that, however, she didn't react other than the indrawn breath.

He pointed out the next step, and the one after that, until they stood so close to the torrent of water that icy droplets soaked their faces. From here, they'd have to pass *through* the falls to get behind it. "Are you ready?" he asked.

She was grinning so hard, he thought at first that she was gritting her teeth so they wouldn't chatter, but her eyes were bright with excitement and her nod of agreement was fast and immediate.

"Hold tight," he said, and felt her fingers clench his even tighter. "Here we go."

He ducked his head instinctively, though it made no difference. He was soaked and chilled to the bone before he'd gone even halfway through the pounding flow. He kept going, not only to get clear of it himself, but to keep Antonia from being stuck under the freezing water if he hesitated. Her delicate frame would be far more vulnerable to the icy cold.

When he stepped free of the water and caught his first glimpse of the other side, he was struck by wonder that nature could create such beauty.

"Goddess," Antonia breathed hunching close under the arm he held out to her, for whatever warmth his body could offer. "Nico, this is . . . amazing. More, it's a marvel itself. My magic . . . . I have to take off my boots."

She sat right down and did so, her cold fingers clumsy on the wet ties, so that she hissed in frustration before she was finished. But when she finally stood barefoot on the rock, she gasped in amazement.

"Nico, my magic can *feel* the roots of this world through the stone to the bedrock. It's as if I'm standing barefoot in my own garden and feeling the plants, their roots, digging into the earth all around me. Oh," she breathed. "Oh, it's marvelous."

He could only stare at her in a wonder of his own. He'd known that her magic was of the earth, but hadn't ever considered that it meant more than growing abundant and thriving plants and trees. But the earth was more than dirt. It was the rock below the dirt, and whatever lay deep beneath that rock, as well. He took her hand, wanting to experience even a shadow of what she was sensing.

She turned to him with joy shining like the sun in her expression. "Can you feel it?"

And he did. He stood perfectly still, shivering so hard that his bones rattled, while icy water continued to spray them with cold, until he finally realized that some of that shivering was coming from the woman at his side. "Fuck. Come on, it's warmer deeper inside."

"What if we're not the only ones who know that?"

He had trouble deciphering her words, because her jaw was clattering so hard. "I'll deal with anything we encounter. We have to get you warm."

Taking her hand once again, he led the way deeper into the cave, following a warm air current that grew stronger the farther they went. He had to duck his head when the ceiling grew lower, but not so much that he couldn't see clearly enough to be prepared for any threat.

"Is it getting warmer, or am I so cold that I'm losing sensitivity?" she asked.

"Definitely warmer. Darker, too, but here—" He snapped out a command and a white flame appeared in front of them to light the way. He had to squint at first, the light seemed so bright after the darkness. But his eyes soon adjusted to what he knew was actually a rather dim flame.

The cave's roof opened up again without warning, and when he straightened, he realized the heated air they'd been following had grown abruptly warmer. A moment later, he saw why. They stood so close to a small, roundish pool, that if he'd taken another step, he'd have been in danger of falling in.

"Ooooh," Antonia breathed, loosening her hand from his to huddle close to the edge and dip her fingers into the water to test its waters.

"Careful, we don't know what's in there."

"Nothing's in there. At least nothing but moss and such. Nothing with teeth."

"How about poison?"

She tsked loudly. "For a man who wasn't worried about interrupting some giant carnivore with foot-long teeth, you're awfully concerned about a bit of moss."

"I can handle a giant carnivore."

She laughed. "If you're poisoned, I'll suck it out of you. But there's nothing in here, Nico. Oh, look!" She pointed at a huge bubble that suddenly shoved its way up to the surface in the middle of the pool, bringing a rush of almost hot air with it. "That's why this part of the cave, and the water, too, are so warm. There must be a hot spring deep underground."

Without warning, she swung her legs around and slid up to her neck into the pool. Nico grabbed for her, but it was too late. And before he managed to snap the necessary trigger for the offensive spell he'd had ready, she was stroking her way to the warmest center of the pool, while cooing in delight.

"Oh, you have to feel this. It's lovely. Come on, I'll protect you!" she added on a laugh.

Well, fuck, he thought. He couldn't huddle on the edge while she called his manhood into doubt. Hoping he wasn't making a mistake, and there wasn't some man-eating beast in the depths of the pool who farted up those hot bubbles to lure unwary males into the water, he sat down, pulled off his boots, and slid into the water, just in time to catch her lithe body as she paddled back his way.

ANTONIA TURNED her head to kiss his jaw when they met, but his lips were already waiting. Their kiss was clumsy and wet, both of them laughing as much as kissing. But the sensuality of the moment, their cold bodies heating as they wrapped around each other, the press of her nipples against his hard, bare chest, soon took over. Gentle became desperate as he reached down and shredded the undergarment that was her last bit of clothing, then lifted her just enough that he could bend his head to her breast and suck the delicate flesh into his mouth. His mouth was so hot on her still cool nipple that she barely felt when his teeth closed over the hard bud, as what might have been pain bloomed into sensual pleasure. She gripped his long hair, impatiently ripping away the leather tie, and taking a few strands with it, though he didn't seem to care. She twisted the wet strands around her fingers and tugged hard, when he switched to her other breast, bringing the same erotic pain that had her crying out in a way she would have considered far too wanton before she'd met Nico. She hungered for this beautiful man in a way she had no other—a way that she knew she'd never experience with anyone else.

Sobs choked her throat and tears sprang to her eyes as her body soared with desire. She loved him so much that she thought her heart would burst with the fullness of it. Given the smallest chance, she'd have abandoned everyone she loved, forsaken every responsibility, and let him spirit them both to another world. Somewhere they could live together, unconcerned with enemy sorcerers and war, with politics and dynasties. But what chance did they have of that? If she left Sotiris, he'd either chase her down and imprison her in his tower, or simply kill her and Nico, both. He would make it his sole purpose in life to erase them both from the history of their world, not only her betrayal but the man who'd been the cause of it. And how could she do that to Nico?

"Hey," he said softly, kissing away the hot tears filling her eyes. "What's wrong?"

"Nothing," she lied and pulled him into a tight embrace. "I'm just happy."

He pulled back to study her face, and she could see by his expression that he didn't believe her, but after a moment more, he hugged her close and murmured against her ear, "Shall I fuck you here, or on the bank?"

She gasped in mock outrage, but quickly wrapped her legs around his naked hips. "Here."

A moment later, he had his back against the side of the pool, and was gripping his cock in one hand, while palming her ass to position her sex until, with a powerful flex of his hips, he thrust deep inside her, while switching both hands to her butt and slamming her against his erection until she felt the slap of his balls.

He paused then for just a moment to meet her eyes solemnly and say, "I love you, Antonia."

She knew it was too soon for such declarations, too fraught with danger to utter such words, but if she was going to lose him, then he would first know how she felt. "I love you," she said and had to hide her face against his shoulder, thankful for the noise of the water that hid her tears of despair that she should have met the one man she would love more than any other at such an impossible time for them both.

Their lovemaking was frantic after that, almost desperate, as if they both knew deep in their souls that this might be the last time they had together, the last time their bodies would join in a climax of such ecstasy that their hearts might well stop beating for the joy of it.

But then, if they were going to die for loving each other, was there any better way to do it, than in each other's arms?

Antonia groaned at the hard thrust of his thick shaft, as her inner muscles strained around the sheer size of him, the dull ache deep inside when he could go no farther, as if he'd run into some hidden part of her body. She drank in each minute of their coupling, memorizing every ache and pain, every spiraling joy, until the orgasm swept through her, starting in the center of her sex and spreading outward like an exploding sun, until she was so full of heat and desire that she could only cling to Nico while her back arched and her body convulsed in his arms.

And just when Antonia finally thought she might return to earth, Nico's shouted grunt of pleasure had his heat filling her womb while his cock bucked in the grip of her inner muscles, and she was thrust into a second orgasm that left her limp and exhausted, while Nico clutched her against his chest, and somehow kept them from drowning.

When she woke, she was lying on Nico's chest, moving up and down to the sound of his breaths. She didn't remember getting out of the pool, and thought she must have passed out, leaving Nico to save her from drowning by lifting them both out safely. And since she was lying on *him,* he had to be lying on the rough ground at the pool's edge, which couldn't be comfortable. Although from his steady breathing, she thought he must be asleep still.

On the other hand, because she was on top, she became aware that the cave was darker, and the temperature colder. The air outside the cave must have cooled with the lowering sun, leaving the pool's heat insufficient to counter the cold air coming inside. Which meant, night couldn't be far, and they had to get back to their world before they were missed.

She sat up abruptly, straddling him while she searched futilely for her undergarment, before remembering it was probably snagged on some sharp knob inside the pool, if it hadn't been reduced to wispy strips of cloth that were bouncing around whatever jet of hot water bubbled up to the top. Thank the Goddess most of her clothes were lying outside on the dry bank, or so she hoped.

"It's late," she said urgently, when Nico grunted awake and gripped her thighs with both hands.

He yawned, but said, "It's all right, love. I magicked us here in sunlight. I can return us home at the same time. No one will know that you took advantage of my weakness, and ravaged me into unconsciousness."

She glared down at him impatiently. This was no time for quips. She wondered sometimes that Nico had managed to defeat Sotiris time and again in battle, when he was so rarely serious.

He smiled crookedly, as if reading her thoughts. "Rest assured, my beautiful Antonia, that I am deadly serious in battle. My fighters depend on me for their lives, and I do not take their courage lightly."

"Can you read my thoughts?" she demanded, eyeing him narrowly as she took advantage of his willingness to support her to pull on her now-damp socks and boots. She'd have to bury everything she'd worn deep in a laundry basket when she returned home.

"I could if I wanted to," he said agreeably. "But that would be an unforgiveable intrusion, and something I would never do. No, my love, you simply have an expressive face, and with every hour we spend together, I learn your thoughts a little more."

Antonia wasn't sure she liked that, and thought maybe she should begin scrutinizing him the same way. "We should go," she said simply.

"We will," he said, sitting up and offering her a hand to help her stand.

Standing after her, he pulled her into his arms for a last, hard kiss. "We'll get dressed outside. If the clothes are wet," he added, stopping her objection, "I'll dry them. And we'll go back to where we started, on a sunny afternoon, and then ride back to the estate as Master Petros and his new apprentice candidate. Would you like to succeed in your ambitions to be my apprentice?"

"I think not," she chided. "And please be serious."

He laughed, then pulling on his own boots, guided her back through the freezing water and into a day that was, as she suspected, well into evening with air that was far too cool to be wading through water all but naked.

NICO HELD THE mare's bridle as they rode through the gates to Sotiris's estate and went directly to the barn. True to his word, as always, the sun was no more than an hour lower in the sky than when they'd left, and the guards gave him a sympathetic look, assuming from his grip on the bridle that his apprentice candidate had proven himself unworthy of the task.

Once in the barn and out of sight, he lifted Antonia from her saddle, sensing her exhaustion despite her best efforts to conceal it. "Go," he said, kissing her forehead. "I'll take care of the horses. It *is* my job, after all."

She gave him a weak smile. "When will I see you?"

"I'll be here whenever I can." He looked at her seriously. "Antonia, I understand why you came to me last night. But I don't ever want you to risk doing that—"

"You're taking risks."

"You're right, I am. But I am also far more powerful than you, and able to conceal or defend myself as necessary. More importantly, there is no one watching *my* comings and goings. No one spying on me, or following my every move. Take this." He took a talisman from the inside pocket of his leather vest and handed it to her. It appeared to be an ordinary gold coin, until one looked closer and saw the tiny imprint of a star in the very center of one side. "Keep it with you. If you need me for any reason, speak these words." He leaned close and whispered a word, which made her smile.

"Very original, Lord Nicodemus."

He grinned, and in that grin, she saw Nico, not Master Petros, despite the seeming still in place. It was reassuring in one way, but in another it made her fear for his safety, should an enemy see him behind the spell the way she did.

"Say that word, love, and I'll come. No matter when, no matter why. Do you understand?"

"Of course. I'm not a dimwit."

"No, you're my beautiful, stubborn Antonia. If you love me, take care of yourself. And use the talisman if you suspect you're in danger. Take no chances. I'd rather you use it unnecessarily, than risk not using it when it's needed."

"All right," she said with a touch of impatience. "I understand, and I promise to use the talisman should I need it."

He studied her a moment, then nodded. "Good. Go now. I'll see you soon."

She looked around quickly, then went up on her toes and kissed his mouth. "You take care of my Nico, too, or I'll be very angry."

He grinned. "I might enjoy seeing you angry."

"Nico," she snapped.

"Fear not. I love you far too much to play reckless with my life. I will guard my safety."

"Good." She sighed. "I really must get back to the tower." She started to walk away, then turned to add, "I love you," in a whisper, before running from the barn.

Chapter Seven

A WEEK LATER, Antonia woke with the morning sun, filled with purpose. Today was the day. Sotiris had declared war on Nico, or Nico on Sotiris, to hear him talk. It didn't matter who had cast the final die, the war had been just over the horizon for months, and no one was surprised when it finally cast its shadow on the sunrise.

Climbing from bed, she bathed her hands and face, and changed into fresh clothing suitable for a long afternoon and beyond cooped up in her tower room doing research. It was time to take the final steps toward the hexagon's completion, including priming the device to designate its target. As she'd told Nico, once the target was fixed, it couldn't be changed. The only uncertainty for her had been the freshness of the required blood sample. She'd worried that the sample would deteriorate if she collected it too soon, since blood retained its liquid form and appearance for only a short time once drained from the body. Those concerns had complicated this most important step, but she'd had a solution in mind and was confident it would work. If it didn't, then no harm, since the device would remain inactive and waiting to be primed. But if her solution *did* work, then she would be ready to deliver a finished weapon to Nico, with Sotiris as its sole target.

In plain terms, if she succeeded in arming the device against Sotiris, she would have no option but to take the hexagon and leave his estate immediately. Because Sotiris would know the instant the weapon was primed and would come looking for her. She had to be gone before then, or he would seize and possibly destroy the device. Though he'd probably kill her first.

She worked through the afternoon and was about to break for dinner—which was the only meal Sotiris expected her to attend on a regular basis. She didn't know why he cared. It surely wasn't because he enjoyed her company. She was a tool, a necessary expedience in his goal to acquire allies among the elites of their society. Beyond the bare requirements of civility, he otherwise ignored her. Except for her research. He paid a great deal of attention to that, and considered it to be *his* property, since she was *his* tool.

Fortunately, just as she'd begun organizing her notes in anticipation of the necessary dinner interruption, she received word that Sotiris wouldn't be able to join her for the evening meal, as he was deep in discussions with his generals regarding the pending battle with Nicodemus.

Sighing in relief, Antonia requested a dinner tray and bent her head to her work. When she next looked up, it was late in the night and the slender moon, which had been high in the sky, was already beginning its descent. She stared at that night sky while something very close to fear choked the breath from her throat, making it difficult to breathe as she contemplated what she was about to do. What she *had* to do.

Turning back to her desk, she contemplated the hexagon where it sat in its velvet-lined box. It was almost beautiful, with its unusual shape, and hidden glints of crystalline color. But evil often hid behind a beautiful face, so why shouldn't a weapon against it share the same beauty?

Inhaling deeply, she stood and gathered the instruments she needed, then clasping them to her breast, she crossed to the small sleep chamber which adjoined her workroom, and closed the door. She wanted privacy for what she was about to do, and since she often rested in the small chamber when working late, the maids knew not to disturb her for anything less than a demand from Sotiris himself.

She lit the bedside lantern from the candle she carried and removed her outer clothing. She'd practiced what she was about to do on a sheep or two, sneaking into the covered pen at night and herding one of the animals into the barn for her experiment. Since she required only a small amount of blood, it hadn't hurt the animals, though she'd still felt guilty at the need to knock them out for a short period of time. She wasn't skilled enough to draw the blood while the animal was thrashing, and besides they were far too noisy and would have attracted attention.

Still, she'd never done it on a person, much less herself. She had considered asking her personal maid to volunteer as a test subject, but had rejected the idea in the end. The woman had kept more than one secret on Antonia's behalf, but this one might have stretched her loyalty too far, and possibly even put her in danger.

Sitting on the bed next to a pile of clean cloths, which might be necessary to control her bleeding, Antonia covered herself with one of the big aprons that hung in the kitchen for anyone to use. Bracing herself for what she was about to do, she picked up the small, hollow, wooden tube she'd carved herself, checked to be sure that the short length of pig's gut was securely attached to one end, then drew a deep breath and stuck the other end into herself, shoving it deep until blood began to flow.

No more than a minute or two passed before the small vial was filled, though it seemed much longer to Antonia. Tears flooded her eyes from the pain, and her face and chest were covered in a cold sweat. Wiping her eyes with one of the clean cloths, so she could see what she needed to do, she withdrew the sharpened tube and set it carefully aside, along with the precious vial of blood. Not until that was secure did she turn her attention to the damage she'd inflicted, which was substantial, if the blood still trailing from the wound was any indicator.

She'd learned wound care at her mother's knee, since it commonly fell to the ladies of any court to tend to fallen fighters who returned injured from a battle. She'd never put those skills to that purpose, since her lady mother hadn't engaged actively in any wars since Antonia had come of age, and Sotiris preferred to treat fighters on the battlefield, and then return them to their own villages and farms, rather than bring them to his own estate.

Antonia was grateful for those lessons as she now found herself treating her own bloody damn wound. The bleeding continued for longer than had been necessary for the withdrawn sample, but eventually it stopped long enough for her to place a thick wad of clean cloth over the puncture hole and bind it tightly. She used care in redressing herself, both to avoid disturbing the wound, and to ensure there was no outward sign of it.

With the worst of it completed, Antonia laid back on the bed for a short rest. Her heart was still beating too fast in her chest, and she was mildly lightheaded, though she thought that was probably due not only to her blood loss, but to the absence of sleep, and frankly, fear. So much could go wrong at this point. She had to be clearheaded for this next, final step. Because it could not be undone.

Finally feeling better, she sat up slowly, poured a cup of water and drank it down, then picked up the vial of blood and walked out to her workroom to prime the hexagon. She couldn't get Sotiris's blood without alerting him to what she planned, but the blood of his child . . . She thought it would work. *Hoped* it would work. Else, she'd have risked her life for nothing. "WHAT HAVE YOU DONE?" The roar of Sotiris's demand shocked Antonia so badly, she nearly fell from her high stool when she spun around to face him. He must have snuck up the stairs for her not to have heard him coming. His usual habit was to storm up so forcefully that she knew he was coming after his first step.

Regardless of how he'd gotten there, however, he knew what she'd done and was livid. His rage was an assault on her senses, surrounding her like a cloud of dirt on a windy road, threatening to invade her throat and choke the air from her body.

Antonia waited a moment before speaking, not wanting her voice to show her fear, not willing to give him the satisfaction. "I'm working on the hexagon, as I have been for weeks."

"Don't lie to me, you little bitch. You've primed it. Whose blood, damn you?"

She drew a deep breath and met his furious gaze head on. "Yours, my lord."

He stared at her, unmoving. To anyone else, he might have appeared to grow calm. But Antonia knew this was Sotiris at his most dangerous. He wasn't an ordinary man. His power was fearsome and deadly, and didn't require any elaborate display to kill.

"You lie," he said flatly, then sneering said, "You haven't been close enough to me in months to have taken my blood."

Bracing herself for his attack, she said, "A child bears the father's blood."

He sucked in a breath. "You wouldn't dare."

"I would dare that and much more to save my world from you."

Sotiris seemed to grow larger then, as if his rage was so great that his body could no longer contain it. Antonia tried to run, but one powerful fist swung out and struck her head, knocking her to the floor. Stepping over her body, Sotiris picked up the hexagon, turned, and walked to the door.

"You're a fool if you thought I'd ever permit you to hand this over to Nicodemus." He turned his head and shouted down the stairs. "Breixo!"

Antonia lay on the floor, ears ringing and blood dripping from a cut on her forehead where she'd hit the desk on her way down. Breixo was Sotiris's personal guard, always with him and fanatically loyal. He was also a brute who'd assaulted more than one serving wench and left them pregnant or permanently traumatized. She didn't think Sotiris was angry enough to let the vicious bastard have his way with her, but she didn't want the man touching her under any circumstance.

When the big fighter appeared, Sotiris jerked his head at Antonia where she lay on the floor and said, "Escort Lady Antonia to a cell downstairs. I want her secure, and not comfortable." He swiveled his head slowly to smirk at her once more. "I'll deal with you after the war is over and Nicodemus is dead. You chose the wrong sorcerer, and now you'll live with the consequences."

Antonia blinked rapidly while she watched him leave the room, desperately trying to remain conscious, and terrified of what Breixo might do if she passed out while in his control. She swallowed an instinctive cry when he reached down and grabbed her arm, yanking her to her feet with no regard for the blood running down her face and blinding her in one eye. Sotiris obviously didn't care, and so neither would Breixo. The man had no emotions of his own.

They passed several servants on the stairs as he dragged her beside him, before finally picking her up and throwing her over his shoulder after complaining that she was slowing him down. The maids who knew her well covered their gasps of dismay lest Breixo turn his attention to them, and one of the younger maids ran at the sight of her bloody face. Antonia had assumed the girl had run in fear, but a few minutes later, the head housekeeper placed herself in Breixo's way and demanded to know what was going on.

"None of your concern," he growled. "Lord Sotiris wants her downstairs, and downstairs she's going."

"She may well bleed to her death before you get there."

"That is no concern of mine. If the lord wanted her injury treated, he'd have said so. He didn't." And so saying, he shoved the older woman out of his way and kept going.

No one else tried to stop them as Breixo descended to a level Antonia had never known existed, deep in the bowels below the tower, deeper even than the prisoner cells, and the cold storage rooms which she'd visited more than once. She couldn't see much of their surroundings, but she could feel the cold, and detect the scent of old, dead things. Or maybe people. She shivered, which made Breixo laugh.

"Not what you're used to, is it? You being a fine lady and all. Pretty, too. I'm hoping my lord will let me play a bit, once he's gotten what he needs from you."

Antonia swallowed hard when her stomach threatened to disgorge the small amount she'd eaten. She'd figure out some way to kill herself before she let him touch her.

Without warning, she was tossed from his shoulder to the floor, bumping her head against the wall before she managed to control her own body. Looking around with her one good eye, she saw a small, dank room, with rough stone walls and no light, other than the small amount shining through the open door from a torch on the wall outside. Scooting backward, she pressed against the cold wall and pulled her knees to her chest, covering her legs with her skirt.

"Are you hungry?" Breixo demanded. He laughed when she shook her head. "Good, 'cuz you ain't getting no food." He left then, laughing at his own wit while he closed and locked the thick wooden door behind him.

She saw then that there was a small round opening in the cell door, no bigger than her fist, which admitted a narrow shaft of light from the torch outside . . . until Breixo took the torch with him, and she was left in utter, complete darkness.

ANTONIA DIDN'T know how long it had been since she'd been discarded by Sotiris, thrown into a black hole from which there was no escape. She had her magic, which was strong, but not useful against this predicament. Her gift lay in nature, in nurturing and growing things of the earth, while her intellect and skill served the crafting of devices and spells which were nearly impossible to unravel. She could have used her power to bring a bit of light into her prison, but she wasn't sure she wanted to see what might be sharing the cell with her. More importantly, reason told her to save her strength for when it would make a difference. She had spells she could use against Sotiris that even he didn't realize she possessed. But as with every other spell, they were driven by her own power, and he was so much stronger than she was that it made sense to hold even those spells in reserve for when they would do the most good.

Right now, she was so cold and her thoughts so murky as a result of her injuries, that all she could do was huddle in a corner, trying to get warm. How long would he leave her here? Would they supply water, at least? Or would someone in the distant future find her bones in this dark, dank hole, and wonder whom she'd been?

Thoughts of Nico rose then. He wouldn't know yet that she'd been taken. She wasn't sure when he *would* know. If she failed to show up for their morning ride, he'd miss her, but might well assume she'd been unable to break away from whatever demands Sotiris had placed on her. And while the servants would certainly have spread the word of Sotiris's treatment of her—more than one had seen Breixo carrying her down the stairs—would anyone think to tell Petros Vasilis *why* she was unavailable for their morning ride? Would anyone *dare*?

Tears threatened as she shifted to one side, trying uselessly to find a comfortable place to lie on the cold stone. She hugged herself into a tight ball, wrists crossed in front of her chest, head bent low against her knees. Something was digging into her breast, and she almost ignored it as one more discomfort and a small one at that. But it niggled at her awareness in a way that had her sitting up to untie the laces on her tunic and slide her fingers under her chemise to find . . . By all the gods, she was an idiot. The talisman Nico had given her was hot against her skin, as if aware of her danger and trying to get her attention.

She gripped the small medallion, sensing Nico's magic in it, magic that was so tinged with violence and raw power, and yet somehow was also as warm and loving as if he was with her. It felt as if simply touching it brought him closer, though she knew it couldn't be that simple. She tried to remember the words he'd given her to say, but her head was pounding so loudly against her thoughts. Every beat was like a smith's hammer sounding in her skull, except this was ice not fire, and every blow splintered her thoughts before she could form them.

Holding the talisman close for comfort, if nothing else, she let herself slide sideways until she lay curled on the cold floor. If she could just close her eyes for a little while, just until the hammer stopped pounding in her head . . . . Her exhausted body began to drift, despite the hurt and discomfort. A person could only survive so much pain, so much shock, before the body shut down whether she willed it or not. And she began to think that sleep might be her best choice, after all. What reason was there to remain awake? What was left for her to wake to? The oblivion of unconsciousness called to her. No pain, no fear. Just sleep . . . and never waking.

And Nico. If she was going to die, she wanted his face to be the last thing she remembered. His would be the memory she took with her into the next life, and maybe, if the gods were kind, they'd meet again. She thought back to their last day together—the beauty and power of the waterfall, the rush of the river as it ran away from the frantic tumble of water over rocks, until it became a peaceful flow that ran for miles. She could smell the warm pool where they'd made love, the bright green scent of the moss, the slight sulfuric taint of the hot spring somewhere deep below when it bubbled to the top. And Nico . . . his beautiful face, the love in his gold-flecked eyes when he looked at her, love that reminded her she was a woman, even as it emboldened belief in her own strength and intellect.

She shoved herself upright, shocked at the path of her thoughts. She wasn't ready to die. She wouldn't give Sotiris the satisfaction, or make her death easy for him to explain. She could practically hear his voice, explaining to her mother how she'd died. After all, women died of ordinary ailments every day. Such a tragedy, he would say. Such a young woman, so beautiful, so gifted. The bastard. Her mother probably wouldn't believe him, but there'd be no one to say otherwise. No one to bring Antonia back from the dead to testify against her killer.

But of all the people who might miss her, all the people she might leave behind, it was Nico who pulled her from the fog of her thoughts and demanded she fight to stay alive. And just like that, as if waiting for her to refuse to surrender, she could see him handing her the talisman, could hear his voice telling her to hold it in her hand and say his name, and he would come.

Closing her eyes and praying to the gods she was right, she gripped the talisman in both hands and with the image of him firmly in her thoughts, she whispered his name. "Nicodemus."

Minutes passed, and her hope dimmed. She was certain she'd made a mistake, that her throbbing head had delivered the memory she *wanted,* rather than the one that had actually occurred, and Nico wouldn't be coming. But an instant later, he was simply . . . there, stepping out of a magic portal into the dank cell, and looking around in confusion, before whispering a single word that flooded the cell with light.

The unexpected light, after so long in the dark, stabbed into Antonia's head like a heated blade, and she bent her head to her knees once more, hands over her eyes. She didn't see Nico move, but she heard the vicious curse when he saw her, the scuff of his boot when he came close, and the tears in his voice when he said, "I'm here, love. I'm here."

He was so warm when he lifted her from the cold stone, that she felt scorched by the heat of his powerful arms when he tucked her against a body so familiar that she added her own tears to his. She had no strength left to sob, no voice to cry out. Her tears were silent trails that burned her skin as they washed the blood from her face.

That was the last thought she had before she was abruptly surrounded by magic so strong that it sang in her bones when Nico stepped back into his portal and took her home.

NICO PACED OUTSIDE his bedroom, fury warring with concern over what that bastard Sotiris had done to Antonia. The man who above all should have protected her had beaten her unconscious and thrown her into a cell that no one deserved, much less Antonia.

Well, that part of her life was over now. He would die before he'd permit her to return to Sotiris's estate for any reason. *He* could provide everything she needed, could sure as hell protect and care for her better than Sotiris ever had. What kind of life had she lived all these years, afraid to speak her mind, to deny his demands, or even to miss an evening meal without his permission? And what about her mother? The woman was powerful enough to have moved her daughter back to her own estate, no matter Sotiris's wishes to the contrary. It was obvious that Sotiris didn't care enough about Antonia to have protested her absence.

Except for her magical skills, he realized. Sotiris would have missed those, and in particular the hexagon. Nico's first thought upon finding Antonia in that dark cell had been that Sotiris had discovered her affair with his enemy, and struck her in anger. But now, he wondered if Sotiris had somehow learned of her plan not only to prime the device against him, but to give it to Nico.

It didn't matter what the reason was, really. There was no excuse for a man to beat a woman into unconsciousness, no excuse for banishing her to a cold, dark cell beneath his tower.

He stopped in front of his bedroom door and raised a fist, ready to demand entry no matter what the healers told him. He needed to see Antonia with his own eyes, needed to know that Sotiris's attack had not injured her so badly that she wouldn't recover, not even with the best healers in the realms by her side. But before his fist could fall, the door opened, and his lead healer stood there, studying him with patient, understanding eyes that never changed.

"Come in, my lord. The lady is asking for you."

"Thank the gods," he muttered, but retained enough couth to gesture for the older woman to precede him into the room. Forcing himself to take measured steps, rather than the headlong rush to Antonia's bedside that was his instinct, he studied the horrific bruises and bloody scrapes discoloring her pale face, her limp hands crossed over her chest above the quilt that was pulled to her chin. She was a ghost of herself, not drained of magic by her injuries, but far too weak to use them. Even more than that, however, was the absence of vitality that brought a blush to her cheeks and a sparkle to her eyes. Looking at her now, no one would know she'd been strong enough to defy one of the most powerful sorcerers alive in order to save the world they all shared. Smart enough, yes. Intellect didn't require courage. But his Antonia was more than smart. She was courageous and brilliant, a woman with her own thoughts and beliefs and the fortitude to see them through, despite the danger it might visit upon her.

No longer "might," he thought angrily. She'd clearly defied Sotiris somehow, to bring about this result. But Nico hadn't spoken enough words with her yet to know what had been said or done. And as selfish as it made him, he needed to know. He would be standing across a battlefield from Sotiris very soon, and needed to know what he might face. His four warriors were already gathered below, waiting to learn what they could of Sotiris's battle plans and especially, this new weapon he claimed to possess which would damage Nico badly enough to shift the battle irrevocably in his favor.

Nico had thought long and hard on that subject. Had even set his warriors to considering the same problem. Yet none of them could claim knowledge of what Sotiris had referred to as Nico's "greatest weapon." Perhaps the man had been spouting bullshit, hoping word would get to Nico, who would then waste time worrying about it. If so, the bastard had succeeded, but only to some small extent.

"Nico."

His thoughts snapped immediately back to the present, and the woman he loved, who was lying in his bed, where she belonged. Dropping to his knees at the bedside, he closed his hands over hers, which brought a faint smile to her face.

"So warm," she murmured, when her eyes opened enough to meet his. "That's what I remember most. Your body was so warm. It felt so good."

Nico could imagine any number of scenarios over the past few days when that would have been true, but he assumed she meant when he'd lifted her from that filthy cell, her body so cold that he'd worried she might suffer injuries from the freezing temperature alone.

"Any time you need warming, my lady, I'm available."

"Nico," she scolded in a whisper. The blush on her cheeks was barely noticeable under the bruises, but her glance over his head to where the healer still waited was unmistakable.

He grinned and leaned forward to put his lips to her ear. "You're in my bed, love. I think they know you're mine."

Her lips tightened briefly, which made her wince, and his jaw clenched at the reminder of how she'd come to be there. "I'll kill him," he growled and forced himself to relax the grip on her hands, which had tightened in reflex.

She shook her head slightly as tears filled her eyes. "He has it," she whispered. "I primed it to target him, and thought to sneak it to you when we next rode, but . . ." She coughed dryly. A cup of water appeared over his shoulder, held in the healer's hand. He took it with a whisper of thanks and placed it carefully against Antonia's lips, letting her take only the smallest sips, before she'd had enough and shook her head against any more.

Nico's healers were the only people in the room, and he trusted them absolutely. And yet . . . the hexagon was the kind of weapon that could win, or lose, wars. The kind of weapon a man, or a sorcerer, would pay a great deal of gold to gain control of, or even information about. Before Antonia could say anything more, he cast a spell to enclose the two of them in a sphere of privacy, so that whatever was said would go no farther than their own ears.

"If you primed the device to his blood, it cannot be used against me. Perhaps it was the hexagon he counted on to drain away my magic, which is surely my greatest weapon. If so, he's lost the device he counted on to defeat me."

She grimaced and tightened her hold on his hand. "That's not it. He wanted to use it against you, but I told him I couldn't ensure it would be ready in time. He's created something else, something new. I couldn't discover what it is. He kept it even from me, though I know he began working on it weeks ago, if not longer."

"We both have new spells and weapons, love, I—"

"No," she insisted, though it was obvious her strength was fading. "He's too . . . pleased with himself. You must beware, Nico. You won't expect whatever it is."

"All right," he said, wanting to soothe her so she could rest. "My four warrior brothers wait below to help plan for the battle and design new strategies that Sotiris won't expect. If we alter our attack strategy, he'll be forced to change his own in response. That might be enough to thwart whatever he has planned. And if not, we'll be ready, because of *your* warning, Antonia. You are the most courageous woman I have ever met."

Her eyes were still dark with worry under the haze of exhaustion, but she managed a smile for him. "My courage is slight compared to the warrior women who fight by your side."

"They are not greater or lesser, simply different. Sleep now, and I'll return soon."

DESPITE HIS reassurances to Antonia, Nico was worried. He'd

received a formal proclamation of war from Sotiris just three nights ago, the message delivered to the night watch. Opening the scroll was well beyond the night commander's authority, but noting who'd sent it, he'd done the right thing and ordered Nico wakened.

Both sorcerers had known war was coming and had been preparing for it almost since the cessation of their last battle. If it was going to happen this year, it had to be before the first snowfall, with enough time to either settle their hatred forever, or declare another truce and retire to their castles to plan for a spring offensive. They each had armies already bivouacked on the chosen battleground, which had been selected by Sotiris. As the two sorcerers had been fighting on and off for years, they'd agreed long ago to alternate the choice of battleground between the two of them. It added a veneer of civility to their ongoing wars, except that there was nothing civil or even honorable about war. Hundreds of men had died, hundreds more permanently injured with many of them no longer able to support their families. In Nico's opinion, it was an ongoing tragedy that had to end, but it would only do so if one of them died.

Thoughts of their endless conflict and the lives it had ruined were nothing new to Nico as he took the stairs down to the conference room where he'd meet the four men who were the greatest warriors their world had ever known. If anyone could devise a strategy to deal with the many unknowns of Sotiris's battle plan, it was these four.

They were waiting for him when he opened the doors to the war room, which had a variety of weapons and maps covering every bit of space on the stone walls, and a huge wooden table that was similarly covered with maps and sketched-out attack plans. All four looked up when he entered, and all four had the same questioning look on their faces. They knew about the hexagon, because he'd told them the same night that Antonia had first visited his castle with word of the device. They'd also been made aware of her presence upstairs, along with the circumstances of her rescue. And every one of them was intelligent and experienced enough to understand what it might mean for the battle they'd be fighting the next morning.

"The lady?" Damian asked. Though they were all close, Damian and Nico had grown up together. Nico had somehow conjured Damian to his side, when they'd both been very small boys. Not even Nico knew if he'd pulled the other boy from a life somewhere else, or if he'd been literally created by Nico's will. It didn't matter to either of them. They were brothers and always would be, though it did mean that the big, blond warrior had a more instinctive understanding of how Nico's mind worked.

"She's been shockingly brutalized," Nico said. "But my healers are seeing to her, and she's safe."

Damian was studying him shrewdly. "She's more to you than a spy in Sotiris's court."

Nico eyed him back, torn between his gut-deep need to protect Antonia, and his loyalty to these men. "I love her, and intend to wed her when this is over, no matter the cost."

Kato gave a low whistle. "That must grate on Sotiris's pride like a rusty blade."

"Fuck Sotiris and his pride. He's the one who beat her."

"Fuck him indeed, then," Gabriel growled. "No honorable warrior would hit a woman, much less one who looks to him for protection."

"Except on the battlefield," Damian commented.

"A warrior is neither male nor female," Gabriel replied. "She is simply a warrior."

Damian, who'd once been worshipped as a god of war, grinned. "A fine distinction, my friend. And one I agree with."

Gabriel snorted to indicate his opinion of Damian's agreement.

Nico let their banter flow over and through him without much notice. No matter what they said or how much they might disagree, they were a single unit on the field, and would each die to defend the others. Instead, he looked to the one warrior who rarely spoke, though he probably had more real battlefield experience than any of them. He'd been chosen by the goddess of his people to singlehandedly defeat armies of invading barbarians who threatened the island where he'd been born.

"Dragan?"

The warrior lifted green eyes to meet Nico's. It was a gaze marked by the nightmare that had been his life before he'd left his island home in response to Nico's spell calling the greatest warriors to join him.

"The hexagon is no longer our concern," Dragan said. "As its designer, the lady understands its use better than anyone, including Sotiris. He may well attempt to reforge it for a future battle, but knowing she's made him the device's only target, he won't dare attempt its use tomorrow. He's no fool, and he also lacks the courage to take that risk. We should instead be looking to this other device or spell he claims to possess, the one that will deprive Nico of his greatest weapon."

"Agreed," Damian said readily. "But I, for one, have no idea what that might be. Our strategies are not dependent on a single weapon, great or otherwise."

The others started to speak, but again it was Dragan whose quiet words had the others going still. "We four are often spoken of as his greatest weapon."

"Well, fuck," Damian whispered.

Silence reigned for several minutes, before Kato said, "He could possibly eliminate *one* of us if he turned a number of his fighters on that one at the same time. But even then, we are rarely alone on the field at any time. Even if our brothers were somehow unable to support us, we're surrounded by multiple soldiers who would come to our defense. It must also be said that even without that assistance, none of us would go down easily."

"Sorcery can overcome even the greatest warrior, if the spell is properly designed and executed," Damian said darkly.

"Perhaps one of us, if he was very fortunate," Gabriel agreed. "But how could he take out all four at the same time? We don't march in line like ducklings on a pond when we fight."

"And yet, Antonia was convinced that his confidence was more than an idle boast, and she knows him and his machinations better than any of us," Nico reminded them. "Having said that, however, I don't see how we can defend against something we know so little about. We can alter our fighting techniques so that the four of you fight in pairs, rather than solitary, and I can shield Dragan whenever he takes to the air."

"Will that severely limit the amount of sorcery you can put into play against him directly?" Kato asked. "Perhaps that was his plan all along, that he would let slip word of this new weapon, so that your magic would be divided."

"He couldn't have known Antonia would come to me with the hexagon. She didn't know herself until the first day she rode through my gates."

"She may have let slip some doubts," Kato replied, although his own doubt flavored the words.

"Would her doubts be sufficient for him to secure his strategy on? That would be risky indeed, and as Dragan rightly pointed out, Sotiris is not a courageous man," Damian said.

"Enough." Nico raised both hands, palm out. "We can't possibly know what Sotiris hopes or plans for, if anything at all. We will take what steps we can to mitigate our vulnerability, but we must fight as we always have . . . with our best skill, and with knowledge of the many lives at stake." He looked around the table. "Agreed?"

Four nods were returned.

"Good. We'll arrive on the field before sunrise tomorrow, and survey Sotiris's deployments, noting anything that appears unusual or suspect. If nothing, then we proceed as always."

Damian stood, flask of ale lifted, and the others joined him. "To our leader, and our brother, Nicodemus." They all raised their flasks in Nico's direction and drank. "And to victory," Damian added.

Five flasks were raised, and five voices shouted, "To victory!"

Nico and his brothers spent several hours rehashing their battle plans, and making what changes they could without knowing more about Sotiris's strategy. But he remained somewhat concerned, especially after Dragan had pointed out that these four, who had fought so many battles by his side and meant so much to him, were truly his greatest weapon. He would die without hesitation if it would save any one of their lives. Yet wars weren't won on emotions, but on superior skill and flexible strategy, both of which he had on his side. It was also true that he was a more powerful sorcerer than Sotiris, and more innovative in the use of his magical skills. He knew he'd done everything possible, short of surrender, to avoid catastrophe in the coming battle. And so, it was with a confident heart that he stood at the foot of the stairs outside his tower, and bid his warriors good night. He remained standing there until they'd ridden through the gates and disappeared into the night. All four would ride to the battlefield tonight, to wake with the army and see to their disposition on the field.

Nico would arrive very soon after sunrise, but first he would spend what might be his final night on earth with Antonia, and see to her safety, whether or not he returned from the field.

Chapter Eight

HE MADE NO ATTEMPT to stifle his footfalls when he climbed the stairs of his tower, and so he wasn't surprised when his head healer was waiting outside the door of his bedroom.

"My lord." The woman's greeting was warm as always, though her eyes showed the effects of one more sleepless night after a lifetime of too many. Healers were born, not made, and they began training very young—as soon as their gifts became evident. It was safer for the healer, and better for their patients that way, and healers were both loved and appreciated, since they treated all, regardless of ability to pay. Nick's healers treated everyone on his estate, and anyone else who came to the gate needing help. It was why he maintained a large staff of them, but also why so many healers wanted to work on his estate.

"Good evening, Magda. Or is it morning by now?"

"Just past the stroke of midnight, my lord."

"Ah. The beginning of an iniquitous day, I'm afraid."

"Only the enemy is wicked, my lord."

He smiled wearily. "How do you know that I am not the wicked one?"

"Because I know you, and because only a beast could have beaten one so vulnerable to a man's fists as Lady Antonia. On my oath, I have never seen a more odious example of brutality."

"On that we can agree. How is the lady faring?"

"Much better than when you left. She's undergone three separate rounds of healing, by myself and two others, thus her physical ailments are substantially improved. Her emotions are still running high, so I've calmed her somewhat. I expect, however, that your presence will do more to reassure her than anything I can do."

"Thank you, Magda. I'll remain with her through the night, so you may go to your bed for now. I shall be leaving before dawn, however, and don't want her left alone. I will also provide additional guards for her safety. Sotiris cannot himself leave the field of battle, but he may well think to take advantage of my preoccupation to send others to retrieve that which he considers his."

Magda snorted in disgust. "They will find no easy target here, my lord. Healers can *cause* injury as well as heal it."

Nico grinned. "I won't tell anyone you said that, but I shall, however, endeavor to keep the number of people requiring your care tomorrow as low as possible."

"Much appreciated, my lord. See to it that you are one of those."

"Good night, Magda."

"Rest well, my lord."

NICODEMUS CLOSED the door behind the healer and cast a locking spell to be sure no one could enter without blowing the door itself off its hinges. He would wake long before that happened, so anyone who tried would be dead well before their attempt succeeded. He needed to know that Antonia was safe before he could rest, and he needed to rest if he was to outwit Sotiris the next morning.

Removing his clothes, he slid under the covers and pulled Antonia into his arms. She hummed with pleasure when she recognized his body, or maybe his scent. What mattered to Nico was that she knew and welcomed him, even though she was still affected by the healer's sleep spell. He lay still, holding her in his arms, content just to know that she was now his forever. There was no going back from what he'd done in taking her from Sotiris's clutches, no longer room for any explanation but the truth when it came to their relationship.

He knew he should sleep, but couldn't bring himself to let it happen. He wanted to slide into her body one more time, to make slow love to her here, in his bed, not on a blanket under the trees or behind a waterfall, no matter how beautiful or romantic. He had a . . . premonition was too strong a word. Call it a gut feeling instead, that he wouldn't return unscathed from the battlefield tomorrow, that tonight might be his last time with her. And still, he couldn't bring himself to disturb her sleep, or worse, to trouble her with his unformed feelings of doom.

And so, he held her close in the protection of his arms until he slept, and didn't dream.

Chapter Nine

Five weeks later

THE MEMORIES THAT had chased Nicodemus into sleep had brought dreams so vivid that when he woke on the floor of Sotiris's tower so many weeks after their disastrous battle, he fully expected to find Antonia lying next to him. It took no more than a moment to realize where he was, and why, as the harsh reality of her loss crashed once more into his already battered heart. He sat up with a tired sigh and noted that someone had covered him with a blanket again, and that the scent of warm food filled the room.

Sotiris's servants took a risk offering such comfort to his enemy, no matter that the sorcerer was gone, and seemed likely to remain that way. Nico would have to provide for them somehow before he left. What would happen to Sotiris's tower if, as Nico believed, the bastard had fled into the same world where he'd sent the four warriors? For that matter, what would happen to his own tower when he did the same? There was little choice in the matter. It was the only route available if he wanted to find and free the people he loved from wherever Sotiris's curse had flung them.

He rubbed his face as he sat up fully and reached for the tea, not knowing how long he'd slept and hoping it was still warm. He immediately snatched his fingers back from the ceramic jug, sucking them like a child, but pleased that he'd have something hot to wet his throat and bring greater acuity to his thoughts. A linen-covered basket next to the jug produced breads as warm as the tea, and a fresh jam which was delicious. He'd have stolen Sotiris's cook for his own estate if he'd been planning to linger. He had duties here, responsibilities to people from the towns, villages, and farms across the lands he'd conquered. But this world held nothing for him anymore. The very air was like dust in his lungs, and the warm sun taunted him with visions of the unknown horrors his warriors might be enduring. And what of Antonia? Was she locked in a dark dungeon somewhere, awaiting Sotiris's benevolence?

She could die of neglect if that was the case, for the enemy sorcerer surely had none to give.

Nico finished the light breakfast, which only served to make his stomach growl for more. He became aware for the first time in days? weeks? that he was hungry. He needed to find the kitchen that housed Sotiris's excellent cook and ask politely for something more substantial, preferably meat. Maybe if he ate a better meal, his thoughts would clear, and he could decide what his next steps should be.

Because he had a critical decision to make. He'd unraveled enough of Sotiris's spell that he now knew his warriors had been cast into the maelstrom of time and place, although that knowledge brought no comfort, nor hope of finding them easily. And he still hadn't found the smallest clue as to Antonia's fate. She wasn't dead. He believed to the depths of his soul that he'd have felt her death as sharply as a knife to his heart. She was that important to him, that much a part of his existence. But the universe was a huge place, with worlds intersecting and time a fluid thing. He'd never thought to travel beyond the world and time he'd been born to—he'd had no reason. But now that he did, he wished he'd paid better attention to the great thinkers who'd hypothesized that structure of reality, some of whom had even taken the leap and ventured forth, determined to prove, to themselves at least, that their theories were correct. None of them had ever returned, however, which meant they were either dead, or had found a world better than this one. It was also possible, he supposed, that they'd simply been unable to return, or that the world they'd landed in hadn't been wonderful at all. But that possibility didn't change his own thinking one whit. If his warriors and Antonia were in a dangerous world, then they would need him all the more.

Nico climbed to his feet and set about straightening his clothes before venturing to the kitchen. If he hoped to make a special request of Sotiris's cook, he should look like what he was—a powerful sorcerer and landholder, born and raised the son of a king. Unfortunately, the shaking out of his clothes only served to make him aware that he hadn't bathed in—he frowned—a very long time. Weeks, he thought. It was a wonder the servants had bothered with him at all.

"Fuck." Well, there was nothing for it but for him to ask the first servant he encountered where he could bathe. Maybe he'd use Sotiris's own quarters. No doubt the accommodations there were of the highest quality and comfort. He considered for a moment whether the bastard would have set magical traps for the unwary in his own quarters. Was he that paranoid? Possibly, although the daily inconvenience of dealing with such traps would have been considerable. And for that matter, since Nico had penetrated his enemy's tower, he could surely manage to invade his chambers, too. The idea gave him sufficient satisfaction that he decided to venture forth and give it a try.

THE SUN WAS WELL into the sky by the time Nico was kissing a blushing cook on the cheek to thank her for the enormous and delicious breakfast she'd prepared for him. He was getting the clear impression from everyone he met in the halls—and especially the servants' corridors— that no one particularly mourned Sotiris's absence. Did they think Nicodemus was their new lord? He was beginning to believe they might, and it only made him feel more obligated to see to their futures, along with those of his own people. His personal assets, now combined with Sotiris's, were considerable, but he would need to assign someone from his own staff to see to their distribution.

He shook his head of the thought. He would do the best he could in the short time he had, but his first duty was to Antonia and his warriors. Bearing that in mind, he returned to Sotiris's tower and began gathering materials. He'd examined his choices going forward while he'd bathed and eaten. Both activities had helped clear his thoughts, thus permitting him to see the alternatives more clearly. And he'd made a decision. He could linger in this world forever and never find the clear answers he required. But while he lingered, the people he loved would be suffering.

Instead, he would gather what he could of Sotiris's notes and work-books, pack those which were the most recent and/or had been the most helpful to him thus far, and take them with him into the unknown future. He knew enough of the various theories regarding space and time that he wouldn't be able to pack a wagon, harness a pair of horses, and trundle into the unknown. Everything he wanted to take would have to be on his person, and even then, some of the materials might be too fragile for the passage, since he might be tossed around, or land badly in whatever place and time he ended. He would have to select carefully, which is what he set out to do with what was left of the day. Before sunset, he intended to be on his way back to his own estate, where he would complete his arrangements as quickly as he could, and then leave this world behind, forever.

The thought of leaving the only home he'd ever known should have been a sorrowful one. And it was, somewhat. But mostly, he found himself exhilarated at the prospect of seeing a new world, perhaps more than one. Would magic still prevail wherever he landed? The same men who hypothesized the existence of other worlds taught that there would be at least some magic in all of them . . . although they might only have been pandering to the wealthy sorcerers and other magic-users who supported them and their work.

Nico was trusting their knowledge with his life, but even so, he had few qualms about the things he might lose along the way. If his magic didn't work, his intellect would, and so would his charm, which had served him well in this world and would in the next.

The only nightmarish thought that continued to haunt him was the possibility that among Sotiris's papers that he was bringing with him—too many of which he hadn't yet read—would be the one journal, the lone page or scribbled note, that would tell him where Antonia was and how he could find her. And that singular piece of information would be the one page or journal somehow lost during his transition to the next world.

But lingering on that possibility would only freeze him in place until he'd read every book, every journal, every scribbled note in Sotiris's tower—which would take decades or more that he simply didn't have. Because in his heart of hearts, he believed it was necessary for him to leave as quickly as possible, if he hoped to end up in the same place Antonia and the others had been cast.

NICODEMUS WAS uncharacteristically somber when he reached his own home that night. It was an elegant castle with white stone peaks, surrounded by orchards that still held the scent of the fruits they bore in the spring and fall. The air carried the first chill of winter, which was usually the case when he was returning home from battle. The winters in this part of the world were harsh, and not even Sotiris had been willing to fight both the elements and his enemies.

Nico was more than tired when he climbed the stairs to his private tower. His heart lay like a stone in his chest, a burden to carry with every step. He knew he'd done everything right, everything possible, to retrace Sotiris's evil spell. And that the best chance his warriors had was for him to follow his instincts, to leave immediately and . . . never return to this place, which was the only home he'd ever known. But his brothers, and then Antonia, had made it a true home. Not his father or mother, certainly, nor his older brother who'd tormented him his entire childhood until he'd learned to use his magic to fight back.

"My lord."

The familiar voice, filled with worry, had him turning away from the stairs to face the man who was the true ruler within the walls of Nico's estate. "Seneca," he said, putting what little warmth he had left in him into the name. The manservant had been with Nico from his earliest years, and during that time, he'd been the closest thing Nico'd had to a father figure. "Everyone is well?"

"All but you, my lord. I look at you and know you need rest. Real rest. And some good food."

He grinned half-heartedly. "Sotiris's cook is a genius. You should bring her here."

"Bring her here? What of Sotiris? The reports we received had him still alive when last—"

"Alive, but well gone into another world, I believe. Never to return." He sighed deeply. "As I will soon be, my friend. Our enemy cast a deadly spell which I am left to somehow undo. I must follow him, Seneca. And I doubt either of us will ever return."

Seneca appeared stricken by the news. "Never return," he said slowly. "But you are victorious, these lands—all of them now—are yours to rule."

"Victory . . ." Nico repeated, as if tasting the word. "It is dust on my tongue, Seneca. He's taken my lady Antonia, and my brothers. Damian, Kato, Gabriel, Dragan . . . they're all gone."

"Dead," Seneca breathed.

"Worse even than that. Cast into a living hell to suffer until I can somehow find their individual prisons and free them."

"But how . . . ?"

"We were betrayed, old friend. Antioch sold his soul and his honor to the enemy, providing Sotiris with possessions from the very men who'd trusted him most, even called him friend. The items he stole were of little value to others, but of great personal value to each of the four warriors. Sotiris then used those treasures to personalize the powerful and heinous spell which sucked them from this world and into another, where they are even now suffering a terrible fate."

"Antioch? But why?"

"Money to buy his family a farm."

"He never mentioned—"

"No, not to me or the others either, I'm sure." Nico's gaze hardened when he met Seneca's eyes. "It's a farm he'll never enjoy, a family he'll never be a part of now. He's naught but mud on the battlefield by now."

"I don't understand such disloyalty to a lord like yourself. If he'd come to you . . . . Ah, but he didn't, and the die is cast." His expression was one of horror when he looked up at Nico. "But . . . Lady Antonia? Surely Sotiris would not—"

"No, not with the others, I don't believe. But beyond that . . . I cannot find her." It took every bit of strength he had left not to surrender to despair.

"But . . . your lands, this estate, and the others . . . . What will happen to them. To . . . us?"

"Everything I have is yours."

"My lord!" The manservant was aghast. "I am not—"

"You are a decent and good man, and more family to me than those who gave me life. You will do well and right by the others. My trust is yours."

Seneca looked from side to side as if searching for something that would make sense of what his master was saying. "When?"

"Tonight. There is no benefit in waiting. I will pack a few things and be gone."

"Will you . . . . My lord, will you share a meal with us before you go?"

Now that the decision was made, Nicodemus didn't want to delay a moment longer than necessary. Having told Seneca of his plans, and having passed to this good man the burden of ruling the estate, Nico wanted to throw Sotiris's journals into a backpack, along with a few necessary supplies and journals of his own, and leave. But it was fit that he end his life in this world by sharing dinner with the men and women who'd served him so well for so long.

"I will," he told Seneca. "But make it within the hour. Instinct is telling me that I have no hope of following Lady Antonia and my brothers if I delay beyond that. The alignment of worlds may shift without regard for my needs."

"Right away, then, my lord. I will see to it." Seneca started away, but stopped when he pulled an envelope from his pocket. "Forgive me," he said, holding it out to Nicodemus. "This came for you in the midst of battle, which I thought a curious thing. But with what you've told me . . . perhaps it is significant."

Nico almost didn't want to touch the envelope. He recognized Sotiris's writing, and knew it wouldn't contain anything good. Nothing Sotiris touched had ever been good. But Nico couldn't afford to ignore it, either. It would be very like his enemy to taunt him with some small piece of knowledge, some obscure clue as to the whereabouts of his people, and how he could find them across the many worlds. He took the envelope, which was worn and wrinkled, as if it had been stuffed into someone's pocket for too many days.

"When did this arrive?" he asked.

"Yesterday eve, my lord. The messenger was a young boy, and not one I recognized. It was, in fact, my impression that he'd been paid only to deliver this one thing."

"Last night," Nico murmured to himself. Sotiris had fled long before that, but if it was as Seneca believed, the boy could have taken far longer to deliver this missive than would the usual messenger.

"Thank you, Seneca. I will join you and the others in the kitchen very soon."

He continued up the stairs without further comment. What he'd said to Seneca was true. The sense inside him that time was running out was growing more urgent with every breath. He almost regretted agreeing to sit down to a meal with his staff, but the promise had been made. He would pack everything he intended to take with him before meeting the others, and leave immediately after.

Leave, he thought to himself. This would be a very different sort of leave-taking than any before. He wouldn't ride through the gates and travel the nearby road. Rather, he'd cast a spell and hope the fates were kind, which was always a chancy thing.

He didn't read the letter immediately, but set about gathering whatever notes and journals he thought would be most useful in his new life. It was a guessing game, since he had no idea where he'd end up. But even sorcery had immutable rules. So he packed what he could, and then stood for a moment simply breathing in the scent of his library, scanning the shelves and titles, trying to commit them to the prodigious memory which was the tool of a truly powerful sorcerer. He doubted these same tomes would exist wherever he ended up, but one never knew. If travel between the worlds was possible, albeit rare, then he might make the occasional fortuitous find in a market stall or library.

His final, and most important, task was to gather the various elements of Sotiris's spell. He had to be precise in this if he wanted to reach the same destination. The physical elements weren't the same. He didn't need the personal items Antioch had turned traitor to provide, since *he* was the only one making the transition. He didn't even need anything of his own, beyond whatever he was taking along. The crucial aspect had been figuring out which parts of Sotiris's spell had been responsible for selecting the ultimate destination for the unwilling warriors, then duplicating and incorporating those elements in his own spell. For all that, the task hadn't taken long, once he'd located and understood the spell itself. The most critical aspects were straightforward sorcery, and for that, Nico needed only himself.

Before he left his rooms to join his household staff for dinner, he rested on the same sofa where he'd first sat talking to Antonia, and opened Sotiris's final missive.

Nicodemus,

The fates have favored you once again, if you are alive to read this. If they were bound by logic or simple good sense, they'd have abandoned you long ago. But the outcome of this battle is no longer in play. Or so it would seem. Even the fates can be fooled if a sorcerer is smart and powerful and motivated by sufficient hatred that the impossible is no longer out of reach.

Your storied warriors have gone where you will never find them. Their lives will be eternal and filled with the agony of endless imprisonment. Every moment they suffer will strengthen the hatred they feel for your arrogance in having ripped them from their lives to serve yours.

Ah, but you are clever enough to have discovered this by now. I will grant you that much intellectual discipline, if not respect. But that is not my final gift to you. No, I reserve that to my treacherous Antonia, who in violation of nature and obligation betrayed me to serve you. I would like to believe she was the victim of ensorcellment on your part, but likely, she was simply weak, as seems to be the curse of all women.

You are no doubt desperate to discover her fate. Is she imprisoned in the manner of your warriors? Does she still live at all? Shall I tell you, my old enemy? And if I do, will you spend your life and power searching for her? That could prove a useful distraction for me, but far too easy a punishment for her. No, I have stolen far more than her freedom. I have stolen her very self, everything that has made her the unfaithful bitch she became. Sweet Antonia lives in the same world as your warriors, though perhaps not the same time. She has no knowledge of herself, no memory of you, or of the world where she was born. Her magic remains, though she cannot use it. The outward beauty that hides her treacherous heart will never fade. She has become a pretty porcelain doll who sits in a child's playhouse and neither knows nor cares anything of the world. Her only memory is of me, but even that is as shallow as she deemed it by act and devotion.

I have granted her eternal life. Eternal, meaningless, empty life.

Which is more than she earned with her betrayal. But lest you think me utterly unfeeling, I give you one more task, Nicodemus. Find her, claim her, and her "self" will be restored. Where shall you look? When shall you look? And whom shall you seek first? Your warriors or the woman?

One final note, Nicodemus Katsaros. I am not done with you. Wherever you go, I will be there, inflicting pain on anyone you dare to love, while I watch you scurry through the worlds searching for the past. That is my promise to you.

The pompous bastard signed the hateful missive with a wax seal and the scrawl of his full name . . . Sotiris Dellakos.

Nico tossed it to the floor, certain he could feel evil sliding off the paper, clinging like oil to his fingers. He wanted to rip it to shreds and burn the bits, but instead he picked it up, folded it neatly, and tucked it into his pocket. Sotiris was just vicious enough to have concealed some necessary bit of information within the text, hoping Nico would lose any chance of finding Antonia by following the impulse to destroy the hateful letter.

Antonia lived. That was all that mattered. That she didn't know herself, that she had no recourse to her magic . . . he couldn't understand how a man who should have cared at least some small measure for her could inflict such punishment. At least he'd let her live, even if he'd done it to further her punishment. There was a chance, and Nico was a powerful sorcerer. Which meant chance was *always* in play.

LATER THAT NIGHT, Nicodemus Katsaros stood in his tower room for the last time. He didn't linger for a final, sentimental perusal of his library. He had a purpose, and it was no longer in this world. Picking up the backpack which held everything he was taking with him, he began chanting the spell that would cast his fate to the mists of time, and the shifting reality of worlds. He would find his warriors. He would find his Antonia. And then he would find Sotiris. And he would kill him.

PART TWO

Chapter One

1824, Paris, France

NICODEMUS ARRIVED on a city street with a burst of magical energy that he quickly tried to contain, for fear it would draw every magic user in the vicinity to his location. He knew Sotiris had been to this place and time, because he'd replicated the other sorcerer's spell to get this far. What he didn't know was whether Sotiris was still here. He'd prefer to avoid confronting the enemy sorcerer until he was in full control of his powers. He also needed to discover exactly where and when he was before he did or said anything to anyone. It would be too easy to insult the wrong person, or say the wrong thing, and end up captured or dead.

A quick internal survey of his physical state told him he hadn't suffered any injuries from the spell that had transported him to this place. His sorcery was another matter, however. His use of Sotiris's curse had consumed a great amount of power, which in his own world, wouldn't have been a problem. Magic had been everywhere. If he'd run low for any reason, he could pull energy from the world around him. Some people said the air itself was magic there.

The reality of the matter was more complex. Magic wasn't in the air. It was in every part of the world. It was an energy force much like the heat of the sun, and just as that heat could be used in all manner of practical ways, so could magic. Unlike the sun's warmth, however, only a born magic-user could sense magic's existence and draw it into themselves. And among magic-users, only born-sorcerers had the ability to sense and use every particle of energy they touched. Not only use it, but store it, so that a sorcerer had immense amounts of magic at his, or her, fingertips.

Using that much magic, however, meant the sorcerer—or on a lesser scale, any magic user—had to resupply his magical energy. But Nico already knew that what had been a simple process in his own world was going to be far more difficult in this one. He drew a deep breath, meaning to evaluate the air, and immediately began to cough as his chest burned and an unpleasant scent clung to the inside of his mouth, leaving an offensive taste. He gripped a metal post with an unlit lantern on top and tried to cough out both the bad air and the foul taste. Footsteps and the sound of a disapproving grunt had him gathering his strength when he turned to examine the first person he'd been close to in this city. He was prepared to defend himself, but the man limited his interaction to a grimace that conveyed both disgust and disapproval, before he strode in a deliberately wide path around Nico. The stranger's reaction wasn't surprising, but it irritated Nico enough that he cast a quick spell on the man. Nothing deadly, just a very simple spell that would make his entire body itch with no relief for the next . . . week or so. No remedy would relieve or lessen the effect.

Watching the stranger scratch his arm as he walked away, Nico smiled, but then took serious stock of his appearance. The simple tunic and pants he wore were clean. The tunic was wrinkled, but then Nico had just traveled across worlds, so what would one expect? His pants were similarly unsoiled and made of very fine leather, as were his boots. Admittedly, he'd lost his cloak in the transition, and it was nighttime, but the air wasn't so cold that he missed it. There were far more important details on his mind than the whereabouts of a cloak he could easily replace. He stared after the figure of the departing man, and noting the difference in their style of dress, scanned the few people still moving about the street, and understood the man's reaction. His clothes—both linen and leather—were of good quality. They'd been sewn on his own estate, cut to his measure, and finished by the best seamstresses in his world. The style of his clothes, however, was markedly different than what he saw people wearing around him.

Even in his own world, they were the kind of clothes worn by farmers and tradesmen, because Nico had always prioritized comfort over style. He'd had other clothes in his wardrobe back home. Clothes he wore when visiting the courts of other nobles, or social engagements of the wealthy. But he'd rarely bothered with such events, and given the urgency of his departure, and the limited space in the lone backpack he'd brought with him, he hadn't given any thought to his clothing.

Now that he'd landed in this place and time, however, he would need new garments if he hoped to blend in. He added new attire to his mental list of necessities, and looked up and down the street studying this new city. It was already past sunset, and most of the shops were closed, though there were several gathering places still open. Music and the sound of men's laughter spilled onto the streets, while lantern light flickered through open windows and doors.

He was surprised at first to discover he could understand the comments shouted by men in the brightly-lit building down the street, and realized Sotiris's spell must have included language recognition. It was a practical element to a spell intended to transport the user elsewhere, but one Nico hadn't noticed in his rush to replicate whatever curse Sotiris had placed on his warriors. His focus had been on unraveling enough of the other sorcerer's magic, that he could follow. Such niceties as language assistance hadn't loomed large in his desperate effort, but now that he'd transitioned successfully, he could admit it was helpful. Especially as he found himself able to read and understand the various painted signs, one of which told him the crowded establishment in front of him was like the taverns back home.

The convenience should have pleased him, since it would ease his adjustment to this or any other world he ended up in. But instead, he only stared moodily at the tavern sign and thought about why Sotiris would have done it. Not for his own convenience, since the bastard had been utterly certain he would first win the battle between them, and then rule their world. It was panic at his inevitable death at Nico's hand that had sent him fleeing into the same sands of time and place where he'd banished Nico's warriors. It was that banishment which explained the language assist. If Nico's grasp of their curse was correct, then his brothers were alert and aware in their stone prisons, able to hear and *understand* everything happening around them, but utterly unable to let anyone know they still lived.

What a fucking nightmare, he thought and could only hope that Antonia hadn't been similarly cursed. He didn't think she had, but Sotiris was an evil bastard, so who knew what punishment he would visit on the woman who'd betrayed him?

Finding determination in the depths of Sotiris's cruelty, Nico began walking toward the closest tavern. It was a short distance, but still gave him time to contemplate his next steps. Clothing was already on the list, but he added a place to live, a reliable source of food, and . . . knowledge. That was perhaps the most important item, although acquiring the others would probably make the acquisition of knowledge easier. If this society was anything like his, men and women of the nobility had both activities and information more readily available to them. If he was clean and properly clothed to go along with his fluency in the language, he would no doubt have many more doors open to him. For that matter, once he met or interacted with a person—male or female—who had information he needed, he could either take it directly from their mind, or *persuade* them to assist, or teach him what was required.

If he was to succeed in doing any of that, however, he needed to replenish his power. He already knew that it would take longer in this world. How much longer, he couldn't say, since magical energy wasn't something to be counted like beans in a larder. He needed to find an inn, someplace safe where he could settle and learn—or as safe as he could be in a place he'd never been. He also needed sleep, since along with his magic, Sotiris's spell had exhausted his body.

The clatter of hooves on stone drew his attention, and he turned just in time to avoid a horse-drawn carriage that was bearing down on him with no regard for his safety. Stepping closer to the buildings where the various vendors had their shops, he continued toward the tavern. The carriage that he'd so narrowly avoided had been fully enclosed, with shaded windows concealing the faces of whoever rode inside. Other than the enclosed box, however, the vehicle wasn't that different from the ones he'd left behind. He found it oddly reassuring to discover something in this new world that was familiar.

By the time he reached the tavern, a tired ache was already growing heavy in his bones, especially his legs. But when he looked through the open doors of the tavern, and saw a room filled with people drinking, he knew this place would never provide what he needed. Perhaps it was his noble upbringing that had spoiled him, but he wanted an inn that was quiet and more . . . refined than this one seemed to be. And there was no guarantee that this tavern even doubled as an inn, the way most did in his world. There was the occasional couple coming or going from the upstairs, but he didn't need to be of this place to understand what that meant. The women were there to serve the men in whatever way they required, including sexual favors. Nico had no problem with the custom, but its presence told him this place wouldn't suit his long-term needs.

He observed a few minutes longer, taking in the back and forth of conversation in this new language, and absorbing what he learned, while forcing his tired mind to come up with a solution. Once it came to him, it was obvious. He was a fucking sorcerer. He only needed to wait until someone of suitable means, probably a man, left the tavern. Then, he would either retrieve the information he needed from the patron's thoughts, or use his dwindling power to convince the man to help an oddly-dressed stranger locate a suitable inn to spend a few nights.

While he waited, he moved out of the doorway, wanting to avoid the smoke from both oil lanterns and the paper tubes that the men were setting fire to and creating yet another unpleasant smell to burn Nico's throat. As it happened, there was a bench to one side of the doors, which he gratefully sank onto, then leaned his back against the wall.

Before he could succumb to his body's exhaustion and fall asleep where he sat, two men emerged, stinky tubes puffing smoke from their mouths as they exchanged words and clapped each other on the shoulders, before departing in opposite directions. Since they were similar in appearance and clothing, Nico stood and followed the man who'd passed directly in front of him. A few steps later and he lengthened his stride to catch up.

Addressing the man's back, he requested assistance, saying, "*Bonsoir. J'ai besoin de votre aide.*"

The man turned in surprise, mouth open to curse or cry out, but before he could make a sound, Nico caught hold of his thoughts and dictated his response.

The stranger smiled graciously and speaking the local language said, "Of course, sir. What do you need?"

A few minutes later, they were continuing down the street, but with sure strides, while Nico's new friend chattered on about the city—which was called "Paris" and was located in the country of France. Cities hadn't existed in Nico's home world. Towns and villages were associated with great estates or kingdoms, with sorcerers controlling the largest swaths of land and people. Nico's estate, for example, had included his father's kingdom, a fact which had been a source of conflict between them, even though he hadn't made any overt attempt to impose his power over his father's rule.

His new friend—whose name was Dorian Duchamp—told him that towns and villages still existed in the countryside, and explained the difference between a town and city—which to Nico, simply sounded like a matter of size and population.

Nico's tired legs were complaining by the time they stood in front of a two-story building. The double doors were closed, but a single lantern still shone through the hazy glass panes. Dorian was explaining that this was a gentleman's inn, which Nico took to mean it was suitable for men like Dorian himself. Nico didn't have a sense yet if this world had a nobility, or some other ruling class, but it didn't matter. If the inn was good enough for Dorian, it was good enough for Nicodemus. He could always move if he determined another place would please him better.

Dorian was bidding him farewell, when Nico "changed his mind."

He would need the local man for a while yet. Long enough to secure a suitable room and determine whether the gold coin Nico had brought with him would be accepted. Nico could alter the coins to whatever form was required, once he established what that form was. He'd brought the gold, along with a supply of diamonds and other gems, guessing that as long as he ended up in a world that bred humans, one or all of those valuables would be present and have some monetary value. If the alternate was true, and he landed in a world that didn't support human life, it wouldn't matter what he carried. He might be a sorcerer, but he was still human and would die quickly in a world antithetical to his nature.

He was contemplating his financial situation, while half-listening to Dorian's exchange with the inn clerk, when his new friend turned and asked what level of *l'hebergement* Nico preferred. A quick mental translation later, he understood that, like most others, this inn had rooms of varying size and quality. Since he expected to be residing there for more than a few days, he told the clerk he wanted the best room available. When the clerk responded with a dubious glance at his clothing, Nico produced a leather bag of gold *francs,* which was the local currency now filling his purse.

The clerk became much more enthusiastic, saying the grandest suite was available and would be his. And after handing him his key, he assured Nico that if he required anything else, he had but to ask. Nico took the key, asked for some food to be sent up, and for the recommendation of a local guide—someone who knew the city well enough to show him around for at least the next two days, maybe longer.

"But of course, sir. I will send the boy up at once."

Too tired to worry about whether the boy would be bringing food or information, Nico thanked the clerk, and turned away from the desk. Dorian shook his hand and bid him a good evening, but paused to invite Nico to dinner with him and his wife on some future date. Nico accepted gratefully, lingered long enough to watch Dorian leave, then turned for the stairs. He wanted food, wine, and sleep, in that order. Anyone who thought to stand in his way would be very short-lived.

NICO OPENED THE door and walked into the room that would be his home for the near future—a future he couldn't define by any number of days or nights. When he'd made the transition to this foreign city, he'd known only that he had to follow Sotiris, had to begin the search for Antonia and his brothers. But standing in this room, where everything except the chairs was utterly unfamiliar, he suddenly knew despair. Was this to be his future? Moving from one strange world to another? Learning new customs and languages, never finding a place he could call home while he searched endlessly, without ever finding the people he loved? He was a sorcerer, with so much power that he was essentially immortal. Would he wander forever? Was that what Sotiris had planned all along, and he'd been fool enough to fall into the trap?

He stared around the room, with its unfamiliar windows looking down on an unfamiliar city. Turning in a circle he stared at a pottery pitcher and bowl standing on a table that appeared too delicate to hold it. Walking over, he found the pitcher empty, and realized he had no idea where to get water. Water. The most basic human necessity, and he didn't even know where to fill a pitcher.

Cursing himself for a fool—though he didn't know if it was because he'd left his home so ill-prepared, or if he was simply impatient with his own helplessness, he gave himself a mental slap. He was a sorcerer, for gods' sake. If he needed water, he could conjure some with a thought. Doing so, just to prove he still could, he washed his face and hands, then set about searching the entire "suite," using both sorcerous and ordinary human senses. It consisted of two rooms, the first with two chairs and a small sofa, all covered in a good quality, though somewhat faded, burgundy satin. An oil lantern sat on a small table, providing the only source of light. He didn't need artificial light, but lit the lantern anyway, since someone would be bringing food soon—he hoped—and they might think it strange for the poorly-dressed newcomer to be sitting in the dark. So he lit it, but didn't bother carrying it with him into the next room, where he found a bed that was smaller than his own, but big enough.

Thoughts of his bed soon brought images of Antonia as he'd last seen her, sleeping peacefully in his arms. He closed his eyes against flashes of what she must have endured in the last moments before Sotiris cast his spell against her. Had she known what was happening? Had the enemy sorcerer taunted her with whatever place or life he'd banished her to? For that matter, how the hell had Sotiris's spell penetrated his tower? Had Antonia left the tower? Hell, had she left his estate altogether? Gone back to Sotiris's tower for some reason, and found him waiting for her? There were too many questions and no answers.

A knock on the door rescued him from a hellscape of possibilities.

Dowsing the "witch light" he'd conjured, he crossed to the door by lantern light and opened it.

"*Bonsoir, monsieur.*" A somewhat gawky young man stood there holding a tray that looked far too heavy for his bony build.

"Bonsoir. Entrez."

"*Merci.*" The server maintained a proper bearing when he walked past and set his tray on the sitting room table, but Nico could tell the boy—for that's what he really was—was fighting a grin, and probably bursting with curiosity. Continuing in the local language, the boy pointed to the cloth-covered tray and said, "Bread, meat and cheese. And wine, of course."

When Nico nodded, he continued, "If you want coffee or tea, I can bring that, too."

A cup of a calming tea would have been welcome, for the warmth and familiarity if nothing else, but Nico wanted to be done with other people, even the helpful ones. "No," he said and reached into his pocket for . . . hell, he didn't know what he should give the server. Finally, he asked, "I was looking for someone who knows the city well enough to show me around for a few days. I told the clerk downstairs, but do you know—"

"Ah! I am that person. The clerk told me what you required, and I offered my services."

"Good." Nico was oddly pleased that this friendly and unassuming young man would be his guide. The last thing he'd wanted was some obsequious social climber who would have his own ideas of what the visitor should be looking for, and at. Fetching a single gold coin from his pocket, he asked, "What's your name?"

"I am David Roche, sir."

"Good. You may call me . . ." He hesitated. What *did* he want to be called in this world? Some variation of his own name, otherwise, he'd forget what he was supposed to answer to and raise suspicions when he didn't respond. But "Nicodemus" was too obviously foreign. He paused long enough that young David's expression turned uneasy. He was likely thinking Nico was some sort of criminal. Why else would a man not know his own name? "Apologies," Nico said, rubbing his eyes deliberately. "I've traveled a long distance, and I'm very tired. I'm Nicholas Katsaros." It was the name he'd registered under downstairs, for fuck's sake. What else could he say?

"What time should I call for you in the morning, Nicholas Katsaros?"

"Call me Nicholas," he said absently. "Not tomorrow, but the day after. I have business to attend to first."

"Of course, Nicholas." The boy blushed at the use of Nico's first name, but seemed pleased at the same time. "Will you want breakfast?"

"Oh, yes," he said absently, then shrugged. "What time is customary in Paris?"

"Whatever time pleases you, though morning is best."

Nico wanted to grin at the tongue-in-cheek comment, but held it back, wanting to seem like a proper gentleman. "The ninth hour of morning, then. With coffee, if you please. And wine."

"Of course. Shall I call for the tray this evening?" he asked, nodding toward the still covered food tray.

"No. I don't want to be disturbed tonight. But thank you," he added, handing over the franc he'd been holding. "You can take this tray in the morning."

"Thank you, Nicholas!"

The boy's enthusiasm told Nico the gold franc was too much, but he didn't care. If the possibility of future generous gratuities encouraged better service, the money was well spent.

"I shall bring your breakfast promptly at nine in the morning. You may count on me."

"Until morning, then," Nico said, herding David through the open doorway. "Enjoy your evening." He shut the door, but waited to lock it until David reached the stairs and was clomping downward. Then, he engaged the door lock, but added a protection spell of his own. He thought he was alone in this city—in the sense that no one from his own world was nearby—but he couldn't be sure. And he wasn't in the mood to take risks.

With a deep sigh, he extinguished the oil lamp, conjured his witch light again, then picked up the dinner tray and carried it into the bedroom. With any luck, the bottle of wine he'd seen under the cloth would be enough to help him sleep the rest of the night. Tomorrow, he would begin his search in earnest, though his mind was too exhausted to think how on this earth or any other he would start.

Chapter Two

WHEN DAVID ARRIVED with his breakfast the next morning, Nico was more rested, and had added several items to his mental list of things to accomplish. First was a proper bath. He'd already learned that the usual method was for someone—presumably David—to run up and down the stairs with hot water, to be poured into a large copper tub in the communal bath down the hall. But as Nico was capable of heating his own water, all he needed was a large, private tub that no one had to run up or down the stairs to fill.

"David, is there somewhere downstairs where I could bathe instead?"

The boy seemed taken aback. Perhaps the usual guests at this inn were less accommodating. But he recovered quickly enough and said, "There is a bathing room, Nicholas, but it's used mostly by the manager and his family. Sometimes the clerk, too."

"I'm sure the manager won't mind granting me this favor," Nico said, as if it was already decided. Which in his mind, it was. "I'll just finish breakfast and meet you down there, shall I?"

"Uh, yes, sir . . . Nicholas. I'm sure that will be fine."

"Bien. Une heure, alors."

NICO GATHERED enough clean clothes to remain decent for the walk back to his room, then donned his dirty tunic and pants, and walked barefoot down the stairs. When he reached the lobby, the clerk—who seemed to be looking out for him—pointed to a hallway opposite the stairs.

Before he'd gone six steps, he could feel the difference in the air. The very narrow hallway began to take on a humid warmth. Nico thought it was probably less warm than it felt, but it was so cold in the rest of the hotel that anything would have seemed warm by contrast. Thus far, Paris was seeming a very cold city. But as he wasn't yet sure of the season, he reserved judgment.

"You found it!" David said when Nico opened the door, as enthusiastic as if Nico had found his way through a dark warren of caves to the bathing room.

"I did."

"You can undress behind the curtain," David said, pointing to a hanging piece of threadbare black fabric. It wasn't much of a curtain, but then, Nico didn't have much in the way of modesty, and so didn't care. "There are towels in there, too. You can wrap the clean clothes to keep them dry. I added extra towels for you."

"Merci."

The towels were as threadbare as the curtain, but they were clean and there were enough of them to make up for the absence of quality. Nico was increasingly aware that he'd been accustomed to a higher standard of life than most others seemed to enjoy. Soft fabrics, good food and wine, a private hot springs pool . . . the list went on and on. If he remained in this world, he'd have to step up the comforts of his life. For now, however, a copper tub big enough for two and filled with bless-edly steaming water was calling his name.

Nico sank into the heat, not realizing until that moment how sore his muscles had become. He hadn't done anything more strenuous than climbing stairs, so he had to assume the strain was from the transition itself. He had no memories of the process. To his senses, the transition had taken no more than an instant, like stepping from one room to the next through an open door. But clearly, his body knew better. He slid low into the water, eyes closed, and leaned his head against one side. He would have liked to lie in the steaming water until his body was completely thawed and relaxed, but the water was already markedly cooler than when he'd climbed in. So he rubbed a surprisingly gentle bar of soap between his hands and used it to wash both his body and hair. After submerging completely to rinse off, he came back up to find David waiting with a fresh stack of towels.

Snagging two towels from the top, he dried most of his body, then grabbed a third to dry his hair and walked back to the curtained area to finish drying and get dressed. He regretted now that he hadn't worn shoes. His feet would not only freeze up again, but they'd pick up every bit of dirt in the hallways and on the stairs. Muttering imprecations to himself, he yanked open the curtain and stepped out.

"David, I need a . . ." He searched for the right word. His French was improving by the minute, but he wasn't yet what he considered to be fluent. "A *couturier*."

David cocked his head thoughtfully, then nodded. "I can take you to the man the owner of this hotel uses. He is much fatter than you, but

I'm sure the *couturier* can adapt."

"That's his job," Nico agreed. "Do you have any duties at the inn today?"

"No, my only duty is to help you."

Nico laughed. "Good. We'll leave as soon as I'm dressed then."

THE DAY WAS AS cold as Nico expected when they left the hotel that morning, and he made a note to have the tailor make him a new cape or . . . . He looked around. The other men he saw on the street were wearing long coats. Nico didn't care as long as it was warm. And since he was quickly losing the delicious warmth he'd enjoyed since his bath, he steered David to a small shop which sold pretty cakes and coffee. They sat there long enough to finish both, then walked two blocks off the street which held the inn, then down another half-block until they reached a tall narrow door adjacent to a smoke-stained window that held several bolts of fabric.

"The shop belongs to Adrien Moulin," David whispered when he opened the door and gestured for Nico to go ahead of him.

A thin man, nearly as tall as Nico, who was counted very tall, emerged from a back room, hands clasped in front of him. He was nicely dressed, as one would expect, his clothes both well-fitted and of good fabric. His gaze skirted over David and landed on Nico.

"*Bonjour Monsieur. Comment puis-je vous aider?*" David glanced at Nico, as if checking if he should do the talking, but Nico spoke up, saying in what was now very nearly fluent French, "Monsieur Moulin, I've just arrived after an arduous journey, during which my wardrobe trunk was lost. I need to replace . . . everything, and your work was recommended to me."

"I shall do my best," he said, eyeing Nico up and down, while trying to avoid being seen doing it.

Nico admitted he looked far from his best, and so didn't take offense. "David," he said, turning to his young guide instead. "Why don't you go pick up something to take back with us for lunch? Standing still for a fitting is not my greatest skill. Once Monsieur Moulin has completed his initial work for me, I'll be in need of food, and a bottle of wine. A good bottle."

David's face lit up. He'd clearly expected to spend the next few hours sitting in a stuffy room watching Moulin take Nico's measure. "Of course, sir. When should I—?"

"Two hours, young man," Moulin interjected. "No less."

The boy glanced at Nico, who nodded his approval and said, "Desserts, too, David."

"Of course, sir." David tipped his cap and escaped the tailor's shop hurriedly, as if he feared being called back to sit instead.

"He's young," Nico commented, watching him go. Then turned to Moulin. "I am Nicholas Katsaros."

Moulin nodded his head. "I am happy to meet you. Please follow me."

BY THE TIME MOULIN was finished measuring, pinning, and muttering, Nico wanted to run from the shop just as fast as David had. He had to admit, however, that the tailor seemed to possess all the right skills. And the fabrics he offered were very fine, including the thick wool he suggested for a long coat.

"Winter has just begun in the city. It will get much colder before spring."

Nico agreed readily and added three wool scarves just to be safe. He hated being cold, in general, but the damp chill of this city was worse.

Moulin offered to have at least one full set of clothing ready for him the next day, since as Nico had explained, he'd lost most of what he owned. He also mentioned casually, that he could recommend a good *chaplier.*

A hatmaker. Nico groaned inwardly. He hated hats, but had to admit that all the better-dressed men he'd seen on the street since arriving had been wearing hats—tall, stiff things that he could only hope warmed as well as a good woolen skull cap. "I appreciate the recommendation. I might otherwise have forgotten, as my trip was . . . arduous."

"I can only imagine, monsieur. I will bring everything to your hotel tomorrow afternoon. Any final adjustments can be made then, so you will have time to dress properly before your dinner appointment."

Nico didn't *have* a dinner appointment, but he appreciated the thought. "Most appreciated." He saw the top of David's head when the boy peeked through the window from where he must have been sitting on the ground, waiting. Since Nico had already provided the tailor with his personal information, including his hotel and suite number, he departed with a nod of his bare head. *"A bientôt."*

David was on his feet when Nico exited the shop. The boy was also holding two grease-stained bags that smelled wonderful.

"Thank the gods," Nico said sincerely. "Moulin says I need a few hats. But first, I need lunch."

The boy grinned. "I have wine, but thought to stop closer to the hotel for coffee. I didn't know how long you'd be, and I didn't want it to get cold."

"Good thought. Stop where we did this morning. It was good."

"*Mais, oui.* My own cousin owns that shop."

"Does he? Why aren't you working for him, then?"

"I like my job at the inn better than I like my cousin."

Nico laughed.

HE SENT DAVID away after lunch, which the boy had seemed surprised to be sharing. Nico noted his wonder, but didn't comment. There were plenty of sorcerers and others, including his own father, who wouldn't have considered sharing their meal with a servant.

He'd intended to visit the hatmaker in the afternoon, to get the chore done with, if for no other reason. But by the time he was pouring a final glass of wine, he was as tired as if he'd worked in the fields all day. Not that he'd ever done so, but a good imagination was required in a sorcerer.

"I'll get hats tomorrow," he told David. "I'm still recovering from the journey here, and would like to rest."

"Will you want dinner in your room, sir? The dining room is quite pleasant."

Nico would rather have remained in his room, but practicality, and the knowledge that this city would be his home for an unknown length of time had him replying, "The dining room it is then. Can you get me a quiet table? Near the window, if possible."

"*Mais oui,* it is no problem. Will the eighth hour serve? Parisians linger over their dinner."

"Of course, they do," he muttered, but said, "Yes. Thank you, David."

The boy left, and Nico locked the door as he had the night before, with both key and magic, then removed his boots, laid down on the bed, and slept so deeply that the eighth hour came and went while he dreamed . . . of home, and Antonia.

THEY RODE TOGETHER across the grassy plains of a land far away from his castle—a land he'd visited more than once on his own. In his dream state, however, he was there with her, wind blowing her hair behind her like a gleaming banner as they urged their horses to a hard gallop. It was so real that he could feel the beast's muscles flexing beneath him, the power of its stride eating up lengths of grassland as if he and the horse could ride forever, with Antonia by his side.

Her eyes sparkled with happiness when she glanced over at him, laughing in uninhibited joy. There was no Sotiris, no traitor, no danger at all to worry about. Just the two of them riding in breathless freedom until they finally tumbled off the horses and fell into each other's arms. Her hair fell over his chest when he held her, filling his senses with her scent, her touch, the sound of her voice.

Until her eyes widened and she screamed.

Nico sat up and stared around the room, searching for the threat, for whatever danger had made Antonia . . . . *Fuck.* He swung his legs to the side and rubbed his face with both hands, realizing he'd slept through the night. That explained the dream, he thought. He'd been exhausted, mentally and physically, and who wouldn't be, in his situation? The exhaustion had leaked into his dreams, slithered into his fears for Antonia, who'd been left alone, at the mercy of an enemy who had none.

It had been a dream, he repeated to himself. Nothing more. But he didn't believe it. He was a damn sorcerer. He had inspirations and premonitions and imminent warnings. He rarely had "just a dream." But this one . . . . He prayed to the gods that this was the exception, that it truly had been a nightmare, and nothing else. But he didn't believe it. Somewhere his Antonia was alone, abandoned, and terrified. And he didn't know how to reach her.

Walking into the sitting room, he poured the final dregs of leftover wine into a glass, and swore. He didn't care if it was still morning. He was going to need something stronger than wine if he hoped to accomplish anything today. A *lot* stronger. He was contemplating the best way to find that stronger drink when a knock came on his door. Puzzled, but sensing no threat, he opened the door to find the clerk from downstairs.

"This came for you, monsieur." The man handed over a sealed envelope with Nico's name written in an elegant script. Since the number of people who knew he was in the city could be counted on one hand, and with fingers left over, he waited until he'd closed the door again before opening the note.

Settling on the sofa, he did a quick scan of the envelope and its contents to verify that there was no sorcery attached. Few people that he *knew* of were aware he was in Paris, but he couldn't rule out the possibility that Sotiris would know where he was, since it was the bastard's spell that he'd used to get there.

Finally assured that the missive was clean, he slid a finger under the sealed flap and opened it to reveal a single folded note from Dorian inviting him to dinner the next evening. Well, apparently the man had been sincere when he'd suggested Nico join him for a meal. Not knowing the appropriate courtesies involved in responding, he penned an acceptance on one of several blank notes left in his room, and walked back down to the reception desk.

"*Pardon,*" he said.

The clerk stood from a small desk and walked over. "Yes, Monsieur Katsaros?"

Mindful of the lateness of his response to Dorian's invitation, he said, "This needs to reach a friend immediately. Is that possible?"

"But of course. David will deliver it at once."

Knowing the tailor would be arriving soon for a final fitting, and wanting to straighten his room before the man arrived, he asked the clerk to send the boy up when he returned from his errand. He had questions regarding Parisian courtesies when dining at another's home. And there was also the matter of finding his way there.

NICO WAS IN A better mood when he woke the next morning. Either he was growing accustomed to early rising, or the local spirits, while enjoyable, were considerably less powerful than anything brewed back home. His mind paused on that thought. He needed to stop thinking of his world as *home*. Though it was the only one he'd ever known, he'd never be returning there. He didn't think it was possible, for one thing. But for another, his home would be wherever he found his brothers and Antonia. If he found one before the others, he'd continue his search with them, until they were all together. The thought put a damper on his mood, and he lay in bed, staring at the ceiling for another few minutes, then forced himself to rise. Incomplete tasks remained on his list, every one of which was necessary to beginning his search in earnest. Some day he would be reunited with everyone he loved, everyone Sotiris had stolen from him, and they would begin their lives again, together. After they killed the bastard, of course.

David knocked at that moment, calling, "Good morning, monsieur. I have your breakfast."

He opened the door, waving a hand to invite the boy and his coffee in. "I told you to call me 'Nicholas.'"

"*Oui,* but the manager will fire me if he hears. So, I address you properly."

"Ah. I understand." He added sugar and drank some coffee, gesturing for David to do the same. "I need information today. And a hat," he muttered. "Moulin will deliver the rest of my clothes tomorrow, once he's completed the final adjustments."

"Information," David repeated, his brow creased in deep thought. "What sort of information, Monsieur Nicholas?"

Nico thought about that for a moment, pondering how much he could say without making the boy suspicious. He certainly couldn't mention anything about sorcerers or magic. Even in his world, there were regions where people believed that magic was the work of demons, and drove out or, worse, *killed* any witches or other magic-users unlucky enough not to escape in time. On the other hand . . .

"History," he said, confident that any arrival in a new city would want to learn more of the place and its customs. "How did Paris come to be a city? Who governs it? And not only Paris, but the entire country of France." He left it at that, figuring any place that could answer those questions would also have other information he might find useful.

David listened, nodding his head, then brightened and said, "*Bibliothèque Mazarine.*"

It was a moment before Nico figured that one out, despite the translation, since his own culture hadn't possessed anything like a public library. Sorcerers had libraries of their own, or as in his case, multiple *rooms* of libraries. But he certainly hadn't permitted anyone else to use it, other than his brother warriors and the healers. The idea of a public library made so much sense, however, that he was rather ashamed he *hadn't* thought of it. Not public libraries of *magic,* the gods knew, but history and generational stories would have been beneficial to everyone. Unfortunately, thinking that way reminded him once more that he would never be going back. If there were to be libraries in his home world, someone else would have to build them.

"A library. Yes, that's exactly what I need. But first, my friend . . ." He scowled. "A hat."

David laughed. "More than one, Nicholas. A gentleman needs at least two, preferably three."

"What? Do you work for the *chaplier?*"

The boy seemed to take him seriously at first, and acted deeply offended, but when he saw Nico's grin, he laughed and said, "If so, I'd have you buy five."

Nico laughed along, then pulled out Moulin's card, on which he'd written the address of the hatmaker. "You know this address?"

David nodded. *"Oui,* when do you wish to leave?"

"Now."

LESS THAN AN hour into his library search, Nico realized that David's reading skills were limited, though the boy was manfully trying to conceal it. Nico didn't blame him. If anything, he cursed himself for not realizing sooner, or for that matter, for assuming the Parisian educational system was any better than the one on his own estate. The only truly literate people in his world had been the sorcerers. The various courts and nobles educated their sons, though not always their daughters, but very few offered any training to servants. And though he thought of himself as a good ruler, he was ashamed to admit that he hadn't provided his own servants anything but the most remedial level of education. So why would he assume David had access to anything better?

To save the boy's pride, he muttered about his own inability to read French, and looked around the library for a solution. When he saw two men sitting at a desk with a sign that read, *"Bibliothècaires,"* he brightened. He wasn't exactly sure what it meant, but it seemed to imply that these two gentlemen took care of the library. So maybe they could at least send him to the right shelves.

When he pointed out the sign to David, the boy's smile matched Nico's. They both walked over, but David hung back, making it clear that Nico—who was now dressed as a proper gentleman, thanks to Monsieur Moulin—should be the one to inquire.

Both *bibliothècaires* looked up when he cleared his throat, but only one responded with a gracious smile and an offer of assistance. The man, whose name was Marceau Girard, listened patiently to Nico's rather rambling explanation of what he needed, then walked them over to a row of shelves in a far corner that included a great number of loosely bound papers and scrolls along with hardcover books. Gesturing at the collection, he then turned to Nico and, speaking in a low voice, said, "The priests will also have a number of historical manuscripts, though I do not know if they would be willing to share them. Some of them will be quite old, while others are illustrated, which makes them very rare and valuable. You may ask, however. Do the people of your country honor the true faith?"

Since the people of Nico's *world* didn't have any faith, true or otherwise, unless one counted the fickle gods of fate, he nodded his head.

"*Mais oui.*"

Girard smiled in relief. "*Ça c'est bon.* I must return to my desk, Monsieur. But I wish you good luck in your research."

"Thank you. Can I . . . ?" He didn't want to offend Monsieur Girard, but the man had been so helpful. "May I offer a donation to support the library?"

Girard, whose face had donned a pained expression, immediately brightened at the offer. "There is a box at my desk. You will see it when you leave."

Nico sent David in search of a nearby café, saying he'd meet up with him in an hour, then used his magic to move everything in the collection to a very high shelf in a very dark corner of the library, so that he could return after hours and read at his own pace. He walked down the long line of shelves and turned for the exit when his attention was drawn to a giant sphere which he quickly understood claimed to be a model of the entire world. Fascinated, he took the time to commit every detail to his sorcerer's memory. He'd be able to draw every nuance of the sphere once he was back in his room. He wasn't a great artist, but his hand was good enough to draw a circle and the outlines of the various land masses, along with their names. This might very well be the most useful thing he learned in the library or from the priests.

He was feeling more optimistic when he left than he had since arriving in Paris. The sun was peeking out from behind the clouds, and he smiled as he strolled down the street to find David waiting on the steps of the café.

"I'm sorry it took so long," he said immediately, squeezing the boy's shoulder. "We have no such libraries where I come from."

"You should not apologize to me, Nicholas. I am at your service."

"You're as worthy of basic courtesy as any other, David. So I apologize. Is there still time for coffee?" Nico had decided to skip visiting the priest until after he'd absorbed the materials in the library. He'd always hated research and had rejoiced when his power reached the point where he could take on assistants and apprentices to do it for him. That path was obviously no longer available to him, so he'd have to do it himself. Although his magical abilities would help. He'd used very little magic since his arrival in the city, and his ability was growing stronger by the day, despite the pitiful amount of free magic in this world. But the core of his magic remained as always, allowing him to observe the world around him without conscious thought. That core would die only when he did. As long as his heart beat, it would continue to function, although it worked better when his magic was also at its peak.

For tonight, however, he was finished with research and learning, and worrying over things he had no control of. As powerful as he was, his brain still required time to process the many pieces of information his senses—both magical and not—he'd picked up during the day. Much of which, he wasn't yet aware that he'd learned. And so, once in his room, he tossed the ridiculous hat boxes on the sofa, freshened his face, and changed his tie, then went downstairs to enjoy his dinner and absorb the city.

"MONSIEUR KATSAROS."

Nico glanced over from where he'd been studying the people promenading on the wide street, idly wondering if this was the entirety of their evenings. And if so, how he would manage to find the people like himself—magic users. There had to be some, else why would Sotiris have chosen it as his destination? It was barely possible that the sorcerer had cast his fortune to fate, and flung himself into the maelstrom of time and place with no destination in mind. But he didn't believe that. Sotiris was far too obsessed with controlling everyone and everything around him to have taken such a chance. And the fact that he'd been prepared to leave so quickly when the battle turned against him, told Nico that the bastard had planned for such a possibility. And if he'd planned, he'd have made sure he knew where he was going.

"Monsieur Katsaros?"

Nico realized he'd been staring blankly while his thoughts churned, and looked up at the man standing next to his table. "Yes?"

"Permit me to introduce myself. I am Monsieur Faustin Tasse, the manager of this inn. As you're dining alone this evening, may I join you for an aperitif? I don't wish to intrude."

Then why are you? Nico thought rebelliously, but reminded himself that he needed to learn more about the city and its people. And who better to teach him than the nosy manager of an inn? He didn't fully understand what an *aperitif* was, but as it seemed to involve alcohol, he was willing to experiment. "Please," he said indicating the second chair at the table. "Join me."

Tasse beamed with happiness and sat down, which had the waiter rushing over to offer assistance. The manager spoke in very rapid French and the waiter went away, only to return shortly with a tray of drinks and food. The routine was repeated several times over the next few hours, since Monsieur Tasse remained for the entire meal. Nico didn't mind after all, since the man had lived his entire life in Paris and talked non-stop. Nico learned about France's recent political upheavals, and something called the Bourbon Restoration, which involved a particular royal line, most of whom had lost their heads. Quite literally, apparently, since France was fond of a form of execution called a guillotine, which very neatly removed a person's head from their body. He found it rather gruesome, but as long as neither he, nor anyone he loved was threatened, he would let it be.

This was not his world, not his estate, nor did he plan on it being such. If he'd dissected Sotiris's spell correctly, Paris had been his first stop. The question was, why? And of course, where was he going next? Nico might have avoided research whenever possible, but analyzing a spell—any spell—was something he not only enjoyed, but excelled at. He'd worked for weeks figuring out what Sotiris had done, and how. But in his urgency to follow on his enemy's heels, he'd identified the spell elements for Paris—the first stop—and put off the rest for later.

That was what he should be doing with his time. Not having stupid hats made. He should be sitting in his room and studying the complex damn spell, so he could take the next step—and all the ones after that— in pursuit of Sotiris more rapidly than the enemy sorcerer might expect. And eventually catch up with him.

The meal finally ended, with Tasse waving off the waiter and the bill, saying grandly that he'd enjoyed Nico's company far too much to make him pay. Privately Nico thought Tasse's enjoyment had come from having a dinner companion who listened to everything, but rarely spoke. The meal had been pleasant enough, though. Informative, if nothing else.

But though Nico was ready for it to end, he had one question that no one had yet addressed. What the hell did people do for fun in Paris? Late at night, when he woke soaked in sweat from nightmares of Antonia screaming, or his warriors trapped in prisons too suffocating to permit even screams, he knew that the answers he sought were not among the promenading couples and well-lit boulevards. Somewhere in this big city, there had to be taverns like the one he'd passed when he'd first arrived, the one his friend Dorian had warned him was not suitable for gentlemen, which apparently Nico was.

Monsieur Tasse, however, held no such prejudices. At Nico's inquiry, he chuckled, took a deep puff of his cigar—the proper name for the paper tubes that smelled bad—and winked. "*Le Palais Royal*," he said know-ingly.

Nick frowned, wondering if Tasse understood his question. What did a royal palace have to do with late night drinking, bad taverns, and dangerous places?

Seeming to understand his puzzlement, Tasse explained with a wave of his hand. "It was owned by one of our Dukes who ran out of money, and turned it into *un parc d'attractions*. Families attend by daylight, but at night . . . *late* at night, it is for gentlemen to enjoy. There are any number of less savory activities and people to be found there. And women, *mon ami. Les belles femmes*."

Nick neither desired nor needed a woman, beautiful or not, but in a world like this, where magic was rarely spoken of, and mostly considered to be either fanciful stories for a winter's night, or the devil's influence, any magic-users would have long ago gone underground, hiding what they were, while offering their services for sale in dusty shops and dark corners. And this *Palais Royal* sounded like a place with plenty of both for people to hide in.

Chapter Three

WALKING BACK TO his hotel late the next night, Nick knew he'd been wrong about the *Palais Royal* holding the promise of answers for him, as well as the people he'd thought might provide them. And he was finally beginning to grasp the reality of his situation, something he should have understood from the outset. This world was a much bigger place than his own, though even his *own* world had been bigger than what he lived in. He'd called his warriors from the four corners of the earth. Did he think they'd traveled from the next town over, for fuck's sake? No, their journeys to join him had been arduous and taken weeks and months. They'd traveled from places that, for all his sorcerous power and battle prowess, he'd never been. He knew their stories of where they'd come from, only because they told him of these places.

So why in the name of all the gods had he thought the answers he needed would be waiting for him in the one city he'd happened to land in? He'd come here, because Sotiris's spell had led him here. But what if the bastard had expected Nico to follow, after all? What if he'd fled to Paris, only to throw Nico off his trail? He could be hundreds of years and a thousand cities away by now. Disgusted with his own flailing about, and despairing of ever finding his brothers, his Antonia, he'd waved off the carriage drivers who'd tried to sell him a ride back to his hotel, and instead began walking. He wasn't worried about finding his way. He knew the streets well enough by now, and if he became turned around, he could always use some of his magic to find his way.

He barely noticed when he turned onto a street that was little more than an alley. All the streets were darker now, as the oil lamps had long since burned out, or been doused. Darkness didn't bother Nico. His night sight was excellent, and if he needed light, he could always conjure it. But as he walked, head down, deep in thought, he became aware of someone else's footsteps pacing his own. He kept walking, but shifted his senses outward to discover more than one person shadowing his path.

He wasn't afraid. In fact, he silently hoped his stealthy friends would come closer. After all, he was a lone man, well-dressed, obviously walking home after an evening at the *Palais Royal*. Tired, perhaps intoxicated even. Even if he'd lost his money in a game of cards, his clothing and/or jewelry—which he wasn't wearing, but they didn't know that—would be well worth the effort. And who was there to witness the death of a man too stupid to comprehend his own peril?

They made their move, and he let them come. Four men in worn and dirty clothes, their hair long and unwashed, hanging around faces that were made ugly not by birth, but by the hatred in their eyes, the bad teeth bared in animal-like snarls. Pity warred with rage in Nico's mind. If he'd seen these four asking for food by the side of the road, he'd have emptied his pockets between them. Part of him wanted to believe they'd been driven by circumstance to such desperate measures, and he could only imagine the hopelessness that would make a man choose to kill rather than ask for help.

But the other part of him, the part that was walking this dark street in a foreign land and time because another man—one with the where-withal to enjoy a life of luxury and power, who could have used that power to improve the lives of those who looked to him for protect-tion—that man had chosen instead to destroy. To take more than his share from his people, and to punish those who complained. That man had taken everyone Nico loved and thrown them away. He hadn't known or cared where they'd end up. He'd known only that Nico loved them, and that losing them would inflict a crushing blow on the man he *hated* with a rage that burned like the fires of hell itself.

Nico spun to face his attackers, surprising them into stillness, but only for the few seconds it took for them to brandish their thin knives, and to snarl their demand that he strip to the skin.

"Or what?" Nico asked. "What will you do if I refuse?"

The biggest of the four, the one who'd voiced the original demand, took a step closer. He reeked of sweat and dirt, and for all his swagger, a touch of fear. "Refuse, and I will kill you, and take what I want."

"No," Nico replied, shaking his head. "I think you'd have killed me anyway. So I'm going to kill you instead."

All four opened their mouths to laugh, but only screams emerged from their throats as unseen knives slashed through their clothes and bit into their skin, as heat boiled their guts until their stomachs split open and spilled charred lengths of innards over their thighs and onto the ground where they lay shrieking in agonized terror.

"Please," the leader gasped, stretching out a broken and blood-soaked hand to beg.

"I knew another man like you," Nico growled. "The only difference is that I didn't *kill* him before I walked away. And I wish to the gods that I had."

Then he walked away, deaf to the howls of the thieves who still clung to life, though they wouldn't for long. Their cries still rang in his ears, but he'd already forgotten them as he strode down the dark streets, his thoughts obsessing over what he'd said to their leader. He *hadn't* killed Sotiris, though there were many times he could have. He'd always chosen to walk away, to permit *Sotiris* to walk away, in the vain hope that his enemy would see the futility of what he was doing, and stop. It had been a mistake, and if he came face to face with the monster, he wouldn't make it again. There'd be no walking away for Sotiris the next time, he vowed.

IF NICO HAD BEEN tired and depressed before the attack, he was doubly so after. He'd killed those four pathetic men, seeing parallels between them and Sotiris. But they weren't the fucking sorcerer. They were killers, no doubt of that, and he had no regrets about taking their lives, confident that he'd saved others by doing so. But they were fleas on a goat's back compared to Sotiris.

So when he heard *more* footsteps shadowing his trail, he stopped walking and spun to face his stalker. What he wanted, *all* he wanted, was to go back to the hotel and drink the bottle of cognac Monsieur Tasse had promised would be waiting in his suite at the hotel.

The man Nico found when he turned was not who he expected. His stalker stood several feet away, well-dressed and smiling, as if they were long-lost cousins finally reunited.

"What?" Nico demanded, letting his power simmer just below the surface where it would be undetectable but ready for his use.

The man gave an appreciative gasp that came out as a long, "Ahhhhhh." He then clasped his hands before him and whispered, "*Mon Dieu, vous êtes spectaculaire.*"

Nico spat out a heartfelt "Fuck," and said, "*Non, merci.*"

The man stared at him in confusion for a moment, then laughed . . . he *laughed* and continued in French, "No, no. I'm simply admiring the power of your magic. I've never seen the like."

Nico stared, then belatedly used his own senses to determine that the man was indeed . . . not a sorcerer, but definitely a strong magic user.

He chose his next words carefully, wanting to discover if Sotiris was, by some chance, operating in the city. And if not Sotiris, then anyone else who might have useful information for him. "You have no sorcerers living in Paris?"

"Of course. But none as powerful as you. You must come with me to meet our leaders."

"*Your* leaders. Not mine."

The man shrugged. "Ah, forgive me. You are new to Paris, and so don't understand. But come with me, and it will all be explained."

"What will be explained?"

"Why, the war against our people. Were you not touched by this where you come from?"

"What war? Who are you fighting?"

"The vampires, of course. You really must come meet our leaders. They will explain everything, and be most appreciative of your assistance."

Nico didn't want anything to do with someone else's war, nor did he have any interest in meeting anyone who considered themselves to be a leader. But he *did* want to meet someone who might have information about Sotiris, even if he wasn't currently in the city. And if these leaders truly did *lead*, they'd have registered the presence in their city, however brief, of a sorcerer that powerful. "Very well," he agreed. "How far is it?"

"No distance at all. Come, we will walk." The stranger started to leave, then turned back and said, "Forgive my rudeness. I haven't introduced myself. I am Vital Bellamy."

Nico considered using a fake name for all of two seconds. What would be the point? He'd already used his real name—more or less—at the hotel and among his new acquaintances. Besides, if anyone knew his history and wanted to challenge him? Let them try. And if Sotiris had a spy who reported to him? Well then, all the better. He wanted nothing more than to get his hands on the cowardly fuck.

"Nicholas Katsaros," he said now. "Lead the way, Monsieur Bellamy."

True to Bellamy's word, their destination wasn't far, although it was still more of a detour than Nico wanted to make. He only hoped it would be worth the effort to get there. He was torn between the hope that it would be fruitful, and the certainty that it would end up dragging him into a war he had no interest in. Especially as it seemed likely he was the most powerful sorcerer in the city. If he got involved, the others would automatically look to him for direction, and that would only take time away from his true purpose.

On the other hand, "hate" wasn't too strong a word to describe his feelings toward vampires. There had been vampires in his own world. They'd peddled nothing but terror and sold their services to the highest bidder. As far as he knew, their social structure consisted solely of small tribes who lived and hunted together, and when they worked, they did that as a unit, too.

Nicodemus himself had never used them, but he'd fought others who had. Vampires were mostly used off the battlefield to weaken the opposing force. They'd been known to kidnap soldiers and either drain them of blood and leave them to die, or after draining the soldier's blood, they would replace it with their own, thus "turning" the human soldier into one of their own . . . a vampire.

Nico had actually designed a spell that was a "cure" for vampirism. He couldn't completely undo what had been done to them, but he could lessen the effects. In fact, when his warrior Gabriel had come to him, he'd been suffering under the curse of vampirism, after being kidnapped and tortured by vampires while fighting under his father's banner. The greatest warrior in his part of the world, he'd been forced to serve his vampire overlords—hating every minute, yet bound by their shared blood to serve his master. It had been Nico's magic-driven call to battle that had freed Gabriel, in a way.

He'd heard Nico's call and had escaped his master, not caring if doing so would end his life. Despising what he'd become, he would have welcomed death if it was the only freedom he could find. Instead, he'd found Nico, whose magic had broken the vampire master's hold. Gabriel no longer needed to drink blood to survive, and while he preferred cloudy days, the sun no longer had the power to destroy him. The power of Nico's magic had saved more than Gabriel's life. It had saved his soul, and his spirit. Now, Nico could only imagine what Sotiris's vicious spell might have wrought on the proud warrior.

But though Nico hated vampires, he would have preferred to avoid them altogether, rather than join in a war against them. They simply weren't his priority. His plan was only to find Antonia and his warriors. And he would keep going, keep traveling from world to world, until he *did* find them . . . or at least one of them. And then onto the next, and next. He would never stop searching, no matter what it took, until they were all free and together again.

When Monsieur Bellamy finally stopped in front of a townhouse that appeared older than many in the city, Nico stepped into the street so he could look up at it. The building resembled the one where Dorian lived with his family, but it was much narrower, with exterior stone that was blackened by soot and age, and a decorative façade that was crumbling on the edges and corners, diminishing whatever impression the long-ago builder had desired to make.

If this townhouse was where the leader of the city's sorcerers resided, he wasn't impressed.

Monsieur Bellamy must have noticed his reaction, because he grinned and said, "It's much nicer inside. You'll see."

Having come this far, Nico wasn't about to walk away because of a shabby house. When someone opened the door a bare crack in response to Bellamy's knock, he stepped up to stand next to him. And when the door opened wider, and they both left the cold night behind, he understood what Bellamy had meant about the inside being nicer. The floors were marble, the walls papered with a fine cloth he couldn't name, and the twisting stairway in front of him, while narrow, was covered with what in Nico's world would have been a finely woven carpet. Brass rods held the carpet in place and were matched by brass detailing on the black-painted bannister. Above him, an elaborate chandelier sparkled with an unknown number of clear cut crystal ornaments, each of which supported a burning wax candle.

Impressed by the beauty of the interior, he wasn't prepared for their host to call from an adjoining room, "Don't just stand there gawking, Bellamy. Introduce me to whatever stranger you've trusted enough to bring into our nest. I only hope you know what you've done."

Nico's attention was caught by the word "nest," since vampires had been known to use that term for their group living arrangements. But since snakes were also known to invade birds' nests and eat the eggs, he let the comment pass, with prejudice. He would hold on to his suspicion, until proven otherwise.

"Monsieur Katsaros," Bellamy urged. "Come meet our leader."

Not my leader, Nico thought again, but he kept silent, willing to hold onto his judgment until he knew more. Following his erstwhile friend into the next room, he found an unkempt man of an indeterminate age—other than that he was obviously much older than Nico—sitting on a small sofa like the one in his hotel room. Only the man Bellamy called his leader was sitting in the middle of the sofa, surrounded by a mess all around him. Nico would have understood if the man had been encircled by notes and inkpots. He himself had been known to sink into untidiness when in the midst of designing a new spell. But it appeared that the "leader," who still remained nameless, had no servants or staff to assist him, because on both sides were plates of half-eaten food, and the sofa's fabric was stained from previous repasts. He didn't dare guess which meal the various foods represented, except that they'd all been prepared hours, rather than minutes, ago.

The man slurped from a glass of red wine, stared narrow-eyed at Nicodemus, and said, "Who's this?"

Bellamy drew breath to respond, but Nico beat him to it. "I'm Nicholas Katsaros. Who are you?" The words were rude, but then, the question had been rude, too.

The man's eyes flared briefly with power, but if he'd expected Nico to quail at the sight of it, he was badly mistaken. Nico waited patiently, unaffected by either the power or the man, and letting him know it.

Obviously trying to interrupt the growing tension, Bellamy stepped between them, and turning to his leader said, "Monsieur Charron, may I introduce Nicholas Katsaros, newly arrived in Paris, and"—he turned to Nico,—"Monsieur Katsaros, our leader, the sorcerer Hadrien Charron."

Nico managed not to scoff out loud. If Charron was a sorcerer, he must have barely made the cut for that designation. He *wouldn't* have qualified in Nico's world. But Nico chose to remain polite in the face of Charron's crudeness. Murmuring, "A pleasure," Nico bent his head the tiniest measure he could manage, while still calling it a bow.

True to form, Charron scowled and asked, "Why'd you bring him here?" The question was obviously directed at Bellamy, even though Charron's gaze never left Nico.

Bellamy fidgeted and gave Nico an uneasy glance. Bellamy clearly knew that Nico's power was greater than Charron's. Far greater. Finally, Bellamy said, "Monsieur Katsaros is a sorcerer. He could be . . . helpful in our struggle against the vampires."

Feeling for him, Nico didn't comment, although privately he had no intention of being recruited into anyone's struggle, no matter the enemy.

"Sorcerer?" Charron scoffed. "His people must judge power by a means inferior to ours, then, because he—"

He got no further, because Nicodemus had had enough. His power rose in a brief, but undeniable display, which had Charron shrinking back against the sofa, one hand raised against the brilliant flare which Nico had permitted to highlight the release of his power. It was the sort of thing he'd have used to intimidate enemy soldiers in his world, not other magic-users. It had never been necessary. But apparently the number of magic users in this world had dwindled so deeply that the few who remained had no appreciation for, or knowledge of, true sorcerous power.

Charron struggled to his feet, face twisted in rage, when he raised his own power in a threatening manner. "What kind of devil's creature is this that you bring into my home?"

"Devil?" Nico mocked lightly. "Are you not a sorcerer, monsieur? And is your power thus the work of the devil?"

"Absolutely not!"

"Why then would you accuse me of consorting with such? Like you, I am a sorcerer. I draw magic from the world around me."

Charron stared. "But you hold too much for this world. There've been no sorcerers that strong since . . ." He shrugged, searching for the answer. "There've been none in my lifetime, though there are stories that tell us they once existed."

Nico nodded in agreement. "Where I come from, there is a great deal more magic available than what you have here. I don't know why. But when I arrived, at the end of a long and difficult journey, it took me much longer to rebuild my strength than it would have at home."

"Where is your home, then?"

Nico sighed and considered what to say. If Charron thought Nico's relatively simple display of power had been so overwhelming that he'd accused him of consorting with devils, then Nico could only imagine what he'd think about a spell that could spin a man between worlds and time. Charron seemed to accept his explanation that there was more magic available where Nico came from. But would he accept that it wasn't another country or state, but another world?

Worried that any attempt to explain the true situation would only delay his quest, Nico made up a story, instead. "My home lies in the mountains to the east and north of your country. The journey was long and difficult. It was foolish of me to undertake it on my own."

"And yet, God saw you safely here," Bellamy observed. "Perhaps He wanted you to reach Paris, knowing that your power was needed to cleanse the city of vampires, who are surely the devil's minions."

Charron grunted his agreement, although it seemed less than heartfelt to Nico. He suspected the leader would have preferred that God dump his body in a deep ravine somewhere. Bellamy, however, seemed to be enamored with his theory of divine intervention, and was eyeing his leader with barely suppressed excitement.

Nico cared little as to Charron's opinion of him, or for that matter, what use he might make of Nico's skills. He was just waiting for a more or less polite opportunity to depart, so he could go back to his hotel, have a glass of cognac, and sleep for several hours. And upon waking, he fully intended to block all memory of the local magic-users and their war with vampires.

The unexpected slap of Charron's hands on his thighs was so loud and sharp that even Nico was startled at the sound. His gaze swung to the French sorcerer, though he managed to compose his expression into one of mild interest rather than surprise.

"Bellamy's correct," the big man announced. "We can use your skills against the vampires. They outnumber us rather badly, and they're able to replace any losses in a single night. The number of magic users in Paris has been dwindling for years, and unlike the vampires, we cannot produce new recruits at will. Your power will be most welcome. You will be commanding—"

Nico held up a blocking hand. "I've no desire to command anyone, Monsieur Charron. It's not even clear to me that this is a war I should be involved with. My reason for leaving the comfort and safety of my home and traveling to this city was to locate a cousin, who set out months before I did, and has never been heard from again. But Paris is a huge city, which is difficult enough, and my own experience in getting here tells me that he may not have been as fortunate as I was in arriving safely."

"Is your cousin also a sorcerer?" Charron's florid face took on a greedy expression.

"He is, but you'll find him even less eager than I am to become embroiled in your vampire war. I am nonetheless set on finding him, or if not that, at least discovering his fate. That search is likely to eventually take me out of Paris permanently, so you can surely see why I want to avoid entanglements that would complicate my departure."

Bellamy gasped. "But Monsieur—"

"I understand, of course," Charron interrupted. "If I were on a similar quest, I would do the same. But think on it, Monsieur Katsaros. As you said, finding one man in a city this large is a daunting task. You could very well remain in Paris for months, if not longer. The vampires will sniff you out eventually, whether you join us or not. It is in your best interest, as well as ours, to do what you can to exterminate them."

The bastard had a point, though Nico would never admit it. But he wasn't quite as lost in terms of finding Sotiris as Charron might believe. The spell which had brought him to Paris had been made with more urgency than thought. The next one would have to be more deliberately planned if he hoped to follow Sotiris to where Antonia and his warriors were being held. The question remained as to whether Sotiris himself knew where the four warriors were, but he had no such doubts when it came to Antonia. The bastard would know where she was, would know where he'd *put* her, which meant he would at least want to maintain a watch on her, and maybe visit her on occasion.

If Nico found Sotiris, he would find Antonia. He had to learn how the spell worked, so he could *choose* his destination, even if it meant following Sotiris from place to place. He'd already decided to remain in the city long enough to break down Sotiris's spell until he could use it toward his own ends, but Charron didn't need to know that.

"I will think on it for a day or two," he agreed. "I do have much ground still to cover here in Paris."

Charron gave a regal nod of agreement, which didn't exactly encourage Nico to get involved with him. But if he did—and that was far from set—he would be deciding what actions to take against the vampires. The day had never been, and never would be, when he was so weakened that he took orders from one such as Charron.

"I will bid you good night, now, and be on my way." Nico gave a bare bow of farewell. "Gentlemen."

THE REMAINDER of his trek back to the hotel was blessedly uneventful. It occurred to him when he was two blocks away that Charron probably could have provided a carriage to drive him back. But the convenience wouldn't have been worth asking Charron for a favor. The man was the type to demand something in return.

The clerk was absent from the desk when he entered the building, the first such absence since Nico had arrived. Ironically, he'd begun to suspect the man wasn't fully human, since he never seemed to require sleep or a break of any kind. Tonight, however, another stood in his place, wearing a jacket identical to the clerk's.

"Bonsoir. Monsieur Katsaros, n'est-ce pas?"

"*Oui. Bonsoir,*" Nico replied, but didn't stop to chat. He went directly to the stairs and climbed to his suite, where he stripped off his clothes, poured a full glass of cognac, and slid naked beneath the sheets. Closing his eyes, he sighed deeply and took a sip of the lovely alcohol. He had to admit that the French vintners and chefs had taken the art of dining to a higher level than he would have believed possible. Even the food sold by sidewalk vendors tasted far superior to anything from his world. Not even Sotiris's excellent cook was so skilled.

"This world is *your world now,"* a quiet voice in his head reminded him. He wasn't yet fully resolved to that truth. Nor was he completely certain it *was* the truth. Maybe he simply didn't want to believe it.

Two weeks later, his beliefs no longer mattered. Because events decided for him.

Chapter Four

NICO STROLLED along the boulevard, glad for even the weak winter sun after too many weeks of gray skies and snow. He'd been in Paris for nearly two months, and though he'd found no clear sign of any of those he'd lost to Sotiris's curses, nor for that matter of Sotiris himself, he *had* moved from the hotel to a townhouse of his own. His search required both magic and the privacy to use it, which had been in short supply at the hotel. He'd taken David with him when he'd left, however, hiring the boy to be his butler. The new position didn't require much more from the boy than he'd been doing anyway, but the working conditions were better, and the job paid more, too. Nico's only requirement had been for David to live in, which he'd been more than happy to do. At the townhouse, the new butler had his own room and a bath that was mostly his, though in the event Nico broke from routine and had guests, they would use it, as well.

Nico, of course, had a private bath and dressing room, as well as a large bedroom suite, and a balcony with a lovely view, when the air and sky were clear. Long before his arrival, the industrial trend had taken firm hold all over Europe, apparently. Nico appreciated the benefits, but he saw the price being paid every day in the toxic clouds darkening the skies, and blackening the buildings. If he'd had a choice, he'd have left Paris for the clean air and empty vistas of the countryside. Unfortunately, his quest demanded he remain. If he was ever going to find his people, or at least some clue as to their location, he had to unravel every element of Sotiris's spell. And when his brain began to rebel against the complexities of that task, he'd set himself to learning as much as he could about this world. If the spell gave a name or location of the next place he meant to visit, for whatever reason, Nico wanted to have a good sense of where and what that place was.

After studying the giant globe and other maps in the library, he now knew that this world had several large land masses. Most of these continents, as they were called, had a large number of people living upon them, just as this one did. He'd learned that France was part of the continent of Europe, and that there were several more countries just like it. Multiplying the number of people he saw every day in Paris by his best guess for all of Europe, equaled a staggering population. If that was true of the other continents as well, then his chances of finding his warriors and Antonia were daunting to the point of surrender. Unless he found Sotiris first and scrubbed every bit of knowledge from the bastard's mind, including the truth about the people Nico loved.

Whether he found Sotiris or not, however, he would never give up searching for them. He'd have done the same even if loyalty and love weren't driving him to work harder, to find *something*, to uncover some small clue for him to follow.

Today, for example, he'd met with a priest at the great cathedral of Notre Dame de Paris. The man had been more than willing to help, but could offer very little in the way of real information. Nonetheless, he'd given Nico *carte blanche* to access the cathedral's records whenever they might aid his research. Nico didn't know if the church records would help, but it was one more source that he could call on if the need arose.

He hadn't, of course, confided his true mission to the priest. Nor had he revealed that he was a sorcerer. Charron's accusation of devil's work at their first meeting was ever in the back of Nico's mind. The sorcerer might have withdrawn the charge, if he'd ever meant it seriously, but the fact that such an accusation would be voiced reminded Nico that not everyone saw sorcery as a gift. He'd come upon records of ordinary men and women being persecuted, tortured, and even killed for not believing in the teachings of the Church of Rome. The simple accusation of such could still land one in prison.

Nico held no beliefs from his upbringing. If any gods were worshipped, they were ancient and earth-based, or the stuff of mythology, which no one truly believed anymore. In this case, however, his lack of belief was a benefit, since he could take on the mantle of whatever religion the reigning church required, and shed it as easily once he left.

The priest had listened to Nico's tale of a lost cousin, and had been more than helpful. And so, Nico was happy to listen to the man in turn and learn what he could of the ruling faith. All knowledge was useful at some point.

It was the great cathedral that he was returning from, walking, which he preferred to hiring a carriage. He had no fears for his own safety. His sorcerous power was fully restored, despite the diminished level of magic in this world, and the physical demands of walking the sometimes long distances were beneficial to the recovery of his strength and stamina.

By the time he'd reached the outer edges of the neighborhood where he now lived, the sun was low enough in the sky that long shadows reached across the boulevard to create dark pockets between buildings. Nico shivered at what he thought must be the first touch of a cold night, but hard on that thought was the premonition of something much worse. He lifted his head instinctively, taking in the scent of the street, weeding out the cooking smells and the sewage, the oily murk of the street lanterns, and leaving . . .

A man was suddenly in front of him, the smooth almost invisible glide of his movements making it seem as if he'd appeared from nowhere. Vampire.

Nico pulled on his power, readying a defensive spell should the creature think to attack. Or should more of them appear. In his experience, vampires rarely travelled alone.

"Your purse, if you please," the vampire purred, his manner so polite that they might have been two friends greeting each other.

Nico didn't reach for his purse, which he had no intention of surrendering. Instead, he studied the vampire, curious but unafraid. "I carry no purse," he lied. It was said that vampires could hear the lie in a man's words. But Nico wasn't an ordinary man.

"Jewelry then," the vampire snarled, no longer bothering with courtesy.

He sighed. "I'm afraid I don't wear jewelry, either. He looked down at himself, as if searching for some random piece he'd forgotten. He touched the lone gold pin holding his cravat in place. "This is gold, but it's rather small, I'm afraid."

"You think to toy with me human?"

Nico didn't answer the question, asking instead, "Who are you?"

The vampire drew himself to his full height and snarled like a wild animal. "No more lies, scum. You have a purse. Give it to me."

He made an offended noise. "I might be new to this city, but even I know that refusing an introduction is terribly impolite." He touched his chest again and said, "I shall go first. I am Nicholas Katsaros. And you are?"

The vampire laughed. "Are you a fool? Or do you simply value your life so lightly?"

"On the contrary. I value my life a great deal, just as I value every citizen of this fine city."

The vampire's eyes flashed red in the growing darkness, and Nico was forcibly reminded of what he'd learned about this world's vampires. Like those of his world, they could not tolerate sunlight. If exposed for too long, a vampire could easily burn alive. But the stronger the vampire, the more resistance he had to the sun. For this vampire to be not only awake, but preying on humans with the sun not yet fully set, meant he was very strong indeed. Unfortunately, Nico's consideration of his vampire assailant was cut short, when two more of the creatures slid bonelessly out of the shadows and into the lamplight of the increasingly dark boulevard.

One of the new vampires spoke to the first one, saying, "We heard your call, Master."

The exchange confirmed something that was only a rumor among the magic users Nico had met at Charron's. The vampires in this world could communicate with their minds alone. He was sure the ability was somehow linked to their shared blood, and speculated that the blood must have some magical aspect to make that possible. His mind automatically wandered to the question of how such a thing had come to be, and how it was continuously passed from one to the other, when they survived by drinking the blood of ordinary humans. Were they the product of some sorcerous spell gone awry? Or were they part of the natural world, just as he was? That seemed more likely, since the trait was shared by vampires in both this world and his own, but—

His attention was snapped back to the present danger when one of the new vampires leaped forward, teeth bared and fingers crooked like claws, with long, yellowed nails. Nico took a half step back, and glanced around, searching not for assistance, but for witnesses. His only hope of defending himself was his sorcery. But he no more wanted tales spreading about his magic, than he did of a battle with vampires. Seeing no one, he lashed out with a bolt of pure power, shoving the vampire so far and so hard that he flew past his friends and slammed into the alley wall, where he slumped to the ground.

The others stared in shock for a heartbeat, and then attacked as one. Rage distorted their faces. Lips drew back from wet fangs gleaming yellow in the lantern light, and their eyes burned with red fire. They reached out not to wound, but to grab Nico and drag him deeper into the alley. They worked in concert, one to each side, with the first, stronger, vampire looping an arm around Nico's neck and squeezing until a regular human would have been choked unconscious. Nico knew they would kill him right there in the alley, not worrying who might see, because they didn't fear repercussions of society or church.

He fought with his physical strength alone. He was a big man, and strong. And so he fought, not to spare the lives of the creatures attacking him, but to give himself the room he needed for an experiment of his own. He could have blown them away in an instant if he'd been willing to use magic, but it would have used too much power, and if too many more had arrived, he could be left without sufficient magic to take all of them out.

Mindful of everything he'd learned from Gabriel, he instead manifested a simple wooden stake, sharpened to a knife point, and stabbed one of the attacking vampires in the heart. But even though he knew the stake was fatal, he still could only stare in horrified intrigue when the vampire froze in an instant of shock, and then crumbled to dust before Nico's eyes.

That stunned reaction to the complete disintegration of a living being almost cost him his life when the one he'd slammed into a wall earlier now joined his leader in a renewed attack. With the stake still in his hand, Nico stabbed out instinctively, striking one in the neck, while a reflexive blast of his power set the other's clothes on fire. The injured vamp yanked the stake from his neck and dropped to the ground, and ignoring the sudden gush of blood, tried to escape down the alley, but Nico didn't want his existence and abilities shared even among vampires. He reached out with a loop of power and grabbed the fleeing vampire, dragging him back until he was close enough to kill. Grabbing the stake from the ground, he thrust it into the vampire's gut, and shoved upward into the heart. A moment later, his dust joined the dirt on the ground.

There was no time to celebrate, however. The leader was still alive and uninjured, and probably summoning more vampires to take Nico down—enough to overcome his magic and kill him. Even worse than death would be if they took him alive and forced their blood into him, making *him* a vampire. Would his sorcery survive? And if so, would he become the deadly weapon that filled the nightmares of Charron and his magic users? Nico would rather die. He had to kill the leader and escape, before any more vampires arrived to witness his power and identify him to others.

Summoning every bit of the power left within him, more worried about the present than some possible future, he raised his hands and filled them with the hilts of two magic-driven blades that arced with lightning as fierce as any storm had ever manifested.

The vampire leader snarled at the sight, but didn't back down.

Bracing himself for attack, he stood knees bent and hands raised in claws before him, his eyes almost yellow with the intensity of the flames that danced there. Nico admired his courage, but wanted him dead. In a move so fast the vampire didn't see it coming, Nico swung both blades at once, crossing each other as they sliced into opposite sides of the vampire's neck, and removed his head. When the head tumbled to the ground, it fell into a dust so fine that Nico could see through it to the lantern lights beyond.

And so he learned another lesson, another weapon to be used against this enemy. A stake through the heart was fatal. But so too, was removing the head. It was a lesson he'd remember to tell his fellow magic users the next afternoon, when he paid a visit to Charron to share the news that he would, after all, be joining their crusade against the vampires of Paris.

NICO DIDN'T ADVISE Charron in advance of his intention to visit. He could have sent a message. It was the polite thing to do. But he wanted his decision to appear sudden, as if he'd been out walking and thinking, and had suddenly decided to join the crusade. When he knocked on the townhouse door, he presented his card and was told to wait on the front step. Standing outside the closed door, he thought it was a particularly rude manner with which to greet guests, but as he was unexpected, he supposed he couldn't complain.

When the door opened again, the butler apologized politely for the delay and invited him inside, gesturing toward the same sitting room where Nico had met Charron previously. The sorcerer was sitting in the same spot, just as unkempt in appearance, though the clothes were different and he was enjoying an afternoon tea, rather than dinner.

Charron greeted him familiarly, but in a sour tone. "Nicholas."

Nico responded in a like manner. "Hadrien."

The sorcerer's mouth tightened in disapproval. Nico didn't give a fuck. If anyone was due respect here, it was him.

Charron sipped his tea and asked, "Have you come to petition our assistance?"

Nico laughed. He couldn't help it. "Hardly. I've come to offer *you* my assistance."

The French sorcerer's eyes lit with an avarice that he couldn't conceal, but all he said was, "What makes you think we require anything you can offer?"

"Let's not play games. I have more power than all of you put together, and far more experience in true battle, as well. I was attacked by several vampires —"

A gasp from behind had him turning to find a woman standing there. Garbed in the latest Parisian ladies' fashion, she was stunningly beautiful, with deep red hair and green eyes that gleamed like emeralds. She was *too* beautiful, actually—a fact confirmed when Nico slid a scan over her body, looking for magic, and found it. The scan was far too quick for anyone but a sorcerer of his caliber to notice, and he was confident she was unaware he'd done it.

He nodded to her. "*Madame*. I don't think I've had the pleasure."

She held out a graceful hand. "*Mademoiselle* Violette Bellamy."

Bellamy? Was this woman related to his friend Vital Bellamy? Not his wife surely. They didn't . . . go together somehow. No. And she'd stressed that she was unmarried by correcting his form of address. "Nicholas Katsaros. *Un plaisir.*" He touched his lips lightly to the offered fingers.

"Enchanté."

Yeah, enchanted pretty much summed her up, didn't it? But he kept the thought to himself, along with the question of her relationship, or not, to Vital.

"*Monsieur* Katsaros has come to offer his assistance in our war with the vampires." The words held a derisive note, as if Nico had nothing to offer, and Charron was only indulging him.

"Ah." Violette moved past Nico with a swish of fabric and a wave of some perfume. Sitting on the chair next to Charron's, she gazed up at him with those artificially emerald eyes, and said, "And *do* you have anything to offer, *Monsieur Katsaros?* Your accent is very nearly perfect, but you are not, I think, from Paris. What do you know of fighting vampires?"

Nico eyed her lazily and said, "I survived an attack just yesterday."

Her eyes went wide. "A vampire tried to—"

"*Five* vampires, *mademoiselle*. One a master. Fortunately, it was barely past sunset, so—"

"Five?" Charron demanded. "Who was with you?"

"No one," Nico responded. "I was alone, walking home from the cathedral."

His audience stared, until a man's laugh broke the silence. "I told you he had power, Hadrien."

Nico turned with a smile and held out his hand in greeting. "Vital, *mon ami.*"

Vital Bellamy returned a hearty handshake. "Nicholas, you have come back. Did you meet my sister?"

That was one question answered, Nico thought, and said, "We met."

"You also met some of our vampires, apparently."

"I did. I was returning from the cathedral, and misjudged the sunset. I was very nearly home when they attacked."

"Did I hear correctly? There were five of them?"

"Yes, and one a master. At first, I thought he would be the only one, given the time of day, but he called the others to him. You know of their ability to do that?"

Vital had moved closer to the others, and so Nico asked the question of all of them.

"We've suspected for some time. But how can you be certain that's what happened?" Charron asked skeptically.

"Forgive my manners," Vital exclaimed suddenly, and dragged an extra chair next to the one where he sat near his sister. "Sit, *mon ami.*"

Nico sat, then crossed his legs and leaned back casually while brushing a bit of lint from his pant leg. "To answer your question, *Monsieur* Charron, the master vampire was the first to attack. He was still alive when two more arrived, and I heard one of them tell the master that they had 'heard his call' and come."

Charron expelled a breath that was harsh with both disgust and regret. "So it's true, then. Most unfortunate, but we've been fighting them all this time without proof, so it doesn't change anything. What else can you tell us?"

"Probably only what you already know. I never fought a vampire before arriving in Paris, and so everything I learn is new to me. But not to you, I would think."

"And yet, you learned something important last night, and you survived, which is most important of all. Five vampires? *Superbe!*"

"Yes, Vital," Charron said sourly. "And now that Nicholas has enjoyed a personal taste of their savagery, it would seem he is prepared to assist us."

"*Merveilleux!* Your strength is very welcome, *mon ami!*"

"*Oui,* Nicolas is *very* welcome." Violette's agreement was a sensual purr, as was the look she was giving him from under lowered lashes.

Charron shot her an irritated glance, which he transferred to Nico. "Am I correct in my assumption that you are prepared to fight these creatures?"

Nico studied him a moment, then said, "I will fight, but in return you will do something for me."

The look Charron shot him then was so filled with hatred that Nico thought for sure he would refuse the offer, and tell him to fuck off, or whatever polite version of the sentiment existed in Paris. Instead, though the expression on his face was so sour that Nico thought he must be in pain, Charron asked, "What do you need?"

"It's not a difficult thing. No one's life will be endangered. But as I said before, Paris is a big city, with endless villages and towns in the countryside. You and the others in your group know the city and its people far better than I. In particular, you have connections among other magic-users, which is most likely where my cousin would be found. Or if not found, then at least known, if only slightly. I want you, by which I mean the entire group, to inquire of friends and colleagues, merchants and bankers, if they've encountered my cousin, and if so, when and where." He shrugged. "Simple enough, as I said."

Charron eyed him appraisingly. "And in return, you pledge to join our fight?"

"My magic and I would be at your service." That was an exaggeration, but the essence of his willingness was accurate.

"Done. You should return this evening, which is when we meet. Several of our number have professional and family obligations most days, but at night we are all free."

"Do you *fight* at night, as well?"

"We prefer not to, since the creatures are at their most powerful then. Though sometimes we must," Vital provided. "We stalk them at night, though only to locate their nests. If the location is sufficiently remote so as not to draw attention, we will sometimes linger until sunrise and burn them out. More often, we return in daylight and eradicate the creatures as you would a nest of rats. We either stake or behead them as they sleep, and then open their nest to the sun."

"It is what they deserve," Violette sniffed.

Nico looked at her directly. "Do you fight as well, *mademoiselle?*"

"Violette," she corrected coyly. "And no, Nicholas. I do not. Do the women in your country take to the battlefield?"

"Some of them do. And they are dangerous and very much feared."

She laughed. "I think I would like to be feared."

Nico was willing to be charming and polite, but that was the extent of his interest in her. He turned to address Charron instead. "What time this evening?"

Chapter Five

THAT EVENING, NICO did as he'd said he would and returned to the townhouse after dinner. He hired a carriage this time. While he'd killed the vampires who'd attacked him, he was certain there had been more back at the nest, wherever that was, and he thought it very likely that they would come after him in revenge. Especially since he'd killed their master, who had probably sired some, if not all, of those remaining.

And if there was no danger from them? Well then, at least he'd arrive at Charron's townhouse with clean boots and his energy unspent. The sorcerer might want a demonstration of his power for the others—and maybe for himself, too. He was probably hoping that Nico's previous demonstration had been a fluke, and that a second conjuration would be Nico's undoing.

Nico didn't care what they thought of his power, and if anything, would be inclined to conceal his true strength. He didn't want to take over Charron's leadership role. He was only joining their group to expand the net of inquiry after Sotiris's whereabouts.

When he stepped down from the carriage, two others were arriving at the townhouse door. One had his hand lifted to knock, but paused when Nico approached and said, *"Bonsoir Messieurs."*

They echoed his, *"Bonsoir,"* but the one lowered his hand and didn't knock, only glanced nervously at his companion.

"Monsieur Charron invited me to join all of you this evening," Nico assured him, then backed a few feet away from the door. "I understand your reluctance, however, and will wait until you can verify my *bona fide."*

The one who'd been about to knock gave him a somewhat apologetic look, but didn't invite him to come closer, when he lifted his hand again and rapped his knuckles on the wood in a clear pattern. Nico looked on askance. Knocking in pattern was a poor system at best, and easily copied by someone hiding nearby. He wondered that Charron hadn't placed a basic spell on the entrance instead. Or if he lacked the power to maintain it, then he should at least have stationed a watcher on the door who could identify members as they arrived. He leaned back to search the upper floors, thinking there had to be at least one window that could serve as a surveillance point, and caught the twitch of a curtain and a flash of red hair.

Violette, he thought. Well, at least she'd proven the existence of a suitable window. He'd ask Charron about the matter. If the sorcerer couldn't power a satisfactory spell, he would offer to do it for him. The thought brought a smirk to his lips, though he hid it well. The two arrivals were nervous enough about him. No need to add to it.

The door opened, and Vital Bellamy stood there, smiling as always. "*Entrez, entrez,*" he said graciously, and gestured behind the two men to Nico. "Come, Nicholas. Violette told me you were here."

"*Merci,* Vital. *Bonsoir,*" he added, gratefully removing his hat when he stepped inside.

Behind him, Vital closed the door and shot the locking bolts. "We are all here now. Follow me."

The other two had already gone ahead, familiar with the group's routine, so it was only Nico and Vital who walked past the room where he'd met Charron before, and down the narrow hall to a set of double doors with an overly elaborate design carved into the wood. The artisanship was undeniable, he supposed. It simply wasn't his taste.

One of the doors was slightly open when Vital pushed it wider so they could enter. Vital glanced first at Charron, received a miniscule nod of permission, and then said, "*Mes amis, nous avons un nouveau compagnon. Nicholas Katsaros.*"

He gestured at Nico, who dipped his head briefly and said, "*Mon plaisir, messieurs.*" He then gave Charron a nod of greeting and followed Vital's direction to a seat between him and his sister at the end of the table opposite Charron. Violette touched his hand briefly in greeting. He managed to avoid yanking his hand out from under her pale fingers, but contrived an opportunity to do so gracefully, by using the hand to toss his hat onto the sideboard behind him, where other hats were similarly deposited. He also cast a silent spell insulating himself from the overwhelming scent of her perfume, not wanting to carry it with him the rest of the night and into his bed.

At his end of the table, Charron took a healthy gulp of red wine, wiped his mouth more or less discreetly, then sat straighter and gave what sounded like a prescribed set of phrases to open the meeting. Nico noticed that the man to the sorcerer's right was writing furiously, and assumed he was taking notes of what was said. That explained the formal opening remarks.

Charron turned his attention to Nico next. *"Monsieur* Katsaros sought us out upon his arrival in Paris two weeks ago. He expressed his interest in our activities at that time, but was understandably occupied with other matters while he settled into living here. I have seen his power, and it is considerable. He is an excellent addition to our group on that basis alone. But I wonder, Nicholas, if you would be so kind as to expand on your talents for us. This will help me decide where you can best be assigned to do the most good.

"Ah," he continued, before Nico could respond. "It's also worth noting that Nicholas was attacked by a group of vampires a few days ago. Obviously, he survived, but he killed five vampires during the assault, including one master. He already gave me the basics of the fight, but if you would, *mon ami,*" he said to Nico. "Could you relate the story to us in greater detail. We do this after every battle so that each of us can benefit from every experience."

"Bien sûr," Nico agreed readily, having already decided to describe the events in a way that emphasized some of his skills, while down-playing others that he preferred to remain secret. "The first vampire—who was master of the nest—surprised me with his attack. It was barely sunset, with light still in the sky, though the sun's orb had already dropped below the tallest buildings. I was passing an alleyway . . ."

And so he continued, repeating some of what he'd already told Charron, while omitting other details. Most importantly, he omitted anything that would lead a knowledgeable magic-user—which he assumed all of these were to some degree—to conclude that his power was anywhere close to what it was. At the same time, he wanted to be sure he was included in every meeting of the group, no matter what was being discussed, or how many other members were included. Which reminded him of Charron's promise in exchange.

"As Monsieur Charron mentioned upon introducing me this evening, I only recently arrived in Paris. It wasn't by chance, however. I traveled a great distance to reach your city, because I'm searching for one of my family who has disappeared. At least, he has stopped communicating with his family since arriving in this city. His parents received a single letter, advising of his safe arrival, but nothing since, and we are deeply concerned. I was sent to follow his trail and find out what has happened, whether the news is good or bad. He is a sorcerer, and though his skills are somewhat different than my own, his power is great. Such a man would not easily disappear into even a city as large as this one, much less the smaller communities in the countryside.

"My cousin's name is Sotiris Dellakos. He is darker in appearance than I am, with dark hair and eyes, and somewhat shorter in height. He is charming, when he chooses to be, especially with women, and not easily forgotten. If any of you have had contact with him, or have heard talk of others who have, I would be grateful if you would share what you know. And also, if you have family or business in the countryside, if you could inquire yourself, or ask others to do so, I would be most appreciative. I will have to return home at some point, and want desperately to have something to report to my family. Or better, to make the return trip with him by my side."

All around the table, there were nods and thoughtful looks that made Nico glad he'd finally thought to use them this way.

He continued then, emphasizing his skill with magical objects, rather than his combat ability. His intention was to persuade Charron to put him in charge of creating devices—powerful devices—that could be used to both detect and destroy vampires. Most would be useable by less powerful sorcerers or magic users, and those he would leave behind, along with diagrams and notes for their design. The more powerful objects he would take with him and destroy any record of their making. Not because he begrudged this group the power to use them, but because he feared their use in the wrong hands—including Charron's, who seemed more interested in his own political power than the welfare of Parisians, or anyone else.

When he finished his retelling of the vampire attack, Charron, who'd been watching him with covert curiosity during his report, now eyed him speculatively, while the others mostly remarked on Nico's good fortune in surviving.

"An excellent report, Nicholas," Charron commented. "And precisely why we take the time for such things. I listened closely to the details, and wonder if we could impose on you to take a lead role in the design and fabrication of the weapons we use to destroy these creatures. Vital currently supervises a small group of us who deal with such matters, but I would ask, *mon bon ami*—" He turned to Vital. "If you would be willing to include Nicholas in your group."

Vital smiled broadly at Nico. "Willing? I would be very pleased not only to include Nicholas, but to surrender my role as leader, if he would accept it."

Nico hoped his returning smile was as self-effacing as he tried to make it. Although only for the others, not Vital, whose own smile had indicated obvious amusement at Nico's diffidence with regard to his sorcerous strength. After all, Vital had witnessed Nico's fight with the four men who'd assaulted him after his evening at the *Palais Royale,* so he *knew* what Nico was capable of.

"I would be honored, *mon ami,*" Nico said now. "Such research has always been a particular favorite of mine." Which also was *definitely* not true.

"*Bien,*" Charron exclaimed, and slapped his hands together. "This has been a very fruitful meeting, *mes amis, n'est-ce pas?* Shall we adjourn to the sitting room for cognac and cigars? And of course, wine for the lady," he added, giving Violette a smile that was on the very edge of intimacy.

Color rose in her cheeks, but whether it was anger or embarrassment, Nico couldn't say. He thought himself a very good judge of women, and didn't believe the two were close, much less intimate. Although his judgment of Parisian women might not be as good as he thought. He'd only been in this *century,* much less this city, for a short time. He shrugged mentally. The existence of a relationship, or the lack of one, between Charron and Violette was purely a matter of curiosity. He had no interest in her, nor would he. His love for Antonia would never fade, regardless of how long it took him to find her.

When the others rose to relocate to the sitting room, he was tempted to excuse himself and return home, but then Vital suggested they use the time to discuss future projects, and make a plan for just the two of them to meet later. Nico didn't mind killing vampires, but more importantly, this group was currently his best chance of discovering news about Sotiris. So, he and Vital selected two chairs away from the others who'd gathered close to the fireplace, and spoke of killing vampires. Mostly.

Vital, as it turned out, was intensely curious about Nico's home country. He responded vaguely at first, not completely trusting the other man's motives in asking. But the longer they talked, the more convinced he became that Vital was simply hungry for anything he could learn about other places and people. Nico knew enough of this world by now to understand that travel was both difficult and dangerous.

Wanting to avoid questions about his "country" as much as possible, he turned the conversation to Vital and learned that he was the head of his family, which included not only Violette, but a younger brother who was married and had three small children. The brother and his family lived on the ancestral estate outside of Paris, while Vital was Violette's official chaperone in the city. Nico also discovered that the townhouse belonged to Vital, and not to Charron. The leader's family had an estate in the same area as Vital's ancestral lands, and the families knew one another. And that was how Charron came to be staying in Vital's townhouse.

It didn't explain the way Charron treated the townhouse as his own, considering he was only a guest, but that wasn't Nico's concern, nor his problem to solve. He liked Vital, but knew they would never be lifelong friends. Nico saw Paris as nothing but a stop on his way to somewhere else. While Vital considered France, and especially Paris, his home, and for all his hunger about other places, he would probably die there, no matter when that unfortunate day came.

When Nico finally stood to leave, he was surprised to note that he'd spent more than an hour learning about Vital and recent French history. He still didn't understand the many changes of rulers and rules in a relatively short period of time, but he did understand Parisians better than he had, which might turn out to be useful.

"You should come to my home for dinner, Vital. We'll have greater privacy to discuss our projects."

"You have no family living with you?"

"No. My family is gone." Which wasn't even a lie. He'd left behind his blood family, and didn't expect to ever see them again. And the five people he considered to be his *real* family were out of his reach . . . for now. "There is only me and my butler," he told Vital. "And the house is more than big enough that I can set aside a room to be our regular meeting place, somewhere we can leave research and fabrication in place and untouched."

"It sounds like a very peaceful place to work," Vital said with a wistful note. "If you're certain it wouldn't impose."

Nico laughed. "I'm not easily persuaded against my will, *mon ami*. Once I commit to a project, I devote every resource I can muster to it."

Vital chuckled in agreement. "Then I accept your invitation."

He fished out one of his cards and handed it to Vital. "Shall we say, two days hence? At the sixth hour of the evening, if that's amenable to you. Shall I send a carriage?"

"*Mais non*, I'll make my own arrangements. I don't want Violette getting too curious about my destination and inviting herself along. She is very persistent, and was overly indulged by our parents. Even I have difficulty denying her what she wants."

Nico suspected his friend was gauging his response, wondering if Violette would be welcome in his home. Since she definitely was *not*, he said only, "Best if we keep this between us, I think. Until we have something to share with the entire group."

"Just so. I agree. Do you require a carriage now? It's very late."

"No, my man will have sent one to wait for me. *Merci, Vital.* I expect our next meeting to be both enjoyable and productive."

"Moi aussi. Bonne nuit, Nicholas."

David was surprisingly excited at Nico's announcement that he would have a dinner guest on *Mercredi*, as the third day of the week was called in France. The boy was somewhat less enthusiastic when Nico explained it was dinner with a male colleague to discuss business, but was still eager at the opportunity to be a "real butler," as he said.

"If you're bored with your duties, I can contrive something more for you to do. The shutters could use painting," Nico commented, his tone dry enough that David seemed to take him seriously.

"*Mais non,* Nicholas. I would be terrible painter."

"And that is why you're a butler whose duties don't include painting. I have an excellent chef in mind for dinner. I'll provide you with a list of everything he'll need, including good wine and cognac. *Very good, non?*"

"I would offer you nothing less, my lord."

Nico fought back a wince at the boy's jocular use of the title. He wasn't a lord in this world, and didn't want to be. But he'd owned the title in his home world for so many years that hearing it brought an unexpected pang of longing for the life he'd had before . . . . Hell, just *before.*

He shook off the feeling, reminding himself that there was no going back to that time or place, and that every day, every act he took, was aimed at restoring his people, if not his former place. He would build a new sort of empire for this new world, with Antonia by his side, and his warriors all around him. He considered that future, and amended it to include Sotiris's death, so that his warriors would remain lifelong friends, but have a chance to build lives of their own that didn't revolve around constant warfare. And families. What an idea! Neither he, nor any of his four had ever included wives and children in their futures, not with always planning for the next battle. But they would. Once Sotiris was dead, they all would.

"Nicholas?"

He was jarred back to the present by David's concerned voice. "Yes?"

"Are you well? You seemed . . . not here."

The observation was more astute than he'd given the boy credit for. "Just thinking. Vital and I are joining forces with some others to rid Paris of its vampires."

"Oh, sir, please be careful. There are more of the creatures every day, and they're very dangerous."

Nico clapped a hand on the boy's shoulder. "So am I, David. So am I."

Chapter Six

1824, Outside London, United Kingdom

ANTONIA STOOD AT one of the large windows in the big, cold room, in the huge, cold house that the man had brought her to. *Yes,* she thought, *that much was true and accurate.* She found it difficult to keep useful thoughts in her head lately. Whenever she tried, her mind would . . . go elsewhere for a while. And when she returned, she always found herself at the same window, in the same room, in the same house. She had no memories of what happened in between. She didn't know how much time had passed, but she knew it had, because the light would be a little bit different, the sun higher or lower in the sky, the clouds high above and raining, or foggy and low to the ground. And sometimes, there would be no clouds or rain, just sunshine. She liked those days best, though she didn't have the words to say why.

Her attention returned to the green forest outside the window. It was no wonder these trees were so green. It seemed always to rain here, or if not rain, then it was so foggy that the clouds seemed to have settled on the forest with no intention of ever lifting again.

Green, she remembered suddenly. Yes, she'd been thinking how green the trees were, because of the rain. She understood that sort of thing, she realized. Understood why some hills were green and others brown, why some trees flourished in this wet place, while others would have withered and died.

She glanced over her shoulder, studying the house, searching for . . . her greenhouse. She frowned, and looked outside instead. A greenhouse wouldn't be inside this elegant mansion. It needed whatever sun could be found in this gray place, and coal pots to warm the air so the plants would thrive. She started for the door, intending to walk around the building and find the greenhouse. She liked working with plants. It was her magic, what she'd been born to. She reached for her coat on the hook near the door, and . . .

Antonia stood in front of the window, gazing out at the rain, and the lovely green trees. Her mind was blank, not a single thought to trouble this peaceful moment. Some part of her—a tiny voice deep in the back of her mind—knew this was wrong. She wasn't a person who had no thoughts, no curiosity or questions. But now, she was so very tired. She turned from the window and sank to the floor. The rug was dense and so soft, and someone was draping a thick blanket over her, making her warm, so she could sleep.

Antonia stood at the window, staring at the fog, watching it tumble slowly, sluggishly, as if hoping no one would notice it had come to earth, so it could stay a while longer. She blinked. That was a fanciful thought, wasn't it? She wasn't a fanciful person. Was she?

"Antonia."

She turned to face the man, the one who'd brought her here. He said she was ill, and he was here to take care of her. She had no memory to say otherwise, and he had provided this elegant mansion for her, with thick rugs and warm blankets. She frowned. That was another odd thought. Rugs and blankets? But then, her mind was so utterly muddled recently. Some days, she didn't even know her name.

"Antonia," the man said again, and she knew she'd drifted off the way she always seemed to do lately. Was it only lately? She glanced at herself and saw a grown woman. So there must have been something before "lately," mustn't there?

"How old am I?" she asked the man.

He regarded her in silent appraisal and said, "Why do you ask that?"

"Because there must have been something before 'lately.'"

He frowned, as if her answer displeased him. But then, he raised his hand and . . .

Antonia stood by the window, staring . . .

Chapter Seven

1824, Paris, France

MERCREDI ARRIVED right on schedule, as it had for countless millennia, regardless of its designation. Vital Bellamy was equally prompt, tapping the door while the pendulum clock in Nico's sitting room was still tolling the sixth hour. David, who'd likewise benefitted from a visit to the tailor, was dressed in his finest garb. And with his neat hair and clean-shaven face, he looked a proper butler.

The house smelled wonderful, the air redolent with the scent of spiced meats and other delicacies, which had been prepared by the chef at Nico's favorite café. He'd stolen the man's services for the night, paying him well enough that he'd been willing to make an excuse to the café's owner to come cook for Nico. He and Nico had sat together late after dinner a few nights ago, planning the menu. The chef had also given Nico a detailed shopping list that included the tools he would need available in the house. Nico ate out most evenings, while his other meals were fairly simple and prepared by a woman who came in every morning to cook and clean. He didn't have any idea what implements his kitchen cupboards might be hiding, so he'd simply turned over that list to David as well. The boy *had* wanted more excitement, after all.

"Vital, welcome," Nico said.

"Thank you, Nicholas. You have a beautiful home."

Nico looked around, as if seeing it for the first time. It was a very nice house, he supposed. Most of the furniture and décor had come with his purchase, though he'd replaced a few pieces that David had pointed out as too worn to be suitable. Nico would have left them as they'd been. He'd bought the house for privacy, not to impress anyone. But now that he had a guest—something he hadn't envisioned even two weeks ago—he was glad his home was elegantly inviting.

"Thank you. Join me for an *aperitif* while the chef completes the meal."

Once they were seated, with drinks in hand, they settled into the true purpose of the evening—the most efficient means of finding and killing vampires.

"Tell me, Vital. I know why I hate vampires. They very nearly destroyed someone close to me. I admit, I'd hoped all of that was well behind me, but the viciousness of my recent encounter with them made it clear they're as deadly as ever. The only way to stop them seems to come down to wiping them from the earth."

"I am as reluctant as you to destroy an entire species of God's creation, but I can see no alternative."

"You believe God created such vile creatures?" Nico asked, questioning Vital's beliefs, not his own. He'd been raised with a plethora of gods, none of whom had shown themselves to have the slightest concern for humans or any other creature, other than as occasional playthings to be used for their own amusement.

"God's truth permits no other interpretation," Vital replied. "Man was expelled from paradise for disobedience. This earth is man's chance to earn his way back into God's grace and return to paradise, is it not?"

Nico made a noise of agreement. He'd been made aware early on of the importance of religion in almost every aspect of French society and culture, and had made a point of studying its tenets and history. It was a topic that he and the old priest at the cathedral had discussed at some length. He'd even permitted the priest to baptize him, simply because it had made the old man happy. As a result, he probably knew more right now about the Catholic church's teachings and history than Vital did, despite having been raised in the faith. That knowledge had more than once eased his assimilation into this world and time.

"But you agree they must be eradicated?" he asked.

"Oh, yes. I've wondered more than once—privately, of course—if they might be the devil's creatures, sent to tempt us."

"How do they tempt? Surely, their lives are dreary by comparison to our own?"

"What does man fear most, *mon ami*, despite the teachings of the holy church?"

Nico didn't have to think about that one. The fear and denial of death was everywhere—in the religion and culture both. "Death."

"*Exactement*. And vampires offer eternal life."

He frowned. "But at what cost? And what kind of life? I would not trade my life for theirs." Of course, he thought privately, he didn't have to worry about dying after a few short decades, either. Maybe if he did, he'd have made a different choice.

Vital shrugged in a way Nico had come to equate with other French-men of his acquaintance. "I agree with you, but I know many who wouldn't."

Nico smiled. "Perhaps their lives are such that they fear the final judgment."

Vital chuckled. "You might be correct."

He took another sip of his wine, then set the glass down, and leaned forward slightly. He enjoyed talking to Vital, but this evening was about more than polite conversation, even if it was also interesting. "Tell me," he asked intently. "What is your strategy, or that of the group, for eliminating the vampires? For every one we kill, their masters create two more."

"Then we must destroy the masters."

"That is not an easy task. The old ones can repair almost any injury, and their creations will sacrifice themselves ten times over to keep their master safe."

"So we do as we have always done. We search out their nests, the places where they hide during the day when they are vulnerable, and kill them as they sleep."

Nico tilted his head curiously. "How long have your people been fighting this war with vampires?"

"A very long time. Any records we know of, ones that go so far back, are scattered and not always precise in their descriptions. But we believe it began hundreds of years ago, perhaps even before the time when written histories first began."

Nico thought of his own world and the vampires who lived in it. Thought, too, of the progress of time evident between then and now. It had to be several hundred years, he thought. And the vampires he'd had knowledge of—those who'd kidnapped and turned Gabriel, for existence—had been old already. "I believe," he said quietly, "that you must be right. The stories from my own country are very old, and yet there is no description of how vampires came to exist."

"Do we conclude from that that we've been fighting them as long as man has existed?"

"Perhaps not that long," he said. He'd never thought much about vampires before, not until he'd met Gabriel.

He was tempted to tell Vital of Gabriel and the spell he'd created to cure him, but that would only reveal too much about his power. He did, however, have a set of rather unique manacles that could be very useful in capturing and holding even the strongest of vampires. The handcuffs would then permit him to do whatever was necessary to gain the knowledge he needed to wipe vampires from the earth. It was an odd stroke of luck that he'd brought the manacles with him at all. It had been a last-minute addition that he'd spontaneously decided to shove into his pack, and it was fortuitous enough that he wondered if it had been a flash of foresight, more instinct than premonition.

At that moment, David entered the room to announce dinner, sparing Nico from deciding how much to share about the amber manacles, as he called them. They would probably require a design change or two, since he'd created them to hold human prisoners, not vampire masters. Yes, he decided. He would tell Vital about them once they were better suited to the task.

He stood with a smile and said, "Let's see what the chef has prepared for us, shall we?"

Chapter Eight

THE NEXT DAY, Nico finished unpacking everything he'd brought with him into the unknown future of Sotiris's spell. He'd removed the notes and journals as soon as he'd moved into the townhouse, but had left the manacles and a few other objects hidden. When he'd purchased the house and moved out of the hotel for good, he'd still considered this to be a temporary home. If he discovered any sign of Sotiris, or his own people, he would stay as long as necessary. But if not, he would search elsewhere.

He was carefully optimistic that the sorcerers and other magic-users in Charron's group would turn up some hint of Sotiris. His enemy might be using a different name, but he couldn't disguise his power. He might shield himself long enough to fool a single person, or even a group, but he couldn't hold the disguise forever. Besides, Sotiris had never been one to hide his power. If he was around, he would make himself known, one way or another.

But if Nico wanted information from the group, he had to contribute something valuable in return. And the amber manacles were certainly that. Made of ensorcelled steel, they were powerful enough that even he preferred to wear gloves when handling them. They were icy cold to the touch, even through gloves, as if the spell that had made them so dangerous had somehow touched them with evil. That touch had troubled Nico when he'd created them, but it hadn't stopped him from using them, just as it wouldn't now. He'd designed them for human prisoners, but had used them only in the most extreme circumstances. They were a terrible weapon. The pain they caused the confined individual was to the mind and spirit, rather than the body. The few prisoners he'd questioned had quickly lost the will to live, and eventually stopped responding even to threats against their own families. Before they reached that point, however, they'd been willing to tell him anything he wanted to know. Because if *nothing* mattered, then any secrets the prisoner held didn't matter either.

He suspected, however, that they would work very differently on vampires. He wasn't convinced that vampires retained human emotions after their transformation. The only sign of caring that he'd ever witnessed, or read about, had been a vampire's slavish need to defend his master.

That was why Nico wanted to capture a master. But what would a master care about? What would cause him to betray his people? His own life, perhaps. That was the one thing most humans would sacrifice anything for, including any loyalties they possessed. He wondered if that effect would manifest differently in vampires, who lived potentially forever. He was going to need a vampire subject.

"David!" he shouted. The butler answered from another room, and quickly appeared in the door to Nico's workroom.

"How can I assist?"

Nico looked up from where he'd been lifting a carefully wrapped piece of amber from his pack. "I'll be going out later tonight. There won't be any need for dinner."

"Will you need a carriage?"

David had made a point of asking that ever since Nico had been attacked. Most times he agreed and let the boy arrange for one. But not tonight. He wanted no witnesses to what he was about to do.

"Not tonight. It's not far."

The boy's expression said he disapproved, but he didn't say it. "Would you like lunch a bit later then? In case the food isn't to your liking?"

That had happened once. Nico had come home as hungry as if he hadn't eaten all day, and made enough noise that David had come downstairs to deal with it. He'd ended up making eggs and potatoes for both of them.

Nico chuckled to let David know he was remembering the night. "We're going to a restaurant, so I think I'm safe."

"Very well. If you change your mind about the carriage—"

"I will let you know."

Nico waited until he heard David take the stairs down to the kitchen, then unwrapped the roughly cut chunk of amber, to reveal the metal key hidden at its very center. Nico had called them the amber manacles because of this key. Once they were secured on the prisoner's wrists, this key—trapped in amber—was hung from a hook or placed on a shelf in full view of the prisoner. It was the key to his freedom, his salvation—so close, and so very unattainable.

There was a second key that Nico now freed from the silk cloth surrounding the manacles, careful to keep the silk between him and the cuffs themselves. This key, a twin to the one in amber, was completely ordinary—a metal key to an ordinary lock. Nico slid the second key into his pants pocket, and placed the amber key in a metal-banded wooden box. He then locked the box and placed it in his desk drawer, and then locked the drawer. It wasn't that the amber key was valuable, other than the value of the amber itself, but it was the last and only chance to free someone who'd been locked in the manacles without Nico's permission.

The clock in his sitting room chimed, reminding him that he'd wanted to return to the library and his purloined stash of reading material. He considered foregoing his usual research routine, but decided against it. He didn't have a clear plan for how to proceed with the manacles, and sometimes when he read texts that were necessary but which contained numbingly bad prose, his mind wandered onto other topics and came up with unexpected conclusions. Some of his best spells had been created that way. And so, he rewrapped the manacles and restored them to a deep corner of his backpack, and went off to the library.

That night, however, he would go hunting.

NICO DRESSED IN common clothing beneath his elegant top coat, to avoid any questions from David. The boy . . . . His butler, he reminded himself. He had to stop thinking of the young man as a boy. So, *his butler* had appointed himself Nico's protector, and worried like an old gran sitting by the fire.

Once out of the house, leaving it securely locked and warded behind him, he stashed the too conspicuous coat behind his house, and went back to the alley where he'd first been attacked by vampires. Despite the tales of impossible-to-find nests from Charron and other members of the group, he was confident he could locate the place used by the vampire master who'd attacked him.

He'd reasoned that it had to be somewhere near where he'd been attacked, since the master had appeared so soon after sunset. He'd also kept the unwashed shirt he'd worn that night, hoping the vampire blood staining the cloth would help him locate the creatures later on. Fingering a square of that cloth now, he cast a simple location spell that he'd learned as a small child and began to hunt. For all that he had sorcery working for him, he wasn't naïve enough to believe his search would be easy. The vampire master he'd fought was dead, but most of his vampires were still alive. Vampires must have a procedure for a new master to rise up and take over when the old master died and left a territory empty. That said, whoever took over wouldn't have been foolish enough to remain in the same building.

Wanting to test the spell, since he'd never before used vampire blood this way, Nico let the magic pull him where it would. The first tug came two blocks before he reached the site of the fight, and very quickly led him to an obviously empty nest. He took the time to search it, but was soon convinced it had been abandoned and no other vampires had since taken up residence. Simple bedding had been left behind—straw mattresses mostly, though there were a few that looked to be feather-stuffed, given the occasional lone feather poking out. He found it curious that the vampires hadn't simply stolen what they needed, and obtained something better than straw. There were no blankets, as if the surviving vampires had taken those and left only the beds. As the mattresses were the best indicator of how many vampires had once used the nest, he studied the rows. Most were clustered in the center of the room, probably to avoid any sunlight seeping through narrow openings in the poorly constructed walls. In the very center, a few tattered blankets still hung in a square of sorts, surrounding the center pole, but leaving enough room for a pile of three mattresses which formed a single bed.

The moderately better conditions led Nico to assume that this was where the master vampire had slept. The other vampires were utterly committed to their master's defense, so it made sense that their sleeping arrangements would reflect that. Anyone thinking to come at the nest from outside would have to fight their way through every regular vampire before reaching the center and the master. For all Nico knew, it was designed that way to permit the master to escape alive, while the others died to give him time. It seemed an odd system to him. He'd been told from the time he'd been a toddler with a wooden sword that the lord of the realm—whatever that realm was—always led his people into battle.

Even after his powers had developed, and his training had changed radically, he'd held to that basic principle. It was one of the many reasons that he had no respect for Sotiris—his enemy always sat above the battle, isolated from danger. The bastard had once told Nico that he did it to facilitate the use of his sorcery, because it gave him a better view of the battlefield. But Nico had led enough armies to war that he'd known the "reason" was nothing but an excuse to remain safe while others died on his behalf. It was a despicable quality in a leader.

Once he'd walked the entire room, Nico left, not wanting to waste time. He was careful not to be seen, lest he gain a reputation for being strange. The last thing he wanted was to find himself questioned as a murderer ... or a vampire, the first time some innocent died on the street. He could have used his power to block others from seeing him when he went out, but unless absolutely necessary, he didn't want to do that. His magic was as powerful as ever, but the magic available in this world for resupply, as it were, was pitiful. He was fully charged just then, and wanted to keep it for something more serious than walking around unseen.

Casting the location spell once more, he closed his eyes and set his senses free, letting the spell take him where it would. When he felt another tug, he opened his eyes again, lest he trip, or run into a wall. He maintained a steady stride, turning this way and that, sometimes worrying that the spell was sending him in a circle rather than anywhere useful. He'd almost decided to stop and recast the spell, when the path became as clear and straight as if it were lit by a solitary beam of moonlight. But rather than race ahead, he slowed his steps, holding a pace that permitted him to study his surroundings, noting every door and window, every dark alley or space. He called up a defensive spell and held it in hand, ready to use. All he would have to do is raise his arm and point toward his attacker, and the spell would shoot a line of magic-based fire, which was a thousand times more deadly than ordinary fire and impossible to douse.

When the attack came, it was from behind. The vampire landed on Nico's back with such force that it drove him to his knees before he had a chance to react. Long nails dug into his shoulder and head as the vampire tried to bare his neck, stretching it tight to assist him in sinking fangs into his human prey.

But Nicodemus was no one's fucking prey. Reaching behind, he gripped the vampire with both hands and threw him over his head to land with an audible crunch on the filthy ground in front of him. The vampire howled in pain and anger, but sprang to his feet with shocking speed and turned to face Nico. One shoulder was visibly damaged, the arm hanging limp, but the vampire didn't appear slowed by the injury. If anything, the pain seemed only to make him angrier and more determined. As if to prove it, the vampire raised his uninjured fist and swung it in a hard upward arc to smash into his own damaged shoulder. He howled again, but when his fist lowered, the shoulder was no longer hanging quite so unnaturally, and the vampire had bared a mouthful of bloody teeth and fangs.

"I don't feel pain, human," the creature rasped.

"Lie," Nico snapped. "You may ignore it, but you still feel it."

"Why are you here? Do you wish to die?" The vampire laughed, his bloody mouth a gaping and gruesome hole in his pale face.

"I've no intention of dying, vampire. What about you?"

"We don't die, fool. The master's blood grants life eternal."

"If that's true, then why do you fear me? I am but a mortal man."

The creature narrowed its red-tinged gaze. "What game do you play? Were you sent by an enemy to test my master's strength?"

"So your master doesn't rule this entire city? How disappointing for him."

"No one master can rule Paris. The city is too large. Even a stupid human should understand that."

"Yes, I am stupid . . . about vampires, at least. Don't make the mistake of thinking me stupid in all things, however."

The vampire sneered. "Or what? You have no power to threaten me."

"Then come closer." Nico tilted his head to bare his neck in invitation. "Taste."

The vampire's eyes flared with hungry desire, but the barest hint of distrust lingered on his face.

Nico shrugged. "Perhaps that's one more thing I've gotten wrong about you, then. I'd heard the vampires of this city were all but fearless. That the human population dreaded sunset, cowering behind—"

The vampire's attack was a blur of silent death. He came head on, with not so much as a nod on the side of caution. The deadly creature had been right in one aspect. Nico *didn't* understand vampires. He'd been so confident of his own strength that he hadn't anticipated a vampire could take him by surprise. Not when he was forewarned of their presence, with the vampire standing right in front of him.

But as shockingly fast as the attack had come, Nico was ready for him. With a single word, he had the vampire frozen in midair, and from there dropping helplessly to the ground, unable to move or protect himself. But while the spell was good, its effect wouldn't last long, especially Nico suspected, on a vampire. Whipping the manacles from the pocket of his peasant jacket, he jerked the vampire's arms into position, then slid the cuffs on and locked them in place, using the plain, metal key.

The vampire's eyes watched him with twin flames burning in their depths. "You will pay for this, human. Your pathetic spell will wear off, and these will never hold me." He rattled the cuffs hard enough that

Nico's attention snapped downward, wanting to be certain the manacles were still locked. That freeze spell of his should have lasted much longer, even on a vampire. He made a mental note to add that to the journal he'd begun, listing everything he thought he knew and everything he'd learned about the bloody creatures.

"I think they will hold," Nico told the vampire casually, as if the two of them were having a learned discussion. "But . . . you asked why I was here, and said I knew nothing of your kind. And these—" He tapped one metal cuff. "—are the answer to both question and assertion. I design weapons of power, and I'm here to learn. You, unfortunately, are to be my teacher."

"Never," the vampire snarled.

"You say that now. But will you say it still when you're starving? When your skin shrivels and your bones soften for lack of blood? You may think so. But I've used these on enemies who were both stronger and smarter than you. And they told me everything before they died. And so will you."

Casting a second immobility spell, he tied the vampire's feet, and risking his fingers, slid a thick wad of cloth into the creature's mouth, then tied a scarf over his lower face, holding the wad in place. He waited several minutes after that, letting the manacles begin to take hold, to drain both consciousness and power from the vampire's mind. At that point, Nico cast a concealment spell, covering both of them. It wouldn't hide them from someone specifically looking for them, or from one who knew what to look for. But he was willing to take that risk, since their destination was nearby.

Part of his planning for this night had included the need for a place where he'd have absolute control, and could muffle any sound, so he'd rented a building not far from where he'd been attacked, one that had been abandoned for some time. Many of the windows had been broken, and the interior had been scavenged for anything a thief could steal. But it had a basement, which was its most important feature. Nico didn't bother with repairs, but simply placed a warding spell on the entire building, which inflicted anyone approaching with a terrible fear that grew stronger with every step they took closer.

Approaching now, Nico sent a small thread of his power into and through the property to make sure it was secure, then unlocked the rear door and slipped inside, where he took the stairs down to where a locked, heavy wooden door blocked access to the basement. He slid a key into the thick lock, which appeared ordinary, but was actually ensorcelled to unlock only when Nico himself held the key.

Once inside, he went directly to a sturdy cabinet against one wall, shoved the vampire inside, then closed and locked the iron-banded doors. Confident that his multiple security measures would guard against discovery of the prisoner, he left the basement. Locking the door behind him, he climbed the stairs, checked to be certain his various spells were still in place, then left the building and went home, remembering to retrieve his coat before going inside and to bed, pleased with the night's work.

NICO WOKE LATER than usual the next morning, due no doubt to his late-night wanderings. He was eager to question the vampire, but had to wait until after sunset, and so was meeting Hadrien Charron for lunch. Charron had suggested a café in the *Palais Royale* and had made a point of saying it would be just the two of them. Nico and the group leader were no more than politely cordial during the group's weekly meetings, and so the invitation had been both unexpected and intriguing.

The day was unusually warm, and the two men chose to sit on the patio. Once they'd ordered their meals, and were enjoying the first course, Charron slowly broached the subject of why they were there. "Vital tells me your work together has been productive."

"I'm pleased that he finds it so."

"He's very enthusiastic, although he refuses to say what you're working on."

Nico lifted his wine glass and regarded the other man over the rim, then took a sip. "We have several projects in early stages, but agreed not to discuss them with the rest of the group until we're certain we can make them work. There's no point in raising hopes, only to disappoint."

"Yes, I understand. Although as the group's leader, surely I should be consulted before any decisions are made about whether to proceed or not."

Nico regarded the other man quizzically. "I wasn't aware you had any particular talent for designing spelled devices."

Charron drained his wine and poured more. "I don't. I do have a wealth of experience in the use of sorcery, however."

"True," Nico agreed. "And once Vital and I have a design that has been tested and proven to work, we will consult you and the rest of the group regarding refinements or resolutions for any specific problems we've encountered, in either spells or fabrication."

Pushing away his empty plate, Charron spent some time lighting his cigar before saying, "Look, Katsaros, we both know you're somewhat stronger in magic than I am."

More than somewhat, Nicholas thought, but said only, "That's probably true."

"And yet you volunteered to assist Vital with his work, rather than assuming the leadership role, which would have been the more logical course."

"Logic would depend on my goals, wouldn't it? I enjoy working with Vital, and I enjoy creating magical objects. I am content."

"Are you? Let me be blunt, then, since you are far too adept at contriving palatable responses to my queries. Why are you here in Paris? I want the truth, and I will know—"

Nico chuckled. "If I chose to prevaricate, regardless of the topic, you would never know."

"There!" Charron slapped the table hard enough that the dishes rattled. "You say such things with neither modesty nor concern. I sit across from you at meetings, and can almost feel your power filling the room. But never more than "almost," because you do such a masterful job of concealing your strength. Why? What do you truly want from us?"

Nico regarded the sorcerer for a moment, deciding what to tell him. He hadn't been bragging when he'd said Charron would never know if he lied. But neither was he about to bare his soul to a man who would as soon see him dead in the street as a member of his precious group.

"What I want," Nico said slowly, "is none of your affair. What I have already told you and the others is the truth. I am in this city seeking a member of my family, a cousin, who left on a great journey and never returned. Or at least, he had not returned as of my own departure. I know from the last letter we received that he arrived in Paris safely, but there has been nothing since."

Charron paused while the waiter delivered their main course, and cut into the meat and chewed before continuing. "I'm better-connected in magical circles than Vital or the others, especially outside the city, since my home lies there. I've sent inquiries. But tell me, if you learn that your cousin has left the city, will you follow him?"

Nico watched the other man in private amusement. It was obvious that Charron wanted him gone, and was willing to help as long as it would mean Nico's departure from the city.

"I will. Though if anyone were to give false report of his departure, they would regret it before they died."

Charron snorted. "I'm not deceived by the false image you show to the others as to the strength of your magic. Only a fool would cross you, and regardless of what you may think of me, I am not a fool. I suspect, as I think you do, that your *cousin* is no longer in this city. You've said that he's nearly as powerful as you. But not even you, Nicholas, could conceal that much magic forever. If this Sotiris were still in the city, he would have given himself away by now. There are those in Paris who might have detected a great use of sorcerous power, but kept quiet about it, for reasons of their own. I will inquire of them, and share my findings, as well as any reports I receive from the countryside."

"*Merci,*" Nico said, miming a toast with his wine glass. "But tell me, Charron, why would you extend me this courtesy?"

The sorcerer pulled hard on his cigar and exhaled it deliberately across the table and into Nico's face.

Having anticipated the action, and surprised only that it had taken so long, Nico puffed a soft breath that, with magical help, sent the smoke on a sharp turn away from his face. He regarded Charron with a too-pleased expression, which had the man's jaw muscles flexing with irritation.

"I want you gone," the sorcerer said bluntly. "Violette is mine. She was promised to me the day she was born. Our child will unite our family estates into one large enough to control prices."

"Prices of what? What do your lands produce?"

"Grapes, of course. We are vintners, and the wines of both our houses are well sought after."

"Vital has contributed truly excellent wines to our shared dinners. Perhaps I've tasted one of yours." He sipped the delicious cognac the waiter had just placed in front of him, then said, "I've no interest in Violette, if that's your concern."

"I doubt she would intrigue you in any event. Her skill with magic is considerable, and her mind is excellent. But her behavior . . ." He shook his head, tsking in disapproval. "No young woman of my house would be permitted such obstinance, much less such freedom."

"And yet you will marry her in the holy church?"

"Of course. The alliance was signed two decades ago."

"I see."

"Such agreements are not common in your home country?"

"Very common. I myself am the second son of a powerful house."

"The *second* son. Now I understand your lack of urgency in returning home."

The man understood nothing, but Nico said simply, "Just so."

"Let us toast then, Nicholas." He raised his glass. "To a vampire-free Paris."

Nico tipped his glass, but didn't join in the sentiment. He doubted Paris or any other city would ever be free of vampires. They reproduced too easily. But the truth was that what he wanted wasn't in Paris. And the only outcome he would be toasting to was the return of his warriors, and Antonia. Which he pledged again would happen, no matter how long it took.

Chapter Nine

NICO TOOK A NAP when he returned home after lunch. Sleeping in the afternoon wasn't his usual routine, but the combination of a night spent hunting vampires, a midday meal with wine flowing freely, and a coming night that included questioning a captive vampire, convinced him to take to his bed. If any further rationalization was necessary, he told himself he could come up with a strategy for the night's interrogation while he lay resting. The plan worked somewhat, in that he did a considerable amount of thinking about how to proceed. The subject eventually taxed his thoughts sufficiently that he slept deeply and woke not only refreshed, but looking forward to both questioning his prisoner and observing the manacles' performance on a vampire.

David was waiting when he came downstairs, a look of concern on his face. "Are you unwell, Nicholas?"

"Not at all. Why do you ask?"

"You . . . rested this afternoon. It's not your habit."

"Ah. I had lunch with *Monsieur* Charron, which required a great deal of wine to survive."

His butler chuckled. "I understand. Dinner will be ready in one hour. Will you want an *aperitif* in the sitting room?"

"An *aperitif,* yes. But in my office. I've neglected my research."

HE WORKED IN his office until dinner, returned there afterward, and remained until David was long asleep, and the house was quiet. Then, placing the notes he'd written about the manacles in a satchel, including what he could remember of his original research, he took off for his clandestine work.

Once inside the basement of the rented building, he locked and warded the heavy door, crossed to the simple wooden table he'd found upstairs, put his satchel down, and removed his coat, then stood perfectly still and *listened* with every sense he possessed, both magical and not. Satisfied he was truly alone with his captive, he opened the cabinet to find the vampire was already awake. His gaze was fierce when a growl rumbled from his chest at the sight of Nico. But despite the rage in his eyes, the manacles had reduced his strength so much that the growl sounded more like the purr of a lazy cat, and not at all like the arrogant vampire he'd first captured.

Curious, Nico nonetheless ignored the creature while he set out his journal and writing tools, then finally sat at the table and studied his captive. He wished for a moment that he was a skilled artist, because the change in the vampire's appearance after a single night in the amber manacles was so obvious that he doubted any words he might write in his journal could capture it. He was . . . diminished. His skin was dry and stretched, as if it would tear if touched. His lips and gums were pale when he tried to snarl, and the fangs he'd displayed so prominently the night before were either shorter, or he was unable to display them completely.

The vampire raised his head slowly, struggling to hold it up. "What have you done to me, human?" he rasped.

Nico felt almost sorry for the creature, which was just wrong. This vampire would have drained him dry, given the chance. Still, he wanted answers and wouldn't get them from a dead vampire. "If you continue to struggle," he warned, "you will only weaken yourself more. I'm a sorcerer, and the bindings are of my own making. You cannot free yourself."

The vampire let his head fall forward, though whether in defeat or to conserve his strength, Nico didn't know. He wasn't willing to assume the vampire was neutralized, but he was confident that the creature couldn't break the manacles. Even without the restraints, Nico's power alone was great enough to contain one vampire. But he preferred it not come to that, since any use of his power to that extent might warn those listeners in Paris that Charron had spoken of. Nico needed this vampire alive, however, if the vamp was going to help Nico capture the master. And he needed to do that—to prove himself to the group, and obtain whatever they might learn about Sotiris in return.

Hating the necessity, but admitting that it *was* necessary, he manifested a tiny blade of magical energy, made it real, and pricked his finger, hoping it would bleed enough to restore the vampire to where he could answer questions. He walked around the table to stand in front of his captive.

"Open your mouth," he commanded.

The vampire obeyed the authority in the command, tilting his head back and opening his pale lips. When the first drop of blood hit his tongue, his eyes shot open to stare at Nico.

"Ah yes, this blood is richer than any you've ever tasted," Nico thought.

With the second and third drops, the vampire's face flushed pink and his fangs dropped completely into view. Deciding that was enough, and tired of squeezing his finger, Nico pulled it back and sealed the pinprick of a wound, then went back to sit down.

The vampire was watching him carefully, fear and hunger waging a war in his gaze.

"You should know that I have no compassion for your kind," Nico said. "One of you tried to destroy the life of someone I love. He was the champion of his people, an honorable man who fought to defend them against an unprovoked invasion by those who would have wiped them from the earth and built a new empire on their bones. When your people took him, they perverted everything he believed in, everything he lived for, and forced him to prey on the same people he'd defended so courageously. When he finally came to me, he hoped only for his own death. Not a cure, not salvation, but death, so that he could stop existing as the monster they'd made of him.

"Even so, I didn't come to this city to kill vampires. I came here chasing a man whose evil is far greater than anything even your master's master could possibly hope to achieve. But when I arrived, I found that the man I sought was gone. However . . ."

He gave the vampire an assessing look, making sure he was paying attention, then continued. "There are others in this city who *do* want to kill vampires. People who, in fact, want to cleanse Paris of every last one of you. And they have information that could lead me to the man I seek. Do you understand so far?"

The vampire glared silently for a moment, and then—possibly because he realized that Nico could and *would* kill him if he didn't cooperate—nodded.

"Good," Nico said. "In order to gain the cooperation of these people, and thus learn the information they possess, I had to convince them that I shared their hatred of vampires. Which I do. But since I've no desire to run around killing one vampire after another, I've built a weapon which will be very useful in their pursuit of your kind. A weapon that I now need to test."

The vampire stared, his expression definitely more fearful than angry.

"Not on you," he dismissed immediately. "On a master. And yours would do nicely, if you'd just tell me where to find him."

The vampire tried to conceal his reaction, but Nico was watching for it. When he'd said he wanted to know the master's location, the vampire's pupils had flared in alarm for a bare instant.

Nico sighed. "I've heard that vampires are incapable of betraying their master. That they'd rather die than do so. Unfortunately, you and I are about to discover if that's true."

Nico stood, and once again walked around the table to stand in front of his captive. It wasn't necessary, but physical proximity heightened a prisoner's stress. He'd always begun his interrogations this way in his own world, though he couldn't say he'd participated in a great number of them. And he'd never before questioned a vampire prisoner, which made tonight different from any other, and rather morbidly excited Nico with the prospect of a new experience.

"How do the manacles feel against your skin?" he asked curiously.

The vampire stared stubbornly, before apparently deciding that he could answer the question without betraying anyone. "Cold."

"Really? How cold? Like the brush of snow on your fingers, or more like a freezing wind on bare skin?"

"Neither of those. It's as if these things—" He lifted his hands and shook them, making the manacles rattle. "—are trying to steal my soul."

"Do you have a soul?"

"Yes," the vampire hissed angrily.

"So you believe, anyway."

"It's all belief, isn't it, sorcerer? Even you cannot prove the existence of a soul, *or* the lack thereof. Even in a vampire."

Nico grinned, inordinately pleased to discover his prisoner knew how to use his brain, and might have been an educated man in his previous life. "Very good, vampire. How old are you?"

"I was born to my human mother fifty-seven years ago. But my master gave me the gift of eternal life when I was but nineteen."

"So young, and now so old," Nico whispered, sorry for the young man on the cusp of adulthood who'd had his life torn away. And yet, he was also pleased that this vampire was old enough to have come to terms with his new life and remain sane, so that he'd survived thirty-eight years as a creature of nightmare. He was intrigued, too, to learn that a vampire this old remained loyal to his master, and continued to live with him, when most humans would have long since moved on to a family and home of their own.

Nodding thoughtfully, Nico bent to the table and scribbled a few notes, before looking up. "Try to break free of the manacles, by whatever means you choose."

The vampire met and held his gaze, while his shoulders and arms bunched and flexed. He gave a single grunt, then lifted his hands halfway to his chest, while his shoulders strained and he fought to break free.

Nico watched intently, tension rising when the vampire's struggles increased until his face darkened, and a vein in his forehead swelled as if it would burst. Finally, he let out a deep groan and let his manacled hands drop to rest limply on his thighs. His head was lowered, his chest heaving as he worked to pull in air.

"What are they?" the vampire finally ground out.

"They are the amber manacles."

"What the fuck *are* they?" he repeated. "Not the fancy name you and your high and mighty sorcerer friends gave them, but what they *are*."

Nico finished what he was writing before he looked up. "I told you, they're magic and unbreakable by humans, most sorcerers, and by vampires, as well, it seems. Don't worry, this next bit will be easier." He paused until he had the vampire's full attention. "Who is your master?"

"My master is my master. What is the question?"

"You're not stupid. Don't pretend you are. What is your master's name, and where is he from?"

The vampire didn't want to answer that one. He stared stonily straight ahead while Nico applied pain, using his magic, rather than any physical implement. He'd already decided that this vampire, who'd once been a man like any other, wouldn't surrender to ordinary pain. It would take something extraordinary to make him forswear his oath and loyalty to his master. Unfortunately for him, Nico was capable of extraordinary cruelty to get what he wanted from a murderer of innocents.

He began with the thinnest thread of magic, sliding it into the vampire's lungs on an indrawn breath, weaving it around and through every organ in his body, until he was utterly at Nico's mercy. The vampire hadn't felt the magical intrusion, however, and didn't yet realize his vulnerability, until Nico withheld air from his lungs.

The vampire gasped, eyes wide and staring around the room, as if searching for whatever had caused this sudden loss of breath. His mouth hung open like a hooked fish, blood and drool dripping from his lips, while his pale face flushed red, then purple . . .

And Nico released his hold.

The prisoner slumped for a moment as if he'd fainted, but then he snapped upright, sucking air when his lungs began to work again. He coughed hard enough that Nico worried he'd do damage, but finally the coughing ceased, and he breathed with deep, harsh rasps, until he sat up and stared at Nico. "What are you?"

"I told you. I'm a sorcerer. I can steal the breath from your lungs, or stop your heart from beating with a thought. I can make you take this knife—" He took the knife he'd used to prick his finger and lifted it to the candle flame, so that the honed edge gleamed. "—and slice your own throat, then watch your life's blood pour out, helpless to save yourself. There is nothing I cannot compel you to do, and nothing I *won't* do to get what I want."

"Why?" the vampire asked, almost pleading.

"Because I need what you know, and your kind are merciless killers. Can you say honestly that you have never killed?"

He stared at Nico hopelessly. "No. Can you? Every animal kills to survive, even you, sorcerer."

"But you need only the blood of your prey. Is it necessary for you to kill and mutilate in order to feed? Are the stories of a vampire's ability to mesmerize not true?"

The vampire started to speak, then seemed to think better of it.

"Ah, that is something your master would not want you to tell me. Which means it's something I want to know. Which was it? The question of killing to feed? Or the ability to mesmerize?"

His lips firmed into a tight line of resistance.

"As you wish."

The vampire drew a deep breath, filling his chest with air, anticipating a repeat of the earlier punishment. It might have worked if Nico had planned to freeze his lungs again, but he didn't. Torture worked best if the prisoner never knew what was coming, and with Nico's magic already resident in the vampire's body, he could act on any part of it.

With no visible gesture, Nico caught hold of the wisp of his magic in the vampire's body, and turning it to flame, scored the inside of the creature's gut back and forth until his screams were so loud that Nico feared he would wake the neighborhood despite the basement walls and his own spell of silence. When he stopped, the vampire's head fell forward, blood once more running from his mouth to drip freely onto his chest, though much more of it this time.

Nico studied him carefully, wanting to be sure he was still alive. But then, he reasoned, if the vampire had died, he would have turned to dust, just as those who'd fought Nico in the alley had done. He made a fresh note of the dusting in his journal, rather than go back and check his entry from that night to be sure he'd included it.

It took longer for the vampire to recover this time, and when he did, he was noticeably weaker, his hands trembling in the manacles' grip. "I can be killed, sorcerer. Take care lest you do so before you have your answers."

"You're not the only vampire in the city. If you would rather die than tell me what I want to know, I'll simply capture another."

"You're going to kill me anyway."

"True. So why endure the pain?"

"Have you never sworn loyalty to anyone?"

Nico thought of his father who hadn't *asked* for an oath of loyalty from his son, but demanded it, then said, "Only to the warriors who fought by my side."

"Then you know the answer to your question."

"No, I don't," he lied. "I would have died to protect them, but I don't see how suffering endless pain before you die serves your cause. Tell me what I want, and I'll kill you painlessly."

"I don't trust you."

Nico chuckled. "You're smart not to, though I really would grant you a painless death. It's your master I want, not you."

"And I am sworn to protect him with my life."

"Your logic is faulty, but it's your choice." With no warning of any kind, Nico shaped his magic into a blade and sliced the vampire's thigh so deeply that bone was a white accusation in the wound. The vampire screamed before passing out again. Nico cauterized the wound with fire to ensure his captive didn't bleed to death, then waited dispassionately until the vampire recovered. "I did warn you," he said.

"Bastard," the vampire hissed. "You call me a monster. What are *you?*"

"That's a question I've pondered more than once, with no answer. What matters in this moment, however, is only that I'm more powerful than you. I can remove all your limbs one by one, then slice you open and spill your guts onto the floor . . . and still keep you alive to answer my questions. Or, you can tell me what I want to know, and it will end."

"I cannot reveal the location of the nest," he said hopelessly. "It would endanger my master, and I am *unable* to do that."

"Unable. Not simply unwilling, but unable. Interesting." Nico noted that in his journal before continuing. "What if I ask . . ." He thought for a moment. "What is your name?"

The vampire blinked in confusion. "Greyson."

"And what is the name of the vampire who last slept next to you in the nest?"

"Aurel," he said, frowning.

"And where is the nest in which Aurel might have chosen to sleep this past day?"

Understanding bloomed on the vampire's face, followed immediately by consternation. He glanced at Nico, then down again, as if studying the blood on his shirt and the burned flesh around the open gash on his leg. When he looked up, there was determination in his eyes. But determination to do what?

"Today, Aurel probably chose to sleep—"

Chapter Ten

NICODEMUS LEFT Greyson alive, and free of the manacles, though he was instead tightly bound by ropes that were reinforced with magic. He didn't trust the vampire to have told him the truth, or alternatively, *not* to have sent him into a trap. He also cast a spell to keep the prisoner unconscious and quiet. A less honest man would have said he did it out of pity for the badly injured vampire, who had to be in considerable pain. But Nico considered himself honest to a fault, and whether that was true or not, the real reason he'd knocked Greyson unconscious was to ensure no one heard his cries and tried to free him. That problem would be solved at daybreak, but there were a few hours yet, so he couldn't take the chance.

Greyson hadn't known the building number of the nest's location, but he'd provided the cross streets, which was enough for Nico, since it wasn't far from the basement where they were now.

With the manacles stowed in a small bag tied to his belt, Nico maintained a casual, long-strided walking pace as he made his way toward the nest. In the neighborhood where his townhouse stood, almost every street had pole-mounted oil lanterns to light the sidewalks through the night. But this one, where the nest was located, had no such amenities. The night was utterly dark, without even a moon to see by. Nico wasn't bothered by darkness. He could see well in the night, and if he needed to see better, he could provide his own light. Right then, however, he wanted to avoid drawing attention to himself, and glided silently down the narrow, dark streets, hugging the buildings so as to blend in with the shadows. When his destination was in sight, he ducked into the shallow porch of a solid door, and crouched down on his haunches to observe.

At first, he thought Greyson had steered him wrong. He identified the building easily enough from Greyson's description, but there was no movement in or out, and nothing to indicate there was anyone inside, much less an entire nest of vampires. He reminded himself, however, that the night was their world. They were most likely out killing more innocents to feed upon, and would return before dawn, which wasn't far away. His magic told him that the sun's rise was very near, certainly less than an hour away, so he settled back against the door to watch and wait.

He'd finally found a comfortable position when a small group of men—vampires he hoped—disappeared into the plain, stone building Greyson had directed him to. The windows on both floors were boarded up, and there was just one door visible. Greyson had admitted, reluctantly, that there was a second exit on the back wall, close to a small private room where the nest's master vampire slept, usually alone, unless he brought a blood slave back with him. He also revealed the master's name, which apparently didn't violate his oath. It was Gauvain Fitzroy, which might have marked him as the bastard son of some royal personage or other. But Greyson had hinted that the royal identifier wasn't his real name, which Nico tended to believe. If he were ever forced to become a vampire, he would certainly not continue using his true name. He would, however, contrive to end his own life as soon as possible. He couldn't imagine living as a blood-drinking monster. Never seeing the sun, residing in the gutter end of society, considered unholy at best and demonic at worst, drinking human blood to survive and, the final touch, the loss of his magic. Or so he hoped. Anything else was too horrible to contemplate.

He would have welcomed the challenge of destroying an entire nest of vampires while they were still awake and able to defend themselves. But such a battle, while stimulating, was contrary to his purpose. His strategy was to wait until after dawn, and then slip into the sleeping nest and capture the master with the manacles.

While the sun was near, it wasn't yet light out, and only a few of the vampires had returned. So he bided his time by counting the number of vampires as they entered the nest, listening to what little useful conversation he could overhear, and noting the number of male and female. For reasons he couldn't explain, there were far more men than women among the turned. Maybe he would ask the master about it before he killed him. Because he *would* be killing this master. He'd question him at length and pull every possible detail out of him, all the while testing the manacles. But once he'd gotten what he needed from the creature, he would kill him and count it a victory for humans everywhere.

Perhaps because he had nothing to do but wait, it seemed a long time before the sun began its climb up the eastern sky. But eventually Nico considered it safe to go inside. He walked to the vampires' building and tried the door latch, but as expected, it was secured from the inside. The back door would also be locked, but it was less exposed to the ever-growing number of ordinary people going about their morning business on the street. And it was also closer to the master vampire's private room.

Not wasting time, Nico took the side street, until it met up with an alley barely big enough for a small carriage or wagon to use. Taking the alley, he walked to the right building, and knocked at the door, as if expecting an answer. Using that action as a distraction, in the unlikely event anyone was watching, he touched his hand to the latch, and shot a pulse of magic through the door, which destroyed the inside locking bolt and left a small round hole in the wood.

With no latch to hold it in place, the door swung open on its own. He didn't expect anyone to challenge him, but he went in prepared, with the knife in one hand and a spell ready to cast in the other. A slice of sunlight penetrated the dark interior through the open door, but he closed it quickly. He wasn't interested in vampires bursting into flames and causing enough noise to attract notice.

With his eyes rapidly adjusted to the darkness, he took note of a second row of windows high above the ground floor, most of which were shuttered, rather than boarded over. The shutters were effective, for the most part, but here and there, a sliver of sunlight made its way through a break in the wood or simple poor construction, and admitted enough light for him to see by. And what he saw sent an involuntary and unexpected shudder down his spine.

The vampires lay in rows, side by side, some on their backs, others curled on their sides like small children hiding from danger. In those areas where the sun had managed to make its way inside, the vampires had left empty spaces much wider than the sunbeams seemed to require. Nico supposed it was to avoid rolling over in one's sleep and ending up in a pool of sunlight.

He constructed a mental picture of the nest, memorizing every detail, so that when he returned home, he could sketch what he'd seen. He wasn't aware of any similar sketches available to researchers, and vowed to distribute his own widely enough that they had a chance of making it into official city records for others to find. He would begin by providing a copy to every member of the group, and hoped that some-one among them could draw well enough to prepare better copies for wider distribution. If no one in the group had the skills, then he hoped they'd at least know of someone who could do the job discreetly.

Once he was convinced he could replicate the scene on paper, he turned to the closed door on his right, which according to Greyson, was where the vampire master slept. This was perhaps the most dangerous part of his mission. If the master was still awake, or if masters possessed some level of immunity to sunlight, he could be walking into a full-scale attack by a powerful vampire. He didn't know how powerful, or even if this particular master was stronger or weaker than any others in Paris, but he was prepared for whatever attack might come at him.

The answer was none. No one was waiting for him when he step-ped into the master's private room, nor did the vampire rise to meet him, though Nico remained perfectly still for some minutes, while he scanned the space for any hidden threats. Finding none, he studied the lone vampire in greater detail. The man lay on shimmery gray sheets, with a red silk coverlet pulled to his chest, and his blond hair spread out on a red velvet pillow. Nico had nothing to compare him to, and so made mental notes of every detail—from the vampire's appearance to an aesthetic appraisal of his clothes and bedding. He'd seen nothing so grand being used by any of the vampires sleeping in the main room, and pictured, somewhat facetiously, the master grabbing his bedding if he ever had to run for his life. Or maybe these had been bought just for this location. Not that it mattered. Everyone in this building would be dead before nightfall. Except the master himself, and he might well be wish-ing he'd died with the others, once Nico began asking his questions.

Nico pulled the coverlet off the vampire, and nearly called out in surprise at what he found there. A very young woman, barely old enough to be called a "woman," lay curled next to Gauvain Fitzroy. The sight both infuriated and disgusted him, and he touched a hand to the girl's shoulder, wondering if she was human or if she'd been turned for the sole purpose of warming her master's bed. He couldn't lay that particular sin on vampires, however, since wealthy human men were also known to purchase young girls for their beds.

He touched a hand to the girl's shoulder, trying to wake her. She groaned a protest and opened her eyes long enough to roll over, before closing them again and pulling the coverlet over her head. When she'd rolled, Nico had seen a bloody bitemark on her neck, so either she was human or just turned, possibly that very night. There was too much he didn't know. Like how did the process of turning work? How long did it take, and how was the master's blood used? How much blood did they *need* to survive, as opposed to what they took? Greyson's reaction had seemed to suggest the amount a vampire needed was small and that killing wasn't necessary. So why did they kill anyway?

The master vampire could answer all these questions and more, which brought Nico back to his immediate task. Setting to work, he gently shoved the sleeping blond to one side and covered her once more, since she seemed to prefer it. He then turned the vampire on his stomach and bound his hands first with rope and then with the manacles. He did the same with his ankles, but was forced to use a set of ordinary metal handcuffs. If Nico's experiments on the amber manacles proved fruitful, perhaps he'd construct a second set to be used on the feet. Or maybe not. He'd become very possessive about his various devices and spells in the last year, as some instinct or elusive foretelling had him worrying about the many constructs he'd created and either lost track of, or in his earlier days, sold to support himself and his army.

With the master as securely bound as Nico could make him, he wrapped the vampire in one of the red sheets, tied the two ends above his head, and below his feet, then unfolded the length of ordinary black cotton he'd brought along and did the same. He was counting on the two layers of fabric to protect his captive from sunlight, but also to conceal from anyone who might look too closely, that the burden he carried over his shoulder had a very man-like form.

Stepping to the door, he did a quick scan of the main room, finding it quiet and filled with sleepers. He didn't hesitate after that, but simply crossed back to the bed, hefted the vampire over his shoulder, and left. Once back on the main street, he hurried toward his own building. It might have been safer to get the master vampire farther from his nest, but Nico had weighed that risk against all the others, and decided to use the building he'd rented.

Greyson was, of course, already deep in his daylight sleep when Nico unlocked the basement door and pushed his way inside. Placing the master on the cold floor, he stared at Greyson, whose bonds were still tight and undamaged. Nico couldn't say for sure, but evidence suggested the vampire hadn't made any attempt to escape. In fact, he appeared to be even more faded and wan than he'd been earlier. The absence of a fresh blood infusion on top of more than a full day spent wearing the manacles seemed to be having a devastating effect on the creature's health. His bones were showing beneath paper-thin skin like yellowed stones, and the wound on his thigh hadn't even begun to heal, though vampires' healing abilities were said to rival those of the most powerful sorcerers.

Nico considered putting the vampire out of his misery. He'd honestly answered every question asked of him, but Nico was reluctant to surrender such a useful tool. Once he had the master under his control, Greyson would no longer be necessary, but until then . . . . He was briefly reminded of his promise to kill the captive vampire once he'd fulfilled his half of their bargain, but Nico could come up with any number of reasons to rationalize keeping the vampire alive a little while longer.

He could be a cold son of a bitch, but he knew this as well as anyone, and made no excuses for it.

He shoved the master into the cabinet where he'd originally stored Greyson, and propped the weaker vampire against a wall. Then he sat at the table and opened his journal, wondering why he bothered. He'd always kept a detailed record of the various spells and devices he was working on. Notes on which elements worked or didn't, any ingredients of materials used. But he had no plans to become a great vampire hunter. He'd only taken it this far in order to assure the magical group of his dedication to the cause, so that they'd be motivated to help him find Sotiris. At this point, he thought, it was mostly habit that had him sitting in this abandoned building writing notes. His sketch of the young woman he'd found in the master's bed could be useful if she was ever reported missing. He'd never share it with the authorities, but he could plant an anonymous hint about having seen her in the company of vampires. On the other hand, she was already dead to her family. It might be better to leave her missing, rather than raise hopes that he knew would come to nothing.

With those doubts in mind, he closed his journal without writing anything more, then placed it in his satchel and stood to leave. Regardless of the utility of what he'd learned in the last few nights, he'd definitely made considerable progress in a relatively short period of time, and was confident he'd have something to report to Vital and the group soon. He hoped the next night would be his last visit to this place. The master vampire would spend the day bound by the amber manacles, but there was no guarantee that they would contain him once he woke for the night. That meant Nico would have to be there when the master vampire woke, and be ready with a spell of sufficient power to trap the master in the event he broke free. The tales of garlic or blessed symbols used as weapons against vampires were just that . . . tales. The only real enemy a vampire had was sunlight, and of course, stabbing or beheading, which Nico had already proved to his own satisfaction.

Nico stood with a grimace. He needed a bath and fresh clothes, not to mention a decent meal, and sleep. He pulled on his coat, did a final check on his prisoners, and left, locking all the doors as he went.

Somewhat concerned about the master's ability to summon his nestmates, Nico took the additional precaution of placing a spell on the outside door that would both hide the door from human eyes, and if that failed, a second spell would make every door in the building impossible to open.

Finally, as confident as he could be, he turned for home and his bed.

NICO APPROACHED his house from the rear, using all his senses to scan the building. It was early enough that there was a chance David wouldn't yet be awake, but as Nico approached, he noted the light on in the young man's room. A moment later, a second light flashed on in the kitchen. He smiled, thinking it must be the day for the housekeeper's regular visits, which would work to his advantage. David spent those mornings in the kitchen, having breakfast with the pretty, young woman named Josette. The two young people had begun a courtship, which delighted Nico. He'd be leaving someday and didn't want David to be alone when that happened.

Waiting a few minutes to be sure he was right about the two of them being settled in the kitchen, he let himself in the front door and hurried upstairs, aided by a simple spell that muffled his footsteps. Once in his room, he tore off his clothes and collapsed into bed for a few hours' sleep.

When he finally made his usual late morning appearance downstairs, his tired brain was invigorated by first the smell, and then the taste of fresh coffee, which he considered one of the greatest discoveries of this world. Walking into the dining room, he found his place set as usual, and David waiting with a large envelope of fine linen. Curious about the envelope, but needing his wits alert, he sugared and sipped his coffee first, then held out a hand.

The first thing he noted was Charron's wax seal on the flap. He gave David a questioning glance.

"It arrived first thing this morning, sir."

"Who brought it?"

"A carriage driver hired for the task."

Nico frowned, and his gut tightened with worry. Charron wasn't a generous or ostentatious man, other than when it related to his own comfort. But this . . . . Had something happened to another member of their group? They were always going off on ill-advised vampire hunts, despite his urging that they wait until he had better weapons for them. Abruptly aware that it could be Vital, or even his sister, who'd been injured or worse, he tore open the seal with little regard for neatness, and read the handwritten note.

"Nicholas, mon ami, I have news regarding your missing cousin. If you can, please join me for luncheon today at two hours past the noon bell. Send word only if you are indisposed. Otherwise, I look forward to greeting you once more."

It was signed with Charron's usual flourish.

He read it again, wondering why the damn man couldn't have simply revealed whatever he'd discovered, but knew that wasn't Charron's way. He probably loved the idea of summoning Nicholas to his parlor to receive the news. Mindful of the master vampire waiting in a rented basement, Nico might have sent his regrets and postponed hearing whatever Charron had discovered until the regular group meeting in a few days, but it gnawed at him that the other man had felt it important enough for a separate, personal engagement. What if he really *had* learned something of Sotiris's whereabouts?

"I'll be lunching with *Monsieur* Charron today," he told David. "If you could arrange a carriage?"

"Of course. What time, if I might inquire?"

Nico gave him a dry look at the excessively polite question. "Two bells past noon, I'm told. So . . . I don't know. You decide the appropriate time to ensure a timely arrival."

"Of course. And will anyone be joining you for dinner this evening?"

"No," he said, slightly puzzled at the question. He rarely had dinner guests. Only Vital, and even that was sporadic at best. "I'm continuing my research alone for now."

"Very well."

He glanced up. "Stop hovering, David. Go back to the kitchen with Josette. It smells like she's baking something delicious. Just save some for me."

David choked back a laugh he tried to hide. "Thank you, Nicholas. If you need anything—"

"I'll shout. Go."

BY THE TIME THE carriage arrived to transport him to his luncheon with Charron, Nico was willing to admit a certain curiosity as to what the man's news might be. It had to be something more than a traveler over-hearing Sotiris's name whispered in a village, didn't it? Otherwise, it wouldn't have been worth this private luncheon.

He presented himself at Charron's door just as the cathedral bells rang the second hour of the afternoon. He was greeted by Violette, who had ceased flirting with him once she knew he'd learned of her betrothal to Charron. Nico suspected Vital had also told her of his lack of interest, though no doubt he'd phrased it diplomatically. Either way, it meant he no longer had to dissuade her attention, so he was grateful.

Closing the door behind him now, Violette waved a casual hand in the direction of Charron's parlor and continued up the stairs, obviously no longer seeing the need for formality.

When he walked into the parlor, Charron lifted his buttocks off the settee in a semblance of greeting, and waved a hand at the lone chair sitting at the small table between them.

"Good afternoon, Charron. Thank you for inviting me."

"My pleasure, Nicholas. As I said in my note, I have news you'll want to hear. I also have this."

He held out a letter-sized envelope that was completely ordinary, except for the fine linen paper that it was made of. And once Nico took it from him, he couldn't help wondering at the elegant writing on the outside that read simply, "Nicodemus Katsaros."

Nico stared at his name, his true name, on the envelope. "What is this?"

"I don't know," Charron protested, seeming flustered by the question. "It is addressed to you."

"How is that possible? No one knows I'm here, except family, and *this* is not from them."

"I was told it was left for you by your cousin. I thought you'd be pleased."

"Left where?"

"With a sorcerer friend who lives not far from my family's country estate. He heard of my inquiries, and sent this on. He was told you would be looking for him, and to give it to you."

Nico wanted to tell him that was impossible. No one knew where he was. Not even Sotiris. He'd been long gone by the time Nico had followed, and even if he'd guessed that Nico would come after him, how could he know where . . . . Well, fuck. Of course, he'd known. He'd designed the damn spell. And hadn't Nico just spent days figuring out how the spell worked? That first transition could only go to Paris, because that's where Sotiris had designed it to go.

It wouldn't have taken a genius to guess that Nicodemus would try to use the spell to locate his warriors. And as much as he hated Sotiris, he had to admit the bastard was very likely a genius. He wasn't as gifted as Nico himself, but was still quite talented. But for this message to come now . . . . Had Sotiris already moved on, and left this just in case Nico followed him into this world, this city?

Or by the gods, was the bastard still here?

Nico ripped open the envelope, wanting whatever answers it could give him, and immediately recognized Sotiris's flowery script.

I never doubted you would follow, my old enemy. Just as I'm certain you never believed it would be that simple. Take care with the gift I've left for you. The lives of your precious warriors may depend upon it."

Nico's fingers tightened to a fist, crumpling the letter between them. The evil bastard was tormenting him, wanting to make him believe he could save his warriors. Steeling himself for the rest, he straightened the letter and read the final paragraph.

Oh, yes . . . you may have dissected the curse that binds your warriors, and followed me this far. But do you know yet that each curse is unique to one warrior, and can be lifted only if nearly impossible conditions are met? So even if you find their stone prisons, Nicodemus, your power will not free them. The curses must be broken . . . but not by you. They alone know the keys to their freedom. Now, if only they could tell someone . . .

Nico could almost *hear* the sadistic bastard simpering that last bit in a mockery of care. "Who delivered this?" he demanded in a harsh whisper.

Charron blinked in confusion at the question, or perhaps at its furious delivery. He stared for the blink of an eye, then said, "An ordinary carriage driver. One of the servants answered the door, but when the driver inquired as to your whereabouts, Violette overheard. She questioned the man thoroughly in turn, but he knew only that his employer had been entrusted with this letter by *Monsieur* Sotiris, who had briefly been a guest at his employer's estate." He hesitated, then asked, "Is there a problem, Nicholas? Was this letter not sent by your cousin?"

"No. I mean, yes, it appears to be genuine, and from my cousin. But it says only that he's moved on, not where he's gone." Nico decided against mentioning Sotiris's allusion to a gift that he'd left with the same man. Or maybe it was not with the *man,* but on this estate.

"Where can I find the sorcerer who was keeping this for my cousin? Do you know his name, and where I can find him?"

"*Mais, bien sûr.* I know him well. His estate is several days' ride outside Paris, however."

"I'll need to go there, to talk to him. If you would write me a letter of introduction, I would be grateful."

"You need not ask. But it is a considerable distance. When will you leave?"

Nico thought quickly. He didn't want to waste time, but couldn't simply abandon his responsibilities in the city—not the least of which were the two vampires currently imprisoned in his secret location. "Two days. I'll require one day to finish my research, and a second to set my other affairs in order. I've made certain discoveries regarding the vampires in this city and want to share what I've learned with you and Vital before I leave. My return to Paris might be delayed if I learn of my cousin's plans."

"You should ask Vital to accompany you on this journey. The roads are not as safe as they once were."

"I travelled a great distance to reach your fair city, *mon ami*. My sorcery makes an excellent companion and defender." He gave the other man a smile of shared understanding, one sorcerer to another. Though Charron's power was no more than a shadow of his own, the Parisian had been welcoming in his own way, and certainly helpful.

"Ah, *oui*. Will you stay this afternoon, or—?"

Nico was already shaking his head. "I regret that I cannot. I would meet with you tomorrow, if possible, however."

"Come to dinner, then. I look forward to learning of your discoveries."

"*Bon. Merci.*" With a barely civil farewell, Nico was out the door and, grateful his driver had a habit of lingering, jumped into the carriage and ordered him to return home at all speed.

Chapter Eleven

NICO MADE SEVERAL decisions on the trip home, though none of them were made consciously. His mind raced as he thought of everything he would need to take care of before leaving Paris for an extended amount of time. The length of his absence would depend on what he discovered upon reaching the estate of Charron's sorcerer friend. The only thing he knew was that whatever the "gift" Sotiris had left for him was, it wouldn't be anything good.

He'd told Charron that he needed time to complete his research on Paris's vampires, though that wasn't precisely true. He was already confident the amber manacles would hold a master, though the true test wouldn't occur until that evening. He didn't want to rush his conclusions, since Vital and the others would pay the price for any mistakes he made. But he didn't want to linger, either.

He would get started as soon as he reached the townhouse, but would need to be in the rented basement before the vampires rose for the night. If the manacles didn't hold for any reason, his power would be necessary to eliminate the master vampire before he could escape. That was one task that he couldn't trust to anyone but himself.

As details sped through his thoughts, a fresh possibility arose that had him leaning forward to order the driver to take him to the office of his banker, instead of straight home. There was a good possibility that he would never return to Paris—or if he did, not for many years—and he wanted to make such arrangements as he could for the townhouse and what it contained. Nico's home had been purchased with a single cash payment, which was unusual, but had been explained away by a windfall bequeathed to Nico by a recently dead grandparent. David was already a co-owner of the property, though he doubted the butler knew what he'd signed. But knowing now that he might be gone for some time, he wanted to clarify the arrangements and any legalities with the banker to avoid problems for David later on. He would also leave a letter with Vital, whom he trusted to protect David's legal interests if necessary. He would never have trusted Charron with a similar responsibility.

The banker saw Nico immediately, and their conversation took very little time. The man was honest. Nico had used his magic to be sure of that before doing any business with him. David had been as close to family as Nico had in this world, and he wanted the young man to be financially able to do whatever he wished with his life, including marriage and family. He would have advised him to sell the townhouse, and leave Paris, which Nico thought was on the brink of another revolution. Not to mention that the city was generally an unhealthy place to live. But David was an adult, or would be soon, and would make his own choices as every man had a right to do. Still, he was inexperienced in matters of property and wealth, and so Nico had penned a letter with his recommendations, making clear that was all they were.

With the bank business behind him, Nico arrived home in time for an early supper, after which he retired to his office, pleading a pile of research waiting for him. He wasn't convinced David believed him. The young man saw more than most would give him credit for. Later that evening, he asked David to join him for dinner, so they could discuss his departure.

"I'll be traveling outside the city soon," he told David. "I'll need you to look after this house while I'm gone. Keep it clean and well-maintained and such."

"I should go with you, Nicholas. The roads aren't safe, and your banker can see to the house," David said.

"You forget that I traveled to Paris from my home—which is very far away—and arrived safely."

"And *you* forget that you resembled a peasant when you arrived. No self-respecting thief would have wasted time on you then. Now is another matter."

Nico laughed. "I did, didn't I? But I am still capable of protecting myself."

"There are new and dangerous bands of brigands on the roads, I've heard. And capable or not, you are only one man."

"One very skilled man, who has fought and survived more wars than you've ever heard of."

Seeing that reason wasn't going to work, David said simply, "I'd *like* to come, sir."

Nico's expression softened. "I know. And there is no one I'd rather have by my side. But I'll be moving fast, and don't know where I'll end up, or how long it will take me to get there. I need you *here*, so that I have a home to return to."

David sighed deeply. "Vital could stay here, in your house. He'd probably welcome the opportunity to get away from the others."

Nico smiled. "You're not wrong, I suspect. But his attention is already split between his family estate in the country, and his business here in the city. Besides, if he left the townhouse, Violette would have to come with him, lest he create a scandal by leaving her to live unchaperoned with Charron."

The young butler rolled his eyes. "I don't know them as well as you do, but if Charron tried anything untoward, Violette could run all the way from their townhome to the other side of the Seine before Charron even managed to put on his coat and climb into a carriage."

Nico felt compelled to swallow his laughter, though he privately agreed. "Even so. This house is *your* home, not Vital's or anyone else's. I need you here."

"Yes, sir," he sighed, with all the reluctance of the boy he'd so recently been.

"Besides, think how impressed our young housekeeper will be with your rise in station."

He brightened. "Do you think so?"

"Of course. Women love a responsible man."

"I suppose they have to, don't they?" David said thoughtfully. "Do you think I'm too young to marry?"

Nico choked on the bite of fish he'd just swallowed, and had to drink some wine before answering. "How old are you?"

"Sixteen years, according to my mother."

He was definitely too young, but only in Nico's world. In France, especially outside the city, David could well have been married and a father already. "I think," he said slowly, "that being ready to marry has more to do with the person than the number of years. You, David, are one of the most trustworthy and resourceful men I have ever met."

"Resourceful?"

"It is a quality that can be more important than any other. It means if there's a problem, you don't sit in a corner and cry. You figure out a solution and get it done. *Your* family will never want for food or shelter, because you will figure out a way to take care of them. You're clever, and you're intelligent. Those matter. Besides, you'll always have a home with me. You and your family both." He said it as a promise, knowing that it might well be a promise he'd have to keep from afar.

David blushed. "Thank you, sir," he said in an awestruck whisper. "That means . . . that means more to me than you can imagine."

"I do mean it."

"I've watched and learned from *you*, sir."

"A great compliment. Thank you. Now, enough of this seriousness. Join me for a cognac, and then I must adjourn to my office again, or I'll be up all night."

NICO WAS STILL warmed, his spirited lifted, by his conversation with David, when he slipped out of the house much later that night. He'd kept busy in his office, putting together documents for the young butler to find once Nico was gone, writing a list of things to do and people to contact, as well as a letter expressing his affection and appreciation.

He was eager to get back to the rented building and the vampires imprisoned there. He hoped the master vampire would be sufficiently weakened that the desire to live would motivate him to answer questions, as it had Greyson. And if not, there were other ways to motivate him. As for Greyson . . . well, Nico hadn't decided yet what to do about him. He couldn't simply release the vampire. Driven by the overpowering need to protect his Sire, he'd either attack straight out, or he'd run to the nest, gather more of his nestmates, and return in force.

The neighborhood was very quiet when he let himself into the building and went directly down the stairs to the basement. He paused outside the last door to do a magical scan of the room beyond, and then expanding outward to the building and the surrounding neighborhood. He didn't want to mistakenly assume the master was incapable of summoning his blood-drinking creations to rescue him.

Finding nothing suspicious with his scan, Nico opened the door and stepped into the basement, closing and locking the door behind him. He took the time to reset his warding spells before removing his coat, then set his bag on the table. It wasn't until he brought up a witch light that he caught sight of Greyson lying on the floor. The vampire didn't look good at all. In fact, if he hadn't been a vampire, Nico would have thought the man dead—he looked that bad. There was nothing to be done about it, however, since the only solution to his condition was blood, and Nico was done with providing it.

Going to the cabinet instead, he unlocked and opened both doors to discover that the vampire master was also rather diminished, though not on the edge of death, as Greyson was. The master's eyes, in particular, still burned with a furious flame-bright light that promised a horrible death for his captor once he broke free. Such an escape would never happen, as long as Nico remained alive, but it benefitted him to let the master believe it might.

Once he had the master seated on the other chair, he opened his journal to a fresh page, and made a great show of preparing pen and ink, before using magic to remove the vampire's gag with a quick flick of his finger. The captive's eyes widened at that simple display of magic. He didn't say anything, but just worked his jaw to relieve the stiffness. His gaze wandered to where Greyson lay unmoving.

"He's dying," the master said, moving only his eyes to study Nico's response.

"Is he?"

"He'll be dead very soon, unless he feeds."

"Is he one of yours?"

The master turned fully to regard Nico. "He is my child, if that's what you mean."

He considered that. "Do you have a name? Greyson's loyalty kept him from telling me the truth."

The vampire glanced down at Greyson again, this time with what appeared to be true sorrow. "He was loyal, but he also suffered under certain . . . restrictions as to what he could reveal. You may call me Gauvain."

Nico ignored the name, more interested in what else he'd revealed. "Are these restrictions magical in nature? Or simply linked to the blood you share?"

"Both, neither. It depends on the master."

"I see. And will it pain you if he dies?"

The vampire's pale lips thinned with anger. "I am connected to all my children."

"That's not what I asked, vampire. I want to know if you will experience sorrow at this one's death."

The hatred in Gauvain's gaze was so fierce that Nico would have sworn he felt it like fire against his skin.

"I would grieve his death," the master snarled.

"Surely he is already dead in some sense? His soul has fled."

"Who told you that?" the vampire scoffed.

Nico fought to conceal his reaction. He didn't know why he'd assumed vampires had no souls. He'd never been a particularly religious man, but perhaps his recent conversations with the cathedral priest had influenced him more than he'd realized. He wasn't sure he knew what a soul was, much less who did or didn't possess one. "You believe he has a soul? And that you, too, possess one?"

Gauvain gave him a pitying look. "All men are born with souls, fool. Do they teach you nothing in whatever barbarian place you come from?"

Nico found himself intrigued by their conversation, and a little amused at the description of his home world as barbaric, when he'd have described *this* world the same way. "All *men* are born with souls," he agreed, "but you are no longer a man."

"Neither are you, sorcerer. Do you think I can't recognize magic when I see it? Or *feel* it," he added lifting his manacled hands. "No ordinary cuffs could hold me. So, tell me, do *you* have a soul?"

Nico considered that. "The priest tells me I do."

"Priests," Gauvain snorted. "Self-righteous fools, most of them. I cannot speak for you. But for myself and my children . . . yes, we are alive. And we have souls."

"Do you fear dying, then? For surely you will burn for eternity as penance for the many deaths you've dealt."

"I didn't ask to be made what I am. I do what I must to survive."

He was about to respond when the master shot a sharp glance down at Greyson. Nico followed his gaze just in time to see the emaciated vampire shrink alarmingly inward, as if his flesh was collapsing onto his bones. A heartbeat later, Greyson was replaced by a more-or-less body-shaped cloud of dust, and then even that was gone, when the cloud fell to the floor to form a pile far too small to ever have been a full-grown man.

When Nico looked back, Gauvain's eyes were closed, and a flicker of pain creased his face. "Why?" the vampire ground out.

"Why did he die?"

"Why did he *have* to die? Why did you kill him?"

Nico experienced an unexpected pang of something close to guilt, which made no sense. Vampires were monsters. He'd seen the effects of their evil in his own world, had felt the agony of his brother Gabriel when he'd begged for the release of death. Here in this world, he himself had been attacked and nearly killed for walking past the wrong alley at the wrong time of day. Why should he feel guilty that one of the creatures who'd attacked him was dead?

"I was attacked," he said. "And my brother was made one of you against his will. He longed for death after what you did to him."

Gauvain gave him a quizzical look. "Where are you from?"

"You won't have heard of it."

"Then enlighten me."

"No. How do you feel?"

The vampire frowned. "Did you put these—" he lifted his hands, "—on Greyson?"

Finding the question intriguing, Nico said, "Yes."

"His death was agonizing, then. He wasn't strong enough to endure them."

"But you are?"

Gauvain shrugged, clearly not willing to provide further information about himself, or the vampires he considered his children, vampires he had feelings for. Nico was reluctant to attribute true emotion to the vampire master, but what else was it?

Nico studied him, thinking about the people he loved and the danger they were in. They weren't connected to him by anything but emotion. While Gauvain's "children" had been made with his blood, just as . . . . *Fuck no!* Nico couldn't believe he'd almost fallen for that line of thinking. There was a world of difference between human children and the unholy things created when a vampire drained every measure of blood from a living human, and replaced it with his own.

Uneasy with his train of thought, Nico forestalled any further discussion by hustling the vampire master back into the cabinet. He could die there, he thought. Much easier that way. No more talk of souls or regret. He would return the next night to retrieve the manacles, and if necessary, finish off the master vampire. By then, it would be a mercy to grant his death.

He'd already done everything he'd promised the group, taking up the task of devising a better means of capturing and killing vampires. He had that and more now. The details he'd gathered from the master vampire, in addition to the effect of the manacles, should be particularly useful to Vital and the others. He'd turn over everything to Vital before he left, including the design for the manacles. Not the amber manacles themselves, though. He'd created those before he'd ever come to Paris. They were from his world, part of his life that was gone forever, and he wanted to keep them. Vital and the others would have to fabricate their own, and combine their magic to provide enough.

He frowned. His notes were all in his journals, which he definitely didn't to want to leave behind. But he intended to provide the information they contained to the group. Damn. He considered the number of pages, and the sketches—which suffered from his lack of artistic talent but were still useful—and knew he didn't have time to make copies himself.

There must be someone in this huge city who performed such tasks, and would do so quickly if paid generously enough. But how to find such a person? David was a fount of information when it came to the household, but this was different.

His banker was the one he needed, he decided. Though the entire matter was inconvenient. He might have to remain in Paris an additional day, or at least a morning. Mentally rearranging his plans to include an early morning visit to his banker, he locked up the basement, sealed the door, and the entire building with a protection spell, and headed home to accomplish what he could before sleep overtook him.

Walking down the empty streets, while considering everything he hoped to do the next day, he reached into his satchel for his journal, wanting to check a note he'd made. He found the journal easily enough, but what he didn't find had him shoving his hand back into the satchel to search every nook and cranny, while his heart pounded in disbelief. Finding nothing, he proceeded to do the same with every pocket he possessed, even the tiny inside pocket of his pants that the tailor had suggested for such *personal* items as a gentleman might require when going out for an evening. Nico still didn't know what the man had been talking about, and didn't care.

Because he had a much bigger problem. He'd left the damn key to the manacles somewhere in the basement room. It was probably sitting on the fucking table, since he'd been about to question Gauvain and had wanted the key visible for the same reason he'd created the amber key. To torment the prisoner.

Now, he was the one being tormented. Should he go back and retrieve the key? He was already more than halfway home, and it was cold and late. Plus, he wasn't going to get much sleep as it was. If he went back, he might end up staying awake all night to finish everything. Besides, the building was locked and magically protected, as was the basement door. Gauvain was the only living creature in the building, and he was in no condition to free *himself.*

He sighed unhappily, but decided not to go back. He'd return before sunset the next night, get the key, dispose of Gauvain, dead or alive, and be done with it. He picked up his pace, wanting to get home to finish what needed doing before he slept.

AT A SCANDALOUSLY early hour the next morning, Nico took a carriage to the bank. The banker was already there, though he was surprised to see anyone knocking on his door. Nico described his need for immediate and *discreet* copies of his notes. The need for discretion had woken him in the middle of the night, and made him question altogether his decision to copy the journals. But after a restless night, he'd finally cursed himself for a fool. His notes were in the language of his own world, which had no similarities to French. Nothing was the same, not even the alphabet.

His new worry then, had been that the language itself would be a problem. How could one copy a language he didn't understand? But the banker had taken one look at the notes, and nodded, as if he received similar requests every day of the week. The copies, he'd explained, would be made by men with little to no understanding of French, which was the language they were most often tasked with replicating. Their lack of understanding was a guarantee of discretion, and they were accustomed to copying words that meant nothing to them. Since Nico's papers were completely indecipherable, there would be no problem at all. The copies would be ready, and the originals returned undamaged by the end of day. And would Nico like them delivered to his home?

He considered the convenience of that, and agreed with one modification. He would have his own driver pick up the documents. The banker agreed, so they negotiated a very high price, which Nico paid in advance. After which, he returned to his home and the many tasks still waiting for him.

The night seemed to sink faster over the city that evening, due to heavy clouds which, he was told, promised snowfall by morning. Nico glanced overhead and quickened his pace, not wanting to return home in the snow. A few flakes wouldn't matter, but David seemed to believe there would be a lot more than that. Hurrying down the alley behind the building he'd rented, he cast out his magic to unlock the door before he reached it. It was faster than using a physical key *along* with magic, since magic alone could disable every lock on the building. And since after tonight, he and his captives would both be gone, he'd no longer require any security on the building at all.

His hand flew out once more, using magic to unlock the door to the basement stairs. It creaked open and he shoved it wider, overcome by an unexpected sense of urgency that had him leaping down the stairs. His magic was already flying toward the locked basement door, when he saw that it was open. Changing his spell on the fly, he reached for the open door, and was almost knocked off his feet when a small woman rushed past him, the slender arm that slammed into him as strong and stiff as a battering ram. He sensed the magic powering the arm in time to defend himself if she attacked, but she was already racing up the stairs with inhuman speed.

Nico's first thought upon seeing her frantic dash through the open door had been to protect her, convinced that Gauvain had gotten loose and lured the woman to him to feed upon. But her speed and the magic powering her attack against him told him he was wrong. She was a vampire, and not an ordinary one.

He'd fucked up.

Racing after her, he reached the upper level in time to see her yank open the door to the alley. He shot his power at her back, in a spell intended to freeze her in place, until he could catch up with her. And it almost worked. She did freeze, but no more than an instant. He was still three strides away, when the spell shattered with the sound of breaking ice, and she ran once more. He followed close after, not understanding how she'd managed to break his spell. He didn't have time to think on it, however. He had to catch her first. He was bigger, taller, and a sorcerer. He'd have her before she reached the street where it met the alley.

A single length separated them when he reached for her, but despite his own inhuman speed, his fingers only managed to brush her sleeve before she glanced back, and with the manacles raised like a prize and a triumphant grin on her face . . . she vanished, leaving nothing but a trilled "*Merci!*" on the air to say that she'd ever been there.

Amazed and furious at the same time, Nico raced to look up and down the street, even casting a spell over the entire block, seeking some sign of her, but she was gone. Not *just* gone, but disappeared. He'd felt the touch of a powerful magic when she'd done it.

"What the fuck?" he growled, finally giving up and stalking back to the basement. What kind of creature was she to vanish so fast and thoroughly that *he,* one of the most powerful sorcerers alive, couldn't locate her or even a lingering sign that she'd been there? Devastated by the loss of the manacles, and deeply troubled at having been bested by . . . whatever the hell she was, he remained in the alley for a time, casting spell after spell for some trace of her. She was easily the most powerful magic-user he'd encountered in this world, the *only* one who had enough power to demand a higher level of power than he'd been using so far. He'd become complacent, and it had cost him dearly.

Ultimately, he found nothing useful in the alley, which was no more than expected. He went back inside and down to the basement, where he again found exactly what he expected. There was a mound of vampire dust that had been Gauvain, still so fresh that particles lingered in the air above a pile of recognizable clothing. And an empty space on the table, where he'd so stupidly forgotten the key.

What the hell was the damn woman? Was she another master vampire? If so, she was one hell of a lot stronger than Gauvain. And if she'd killed Gauvain—which seemed likely—how had she known about the key? She might have simply figured it out for herself, or Gauvain may have told her, trusting that she would set him free.

But then, she'd *taken* the manacles, which were, to all appearances, perfectly ordinary cuffs. Again, either Gauvain had to have told her they were ensorcelled, or she had enough power of her own to sense their unique magic. Whatever she was, Nico would wager his fortune that she was no sorcerer. Her power had a different . . . *taste* to it.

Abruptly worried about the strange woman, and what she might do next, he abandoned the now empty room, and the building he no longer needed, and hurried home. There was no reason to believe she would attempt to break into his house, no reason to think she even knew where he lived. But he didn't relax until he opened the back door and slipped into the kitchen, which was still warm from the day's cooking, and the freshly-baked bread still cooling on the hearth. David was asleep upstairs, and the house was quiet. And the protections and wards on his home were far stronger than those he'd put on the empty building.

But Nico was no longer trusting to probabilities when it came to her. He checked every aspect of the house's protection, and strengthened those on the entry points—doors and windows both—before retiring to his workroom to *think*.

He'd assumed too much about the magical creatures of this world, been too arrogant about his own power. Yes, he had power beyond anything most magic-users could imagine, but he hadn't used his full abilities since arriving in Paris. Apart from the overall scarcity of available magic in this world, every so-called sorcerer he'd met thus far had possessed barely enough magic to earn that designation.

He pulled out one of the few journals he'd brought with him from his own world—the one that detailed how he'd drawn the four warriors to him, and also, the spell he'd eventually used to free Gabriel from the curse of his vampirism. Nico didn't need the spell itself. But the journal also contained everything he'd learned about vampires while preparing to help Gabriel. What he remembered of the vampires in his own world was limited, since once he'd freed his brother warrior, he'd had no further encounters with them.

That was the reason he kept journals at all, and why he'd continued the practice, even after leaving his world behind. It would have been impossible to remember every aspect of every spell he'd ever devised or cast. And so now, he poured a glass of wine, found the relevant entries, and began reading.

By morning, he knew what he'd forgotten, or rather what he'd assumed was different in this world. The vampire masters of his home were far more powerful than he'd remembered. During his research, he'd been so focused on reversing Gabriel's curse that he'd forgotten everything else he'd learned about them. The strongest among them were as powerful as sorcerers. He'd made a note in his journal at the time, questioning if it was possible the master vampires had been sorcerers before being turned, which would have explained their power. But he'd never followed up on that idea, too consumed with defeating Sotiris. Now, however, he devoured every word he'd written, every idea he'd considered with regard to their power. The possibilities he'd only speculated about back then, now made perfect sense, even though the result was the very embodiment of his personal nightmare.

Vampires were inherently magical creatures. They had to be. How else could anyone explain their very existence, much less their incredibly long lives and resistance to human disease? Their ability to create others like themselves, and to command those others to do their bidding against their will, was only more proof. Even Gabriel, who was one of the most powerful warriors and possessed one of the strongest wills of any man Nico had ever met, had been forced to commit heinous acts that went against everything he believed as both a man and a warrior. Nico had known that, but had forgotten what it might mean about a vampire's power and magic.

He sat back and sipped his wine while considering these new ideas. The female, who was undoubtedly long gone and whose name he might never learn, must have been much more powerful than Gauvain. She'd not only gotten through Nico's wards, she'd killed Gauvain to get the manacles, presumably after learning what they could do. But would Gauvain have told her anything before she'd freed him? Why give her a motive to kill him? Fuck, he kept forgetting about her power. She hadn't needed Gauvain to tell her anything. She might have come there with the intent to free Gauvain, but once she'd sensed the strong magic that was the very essence of the manacles, she'd wanted them. So, fuck Gauvain. They were useless without the key, but that had been sitting right there on the table begging to be taken.

Feeling like a fool, Nico wrote down everything he already knew, along with what he'd just learned, and how the two finally came together in his own mind. He then wrote out a copy on plain paper for his friend Vital, omitting any comments as to his own stupidity. That copy he placed in an envelope with Vital's name on it. He'd ask David to deliver it along with the rest of the journal copies, after he'd left Paris.

Nico had learned a hard lesson about faulty assumptions and new worlds. He'd learned it much too late, though he took some comfort in knowing that he, at least, could never be bound by the manacles. They were his creation. And he still had the amber key, which might come in handy someday. But for now, the manacles were gone.

Just as *he* would be, by this time tomorrow.

Chapter Twelve

NICO SLEPT LATER than planned the next morning, but didn't regret the extra rest. He'd been up most of the night again, and had a hard day ahead of him. He'd already decided to ride solo, rather than taking a carriage out to the country estate of Charron's friend. He was eager to get there, worried that something might happen to the "gift" Sotiris had left for him. Not knowing what it was, how fragile or even dangerous it might be, only made his sense of urgency stronger.

He had a late breakfast with David, during which he made sure the young butler had everything he'd need for the future. His original journals and notes had been waiting for him, along with the copies, all of which had been picked up by David personally the previous evening. He checked to be certain everything was there, then made sure David understood the importance of their secure delivery to Vital.

"Getting them there safely is more important than the speed of their delivery, you understand? You must handle this yourself, and take a carriage to Charron's. But only turn these papers over to Vital. If he's not available, then wait in the carriage until he returns, or try again the next day."

"But, sir, the cost of the carriage—"

"Is nothing compared to the importance of these notes."

David's expression tightened with determination. "I will take care of it, sir. Just as you ask."

"I know you will. I'll miss you, David. I may never have a friend I can trust as I do you." What he meant was "in this world," but he omitted that to avoid uncomfortable explanations.

The young man blushed, but looked worried. "But you're coming back, Nicholas, aren't you?"

"It is my intention to return, but it makes sense to plan for delays or other mischance. If I find evidence of my cousin at this home of Charron's friend, and if they have some idea of where he was going, I intend to follow his trail. There are others, people I love, whose lives could be changed forever, and not for the better, if I don't find him."

David sighed. "I understand, sir. I will pray for you."

Nico hid his surprise. David had never before given evidence of any particular devotion to the church. He wondered if Josette did, but he'd probably never find out. He'd told David that he planned to return to Paris, and maybe he would. But it was more likely that whatever Sotiris had left for him would send him in a very different direction.

WHEN HE FINALLY left the house, Nico carried only his weapons and the backpack he'd arrived with. The pack held the few clothes he was taking, the journals and notes that had caused his delayed departure, and the amber key, which was all he had left of the manacles. Josette had provided him with a picnic lunch, which reminded him painfully of the times he and Antonia had shared one, in happier times. He didn't see himself stopping by the roadside, but the food was neat enough that he could eat in the saddle, and he was grateful for her thoughtfulness.

He was leaving behind so many good people. How many worlds and times would he have to do the same, before he was reunited with Antonia and his warriors? How long before they could all reclaim the lives that had been so viciously interrupted by Sotiris?

He said good-bye to David, knowing he'd miss him and already regretting that he wouldn't have any part of a life that he hoped he'd shaped in some way, hoped as fervently that he'd made that life better.

He pulled the boy in for a hard embrace and stepped into the waiting carriage, which would take him to a reputable stable where he'd purchase a young, strong horse with plenty of spirit for the long ride ahead.

Chapter Thirteen

1824, Reims, France

NICO HAD BEEN right that riding his own horse would be faster than travelling in a carriage, but he'd forgotten, after so long in Paris, how exhausting hours upon hours in the saddle could be. Or maybe he'd just grown soft sitting in carriages for even short trips through the city, only to sit even longer in the library, or at Charron's, or even in his own home in the city.

At his real home—the place he'd been born and grown to manhood—he'd been constantly outdoors, riding to the villages in his territory, or walking marketplaces or fields. And when he wasn't doing that, he'd been sparring with his warriors or helping train the farmers and tradesmen who would become fighters in his next war with Sotiris. He'd been busy from morning to night, and it was only then, for the most part, that he'd worked with his magic to create new and better spells, or weapons for that same war.

The gelding he'd purchased for the ride was strong and spirited, but well-trained, and with a smooth gait that saved his ass from becoming even more sore than it was after two days in the saddle. He'd arrived too late in the day to intrude on the sorcerer whose estate had briefly housed Sotiris. He had a letter from Charron introducing him as Sotiris's cousin, and testifying to his honesty and trustworthiness. The letter also identified him as a sorcerer of some note, but at Nico's request, Charron had been all too happy to omit any superlatives to describe his power.

Despite the letter, he was too polite and mostly too tired to deal with that introduction and what would follow that night. Instead, he stayed at an inn that was good enough to have a clean stable and a stable master who slept in the barn round the clock, where he could be roused by the stable boy on duty through the night. Nico had grown rather fond of the gelding he'd begun to call "Denis," who, according to the priest at the cathedral in Paris, was the patron saint of France. Nico was yet to be clear on what patron saints were or did, but he liked the name, and it fit the gelding's golden-brown color, which reminded him of all the old gold decorating the cathedral.

The inn was clean, and the owner's boy delivered a large bucket of steaming hot water for a small addition to the night's room cost. It wasn't too late for dinner, and he desperately wanted some equivalent of cognac to take away the strain of the long ride, so he washed quickly and went down to the *brasserie* where he ordered stew—which smelled so wonderful that he didn't care what was in it. Discovering he was in the wrong region of France for cognac, he happily consumed something called a pilsner, which was a darker, heavier version of the ale consumed in his own territory. Although he supposed it wasn't his territory any longer, and wondered briefly what had come of it.

But he wasn't going to dwell on a past he couldn't change—not yet anyway. If he could travel between worlds and times, it wasn't entirely impossible that he might someday figure out how to go backwards to where he'd started. Still, it was best for now that he concentrate on the present—enjoying a stew that was as delicious as it smelled, a pilsner that was the perfect accompaniment, along with a coarse bread filled with seeds, just the way he liked it. But then, he hadn't had a bad meal since arriving in France. Vital had explained that both food and wine were points of honor in the country.

The men enjoying dinner in the *brasserie* along with him were cheerful for the most part. Sitting in groups of three or more, they looked like people who spent their days in the sun, and their nights eating good food. Faces were tanned and lined, giving an appearance of age that was probably exaggerated, and bodies were sturdy and strong. They talked, sometimes loudly, and seemed to know each other well, exchanging words with other tables in shouts across the room.

It was the sort of place Nico would have enjoyed in this world or any other, but by the time he'd scraped the last tasty spoonful of stew, and drained a final tall glass of pilsner, he was fighting to keep his eyes open. So he retired to his room, with its moderately comfortable, but clean bed, and was asleep before he realized there was no pillow.

HE WASTED NO time the next morning, packing the few things he removed from the backpack and heading downstairs for a cup of dark French coffee, and whatever else he could find in the brasserie.

"Bread and ham, sir?" the same young woman asked after he'd leaned his pack against the wall.

"Please, and coffee with sugar."

"Of course," she said with a twinkle in her eye, then did a hip-swinging walk over to the bar to place his order.

Those hips had him remembering the night before, and the same twinkle he'd seen in her eye. Good gods, he'd been propositioned and had been too tired to know it, much less do anything about it. Not that he would have. His heart was still firmly wrapped up with love for Antonia, which was as it would remain until he found her. He took out Charron's letter and began reading, to give him a reason for not meeting her gaze when she slid the coffee onto his table, followed by more of the same bread, and several slices of ham.

He ate quickly, eager to be on his way now that he was so close. Would Sotiris still be there? Had the letter been nothing but a ploy to get him here, so his enemy could kill him? Or try anyway. The only sure way Sotiris had of killing him was a surprise attack from behind. And even then, he'd have to be distracted enough not to notice the bastard was there. This morning, he'd be looking for any sign of Sotiris, so the surprise factor would be all but eliminated.

He stopped at the front desk to ask directions to the estate of Charron's friend, thanked the manager, picked up his horse, who was already saddled and well-rested, and was on his way.

THE ESTATE WAS A vineyard, as everything seemed to be in this region of France, with long rows of staked vines filling the fields to either side of the dirt road leading to what he hoped was the main residence. There were plenty of other buildings, but only this one had a broad, covered porch, as well as a horse and carriage parked to one side. The carriage was open, but empty, and the horse was eating from a feed bag tied to a rail.

Nico dismounted and tied his gelding to the same rail where the carriage was parked, although he left as much distance as possible between the horses, having no way of knowing how friendly or nervous the other animal might be.

Slinging his pack over one shoulder, he started for the porch, still hoping he was right about the building, when the door opened and a man stepped out. "Monsieur Katsaros?" he called.

Nico stopped at the bottom of the stairs and smiling, said, "I am Nicholas Katsaros, and I just realized that Charron never told me your name. It was unforgiveable of me not to have asked."

The man laughed. "Charron is too secretive for his own good. He gives out information like a miser with his centimes. I am Séverin,

Léandre Séverin. Please, come in. We'll have wine, and you can tell me about your journey. And I will tell you what I know of Monsieur Sotiris."

Nico stepped onto the porch. "He's not here, then?"

"Oh no, though I regret to say that you missed him by only a few days. He had important business, or so he said."

"Did he say where he was going?"

"No, only that he would not be returning to France."

Nico swore silently. The bastard had known that *he* was in France, and left, clearly intent on leading him on a merry chase.

"But come," Séverin said, "we can sit inside."

They settled in a spacious room with comfortable-looking furniture and a huge fireplace. Séverin gestured for Nico to sit, while he disappeared into another room and returned with a chilled bottle of light pink wine, and a tray of several cheeses, and some bread.

Nico sipped the wine experimentally and found it light and refreshing, even though it wasn't yet noon. He declined the bread and cheese, explaining he'd just come from breakfast.

"So," Séverin said. "You want to know about your cousin's visit to our lovely part of France." He studied Nico curiously, then said, "I must tell you, Nicholas . . . may I call you Nicholas?"

"Of course."

He tipped his head politely. "And I am Léandre. As I was saying, however, and forgive me, Nicholas, but you look nothing alike."

"Our family is large, but we live very near each other, and have for several generations. Sotiris and I share a great-grandmother, but we aren't close."

Léandre chuckled. "You don't like him."

"No." He didn't see any problem with admitting that. He doubted Sotiris had gone out of his way to be friendly.

"And yet you search for him."

"That great-grandmother we share? She asked the favor of me."

"Ah. Grandmothers hold such power over us, don't they? It's the heart that knows and treasures them."

Nico nodded his agreement, but couldn't help thinking of his own gran, who'd been so afraid of him once his magic emerged that she'd avoided him until the day she died. She had even requested that he *not* attend her deathbed—the only person she'd made the request of. Enemies were forgiven, but not her sorcerous grandson.

While he remained lost in the unpleasant past, Léandre continued, "Your cousin knew little of France, but spoke the language almost fluently. Just as you do, monsieur."

"I've been in Paris for some time."

"That explains it then. But back to Sotiris, who offered no other name and remained quite aloof the entire time he was here. He used magic, and quite a lot of it, though it was never discussed. I didn't ask, as it was obvious he was much more powerful than I, and had no wish to become friends. He ate in his rooms, or in the town, which was the only time he left, and then, only rarely. Whenever he had a window open, which was not often, he was sitting at his desk . . . working, I assumed."

"Where are his rooms?"

"He stayed in the white-washed brick cottage behind us. You might have noticed when you came up our road. It has a blue door and shutters."

"I saw it. When did he leave? I'd hoped to catch up with him here."

"He did leave in something of a hurry. You know about the message, of course, but you should know also that he gave me that message on the day he left, and instructed that it not be sent to Paris until five days had passed." Léandre gave one of those expressive French shrugs and said, "I sent it early. A carriage was returning to Paris, after making a delivery here, and the driver was happy to have the return fee. I couldn't see that it mattered if the message reached you earlier, as he'd already left."

"How long after he left did you send it to Paris?"

"Two days, rather than the five he requested."

So Sotiris had been gone a week or more by now, Nico figured. But it wasn't the specific number of days that intrigued him. It was Sotiris's request to delay his receipt of the message. Why would he have done that, unless he needed time to prepare for Nico's pursuit. What if he'd expected Nico to follow, but there was something—or some*one*—that he wanted to move before Nico could catch up to him?

"Did you happen to see which way he rode when he left?"

"North, my friend, but that covers a great deal."

"Yes," Nico agreed, frustrated as hell by the entire situation. "Have you been in his rooms?" he asked abruptly.

Léandre winced. "I have not, which is unforgiveable, but the girl who cleans this house and the cottage, which is our only guest room, rode into Paris to go shopping with my wife. That is why my own hospitality is so lacking."

"Not at all. The wine is delicious. I've never had it before."

"Ah. I'm pleased to have introduced it to you."

"Could I see Sotiris's rooms? He may have left some clue as to his destination."

"Of course. I should at least allow some air and sunshine into them before my wife returns anyway. Come, the key is in the kitchen."

They walked out together, but when Léandre would have unlocked the cottage door, Nico stopped him. Whatever Sotiris had left for him was in that room. "It would be better if I enter alone. As you said, Sotiris is very powerful, and if there's something he doesn't want seen, he may have . . . taken precautions. Especially since he knows I am trailing him."

Léandre appeared surprised. "He would risk harm to you or to others?"

Nico gave his best impression of the French shrug. "It is apparent that he doesn't want me to find him. I'm curious as to why, but have no doubt that he would harm me if it suited him."

He handed Nico the key with an unhappy grunt. "When you find your cousin, please tell him he is not welcome to return to my home."

"I will tell him." He held up the key. "It would be better if I entered the cottage alone," he repeated, but added a regretful note. This was, after all, the man's own property.

"Of course. I will withdraw to the house. Please be careful, Nicholas."

He nodded. "I will check with you before leaving."

Nico waited until he was sure Léandre was inside and not lingering near a door or window for a better vantage on his possible bloody demise, then turned the key and opened the door. He paused on the threshold of the dark room, scanning the entire building for signs of a protective spell that might destroy him along with the cottage. Finding none, he entered, leaving the door open behind him. The room was very dark and dusty, but rather than search for candles or a lantern, he crossed to the two windows and opened the shutters and windows, admitting the fresh air, along with the warm sunlight.

Turning to survey the small cottage, he saw an unmade bed revealed by an open door to another room, a small hearth with firewood stacked next to it, and what passed for a kitchen. There was a table and chair near one window, which he took to be the workspace Léandre had, on occasion, observed when passing outside.

And sitting in the center of that table was a well-wrapped parcel with his name on it.

Chapter Fourteen

NICO STARED AT what he assumed was Sotiris's *gift*. What else could it be? Sotiris had not only known he was in France, but had assumed he would work out the transition spell, and had *wanted* him to follow. And now this, which wouldn't be anything good. He knew his enemy far too well to believe that. But he also knew it wouldn't kill him. Why would Sotiris go to such lengths to ensure he not only *could* follow, but *would*, only to kill him? The bastard gained too much pleasure from toying with him, letting him believe that he could locate Antonia and his brothers, if only he followed Sotiris, step for step.

The only question was, how bad it would be? His mind was already conjuring images of everything from the severed head of one or all four of his warriors, or gods forbid, some equally gruesome evidence of Antonia's death.

Walking over, he grabbed the package and slid it closer, intending to rip it open and end the parade of horrific images. But a much-delayed splash of cold reason had him slowing down and rethinking such foolish haste. Taking his hands off the box, he considered what he knew of his enemy. Sotiris loved only himself, but would he kill Antonia so early in the chase? After all, she'd betrayed him by helping Nico, thus choosing Sotiris's enemy over him. He'd want her to suffer a more lingering punishment than a quick, if brutal, death. The certainty he was right about that much gave Nico hope that she was alive, which meant, he could still find her and free her from whatever living death Sotiris had conjured for her.

His warriors were another matter, however. Their curses were solely the result of their loyalty to Nico. Their punishment was intended to punish him, as well as them. Their pain was meant to be his pain.

Sighing in resignation, he lit the fireplace and then the lantern, wanting as much light as possible in the room, before closing both windows and door. If he was wrong, and this gift was meant to destroy him, he would do his best to contain the damage. Léandre seemed a decent man, who'd done nothing to deserve being touched by Sotiris's evil.

Pulling the parcel closer once more, he scanned it for evidence of sorcerous meddling, though he didn't expect to find any at this stage. Sotiris might have anticipated the box being handled before it reached him. He couldn't have known that Léandre's wife and cleaning girl had gone to Paris, after all, or that the cottage would remain closed and locked all this time.

He unwrapped the outer sheet of rough paper next. It had a thin coating of wax, which served no purpose that Nico could divine, other than to protect or preserve whatever was inside. And that wasn't the least bit reassuring.

Several layers of wrapping later, including a final swathing of cheesecloth—which seemed an odd choice—Nico lifted the lid, and found even more cheesecloth crushed into balls that filled every empty space in the package, as if to guard against breakage. He frowned, no longer able to guess at what the box might contain.

Removing the four smaller packages, which were more or less identical in size and shape, he split the string on one of them, carefully unwrapped it . . . and had to grip the table lest he fall to the floor, devastated by what he found. Tears blinded him when he hurried to open the other three, until finally he shoved the endless piles of wrapping to the floor, and stood the four statues on top of the table.

"Damian," he whispered, touching the first. "Kato. Gabriel. And oh gods, Dragan." Tears rolled unheeded down his face while he stared at the near perfect images of his warriors as they'd been in the final moments before they vanished. His first thought was that this was the only thing left of his warriors, but he discounted that idea almost at once. Again, Sotiris was far too cruel to end his game so soon.

But for the same reason, they had to be more than they seemed.

A quick magical assessment revealed them to be constructed of some sandy material, not sturdy enough to survive rough handling, but malleable enough to be the product of human carving, or sorcerous creation. None of the four held any spark of life or living matter, for which he was grateful—and so relieved that he had to pause for a time to recover his equanimity.

The few minutes permitted him to regain the cold logic that was necessary to judge the statues for what they were, or might yet become. A taunt from his enemy, certainly. A way to reveal the form of their prisons, but not the locations. It made him wonder if Sotiris himself knew specifically where they were.

Nico had learned enough of Sotiris's spell to reach this world and time, but he been traveling blind, with no idea of where or when he was going. Even now, with all he'd learned since, he doubted he could direct the spell to discharge him in a specific location, or a particular date. Perhaps that was true of Sotiris, as well. He knew *where* the warriors had gone, but maybe he didn't know when. And that meant he and Nico would be in a race to find them.

The possibility of that, which he believed was all too close to reality, brought a fresh wave of fear and desperation for his warriors. What would Sotiris do to them if he found them first? Would he destroy them? Or more likely, would he drop them into the deep ocean, where they would *never* be found?

A small ivory-colored card in the bottom of the larger box caught his attention, and he picked it up, recognizing Sotiris's script.

I caution you once again to take care with my gift. Each of these likenesses is ensorcelled to reflect the welfare of its original. If a warrior's prison is destroyed before he can be freed, he will die. If he dies, the likeness will fall to dust, just as the warrior will do. If, however, a warrior's specific curse is lifted, and he is freed, the likeness will crumble to sand. You will have no knowledge of how or where his freedom was won, but then, since each warrior will, more likely than not, have gone mad by then, neither will he.

My gift to you, Nicodemus, is the knowledge of each man's freedom, whether by death or madness.

Nico could all but hear Sotiris's laughter as he read the card. The evil bastard had succeeded in tormenting him with every word. Tossing the card aside, he sank to the floor, resting his back against the wall, while he stared up at the four small statues that were all he had left of his brothers, of warriors so courageous that they had come at *his* call—a sorcerer they knew nothing about—to stand with him against the greatest evil their world had known. And this was their reward.

Overcome by a despair that not even his rage could pierce, he sat for a long time, his face buried in arms crossed over updrawn knees, until the cold of the stone floor finally penetrated enough to send a shiver rolling through his body. The discomfort—he was ashamed to think of it as such, knowing what his warriors were suffering—drove him to his feet, and rage finally burned through anguish.

Afraid to leave the effigies out of his sight, for fear that they would somehow disappear, he re-wrapped each with precise care, placed them back in the box, then carried them out of the cottage and into the house where Léandre was waiting.

Chapter Fifteen

1824, Outside London, United Kingdom

ANTONIA WOKE TO a single beam of sunshine forcing its way through the clouds and into her bedroom. The sight made her smile in the instant before she realized she didn't know where she was. Why had she known it would be gray and cloudy outside, and so appreciated the lone bit of sunshine? She reached out with her magic, looking for traces of a spell or other mischief that someone might be using to tease her.

Fear, cold and terrible, drenched her in sweat even as her heart began to race and she strained to find some shred of the magic that had been part of her life as long as could remember. "Think, Antonia," she muttered. "Think. What do you remember? What's your last memory?"

She worked to control her breathing, lest she pass out and wake up in an even worse nightmare, and fought to answer her own question. Only she couldn't make her brain work, couldn't make it remember anything . . . except a big window, and forest of trees. What the hell was that?

Throwing back the covers, she jumped out of bed and started searching for something other than the thin linen shift which was all she wore, but didn't recognize. Seeing nothing lying about, she was reaching for the wardrobe, when the door to the room burst open and a man stood there.

No, she thought immediately, *not a man, but* the *man.*

In the same moment she was grabbing the blanket from the bed to cover herself, she couldn't help wondering where that thought had come from. "Who are you, and what have you done to me?" she demanded.

The man smiled, and though he was handsome enough, it wasn't a nice smile.

"I'm pleased to see you on your feet and aware enough to ask questions," he said, sounding as if the pleasure he was feeling came from disdain, rather than sincerity. "There are clothes in the wardrobe. Get dressed. We're leaving."

"I'm not going anywhere until—"

He slapped her so hard that she fell back on the bed and slid to the floor, where she sat staring at him in disbelief. No one had ever struck her like that. Despite her failing memory, she somehow knew that much.

"What do you want with me?" she whispered.

"Get dressed," he snarled, "or I'll drag you out of here as you are." He strode out through the open door, and was gone.

Antonia listened to the soft thud of his footsteps on the carpeted floor, not moving until they became the click of leather soles on marble, which faded as he descended stairs. She was upstairs, she realized. Though it seemed a pointless observation, she thought, as she sat there holding her throbbing cheek and wondering who he was, and what he wanted with her. It couldn't be anything good, if he felt free to slap her as he would a thief after his purse.

Deciding that putting on some clothes was a good idea, no matter what else she did, Antonia got to her feet and opened the wardrobe door. A dress hung there, though it wasn't a style she recognized. It was long with a much fuller skirt than she was accustomed to wearing, though the blouse appeared usual enough—white linen with full sleeves and a gathered neckline, which tied in the front. And despite the excessive bulk of the skirt, it appeared to tie the way most of her clothes did, even if this one was dressy enough for a ball rather than a trip to . . . who knew where? At least she wouldn't be expected to ride a horse. She knew that much, and she clung to every thought she had, trying to fill the hole where her memory used to be.

And her magic. But the possibility that her magic was gone was too devastating to contemplate just now. She had to get dressed, get downstairs, and out of this house . . . and then she'd see.

THE MAN WAS waiting for her outside, standing next to an enclosed carriage that was drawn by a matched pair of gorgeous chestnut horses, who tossed their heads eager to get started.

"Get in. You've delayed us long enough."

"I don't have any shoes," she said faintly. "There weren't—"

"You don't need shoes. Get in."

"But what is all this? Where are we going? And why can't I—?"

"Get in, or I'll throw you in."

Seeing from his hard expression that he'd do it, and with her entire face still throbbing from his earlier outburst, she gathered the heavy skirt above her bare feet, and climbed the two steps into the carriage. She hesitated then, staring at the leather benches to either side.

"Sit the fuck down."

Deciding it would be better to ride facing than with her back to whatever direction they were going, she sat, gathered her cold feet beneath her, and tucked the voluminous skirt under and around them for warmth. When the man climbed into the carriage, he gave her gathered feet and legs a scathing look where they took up the entire seat, but she was too surprised to move. She'd thought the man would be driving the carriage, since she'd seen no one else.

But he'd no sooner seated himself on the opposite bench than the carriage rocked as someone climbed onto the driver's seat, and with a snap of the reins and soft call of encouragement, the horses took off and the carriage went with them.

"Where are we—?"

The man raised his hand, flicked his fingers in irritation, and then . . . nothing.

1824, Reims, France

NICODEMUS RELUCTANTLY left the statues in the cottage, before walking over to knock on the back door of Léandre's home. He would have preferred to keep them not only in his sight, but within his grasp, but knew his host would be curious, and was reluctant to share the contents of his *cousin's* gift. The statues were too precious to him, too *private* a grief to share. After rewrapping as carefully as he'd found them, he cast his strongest protection spell over the box, then added an equally strong spell over the small building, then walked the short distance to the house.

"Come in, come in," Léandre called, hurrying to the door. "What did you find? You're alive, so that's good."

Nico smiled and took the seat at the big, wooden kitchen table that his host offered.

"Sit, my friend. You may be alive, but I can see that things did not go completely well. Sorcery uses a body hard. I don't need to be a great sorcerer like yourself to understand that. Let me make you a light meal, at least. And some wine."

He poured a glass and placed it in front of Nico. It was a different wine, he noticed. Darker and not cold. He took an experimental sip, and then another. "Do you have no wine that is *not* delicious, Léandre?"

The Frenchman grinned and said proudly, "That one is from my own vineyard. A pinot noir, which Alsace Region is noted for, in addition to champagne, of course."

"Of course," Nick replied, having no idea what came from Alsace Region or anywhere else, but having tasted champagne during his stay in Paris, he would have agreed that it was indeed delicious. But then, so was Léandre's pinot noir. "Though I can't say I've tasted a finer wine than this since I arrived in France."

"You're too kind, Nicholas. Here, eat something, you'll feel better, and then you can tell me what you found."

It was more ham and bread. There was also cheese and tiny pickles on the plate. Nico ate at first to be polite, but soon realized that his new friend was right. Despite his sizable breakfast, he was hungry, and when Léandre cleared away the empty plate and replaced it with delicate cookies and more coffee, he ate those, too.

"It seems all I do is eat your food and drink your wine."

"It is a pleasure, my friend. The house has been empty with my wife gone, and my daughter living so far away in Calais, near her husband's family. They have a very profitable shipping business, which my son-in-law is expected to take over when his father retires. I miss her, but am ever hopeful for a pack of grandchildren who will spend summers on their grandfather's vineyard, learning how wine is made, and perhaps one day, will want to take over my business instead."

"It sounds a far more pleasant life than packing ships."

Léandre laughed. "It does indeed. Now, tell me what you found that wounded your soul so dreadfully."

Thinking the winemaker understood people as well as he did grapes, Nico related a made-up, but believable story of his cousin's descent into lawlessness, and the terrible decision Nico now had to make as to whether to go home and tell his great-grandmother that he'd failed to find Sotiris, despite months of searching—though she knew him well, and would surely know he lied. Or should he give his search one more chance, one more attempt to find his cousin. Then he could drag him back to his family, who would take him in hand and stop him from cheating others out of their hard-earned money.

Léandre listened carefully, not interrupting to comment, until Nico had finished. "Do you know where he's gone?"

"He left a great number of papers and scrawled notes. It might be worth a bit more of my time to read through them, and see if I can find anything that would tell me where to look, at least. And if I discover nothing useful, then I'll be able to go home with a clear conscience, knowing I've done all I could." He sighed. "I miss my brothers, Léandre. I need to—" He almost said, "find them," but caught himself and finished by saying, "See them, and the rest of my family, including my great-grandmother."

"You are a good man, a good grandson to have done so much already. You shouldn't have to pay for your cousin's bad deeds or lack of concern for his family."

Nico sipped his wine. "Still, I wonder if I could use the cottage for just one night, in order to be certain there's nothing to find in Sotiris's notes."

"Of course, but, oh! My friend, I'm having dinner with my brother's family tonight. His wife argues that my own spouse is negligent in leaving me to cook for myself, and insists I come over for a decent meal. And as she is an excellent cook . . ."

Nico grinned. "Go. I will be completely occupied with Sotiris's records, and no fit company in any event. In all likelihood, I will leave before dawn, regardless of what I find. Whether it's to continue my search, or turn for home, I will be eager to get started as soon as possible."

"I could cancel—"

"Absolutely not. I won't hear of it. You've been far more gracious and kind to a stranger at your door. I have never felt more welcome, and you may tell your wife I said so."

"If you're certain."

"I am. Please, go and enjoy an evening with your brother's family. And perhaps say a prayer that I will soon be doing the same with my own brothers."

"I will pray for you every Sunday. And I will leave the door unlocked here." He gestured at the back door. "Feel free to take whatever you wish for supper, or if you require anything else."

"You are too kind."

"And your cousin is a fool."

It required a few more invitations from Léandre, and insistences from Nico he would be well enough alone, but eventually he was able to retreat to the cottage with a bottle of pinot noir to "give him strength" for the night's work.

Once Léandre had departed in the horse-drawn carriage, Nico conjured a witch light and began reading. Unlike what he'd told Léandre, however, his reading material wasn't anything that Sotiris had written.

He'd already been through what little had been left and determined it was nothing useful.

No, what he read as he sipped wine and ate more of the excellent ham and bread, was his own journal. He read and re-read every word he'd written about the transition spell, both before and after he left his home for Paris. But no matter how many times he read it, he arrived at the same conclusion.

If Sotiris was set on leaving a trail of clues for Nico to chase, no matter how cruel or useless some of them might be, or how many worlds or centuries the trail took him through, the only way he would ever find Antonia, and free his warriors, was to follow his enemy. It might be years, or it might be centuries, but he *would* someday be reunited with everyone he loved.

LÉANDRE WAS disappointed, but not surprised, when he knocked on the cottage door the next morning only to discover his friend Nicholas was gone. He *was* surprised, however, to find Nicholas's very fine gelding stabled in his own barn. He stared at the horse for a moment, then being a sorcerer who believed in the impossible, he took it in stride and went about his day.

1824, Outside London, United Kingdom

NICO WOKE TO find himself lying in the dirt next to a large building, with a sore head, and no idea of where he was. He'd cast the same transition spell that Sotiris had used to flee France, and assumed it had worked, but the only way he could know for sure was to explore his surroundings. He leaned back and studied what looked like a house. He was lying next to one of its walls, and its brick construction was probably responsible for his aching head.

He gathered himself to stand, and was relieved to see that his backpack had survived the transition, still hanging from a single strap on his shoulder. Worried, he did a quick inventory of its contents, which now included the four, carefully wrapped statues of his warriors. He'd briefly considered setting aside his reservations and leaving those, along with his horse, at Léandre's vineyard, but couldn't know for certain that he'd ever return to that place and time. And the more he'd thought about it, the more reluctant he'd been to part with them. Some might call it instinct, others superstition, or plain foolishness, but he was convinced that parting with those statues, even to safeguard them from harm, would lead to bad things for him and his warriors both.

Once more on his feet, he looked beyond the house, and saw nothing but a thick forest that seemed to go on forever. Closer to the building was a broad lawn of very green grass flanking the walkway leading to a wide, gray door. As for the house itself, it was even bigger than he'd first thought, nearly as wide as the forecourt of his father's castle, with three stories rising overhead. There were no outbuildings that he could see, which seemed odd. The house appeared to be isolated in these deep woods, so where was the barn, or stables for the horses, that should have been necessary for transport to somewhere, *anywhere*, else?

Resigned to play out Sotiris's game, he strode to the front door and knocked. The door opened beneath his fist, and he froze, drawing protection over himself, and summoning an attack spell. He'd dueled with Sotiris for too many years to assume that anything about this place was safe.

Nico shoved the door hard enough that it smacked against the wall, before bouncing back to hang completely open, giving him an unobstructed view inside. He saw no one, heard nothing. The house had an abandoned feel to it, as if it had been empty for a very long time, despite the well-cared interior with its elegant couches and pleasing complement of chairs, the wooden tables gleaming with not a speck of dust in sight.

It was the absence of dust that made Nico pause on the threshold. Every sense he possessed told him it had been years since a family had sheltered under its broad roof. And yet, it was as neat and clean as if held immune to the passage of time. A strong enough sorcerer could work such a spell. Nico could have done it. And he was following a trail cast by Sotiris.

He'd already walked the yard and stone path to the door. If there'd been anything there, he'd have sensed it long before. But now, reaching out as he should have done from the first, Nico cast his magic into the house itself and saw the spell revealed as it unraveled under the touch of his own. It was as if a coating of wax, like that on the paper around the box, was melting away. Inside the house, there was a golden shimmer, like sunlight through a window, that glowed brightly for an instant, and then disappeared with a soundless explosion of light.

He didn't enter right away, but took the time to cast his magic forth once more to be certain, since he now knew that Sotiris had been here. The spell had his stink all over it, but though it confirmed his enemy's presence at some time in the past, it didn't tell him when or for how long. A spell like that, cast by a powerful sorcerer, could last for a century or more. Time was measured differently by those with magic in their veins. Living in the human world like this, it would have made sense to protect the house for that length of time, so that it would be there when they returned with a new identity to suit their human neighbors. Although this house had few neighbors close enough to matter, but there was still the marketplace and whatever town was nearby.

With that in mind, and knowing that Sotiris might well have directed him to this place regardless of whether Antonia had ever been here, Nico took three steps into the house . . . and froze. He'd been wrong, or maybe he'd been right all along, because Antonia *had* been here, recently enough to leave her unique scent in this room. Worried he was wrong, that he was only sensing what he'd so fervently hoped to find, he began a frantic search of every room in the big house. He started with the ground floor, where her scent was so strong in the large sitting room with big windows that looked out on the endless forest, and went from one room to the next, taking time to cleanse his senses upon entering each room to be certain of what he was finding.

Disappointed when he found no trace of her anywhere else on that floor, he climbed the broad stairs to the second floor, determined to find out if his senses were telling him true, or if he was overcome with wishful thinking. Choosing a direction at random, he turned left, walked to the very end of the hallway, and began opening one door after another, intent on checking every room and closet, big or small.

He reached the top of the stairs once again, without finding a trace of Antonia. Once more convinced he'd imagined her scent downstairs, but determined to finish his sweep of the house, he started on the hallway to the right, checking room after room and finding nothing, until he opened the door to a small, sunny bedroom with an unmade bed . . . and was suddenly drowning, not only in her scent, but in the lingering taste of her magic. It was barely recognizable, overlaid with Sotiris's unmistakable taint, but it was Antonia. She'd been in this room. He saw a discarded piece of clothing, a lightweight linen shift, the kind a woman might wear to bed on a warm night. Striding forward, he grabbed the gown from where it lay on the floor and staggered so hard that he had to sit on the bed, before he fell.

The front of the gown was covered with smears of blood. And by all the gods in heaven and hell, it was her blood. Antonia *had* been in this house, *had* slept in this bed, and *had* been wounded so badly that she'd bled.

He knew now what Sotiris had been in such a hurry to do, why he'd tried to delay his taunting message from reaching Nico. He'd needed enough time to reach this remote house and take Antonia away to the gods knew where, before Nico caught up to him. It was the reason he'd left his *gift* of the statues in distant Reims, rather than having it delivered it to Charron's townhouse. He'd probably hoped that the statues and what they represented would break Nico emotionally, throwing him off the hunt, or at least slowing him down.

Taking the gown with him as a reminder if nothing else, he returned to the ground floor, where he sank to the bottom few stairs and, clutching the gown to his chest, leaned against the wall. He was so fucking tired. He couldn't remember his last full night of sleep untroubled by terrifying possibilities, or past nightmares. Was this to be his life now? Racing from one place to the next, only to find himself a day too late? An hour? And all the while he was chasing Sotiris, his warriors were suffering gods knew what horrors.

Fuck. He didn't know what to do next, how to interrupt Sotiris's diabolic plan to torture those who'd dare cross him. Somehow, he had to get a step ahead of Sotiris instead of two steps behind, so he could kill the bastard once and for all and give his people their lives back.

Nearly falling asleep where he sat, despite the next riser digging into his back, Nico walked over to the nearest sofa, and stretching out on its too soft cushions, pulled a woolen throw off the padded back, and surrounded by the scent of Antonia, he slept.

He woke the next morning to the sound of a horse blowing restlessly somewhere outside. Abruptly wide awake, he rolled to the floor and, half-crouching, made his way to one of the big windows that looked out over the front. A carriage stood there, with a pair of chestnut brown horses dancing restlessly at the front. A man in work clothes was removing the harness from one horse at a time, then walked them to a nearby pair of iron posts, with hitching rings on top. As Nico watched, he slid feed bags over the nose of each horse, then leaving the carriage where it stood, walked out of sight, around the house to do whatever he'd come for.

Nico hated to steal another man's horse, but if he left it at a stable in the next town or city, with enough financial incentive and information for the stable's manager, there was a possibility at least that the man could reclaim the animal. And it wasn't as if he'd be stranding the owner at this remote location, since the other horse would still be available to him.

Wanting to be sure before he tried to steal a horse and sneak away, Nico slipped quietly through to the back of the house and peered through the windows there. The man was chopping fat lengths of tree logs into firewood. Nico had seen multiple fireplaces not only on the ground floor, but in the larger rooms upstairs. And since he was currently spying through the kitchen window, he could tell that the pile of wood next to the big kitchen hearth was woefully inadequate.

If the workman was chopping firewood, it might mean that someone was about to visit. Not Sotiris, however. He wouldn't come back, knowing that Nico was likely to have found the place. But the imminent arrival of others might have been another incentive for him to move Antonia someplace else.

And damn but Nico would have loved to know how Sotiris had left this place. Had he cast his next transition spell from right there in the front yard? Or had this man possibly driven him to a nearby city, where he'd been better prepared to undertake travel to another place and time?

Nico could ask the man. A simple truth spell would tell him what he needed to know, and he could make the man forget without harming him in any way. The tricky part would be approaching the workman without frightening him into doing something unwise, like tossing that big fucking ax at Nico.

Deciding he had to find out what he could if he was to have any hope of following Sotiris, he went back to the front of the house and walked around, as if coming from the road. "Good morning!" He realized he was still speaking French, and had no idea if he was still in that country, or had "traveled" somewhere new.

The man stopped working and stared, obviously not expecting casual visitors. "Stop right there," he called. "What do you want?"

Nico walked a few steps closer before he stopped, since distance was a factor when attempting to take over a person's mind without consent. And also, because he didn't understand what the workman had shouted, since it wasn't in French. But neither was it enough for him to make use of the only fortunate aspect of Sotiris's spell, and understand the new language.

"I need answers," he called back, once more in French, but his magic didn't care what language he used, as long as his intent was clear when he followed the words with a whispered spell, which would both ease the man's fears and ensure he would speak truthfully.

The workman went perfectly still for a moment, then shook himself all over, and stared at Nico. "Do I know you?" he asked calmly.

"No, I've just arrived and need you to answer some questions for me."

He nodded slowly. "All right."

Nico walked over, and sitting on a fat log, said, "Let's sit and be comfortable. You can leave your ax there."

"All right." The man lowered the ax to the ground, then came over to sit on the log, a short distance from Nico.

"What's your name?"

"Marlin Padmore."

"What country is this, Marlin?" Nico asked.

He frowned. "The English part of the United Kingdom."

Nico had heard of the country during his stay in Paris, but knew little of it. "What's the nearest city?"

"London."

"Is it a large city?"

"One of the largest in the world, I'd say."

"Thank you," Nico said politely, although it made no difference to Marlin. "Was there a man here recently? He had a young woman with him."

"Yes. Mr. Dell and his daughter."

Sotiris's true last name was "Dellakos," which fit. "What did they do here?"

"The daughter wasn't well. Mr. Dell rented this house hoping the country air would benefit her."

"And did it?"

"I can't say, sir. I rarely saw her."

"When did you last see her?"

"When I drove them up here from London the first time, and then again when they left."

"And when did they leave?"

Marlin seemed to think about it for a moment, then said, "Five days ago, I believe. My mum's been unwell, and the days mix together when I'm staying with her."

Nico didn't need anything more precise, since anything more than a single day undoubtedly put Sotiris and Antonia not only out of his reach, but most likely on the other side of yet another transition.

"Do you remember where you took them?" When the man nodded, he asked, "And where was that?"

"London."

He had a sudden thought. "Can you take *me* there?"

Marlin scowled. "The carriage is for hire, sir, but it's a long journey. It will put me behind on my chopping, which has to be ready before the next renters arrive."

"I understand. Could you hire someone to help you with the wood, so it would go faster?"

"Yes, sir. Though it would cost a fair bit."

"I would pay you for the helper as well as the carriage. Will you take me to the same place in London where you delivered Mr. Dell?"

"Yes, sir."

"Good. When can we leave?"

1824, London, United Kingdom

NICO SAT ON THE driver's bench with Marlin for the entire ride to London, needing conversation in order to learn the language, which was also called "English." Marlin was startled at first, but then happy to have someone to talk with, to make the journey seem faster. They spoke of everything that occurred to Nico, from the kind of trees they were passing, to the expected length of the journey, and Marlin's mother's illness, as well as the rest of his family, which included a wife and three children—a son and two daughters.

By the time Marlin stopped the carriage in front of a hotel that he explained was the best in the city, Nico was confident that his English would pass, not as a native, but as a well-versed foreign visitor. After paying Marlin in gold francs to make it easier for him to exchange for the local currency, Nico alighted from the carriage and strolled into the hotel as if he owned it. He'd learned as a young teenager with an incredibly powerful magical gift that attitude was everything.

Approaching the front desk, he requested a large room, with a private bath, which he now knew was no more usual in hotels and inns in this world, than it would have been in his own. A sudden idea had him eyeing the middle-aged man flipping through a list of available rooms. Applying just enough magic to make the man cooperative, he asked, "Is Mr. Dellakos staying at this hotel? He sometimes calls himself Mr. Dell."

The man glanced up and said, "Mr. Dellakos. Yes, he was. He left this morning."

"Is his room available?"

The look the desk manager gave him this time was shrewd. "He was in a suite. His daughter was with him."

"Yes, so he told me. Is the suite available?"

He flipped the page, and replied, "It is," then quoted the fee for one night, which was ten times the cost of anywhere Nico had stayed thus far.

"Excellent. I'll take the suite then, for two nights. The same suite as Mr. Sotiris," he said, meeting the man's gaze and adding an extra punch of persuasion—essentially compulsion—which Nico rarely used. But this was only for a hotel room, and it was, in any event, critical to finding Antonia.

The suite itself was a pleasant surprise. A much-improved version of his suite at the hotel in Paris, it had a private bath that included hot water on tap. Nico couldn't strip fast enough. The tub was deep and the water so hot that he had to use a touch of magic to cool it somewhat before he could step in. It was marvelous to soak away the days of stress and dirt, but he didn't, *couldn't* truly relax. As he lay there, replaying every step he'd taken, thinking of ways to outthink Sotiris in hopes of catching up to him faster, he also contemplated how much magic it might require, and became aware that he'd been using a great deal of his power since arriving in this country. And after the extraordinary amount of power it had taken to follow Sotiris's transition away from Reims, he knew it would be necessary to somehow recharge his magic before attempting another transition spell.

Deciding to examine the suite for some indication that Sotiris had worked magic in this room, he donned one of the heavy robes provided for guests and began to explore the suite more carefully. He'd known the minute he stepped through the door that the bastard had been there, because the scent of his magic was immediately obvious. Nico was assuming Sotiris would have performed the transition casting some-where in these rooms, for privacy's sake, if nothing else. The magic which remained from that casting, in addition to what Nico already knew about the transition spell, should enable him to duplicate the specific elements Sotiris had used to whisk himself and Antonia away again. But while the scent was unmistakable in the main room, it wasn't until he entered the larger of the two bedrooms, that he found the leftover *taste* of Sotiris's magic. It was so strong that Nico knew, without a doubt, that *this* was where Sotiris had cast the latest transition spell.

But while evidence of Sotiris was everywhere, Nico had found little to indicate Antonia had ever been there . . . until he walked into the tiny second bedroom, and was swamped by a scent that was uniquely hers. The bed was small, but he'd lain down on it anyway, needing the reassurance that no matter what else Sotiris was putting her through, she was alive, and well enough that her magic was still with her. That, in point of fact, her magic seemed stronger in this room, where she'd slept no more than a single night, than it had in the bedroom of the empty house, even though she'd bled in that room not long before leaving.

Frowning, he considered what that might mean. It could be that Sotiris had kept her unconscious, or close to it, until they left the house. There were many ways that a sorcerer of Sotiris's, or Nico's, strength could incapacitate a magic-user with less power. Ways that would keep a prisoner, like Antonia, compliant and cooperative. If her magic was returning, however, the question became whether Sotiris was allowing it, or whether Antonia's magic was strong enough to rally by itself, despite Sotiris's best efforts.

Nico wanted to believe the latter. Antonia had served Sotiris as both researcher and designer of spells, and weapons of war. But the truth was that such activities went against the true nature of her magic. She was smart enough to do the work Sotiris required, but it was her intellect more than her magic that went into those projects. Her magic was of the earth, of growing things, and the preservation of life, not of wars and killing.

So maybe, he thought, Antonia's magic was reasserting itself now that Sotiris wasn't pushing her to use it to serve his needs. And maybe she retained enough of her true self that she instinctively knew to hide that resurgence. Nico thought his logic was sound, but whether or not his assessment of Antonia's magic was accurate, the possibility comforted him, and made him believe that when they were finally reunited, she would still be his Antonia.

With any luck, he would find someplace in London where the magic was strong enough to restore his power to its optimal level. He regretted the delay, but if he tried the transition spell with his own power compromised, he could end up stranded in the wrong place or time. If that happened, he'd have no option, but to try Sotiris's spell multiple times until he happened upon somewhere he knew. If he was lucky, the spell would return him to Paris on the same day he'd originally arrived. That wouldn't be great, but it would be better than circling back to the house outside London over and over again. A mistake like that could cost his warriors their lives. And even if he eventually found the right place, Antonia might have lived and died, without ever knowing he'd spent his life looking for her.

He sighed and rose from the small bed. He'd have preferred to sleep there, surrounded by the essence of Antonia. But it made more sense to sleep in the bigger room, where Sotiris had not only slept, but used his sorcery. As with the hot water in the tub, soaking himself in his enemy's magic would help him identify and dissect the spell he would need to follow the trail to Antonia. He fell asleep thinking of only that, hoping it would direct his unconscious mind to the necessary task.

THE NEXT DAY, Nico was wandering London in search of even a modest magical vector that might have survived the rampant industrialization all around him. He was close to giving up, and was contemplating a visit outside the city. Before leaving the hotel, he'd inquired of the hotel concierge as to places of historic significance. He'd thought a cathedral or palace might retain enough ancient objects or shadowy corners, even, to create small pockets of magic. The concierge had very patiently listed several such places in the city, but had also commented that if Nico wanted truly historic ruins, he should venture into the countryside. He'd also offered to acquire a map and mark those places, to make it easier for him to explore, although he would need a carriage and driver for the journey.

Nico had thanked him, then set off to explore the city, hoping it would provide what he needed. He wanted to leave that night, but if he had to travel away from the city to restore his magic to full strength, it would take more time, and every delay meant a longer head start for Sotiris in hiding both himself and Antonia so thoroughly that Nico wouldn't ever find them.

Finding himself deep in thought, and standing in front of a magnificent cathedral, he climbed the wide stairs and went inside. The elderly priest in Paris had been not only helpful, but knowledgeable about history and his church. Maybe he could find such a priest in this church, too.

Once inside the cathedral, however, he didn't bother looking for a priest. The building echoed with magic, though it was different than what he was used to. The magic in his world had been a natural part of the environment. This magic was more like . . . . He smiled, despite himself. It reminded him of the magic generated by those who'd worshipped his brother Damian as a god of war, because he was so very good at it. The old places in his world had felt the same. Places of such ancient gods, and so many centuries of prayers, that they'd created a magic of their own.

But though it was different, it was still magic, and Nico was a very powerful sorcerer—powerful enough that he could drink in the magic of this cathedral and his own magic would adapt to it. Relieved to have found this place, and more grateful than he could have expressed to the century's worth of worshippers who created such powerful magic, Nico sank onto one of the wooden benches, and let the magic flow.

HE WAITED UNTIL after sunset to make use of Sotiris's spell. The effects on the surrounding area of such a powerful casting were unpredictable, and he didn't want any loud noises or unexpected lightning in the sky or, even worse, in the hotel, to draw attention to his departure. He'd used the time walking back to the hotel after sitting for hours in the cathedral, to search for a quiet spot to disappear, and decided on a narrow road which ran along and above the river. He didn't see any lantern poles, as there'd been in Paris, and thought the area might be both unlit and mostly empty after dark. That should be especially true tonight, he thought, since judging from the previous night, there should be no moon to provide even the slightest illumination.

Having left the hotel carrying his backpack and wearing his workman's clothing, he was about to descend to the river bank, when a pair of men appeared from between two buildings. Nico tensed, prepared to defend himself if necessary, when a third man appeared, dragging a young woman by the arm. Nico slowed. The woman was tiny—not simply short, but with arms so thin that he feared the man would break a bone with his tight hold on her.

"What's this?" he asked, his voice pitched to a bored curiosity.

"Ah, young sir. She is beautiful, yes? So young and fresh. Do you like her?"

Nico shrugged, already seeing where this was going. He didn't hire prostitutes, and wasn't interested in this one, except . . . she didn't appear to be a willing participant in the sale, and that angered him. If a grown woman decided to offer herself for sex, that was her choice. As long as she was treated well and paid fairly, he had no problem with it. But this girl didn't appear to be either fully grown *or* willing.

Drawing closer, he took the girl's arm and pulled her away from her handler.

The man shouted his objection, but the girl said nothing until she was close enough to speak without being overheard by the men. "Please, sir, take me for an hour. It won't cost much, and . . ."

She stilled with a gasp when Nico shot a hard glance down at her, noting the bruise on her cheek, and reddened eyes above smeared makeup, as if she'd been crying. "Did they hurt you?" he asked softly.

"It doesn't matter," she said quickly, turning her face away. "I'll heal."

"You wish to buy her?" The largest of the three men had drawn close while Nico had been talking to the girl. "Ten pounds sterling gets you the entire night. And, young sir," he added sidling even closer, and lowering his voice to a near whisper. "She is vampire. If she bites, it is heaven. And if you strike her, no matter how many times, she will heal. You understand?"

Nico froze. He didn't let go of the girl, but turned his stare on the three men, looking for signs that they, too, were vampires. The night was too dark to see much, but the one who'd spoken had his lips pulled back in a leer to reveal a definite pair of fangs. And while the others said nothing, he noted for the first time that they carried no torch or lantern, and yet moved easily through the deep shadows between the buildings. Even he, with his sorcerer's enhanced night vision, couldn't see more than a foot or two into that darkness.

Switching focus, he drew the girl closer and studied her pixie-like features. She lowered her eyes, as if ashamed at what he would see. "Are you a vampire?" he asked.

Her response was whispered so faintly that he only heard because he saw her lips move. "Yes."

"How long?"

That startled her into looking up at him for a moment, before immediately lowering her head again. "A few months. Or so I believe. Time is . . . difficult to remember."

Nico frowned. Time loss wasn't something he'd learned from his recent vampire studies. He wondered if it was common to all vampires, or unique to this one girl. Or was it the result of having been captured and forcibly made a vampire at such a young age? He lifted his gaze to the talkative male. "How old is she? When was she turned?"

The vampire shrugged. "Our master took her to his bed, and made her a woman first—" He snickered when saying that. "—and then a vampire, perhaps four months ago. As for her age? She is old enough to have breasts. That is enough, no?"

He gave the vampire a dark look, wishing he could kill all three males and set the girl free. But she wouldn't remain free for long, he knew. None of these vampires were her master—the one who controlled her. If these three were killed, the master would call her back to his side and simply send her out with someone else. Or decide she was too much trouble, and kill her.

"Look at me, girl," he demanded, and waited until she raised pale blue eyes filled with fear. "Did you ask to be made vampire? Did you go willingly to his bed?"

Her eyes widened, going from fear to something close to terror as her gaze swung to the three men.

"Never mind," Nico said immediately. He didn't need her to say the words. Her fear told him the whole story. "I'll take her," he told the vampires, and dug ten pounds from the small purse on his belt. Then, gently holding her slender arm, he tugged her to his other side, so that he stood between her and the three vampires. "For the night," he reminded them.

"Yes, of course," the talkative one crooned. "But she must return before dawn, you understand."

"I understand. Should I bring her here?"

"This will do."

"Good. Enjoy the rest of your evening." He turned his back on the vampires, and still holding the girl's arm, got her moving alongside him.

Once they were far enough away that he was assured the vampires couldn't overhear, he put an arm around the girl's waist to steady her and asked, "What's your name?"

She gave him a startled look.

"Your real name," he clarified. "I won't hurt you."

She studied his face, as if those pale eyes could see into his soul. "No," she said so softly that he had to bend closer to hear. "I don't believe you will. My name is Lilia."

"How old are you, Lilia?"

"Seventeen, I think. Though I don't know for sure, as my mother died when I was small."

"Fuck," he whispered. He knew what he had to do. He also knew it might be a huge mistake. But he was reminded of his conversation with the master vampire about souls—who did or didn't have one. And his comment about Greyson having died a horrible death.

What if Nico had been wrong? What if the vampires in this world were as human as he was? He was a sorcerer, and while that had been normal in his world, it wasn't here. In this world, he wasn't any more "normal" than Greyson had been. Or even the master vampire. And what about this young girl, who could only *think* she was seventeen, because no one alive remembered her birth? Was she a bloodsucking monster? Or a child who'd been caught up in something she'd never asked for, only to find herself sold on the street like meat.

He looked into those clear eyes, and saw no evil, only more questions. He sighed. What the hell? He could take her with him. At least, he thought he could. He was powerful enough to protect her during the transition. And if it worked, and they both landed in the same place and time, then he'd have someone who'd shared at least this part of his unusual history. And moreover, someone who could live as long as he did and share whatever came next. Not as a wife or a lover. He neither wanted, nor needed, that. But as a friend . . . and a witness.

"I'm leaving London tonight," he told her. "Would you like to come with me?"

"Tonight? You would take me where you're going?"

"Yes. I don't require sex from you, don't worry about that. But where I'm going . . . it might be frightening for you. But I'm—" He hesitated then thought, hell, if she was a vampire, why couldn't he admit to being a sorcerer. "I'm a sorcerer, Lilia. I'll keep you safe no matter what happens."

She took two steps away from him, head bent, as if considering what he'd said. When she stopped, she turned and looked back at him, meeting his gaze without fear. "This city holds nothing good for me. Only more danger. I will go with you."

Nico's soul lightened unexpectedly. "You have courage, Lilia. It will serve you well in the coming years."

PART THREE

Chapter One

1963, Chicago, Illinois, USA

ANTONIA WOKE TO sunshine filling the room on a beautiful spring morning. She hated the isolation of Chicago winters, that trapped her in the house, with nothing but her precious greenhouse plants to keep her company, while others waited in the frozen ground for the sun to return. She'd have sworn she could *feel* every one of her trees and shrubs, and even the hibernating bulbs of her perennial flowers, all warm and cozy and waiting.

She'd never have said such a thing out loud, lest the neighbors think she'd gone mad in solitude, or at the very least, become eccentric—like old man Conroy down the block, who sat on his porch and yelled at every car that drove by at what he considered too fast a speed.

She stretched her arms over her as she sat up, and decided she didn't care about the neighbors or Mr. Conroy. She wasn't going to entertain any negative thoughts this morning. She'd rested well, with no strange or frightening dreams to trouble her sleep, and her mind felt clear and refreshed. She had a list of chores she wanted to accomplish on this sunny day, because tonight, for the first time ever, she was entertaining a gentleman guest.

Antonia wasn't altogether sure how old she was. She was strong enough to spend a day in the garden, digging and planting, without aching for days afterward. And she always walked to the grocery to do her shopping, carrying the bags home herself, rather than relying on a delivery boy. Her *father* said she was twenty-six, and that age seemed to match what she saw in the mirror, as well as pictures of other people in the magazines she read. But she wasn't altogether sure about the man who told her how old she was, who visited rarely, and who had until recently managed her accounts and paid her bills . . . . She grimaced, thinking about it. She just wasn't convinced that man was her father.

For one thing, she should have some feelings for him, shouldn't she? Everyone she knew had feelings for their parents, if they had them.

Sometimes the feeling was hate, or intense dislike, rather than love. But hate was an emotion. On the other hand, when her father—if he was that—visited, she felt almost nothing. And what she *did* feel leaned more toward the intense dislike end of the spectrum. Goodness, she had warmer feelings for the checkout clerk at the grocery than she did for her father.

She got up, brushed her teeth, and washed her face, then pulled on what she considered to be her work clothes. She kept her house clean, and she was by nature a tidy person, but she wanted everything to be perfect for her date. It still felt odd to call this evening a date, but what else was it? Mr. Boyd had been her attorney as long as she could remember, though he'd been a very junior partner the first time she'd met him, which had been soon after her move to Chicago. The move had been her father's idea, though he'd never lived in the house they had been meant to share. She managed her finances now, paid her own bills, and took care of the mortgage, along with all the other expenses that came with owning a house. The money to do all of that came from a trust fund in her name that had been established by her maternal grandmother, and had become hers to manage when she'd turned twenty-three. Before that, the income from the trust had gone through Mr. Boyd's law firm, as managing trustees.

She herself had no memories of buying the house, or even of moving into it. Her father said it was because she'd been in a terrible accident and had suffered a severe concussion, which had taken every memory she'd had before then . . . including any recollection of her grandmother or even her mother who, according to her father, had died in the same accident. But though he also insisted she and her mother had been very close, she didn't have a single photograph of them together, or even one of her mother alone.

"Stop," she scolded. She had the bad habit of dwelling on matters she couldn't change. She might never recover the memories she'd lost. And while she had a deep conviction that her mother had loved her, she never spoke of it, especially not to her father. He became agitated whenever she asked or even mentioned the past, and she'd learned to avoid it altogether. Which, considering he rarely visited, didn't require much effort.

It was much healthier for her to focus on the present, which she did now as she looked over her menu for the evening, double-checked to be sure she had all the ingredients she needed, then pulled out the vegetables and began chopping. It was something she could do well in advance, to make the night's preparation go more smoothly.

Mr. Boyd was very handsome, in addition to being kind and oddly charming, and he'd been patiently courting her for over a year, before she'd finally invited him to dinner. Until now, they'd met only at parties associated with his law office, and had never been alone, except for a single moment during the New Year's party this year, when midnight had struck and he'd kissed her. Her cheeks still flushed at the memory, though their lips had barely touched.

That touch, though, the brush of his lips on hers, had triggered something in her brain, as if she *had* kissed someone before, but had lost the memory of it, along with all the others. Though she'd asked her father about anyone she'd dated in the past, he'd dismissed the idea, telling her she'd attended a private, girls' preparatory school, and that there'd been no contact with boys at all, much less any dating.

She wanted to believe him. But just as she wondered why she didn't at least like him, if he was her father, she also held that deep conviction that there was more to her past than her father knew. Or was willing to tell her.

"Stop it." She scolded herself out loud this time. Whatever the truth about her mother, her schooling, or anything else from her past, it no longer mattered. She had a date this evening with a handsome man who laughed at her jokes, who discussed serious matters of finance, and even politics, with her, and who seemed to value her opinion. She was lucky to have survived the accident that had killed her mother, and she intended to make the most of the life she had.

Chapter Two

Present day, Pompano Beach, Florida

NICK LEANED BACK, his legs stretched out in front of him, and soaked in a scene he'd never thought to see again. His warriors sat around him in the big living room at the back of the house, all of them alive and healthy and free. It hadn't been easy for any of them, not even when their curses had finally been lifted, and they'd been released, one by one, from the stone prisons that had trapped them for millennia. But even then, they'd continued to fight, emerging only to find themselves caught up in the ongoing war against Sotiris, the same sorcerer who'd cursed them in another world so long ago.

But today wasn't for memories or regret. Today was the first time in all those centuries, the first time in this world, that Nick and his four warriors could sit together, could share a drink and after all the horror, could laugh. That the four amazing women who'd made this day possible sat next to them was a miracle in itself. They were the ones who'd freed each warrior from his curse, and then remarkable as it was, they'd fallen in love, and *joined* their warriors in the battle against Sotiris. They sat now with their warrior mates and lovers, quiet or laughing according to their personality, and all of them now a part of the family Nick had thought lost to him forever in another world, another time.

Damian's phone chimed where he sat next to Nick. He glanced at it, then slapped Nick's shoulder and stood. "Come on, dinner just arrived, and I'm starving."

Everyone rose at the same time, but Nick raised his voice, stopping them when they would have trooped out to get the table ready and let the delivery guy through the gate with their food.

"Just one more thing," he reminded them. "We have a huge advantage, now that chance and Maeve's curiosity—he smiled at the quiet woman who sat so close to Dragan—have returned the hexagon to where it belongs, to *us*, to those who fight *against* Sotiris. Its creator never intended it to be displayed under glass for Sotiris to gloat over. It was designed and built at immeasurable personal cost for one purpose only—to destroy Sotiris. And I will *not* let that sacrifice be in vain.

"All of us are finally together again," he continued. "He can no longer hold your lives as blackmail to get what he wants, to hobble our efforts. *We* are the hunters now, and *he* is the prey."

There was still no rousing cheer, because there was still no victory, but there were subdued kisses from the women, hugs and claps on the back from the men. Until Damian's phone chimed again, reminding them that dinner awaited.

Nick lingered after the others left, wanting a few more minutes before he joined the others, a few more minutes to remember the one person who was still missing from all this. The one who might have made their future victory possible. He sighed, and was about to rise, when he looked up to find Maeve standing on the other side of the coffee table with a laptop case under her arm. It almost made him smile. The damn computer was attached to her hip. But she was good on it. No question of that.

"Nick? Can I show you something?" her voice was soft, her manner hesitant, but she stood her ground and met his gaze evenly. "I've found something that I think might be important. Something I think you should see."

Nico had been feeling sad, and maybe more than a little sorry for himself, but he smiled and waved a hand in invitation to Dragan's mate. "Of course. Join me."

She walked over and sat next to him on the couch, placing her laptop between them. While unzipping the computer case, she explained. "When we were going through the files I copied from Sotiris's computer, Lili found something interesting. It was in the trash can—on the computer, I mean—an email that had been read and deleted. Lili said it had nothing to do with Sotiris, and to let it go, but—" she shrugged. "I'm not very good at letting things go."

Maeve had been Sotiris's assistant before she'd saved Dragan from his stone prison, and then stolen the hexagon from Sotiris's showcase in the moments before they'd made their escape. Her inside knowledge of Nico's greatest enemy had proven priceless more than once, and he was inclined to trust whatever instinct or intuition she thought worth mentioning. Right now, her head was bent over the case, but she looked up through her lashes, waiting for him to comment. When he only waited for her to explain, having no idea what she was talking about, she continued.

"Anyway, last night I needed something to turn off my brain, and the email was still sitting there, pinned to the top of my inbox, so I did a little searching. Long story short . . ." She took a small square of paper from the inside compartment of her laptop case and handed it to him.

Nico glanced at what she'd written on the paper, not knowing what to expect. But what he found had him staring in wordless shock. It was only two lines, but it was the most important two lines of his life.

He read, "*Antonia Rosales,*"and on the second line, an address. Gods save him, an *address*. He'd spent a thousand lifetimes searching for any sign of her, had almost given up more times than he could count. And she'd been found by such a slim chance. There were so many ways this could have been lost. *Antonia* could have been lost.

He didn't join the rest of his family for dinner. He ran, instead, to his office to call the airlines. And the next morning, he flew to Chicago to discover just how much the fates had been willing to hold onto for him.

Chapter Three

Chicago, Illinois, present day

NICK DROVE ALONG the wide streets of an upscale Chicago suburb, barely noticing the graceful curves, the long lawns, and elegant mansions behind gates of every size and design.

He watched the house numbers flash by, though he didn't need them. Antonia's magic had been diminished, but she would still be who she'd always been. Born of magic, *with* magic. She didn't need great power, or the ability to cast spells to be what she was. Every bit of her being—body and soul—was intrinsically magical.

He was nervous when he left his car and climbed the few stairs to a wide front porch, the door framed in gracious plants that spoke of someone who understood what made a plant thrive, and offered a warm welcome. He rang the bell and wondered if that welcome would still include him.

The door opened, and she stood there, a figure out of his dreams. Her dark beauty was as stunning as ever, her warm brown eyes just a little cautious, and more than a little startled until he spoke to her and they filled with tears.

"I found you," he said simply. And walked into her arms.

TWO HOURS LATER, Nick tightened his arms around Antonia where they lay on the couch together. He was so hungry for the warmth of her flesh, the sweet scent of her hair—simple things that he'd feared he'd never have again. None of it was quite real to him yet. He was more than half-convinced that he'd wake up and find it had all been a dream. That Antonia was still lost to him, while he scoured the world, never finding her.

His saying the words, "I found you," had broken the spell which, until then, had kept her from remembering most of what she'd known of their world, and everything about him specifically. Neither one of them had known that a specific phrase was even required, much less what it was. Nick was haunted by what might have followed if he hadn't just happened to say those *specific* words. Would she have been lost to him, to her own memories, for another century or two? Could even Sotiris have been *that* cruel?

Antonia reached her hand around to caress his neck. "He'll never get between us again, my love. I'll kill him first."

"*I'll* kill him," he growled, resisting the idea that she might endanger herself on a task that he was, quite bluntly, better qualified to execute. Ha, good choice of words.

"I can get closer to him than you can," she said.

"I've been plenty close to him over the last few years. We've battled more than once, and he's run every time. Besides, I don't trust your safety anywhere near that monster."

"He trusts me more than . . . . No that's not right. He doesn't trust me, but he's become used to the me he created, the one who's lived where he put me for so long."

"He'll know the curse is lifted. He won't expect you to be that person anymore."

"No, but if I play it right, he might believe that I'm not myself yet, either. That the shock was so much that I didn't believe what you told me, and threatened to call the police."

"And I ran?" he asked dryly.

"And you left, rather than see me so upset."

Nick rolled his eyes, but said, "Fine. Then, we'll kill him together." He'd meant it as a jest, but as soon as he said it, he knew it was true. They *would* kill Sotiris, but they wouldn't be doing it alone. His warriors, and their mates, would want a piece of their tormentor's flesh.

Nick reined in his anger, reminding himself that the nightmare hadn't come to pass, that by some freak chance he *had* said the right words. Antonia's memories of her life, both *before* and after the curse, had come roaring back in a flood of image and emotion, and only his arms had kept her from falling. She'd been shocked to the point of passing out by the overload of memory and sensation. Nick had scooped her up and carried her to the couch, and they hadn't moved since, other than to tighten their embrace and combine their magic to weave an impenetrable web of protection around the house.

Sotiris was sure to sense the collapse of his curse soon, if he hadn't already, and it would be just like the evil bastard to attempt a fresh curse that would cast them away from each other once more.

The incredible serendipity of *how* Nick had found her—through the determined efforts of a computer geek who'd found Antonia without even knowing who it was she'd been looking for. And then to find her in Chicago—a city Nick had visited a hundred times or more, without ever knowing Antonia was close. He'd always known the fates were capricious bitches, but this . . . . If he'd had the power, he'd have strangled every one of them with his own hands . . . even if, in the end, they'd delivered her to his arms.

"How long have you been here?" Nick asked her on that thought, regretting that he had to lift his mouth from her hair to do so. "Have you been living in Chicago the whole time?"

It had taken them a while to speak of serious matters, to ask where they'd been and what had happened in all the time they'd been apart. He'd related his story first, since it was longer and more complicated, and also because he remembered every day of it, though he didn't know if that was an advantage or not. He'd started with the day of that final, fateful battle in their own world, and worked up to his arrival, with Lili, in what was then the post-colonial United States.

"To answer your question," she said, "my only sure memories are of this city, and mostly this house, which together go back a little more than sixty years, as far as I can figure. That's a lifetime for some."

"How did you endure it?"

"How did *you*? You've lived centuries, aware of what you'd lost for every minute of your life. There is enough magic in my blood that my life might eventually equal several average human lifespans. But had you not found me today, I would have lived all that time without ever knowing what I'd lost, much less suffering for it."

Her words were a knife to his heart, and his arms tightened around her, as if to protect her from a future that now would never happen. "Were you ever aware of who you were? Or did he provide a reasonable fiction of your history? As you say, many humans don't live to be seventy, and none without aging. How did you think it was possible for you to do so? Who did you believe you were? And did you—?" He'd been about to ask if she'd loved anyone during that long time, or if she'd married. But he couldn't make his brain shape the words. Not when his own sexual exploits had only gotten wilder as time went on, and were nothing to be proud of.

"I knew I was unusual, of course," she said slowly. "But I believed it to be an inherited trait. And until today, I was only aware of living one life. I had no memories of moving from place to place, and certainly not through time. Sotiris visited often when I first moved into this house. I think now that he must have been testing to see how much I remembered. His visits became sporadic after a while, and it's been a few years since I've seen him. We had an argument last time he was here. I was remembering more, having dreams of other people and places, and demanding answers. When he refused to give them to me, I ordered him out of my life and set a ward on the house denying him permission to enter." She laughed. "He was so furious. I don't think he realized until that moment that my magic had not just survived whatever he'd tried to do, but that it had continued to improve, despite the pitiful levels of magic in this world. You must have noticed that."

"I did. As did my warriors."

"Your warriors." Her eyes went wide with excitement. "Your warriors? Sotiris didn't tell me what he'd done to them, only that they'd wish for death. They *survived*? But how are they *still* alive?"

"Sotiris designed a special curse for them, one meant to torture me as well, although my pain was nothing compared to theirs. He cast them into the same maelstrom of time and place that he used to escape with you. Except with his own escape, the transition spell included a target destination, to the extent that such a thing can ever be counted on. My warriors, on the other hand, were trapped in stone effigies of themselves, aware of everything around them, but unable to let anyone know they were alive. They spent centuries buried in abandoned ruins or museum basements, as garden adornments or rooftop statues, weathering year after year with no end in sight."

He had to pause, to avoid screaming at the thought of the horrors his brothers had endured. "That they survived, all four of them, with their minds and bodies intact is incredible, and a testament to their strength and courage."

"How did you find them?"

"They found *me*. And when you're ready, I'll take you to meet them." He hesitated, then added, "I want to take you home, Antonia. To *my* home in Florida, I mean. I can protect you better there, and Damian and Casey . . . . You remember Damian? He's one of my warriors. And Casey is the one who broke his curse and freed him. She's his wife now. They're in Florida, too, and live very close."

"But all four of them are alive," she whispered. "Oh, Nico, that's wonderful. And what about Lilia, the young vampire you took with you when you left London? She must still be alive, too. Does she visit?"

"Lilia, or Lili as we call her now, works and lives in my house, which doubles as the headquarters for the work I do for the FBI."

Antonia burst out laughing. "Nico, my love, I know *you*, and I know what the FBI does. I don't believe that *you* would work for any government bureaucracy, much less the FBI."

"I didn't say I work *for* them," he said, unreasonably peeved. "I work *with* them. And only loosely at that. The work I do serves their interests, and so they grant me their imprimatur of authority to expedite that work. They also serve up the occasional freshly-trained FBI agent when I need one to work for me."

She stared at him in disbelief. "By the Goddess, what do you *do?*"

"Mostly I locate and . . . *obtain,* by means lawful or otherwise, dangerous magical artifacts, which have fallen into the wrong hands, usually out of ignorance. But in too many cases, they've been acquired by people, like Sotiris, who intend to use them with nefarious intent."

"I imagine your methods and those of the FBI differ rather dramatically."

He grinned. "In this case, they're more interested in the ends rather than the means. I do my thing, they do theirs, and never the twain shall meet."

"All this time, and you haven't changed who you are at the core." She smiled in fond bemusement, and cupped his face in both hands. "What did you want to ask me, love? I saw it on your face, before you wiped it clean."

"It doesn't matter. Not anymore."

She studied him. "You've told me everything that happened to you after . . . *everything.* And now you want to know about *my* life. You want to know if, in all this time, I've loved anyone."

"Damn it, Antonia. How do you do that?"

"Because I know you," she whispered, then kissed his mouth softly. "Have I loved? Yes. Have I married? No. Even though I couldn't remember you, I knew you existed . . . knew in my heart that someone already lived there, and there was no room for anyone else."

Nick bowed his head, hiding the tears of shame that filled his eyes. He'd loved her forever, but living with the dwindling belief that he'd ever find her again, he'd strayed from his intent to remain true, and fucked his way through the world, instead.

"Nico," she said softly. "My love. You are not a man to live alone, no matter how much you longed to find me. I told you that I loved. Why would you be different, when you *lived* every day of so many more years? Sotiris sent me to this place no more than a century ago, though I don't even remember all of *that.* But your story is far longer, and far more

249

lonely. Tell me, does it matter to you that I loved someone else?"

His head snapped up. "No. I didn't know where or when Sotiris had hidden you, but wherever it was, or however much time had passed, I never wanted you to be alone. We may be magical creatures, you and I, but we are fully human when it comes to needing contact with others. We are not meant to live alone and isolated."

"Then why would I expect you to live that way?"

He sighed. "I didn't love, I fucked. One woman after another, none coming close to touching my heart. Because I didn't want them to."

"Never? There was no one in all those years?"

"There was one who came close. We loved each other, but I think we only permitted that much because both of us feared commitment."

"What was her name, if you don't mind telling me."

"Cyn."

"Sin? Who would give that name to their daughter?"

"Cynthia, actually."

"That makes sense, then. Was she beautiful?"

He chuckled. "I didn't ask about *your* love. But, you should know . . . she's still alive. And, yes, she's beautiful. Though that wasn't what drew me to her. It was . . ." He paused, thinking. "She doesn't have magic— not the way we think of it—but she draws it to her. The first time we met was at a reception of some kind—a political fundraiser, I think. I still make a point of knowing who governs what, since too often, it's politicians who seek magical means of achieving power. I can't tell you how many artifacts my people have retrieved from them."

"That's not hard to believe. I may not have remembered most of my history, but I followed current events during the time I *did* know. And while our own world may have been bloodier, I'm not sure their world is any better."

Nick found it interesting that after living so long among humans, she still spoke in terms of "theirs vs ours."

"So tell me," she persisted. "What happened to your Cyn?"

"We . . . dated, I guess. I live in Florida, she lives in California. Whenever I was in her area, we'd sometimes have a drink or a meal, but mostly we just fucked. It worked for both of us. Or it did, until she met that damn vampire."

"A vampire?" Antonia laughed. "Oh, Nico, that is so karmic. Even you must see it."

"Yeah, yeah. I offered to kill him for her once, after he broke her heart."

"Oh, no." She sounded genuinely distressed. "I hope she let you."

"Nah. He saw the light and came crawling back. I ended up helping her save his life, for fuck's sake. They're still together. He's very big in vampire circles."

"Really? What's his name? I have too much time on my hands, and gardening only uses up so much of it. I read a lot, including gossip magazines. They occasionally manage to grab a picture of a big vampire or two."

Nick didn't want to tell her, because he *knew* Raphael was one of the vamps that magazines loved to feature. But if he didn't, Antonia would think he still carried a torch for Cyn, which wasn't true. The only woman he'd ever truly loved was sitting next to him. "Raphael," he said.

"Well, goodness, Nico. You should have led with that. I probably have a magazine with his picture in it somewhere." She gasped. "I bet there's one with his mate, too." She gasped again, louder. "Is that Cyn?" At his nod, she laughed and said, "Oooh, I'll have to look."

"Not unless your old boyfriend is a movie star that I can ogle."

"No movie stars for me. Just a lawyer." She leaned close enough to nuzzle his jaw and murmur, "And law just doesn't compare to magic, my love."

He pulled her into his lap. "Magic or no, there has only ever been one woman I truly love."

"Then make love to me, Nico. I've waited long enough."

Chapter Four

THEY REMOVED THEIR clothes in a frenzy, with him helping her at the end, since she was wearing more. But when they were both finally naked, and she lay in his arms, her head on his chest, he didn't know what to do. "You're so beautiful," he whispered.

She stroked his chest. "So are you."

Nick just held her, feeling awkward about sex for the first time in his life. He wasn't used to having sex with someone he loved. Though it wasn't only that. He still couldn't believe that Antonia was in his arms. That this wasn't just another cruel dream that he'd wake up from any minute. He had the strange urge to pinch himself to be sure.

"Ow!" He stared down at Antonia, whose fingers had just pinched his side hard enough to bruise.

"I'm not some fragile treasure, Nicodemus. I am the woman I've always been."

"But you're not. I mean, yes, you are, but you haven't . . . it's been a long time. You don't know what I've—"

"Nico, my love. For me, for my memories, a single day has passed since we were last together. My body is older, and no man has been in my bed. But that doesn't mean I've forgotten how it feels to have you inside me, how natural it is when we join our bodies."

"I'll go slowly, then."

"I appreciate that. But not too slowly."

He stared at her for a moment, then rolling her to her back next to him, he slid his hands up her arms to her wrists. Lifting them above her head, he pressed her hands against the iron bars of her headboard. "Keep them there," he whispered.

Her dark eyes widened in surprise, but she wrapped her fingers around a curve of iron, then said, "I trust you."

Nick could feel her heart racing against his chest when he bent down to give her a deep, tongue twisting kiss, which left her breathless, her gaze locked on his. Biting her lip just enough to be felt, he began a slow slide down her body. He lingered at her neck, nibbling the soft skin, then dropped his mouth to the swell of her breasts, licking first one, then the other, drawing a groan from her when he slid his tongue slowly over each nipple. He was tempted to take his time there, to suckle her pretty nipples, maybe even bite.

But remembering how long it had been for her, no matter what she said about memories, he slid his hands to her hips, and laid a line of brushing kisses below her breasts, down her abdomen to her pubic bone, where he lingered again, laying teasing strokes of his tongue down to the edge of her inner thighs and back again.

Antonia arched against him, her hands gripping the iron bars so tightly that he knew she was fighting the desire to reach for him. It made his cock harder than it already was, and when she moaned softly and spread her legs so that her bent knees fell open to bare her pussy, he had to close his eyes and beg for strength.

Raising his eyes up to meet hers, he managed to shake his head, then slid down far enough that when he turned his head to one side, his mouth met the tender flesh of her inner thigh. He kissed the warm, soft skin, and let his wet tongue glide up and down her thigh, before kissing some more. And then bit her flesh, barely enough to sting, but enough that she cried out in surprise more than pain. Licking away the tiny hurt, he kissed the mark of his teeth on her pale skin, then turned to the other thigh and did the same.

"Nico," she whispered, pleading for something, but not asking him to stop.

Smiling against a thigh still wet from his kiss, he slipped both thumbs between the swollen folds of her sex, spread her inner lips, then bent and slid his tongue in a long, slow caress through the honey-sweet juices of her opening. Once, twice, and then up to her clit, which made her gasp. Letting go of the bars, she gripped his hair in strong fingers.

Not minding the slight tug on his hair, Nico circled around and around the blood-swollen nub, feathering its edges, but never licking it fully, teasing her right to the edge of orgasm and gliding away, over and over, until he could feel the growing heat of her pussy against his jaw, could smell the sweet honey of her arousal, and knew if he licked her now, she'd be wet and open, waiting for him.

Antonia suddenly fisted his hair tighter, and with a cry, tried to shove his head lower, pushing his mouth where she needed it so badly.

Nick immediately lifted his head and met her eyes with a flat stare, until she hissed a curse at him, then gripped both hands around the iron headboard once more. He stared a moment longer, and when she opened her mouth to protest, he slapped her ass cheek lightly and growled, "You asked for it, darling."

"I hate you," she snapped.

He laughed and bent his mouth to her clit until he felt her body begin to tremble in orgasm. Sliding one finger into her pussy, he felt her sheath clench and withdrew, only to slide the finger back in. Her hips flexed slightly, forcing his single digit deeper, and when he withdrew this time, it was to shove two fingers deep inside, making her cry out when her inner muscles squeezed hard, trying to hold on as he slowly, seductively glided his fingers out, then in again, perversely slowing down when she begged him to go "faster."

Continuing the leisurely movements, he began torturing her clit with his tongue once more, repeating his grazing touches on the swollen cluster of nerves, while Antonia gasped for air, breathing faster and faster, her muscles rigid as she fought to follow his instruction not to move.

"Nico!" she finally sobbed, begging him to release her.

As if that was what he'd been waiting for, and maybe it was, he sucked her clit hard between his lips, closed his teeth over the engorged bit of flesh, and when Antonia screamed, he pulled the two fingers out and added a third, pushing them deep into her pussy and out again, his knuckles slick with the hot juices of her, as he readied her for his cock.

Lifting his head, he met her frantic gaze while lapping the juices from his fingers, slicking them down and through the creamy slit of her sex, then up once more to his mouth, where she watched him lick them clean of her arousal before pushing inside her once more.

Antonia was moaning in an almost continuous orgasm, her inner muscles trembling around his fingers, until even the firm muscles of her thighs shivered against his head. Gazing up the length of her body, he saw that her hands, bloodless and white, still gripped the headboard.

"Such a good girl," he whispered. Then bracing on his knees, he fisted his aching dick, fit it to her flushed and gaping pussy, and slid deep inside her. His cock was thicker than the sheath of her body, and though he'd made sure she was ready for him, her inner muscles still clamped tight around him, as her climax continued to ripple through her pussy, flexing and releasing while he pushed. Finally, his body was flush against hers, and his cock could go no deeper.

Not wanting to pound in and out of her, the way his body wanted, he lifted her to a sitting position on his thighs, and filled his mouth with her lovely pale breasts and swollen nipples. Pulling back just enough, he gazed down, and found himself unreasonably pleased by the careful bite marks he'd left on her white skin, and the blood-swollen jut of her dark rose nipples. She was his Antonia—beautiful, brilliant, and *his* forever.

No more fucking lawyers, no matter how boring she might find them.

When he was satisfied with the clear marks of his possession all over her breasts, and pleased with the knowledge that they wouldn't fade before he had a chance to renew his claim, he slid her back to the mattress and with her long legs around his hips, gave her what her body, and his, were begging for.

Nick drove himself so deep inside her that she gave a shocked gasp when his cock brushed her cervix. Pulling out, not wanting to hurt her, he slowed his thrusts again, moving in and out, again and again, until she was so slick and wet, her body so open to him, that he was sliding balls deep with every thrust, while her gasps had become breathy moans of need.

And with every hungry moan, his own desire grew until the need to climax was an urgent demand low in his body, a hot tightening of erotic pain in his balls that made him desperate for release. Sliding his hand between her thighs, until his fingers found her clit, he pinched hard.

When Antonia screamed into a hard orgasm, he finally released his own climax in a liquid rush down his cock and deep into her body, filling her at last with his heat.

Eyes closed in pure ecstasy, overwhelmed by the erotic hum through every inch of his body, he slid his cock lazily in and out of her, heightening the delicious sensation of her inner muscles caressing his penis. He could continue this slow fucking all night long.

But as his senses returned, he became aware of Antonia's thighs trembling around him, and pulled out slowly, then eased down to lie next to her on the bed. Her hair was a sweat-soaked tangle down her back when she turned on her side and placed a hand on his chest. Her face was flushed, as damp as her hair, and tear tracks were leaving pale streaks down her cheeks.

"Antonia?" He cursed, thinking he'd hurt her, but she only smiled, her eyes still closed.

"I know," she murmured. "You warned me."

"Did I—?"

"Hurt me? You would never do that, my beautiful Nico. No, I feel wooooonderful."

Nick bit his cheek to keep from laughing in relief.

Cracking one eye open, as she snuggled against him, she looked up and said, "Don't feel too smug, my love. Your turn is coming."

"Oh!" Making no attempt to conceal his anticipation, he said, "That sounds promising."

She made a half-hearted effort to slap his chest, but managed no more than a light pat, before she was sound asleep, her breathing a soft whisper in and out.

The sound, and the sensation of her warm naked body next to his, gave Nico an overwhelming feeling of peace—something he'd never felt before. Not in all the centuries he'd lived. He lay there a while longer, just *feeling,* then closed his eyes, checked the protective wards already in place, added another one, just to be sure, and with a final scan of the house and surroundings for danger, he fell asleep next to the love of his life.

IT WAS EARLY THE next morning when Nick finally woke. His first act, even before fully opening his eyes, was to check the wards and scan the neighborhood for danger, just as he had before going to sleep. Sotiris had to have felt the release of Antonia's curse, by now, and if nothing else, he would likely come to Chicago to see for himself what had caused the collapse. The only question was whether Antonia preferred to wait to confront him, or whether she'd agree to fly to Florida with Nico today.

He knew which option he'd rather take, but one way or the other, a decision needed to be made and soon, so that he could gather his warriors for what Nico was determined would be the final battle against their enemy. Because no matter *where* they ended up fighting, he was going to kill Sotiris this time. He would surrender his own life before he permitted Antonia to spend even one more day under the bastard's thumb.

"What are you thinking about so seriously," she whispered, as she scooted under his arm and smoothed a soft hand over his chest.

"I like to review the previous day's events as soon as I'm awake, to bring myself up to date, and make note of any leftover issues."

"And what did you decide?"

Smiling, he rolled her beneath him. "That I need to be inside you again."

She purred in welcome and spread her legs around his hips, pulling him closer into her embrace. "I hoped you'd say that."

He went slowly anyway, knowing that although her pussy was hot and slick, she'd be tender after what they'd already done. She sighed a soft moan which wrapped around him like a sweet balm, reminding him that she was real, and in his arms, and that he'd never let go of her again. He slid carefully deeper, lingering for a moment to enjoy the flutter of her inner muscles, before withdrawing until only the tip of his cock remained inside her.

Antonia arched beneath him, hips flexing against his in pleasure, as if wanting every inch of her to touch every inch of him. Her eyes were closed, her mouth slightly open, her teeth pressed into her lower lip. She gave a throaty moan, then whispered, "Nico. My Nico."

He was ashamed to feel tears pressing against the back of his eyes. He was just so happy—so damned happy—after so long, wondering if he'd find her, wondering why he persisted, and then fearing that even if he did find her, she'd have moved on, had a life without him, a husband and children, grandchildren even.

But instead, she was here with him, having waited all this time despite never really knowing who or what she waited for, proving if anything could, that they were meant to be together, and now, always would be.

Antonia cried out as her pussy suddenly clenched around him. Her hips rose again to meet his, her muscles tightening around him as she sank her teeth into his shoulder. Nick had to grin at that. It seemed he wasn't the only one who felt the need to mark his territory. His grin fled when her abdominal muscles spasmed and her body clamped down so tightly around his cock that he couldn't move. She was saying his name over and over again, a warm whisper against his skin, her legs linked behind his back, while her heels dug into his ass.

He tried to pull out, wanted to fuck her, but couldn't move without hurting her, because she was holding him so tightly. Reaching behind his back, he stroked from her thigh to her calf and back again, relaxing her hold just enough that he could lift his hips and withdraw from her sweet, little body. But only long enough to plunge back inside, making her pussy grow ever wetter and more welcoming, until his balls were coated with the creamy proof of her desire.

He had to make love to her, to show her with his body how much he loved her, and to vow that he would never let her go again. But when her pussy grabbed hold of his straining cock and wouldn't let go, he forgot all about control and they fucked frantically until finally climaxing together.

They must have slept after that, because the next thing Nick knew, he was waking up all over again, but feeling so lazy and contented that he could have remained in bed all day, dozing and making love.

"That was nice," Antonia said, both arms raised over her head in a full body stretch.

"Nice," he repeated dryly.

She laughed and smiled up at him. "I like nice sometimes. Don't you?"

"Yes, but only with you. Forevermore, my love."

"Oh," she tsked. "You're so charming."

He grinned back at her, then sighed. "We have to decide what happens next."

Her sigh echoed his. "I know. But that will require energy, so first we'd better eat."

"No."

She gave him a surprised look. "No?"

"First, we shower, babe. *Then* we eat."

ANTONIA SMILED IN amusement while she poured more coffee into Nico's cup. He'd already eaten three fried eggs and a stack of bacon, and was now plowing his way through the cinnamon rolls she'd popped out of a can and baked, mostly for herself. Americans loved bacon, but somehow, she'd never developed the taste for it. She liked coffee, but sometimes preferred hot tea and a pastry for breakfast, hence the cinnamon rolls which Nico was making short work of, though he had been polite enough to first ask if she was finished.

"How can you eat all of that and still look so good?" she asked

He looked up with a grin. "You think I look good?"

"Sure, for a guy who's a few hundred years old."

"Ouch. You used to be sweeter."

"You used to be younger," she teased. She figured he knew very well how good he looked. Humility had never been a problem for Nico.

"I work my ass off every damn day. In the gym, with weapons, on the track. I told you how my people and I spend our time. Any artifacts that we can't buy, we steal. And if they're too dangerous, we don't bother negotiating. We just take them. Not everyone agrees with our methods, so sometimes they fight back. And as you well know, using magic requires energy, especially when you're in a battle with someone who has magic of their own."

She studied him seriously. Once he'd said he worked with the FBI, she'd envisioned men in suits and sunglasses, tracking down magical miscreants. Sure, Nico would have identified the evil doers for them, but it hadn't occurred to her that he and his people would be directly involved. "Do the people who work for you have magic of their own?"

"Most of them are drawn from the FBI Academy. All the cadets there are given so many tests over the course of their training, that it was simple to add a short series of tests for magical aptitude. If they score above a certain level, they're offered the opportunity to work on my projects. And if their talent proves useful in the field, they're offered a job with me."

"Do you find many candidates with useable skills? There's so very little magic in this world."

"True. And most have nothing more than a strong sensitivity for it. But when combined with the martial skills they acquire at the academy, that's enough for most of what we search for. There are a few, however, who have a very strong, specific talent. Damian's wife, Casey, was working for me when she discovered his statue on a rooftop and set him free. Her magical sensitivity is extremely strong, and she's a total badass in the field. In fact, it was Casey who figured out that Sotiris had taken the Talisman—"

"He talked about a device he simply called the Talisman, as if there was only one in the world. But that was back in *our* world, long before I ended up here."

Nico gave her a thoughtful look. "I went after it when I was very young. The sorcerer who created it had no idea what he'd built, and to be honest, neither did I. I only knew it had the potential to generate a great amount of power, and he didn't have sufficient strength to control it. Unfortunately, we were subsequently involved in a war and the device disappeared."

"Maybe Sotiris took it."

"Did he ever show it to you? It looks—or looked—like a big emerald."

"Not that I remember."

He nodded. "I suspect it tumbled through the ages in the hands of the ignorant, until Sotiris saw it for sale, recognized it, and bought it for his own use. Fortunately, Casey figured out enough about how it worked to nullify its power before Sotiris could use it. It was powerful in *our* world, but in *this* world . . . it disabled electronics. All of them. And Sotiris planned to take down a major air traffic control hub, as a *demonstration* to ratchet up the sale price."

Horrified, she could only stare. "Goddess bless, Nico, I knew he was ruthless and cared only for himself, but that's . . . evil. Is that what he's become?"

"It's what he's always been," he said bitterly. "It's only the greater technology of this world that's permitted him to grow into his true nature. Why do you think I want him dead?"

"For what he did to your warriors, to you, and to me. He destroyed our lives to win a war that he didn't even stay to fight. He fled before it was over."

"Not quite," he corrected. "He'd already taken my warriors, but I defeated him in that final battle anyway. When he ran, he was running from *me*."

"Ah. I was told a very different story, one in which he acted to save *me*. Although I stopped believing that a long time ago, when the block on my memories first began to weaken."

He sipped his coffee, watching her over the rim of his mug, as if he wanted to ask something, but wasn't sure he should. "You've said that before, that the block he put on your memories had begun to weaken. But it wasn't until I showed up that all of them returned. Is that right?"

"I probably should have said 'magic' rather than 'memories.' When I first . . . *woke* up here, I didn't have any of my magic or even my skills with spells work. Or if I did, I wasn't aware of it, and so made no attempt to use it. About fifty years in, just before he moved me to this house, I began to have dreams of what I now know was my old life, my *true* life. My progress was painfully slow, but I began to remember, and with the return of memory came the return of my magic. My skills followed more slowly. Obviously," she said, gesturing out through the big kitchen window to where her greenhouse was located, and where her yard was thriving despite the still-facing winter, "my earth talent emerged first, and it's still the strongest. But as my suspicions grew about Sotiris, and the history he'd shoved into my memories, I began to experiment with other uses of that energy."

She took a sip of tea to wet her throat, before continuing. "The last three or so years, my magical strength has accelerated. Now that I know about the release of your warriors, I suspect there was a connection between the collapse of their curses and the gradual return of all my magic. The five of us—your warriors, Sotiris, and I—were cast into the maelstrom at roughly the same time and using the same curse. And although that curse was adapted to fit each of us, we were taken so closely that the variations must have used the same stream of Sotiris's magic. You said the collapse of Damian's curse seemed to have accelerated the others. It only makes sense that my curse would have been similarly affected."

He seemed to think about that for a moment. "You're probably right. Are you telling me that your magic is fully returned then?"

"Not fully until yesterday, when my own curse fell completely. But these last few years, I've regained enough that I believe I can help you locate and *fight* Sotiris."

"Okay. But first, we have to get out of this place before Sotiris shows up on your doorstep."

"He's already on his way here."

"You know where he is to that degree?"

"No, it's more a pressure inside me that grows heavier the closer he gets."

"Right. How do you feel about flying?"

Antonia had to think about that. She knew what planes were, of course, but realized she'd never flown. Actually, she'd never even tried to leave this area of Chicago, much less go any farther. "I don't know," she said slowly. "I've never done it."

"Well, then, darling, you're in for . . . an experience. Is there anyone you need to advise that you're leaving? Any details that need taking care of, since you're going to be gone . . . . Well ultimately, you're probably going to be gone forever, but we can return to handle whatever needs handling. Even so, it might be a while."

"My gardens, then," she said, thinking with regret of the magic she'd invested in her yard, of the days spent digging in the warm, fertile soil, and the joy she'd taken not only from the work, which was no hardship, but of the magic that grew with the plants and surrounded her home with a special peace. "I have a gardener I trust," she said slowly. "He can maintain it while I'm gone, but—"

"I could sense the magic when I stepped onto the porch," he said, coming around the island to take her in his arms. "You don't have to leave if—"

"I do have to leave. This is my battle, as much as yours. And I know him better than you, *differently* than you. You won't win without me."

"Won't I?" he asked dryly. "And what about your gardens?"

"They'll thrive while I'm gone. When it's over, I'll come back and take what I need to grow them again wherever I end up. And after I'm gone, this home, these gardens, will retain some of that magic forever, and be a blessing to whoever lives here next."

He sighed. "God, I've missed you. I'm like one of your plants, I think. Your magic brings me peace, and helps me thrive."

She laughed, blushing with pleasure because she knew he meant every word. "Maybe I should give you a new name, then. Something appropriately plantlike and Latin, I think."

"Uh, yeah. I know more than a little about plant nomenclature.

That's a hard pass for me, but we can discuss it later. What about your mail? Do you get it here?"

"No, I have a forwarding service. My mail goes there, they forward the good stuff, and recycle the rest. If I call, they'll hold all of it."

"Good. Then you need to pack."

"Oh, right. I was about to rotate my clothes for spring, so if we're going to Florida—"

"We are. At least for now."

"Then I'll just leave the warm stuff here. It's hot there all the time, isn't it?"

"Degrees of hot, but yeah, always warm at least. And humid. I'm on the water, and I have air-conditioning, so you'll want to bring sweaters, just in case. And maybe a light jacket or two for going out in the evening, and maybe *some* of those warm clothes, since we don't know where—"

"Nico, that's a lot of suitcases. Probably more than I own, and definitely more than the airlines allow. And we'll need reservations. This time of year, everyone in the northeast is flying to Florida. Unless you're planning to drive."

"Hell, no. I already told you I fly private."

"I heard you, but what does it mean?"

"It means, my darling Antonia, I'm loaded. I have my own plane. Well, a jet actually, but it's a small jet. *Relatively.*"

Antonia shook her head, not even surprised. "I should have known. You always were smarter and more clever than the next guy. If anyone could be thrown into the maelstrom of time and space, and somehow thrive, it would be you, Nicodemus Katsaros." She laughed. "I guess I'd better start packing."

NICK STRETCHED back in the soft leather seat, taking irrational pleasure from Antonia's reaction to the comfort and amenities of his jet. The aircraft was larger than it appeared from inside the passenger cabin, since he'd had it modified to provide enough cargo space to bring his Ferrari with him when he traveled. Not everywhere—he wasn't a total ass. But he despised rental cars and avoided them at all costs. And besides, he loved high-performance vehicles, and those were hard to find in a rental.

But Antonia was stroking the leather and stretching out her legs, as if amazed at the comfort. She'd already paid a visit to the bathroom, not because she needed to go, but just to see what was there. She was like a kid, on her way to Walt Disney World for the first time.

He knew he was staring at her, but didn't even try to stop. He loved her so much, and still couldn't believe he'd finally found her—that she was his to make love to, to hold in his arms while they watched a movie, or even to drop a casual kiss on her cheek at the breakfast table.

She turned, saw him watching her, and wrinkled her face in embarrassment. "You have to stop—"

The pilot interrupted to announce they were cleared for take-off and reminded them to put their seats upright and fasten their seatbelts. Antonia promptly complied and turned to him with sparkling dark eyes. "This is so comfortable. Why are people always complaining about how crowded planes are?"

Nick couldn't help but kiss her beautiful face.

"What was that for?" she asked, patting her flushed cheeks.

"Just because I'm happy to be sitting next to you."

"That's because there's no one else on the plane."

He grinned. "And *that's* because I own this plane, and no one gets to fly on it but the two of us. And our friends. Occasionally."

She laughed. "That's a lot of qualifiers, my love."

"They call this jet *private* for a reason."

"Now that's the grumpy Nico I remember."

"I was never grumpy. I just didn't like to be around people."

"Uh huh. Do your friends know this?"

"My only *real* friends are my warriors and their mates, so yes."

"Well, I love your jet. Thank you for including me on the approved list."

"Any time, my love. And speaking of love, did you notice the bedroom?"

She gave him a disbelieving look. "Ha ha."

"No, really."

She looked around. "Where?"

"Across from the bathroom." She started to unbuckle her seatbelt, but he stopped. "Not yet. We're still taking off. Wait until we're airborne, and I'll show you."

Antonia eyed him suspiciously. "It's a very short flight from Chicago to Florida. Even I know that."

"Are you accusing me of something?"

"Yes."

He took her hand and kissed it. "The flight isn't *that* short. But if you don't want to see it—"

"Not a chance. If I'm going to be flying private, I want to know all of my options. Oh!" She reversed his hold on her hand, gripping his fingers tightly, when the plane lifted from the runway.

Cursing himself for forgetting that she'd never *flown*, private or otherwise, he held her hand and leaned closer. "That sensation is perfectly normal. It feels a little weird when the jet first leaves the ground and powers into the sky, but once we're up there, you won't even know you're flying, unless you look out the window."

"What about turbulence?"

"Have you been reading up on flying since yesterday?"

"No, I saw a movie with Alec Baldwin. He had to fly from England to Washington DC, and he was nervous about turbulence. Something about warm air rising and cool air descending, making the plane sort of bounce. It was a good movie."

"Right, it *was* a good movie. I'll be honest. We could hit some rough air, as they call it. But even if we do, my pilot is a former Air Force pilot, a former passenger jet pilot, and is also an instructor for current pilots on this and other jets. He's super-qualified and can handle even the roughest air, which—I hasten to add—we will not be hitting, because the weather between here and Fort Lauderdale, which is the city we'll be flying into, is clear. And lest you think I'm just telling you that, the pilot will tell us himself, just as soon as we reach cruising altitude. You know what that is?"

"Yes. That one I know. It's used in a lot of books and movies."

"Good. You want a drink? Some wine?"

"No. It's too early. Is there a bar?"

"Sure. I fly this baby to California. There's also food, though we should wait until we can take off our seatbelts for that one."

"I think I'm too nervous to eat."

"Don't be nervous. In a pinch, I can fly this plane. And we have parachutes onboard."

"Now you *are* teasing me."

"I am, but only about the parachutes. I've had a lot of time to learn new stuff, so I really can fly the jet. Although I feel much safer with the captain doing it."

She squeezed his hand. "And now we'll have time together."

"You need to be thinking about what you want to see, where you want to go. Anywhere in the world. Better yet, make a list."

"Let's just get to Florida first, okay?"

"Sure. How about a movie? Here." He opened the control app on his cell phone and brought up the oversized screen on the bulkhead in front of them. "Take your pick. Use my phone for now, and I'll add the app to yours."

While she scrolled the menus like a pro, proving just how very comfortable she was with a computer, he put on headphones and keyed in a private conversation with the pilot, asking him about the flying conditions to Fort Lauderdale. When the pilot responded with pretty much the same forecast that Nick had told Antonia, he asked him to make an announcement at the appropriate time, unless conditions changed. In which case, he should buzz Nick privately.

"Understood, sir."

The note of humor in the man's voice said he really *did* understand. But with any luck, the weather would hold. And if it didn't, then hopefully he and Antonia would be in bed, and much too busy to worry about a few extra bumps.

Chapter Five

Pompano Beach, Florida

"IS THIS THE CAR you take with you everywhere you go? It's awfully big, isn't it?" Antonia's voice betrayed the nerves which had reappeared as soon as they'd left the plane.

Nick glanced over and saw her staring at the Town Car that was picking them up at the airport. Walking over from where he'd been showing the porter which car was theirs, he pulled her into a gentle hug. "With everything you know about me, darling, does this look like the car I'd choose?"

Her head tilted as she studied the Town Car, and then glanced around at the other vehicles in the Executive Airport terminal. "No. Definitely not."

He kissed the side of her head, pleased that the distraction had somewhat lessened the nervous quaver in her voice. "I'll show you the real thing when we get to the house. It's red."

"Of course, it is." She rolled her eyes with a soft chuckle, only to stiffen against him when a big man approached.

Nick tightened his hold in reassurance. "Antonia, this is Abe Putin. Abe's my Head of Security. He usually wouldn't be ferrying me from the airport, but these aren't usual times."

As tall as Nick, but much broader and thick with muscle, Abe turned his disarmingly sweet smile on Antonia. "A pleasure to meet you, ma'am. Welcome to Florida."

Proving she still possessed the strength that had gotten her this far, Antonia bestowed her own megawatt smile on the big man, and held out her hand. "Thank you, Abe. And please call me Antonia."

Abe ducked his head, took her delicate hand in his wide paw and shook it briefly. "Antonia it is then. I'm at your service." He glanced at Nick. "We should get you in the car."

"Right." Opening the back door, Nick waited until Antonia was sliding across the back seat to ask Abe, "Any new developments I need to be aware of?"

"Nothing that can't wait until we're behind the gates."

Nick got into the car, then closed and locked the door, while Abe finished helping the porter, tipped the man generously, then closed the trunk and climbed into the driver's seat. Once they were on their way, Nick asked, "Did you let Lili know we're here and on our way?"

"I did. Damian and Casey are already at the house. Dragan and Maeve are close, and might actually beat us there. Kato and Gabriel are on hold. Once we have a target location, they'll travel together. Raphael's offered the use of his plane, if they need it."

Nick held back the sour retort that always leaped to mind when the California vampire lord was mentioned. He hated to admit it, but Raphael had been helpful more than once in pursuing Sotiris. But even that paled when compared to the fact that he'd saved Gabriel's life after the curse was lifted. Nick's spell, which had "cured" Gabriel of much of what had made him a vampire, had been broken along with Sotiris's curse. Raphael was an old and incredibly powerful vampire, and the only one who'd immediately understood what was happening in time to save Gabriel. After seeing the way vampires in this world lived, specifically those in Raphael's territory and thus under his protection, Gabriel had decided to accept his true nature as a vampire and serve as a member of Raphael's security team. He remained totally loyal to Nick and his warrior brothers, however, and was as eager as any of them to see Sotiris dead.

"Everyone's excited to meet you, Antonia," Abe said, glancing up at her in his rearview mirror.

"Don't worry, love," Nick reassured jokingly. "They'll be cool. No bear hugs."

She laughed. "There better not be. I've been experimenting with my magic, you know. I'll bear hug 'em right back."

Abe laughed with her. "I think you're going to fit in just fine with that crowd."

She leaned against Nick with a tired sigh, and he put his arm around her, pillowing her head on his shoulder. "It's a lot to take in," he murmured in understanding.

"It is. But it's also wonderful to be free again. To leave my safe neighborhood and see the world—at least what I've seen of it so far—is amazing."

"We'll travel the world, love. Anywhere you want to go."

She nodded against him, then, her voice hardening, she said, "But first we have to fight, not only for ourselves, but for a world which doesn't yet recognize its peril."

"First we fight," he agreed grimly.

ANTONIA'S FIRST glimpse of the "house," left her speechless. Nico didn't have a house. He had a compound, with full-size houses, and several smaller outbuildings both in front and behind. She caught the shine of turquoise pool water, too, and behind that, what had to be the ocean. Or probably one of the so-called waterways that she'd read were so prevalent in Florida. This would be her first sight of them, and for that matter, her first sight of the ocean—any ocean. Chicago was on Lake Michigan, which was huge, but this was the Atlantic Ocean, covering twenty percent of the earth's surface with its water. She could hardly wait to see it.

"Do you have a boat, Nico?"

"Of course."

"Can we go out on the ocean?"

"Any time you want, if the weather suits."

"Oh right, hurricanes. I've seen those on the news. So many lives destroyed," she added sadly.

"I can't disagree with that. We're out of the official hurricane season now, but the ocean has its own mind."

"How inappropriate to call this planet Earth, when it is clearly Ocean." She glanced up at him and smiled. "Arthur C. Clarke. I told you. I did a lot of reading."

He kissed her upturned lips. "That's why you're so good at spells. You love research."

"Thank the goddess. One of us has to." She gave him a questioning look. "Unless you've changed?"

"Nope."

"I thought as much. Oh, Nico, the house is beautiful. This one anyway. Why two houses?"

"That's a long story, but basically, the last time we fought Sotiris, a lot of this house—" he nodded at the one directly in front of them, "—was damaged. That encounter, especially the way it unfolded, made me aware that I needed a bigger margin of protection. The house next door just happened to come up for sale while I was getting ready to repair this one, and so I bought it and combined the two properties into one estate."

"Wouldn't that require all sorts of permits and, I don't know, exceptions to code or something?"

"Oh, yeah. I told you I keep track of local politics. That includes generous donations to various campaigns and causes, which helped speed up the approval process. It also helped that none of neighbors objected or complained, because they were aware of the violent "break-in" attempt, which was our explanation for Dragan's courtyard fight with Sotiris. And since more security is good for everyone, and the property values went up with the enlarged estate, everyone was happy."

As the car rolled to a stop, the front door opened to reveal another big man. But this one, she recognized. "Damian," she whispered, questioning her own memories. After all, she'd never actually met the warrior. She'd only glimpsed him from across the battlefield.

"That's him. And the woman behind him is Casey, his wife."

Suddenly nervous all over again, she ran her fingers through her hair, wishing she'd thought to brush it before they got this far. She pressed her lips together, confirming that her lipstick was still in place, and was checking her skirt for wrinkles when Nico took her hands in his.

"They won't care about anything except that you're here, safe and sound. Take a minute and look at Casey. Does she look like someone who judges another woman by her hair and makeup? Or cares about a wrinkled skirt? Not that yours is wrinkled," he added quickly. "I'm not saying that. I'm just saying if they can love me, then they'll sure as hell love you."

Antonia breathed a long sigh. "It's just . . . I can't remember the last time I met someone new. Isn't that pathetic?"

"No," he said firmly. "Am I pathetic because it took me fucking *centuries* to find you and my warriors? And even then, it wasn't my doing that you or they were found."

"So you were smart enough to get others to help you."

He laughed. "That's a charitable way to look at it. But that's not my point. You and I know what magic can do in the hands of a powerful sorcerer. We know how much damage a curse from that person can do. What we've endured, my failings and your isolation, are the result of a very destructive curse cast by a master of the craft. Neither of us bears any responsibility for his evil. You got that?"

She smiled slowly. "I love you so much, Nicodemus. I'm so glad you found me."

He bent his head and pressed his warm mouth to hers, rubbing his lips over hers slowly, softly, then gliding his tongue into her mouth. Antonia's breath caught as emotion flooded her chest, and she clutched his arm, holding him to her. They took their time, not caring that there were people waiting. They took this moment for themselves in the quiet of the Town Car, before the hordes descended, demanding attention and asking questions, all with good intentions.

Nico lifted his head, gently breaking the kiss. "You ready?"

"Just one minute," she said, and snatching a tissue from the box on the back of the seat, dabbed the tears from her eyes. "Happiness," she assured him. "Happiness."

He took the tissue and dabbed his own eyes, though she wasn't sure it was needed. "Happiness," he said back to her. "Happiness."

And so, when he opened the door at last, the first sound his people heard was her laughter.

NICK WASN'T WORRIED whether his people would love Antonia. As he'd told her, they loved *him*, and she was far more loveable than he was. Her magic was nurturing by its very nature. She was warm and giving, to his suspicious and doubtful. He liked to be alone, or with only a small number of trusted friends, while she enjoyed meeting new people, getting out in the crowds and just watching. She soaked up and shared the happiness around her, while he couldn't help wondering what the hell they had to be so damn happy about.

Damian walked over to greet them, doing his best to seem non-threatening, which was a tough sell for a man that big and powerful, who looked exactly like the warrior he was—not to mention the magic that was an integral part of who he was as a result of the way Nick had summoned him into his world when they were just children. Antonia would not only sense that magic, but would identify it as belonging to Nick, as if Damian had bitten off a portion of Nick's magic and made it part of himself. That wasn't far from the truth, except it was Nick who'd made it happen, when he'd been too young to know what he was doing. Not that he'd change anything about Damian, or his summoning of him, even if he could. The big warrior was his first and most loyal friend.

There was no need to worry, however. True to her nature, Antonia closed the distance between them, smiled, and said, "Damian. It's wonderful to see you . . . alive and well."

He smiled in return. "That 'alive and well' goes for both of us. I'm surprised you recognize me."

"You're a hard man to miss in a battle, and I watched too many of those to forget."

Grinning, Damian put his arm around Casey, who'd held back half a step, and pulled her to his side. "This is Cassandra, my wife, as of two weeks ago," he added proudly.

"He always says that now, as if he's claimed his fucking prize," Casey commented. "And it's Casey. Not even my father calls me Cassandra." She held out a hand that was rough with callouses from various weapons.

Antonia took it easily. "I'm Antonia. Congratulations."

"We should go inside," Nick said. Despite the new security measures and his total confidence in Abe and his team, he disliked hanging around outside. And he probably would until that bastard Sotiris was not only dead, but chopped into pieces, and scattered over the globe.

Lili waited inside for them, still uneasy about going outdoors in daylight. Nick had assured her over and over again that the spell he'd cast to "cure" her vampirism had made sunlight safe, but he doubted she'd ever be completely comfortable. It had taken years for him to persuade her to leave the house even at night, and then only when absolutely necessary.

The first thing Nick did once he and Antonia were inside was to tug Lili out of the dining area where she was holding back from all the traffic—what with luggage coming in, and people going out and now coming in again. Taking her hand, he led her to Antonia and said, "And this is Lilia, who's been with me since Paris. I told Antonia all about you," he said to Lili. "I don't know what I'd have done without my Lili all these years. She knows more about my business than I do, but she's far more important to me than that. She's a dear friend, and I love her as the sister I never had."

Lili blushed at the effusive praise, but that didn't stop her from saying, "He's right. I do know more about the business than he does, but I love my work." She glanced up at Nick, and added, "And the people I work with."

"That sounds like Nico," Antonia confided. "He was never one for paperwork."

Lili's chiming laughter seemed to sparkle in the air for a moment, before she turned to Nick and said, "Maeve just called. She was feeling a bit "car-sick". That's what she called it, but I think we all know it's morning sickness, even though she insists it can't be. For such a scientific and intelligent woman, she's being awfully stubborn about this. I don't know why it matters. Anyway, they stopped for a rest, and they're just getting back on the road. So they'll probably arrive an hour or two later than planned, depending on traffic.

"Also, I set up a video conference for later tonight. Kato and Grace will be driving over to Raphael's estate, so everyone on the west coast can be in one room. And we'll all be in the conference room here, so that will make conversation easier than zooming everyone in."

"Noisier, you mean," Nick commented. "No mute buttons."

"Well, yes, but still easier."

"Depends on who chimes in from the other coast," he said sourly.

"Oh, get over it, Nick. We have Antonia, and she knows more about Sotiris than anyone, so I'm sure *she'll* do most of the talking."

"Oh, I don't know about that," Antonia demurred. "When it comes to battles or strategy, I know very little. Although yes, I probably do know Sotiris better."

Damian gave her an even look and asked quietly, "Are you married to him still, or—?"

"Good goddess, no!" she said, giving him a startled look. "He's my father!"

Damian's brow shot up in surprise. "Fuck me. Did anyone else know that?"

"Well, I sure as hell did," Nick said.

"And my mother certainly did," Antonia added, her mouth now twitching in amusement. "*She* was his wife, by the way, though they stopped living together when I was still a small child. It wasn't until my magic became too strong to ignore that she arranged for Sotiris to visit her estate, and provide me with suitable instruction. But when I turned sixteen, he insisted they change the arrangements. He wanted me to live with him for a time, so he could provide more advanced training. Mother wasn't thrilled at the idea, but all I saw was that the great sorcerer Sotiris wanted to tutor me. Lucky me, or so I thought at the time. The idea of parental duty never crossed my mind. It wasn't important to me that he was my father. I had no feelings of affection for him. I just wanted to study with him."

She shrugged, as if unsure what else she could say. And Damian appeared half-apologetic and half-awkward, as if he'd said something taboo. Nick broke the silence. "We're tired from the flight, after the time we spent getting Antonia's house and affairs ready for leaving Chicago. And I need her to help me with some research before we tele-conference with the west coast."

The door opened before he could continue, and Abe Putin walked in. Lili's face brightened with joy when he walked over, and without hesitation bent down to place a lingering kiss on her mouth. Lili blushed charmingly, but since her cheeks were already warm with happiness, it barely showed.

"I'll want you in on the video meet later," Nick told Abe. "We're definitely going to war. The only question is where and when."

"I'll bring him up to speed," Lili said, then turned and with Abe's hand on the small of her back, the two of them retreated to her office down the hall.

"Is that new?" Damian asked, staring after them.

"Not really," Nick answered. "They just decided to go public, I guess. Since it wasn't much of a secret anymore. Not to me anyway, since I live here." The truth was, he'd suspected something was going on with those two, probably longer than they'd admitted it to themselves. Their respective positions with Nick had inevitably brought them together, sometimes several times a day when they'd first been getting the new compound wired and up to speed. And for all Lili's shyness, she was fiercely intelligent. When it came to her work, she didn't tolerate fools, nor hesitate to argue when she knew she was right.

For his part, Abe had been more than a little surprised to discover that the tiny mouse, who could barely meet his eyes when introduced, argued with him like a politician, or someone who knew what the hell she was talking about and could talk circles around anyone who didn't. He'd mentioned it to Nick with such admiration, while also complimenting her sweet side, telling him how she'd been so helpful and friendly, so kind to the workman who'd cut his hand severely, and had been in danger of fainting, before Lili had stepped in and fucking mothered him.

Nick had known then that Abe was a goner, but it was the first time he'd seen them having lunch together that he'd known Lili was falling, too. Abe had been so gentle and old-fashioned in the way he'd treated Lili, while she'd poured his tea—even though he drank coffee—and brought over cookies on a *plate*, instead of just plopping the bag on the table. But Abe had realized something even Nick had missed—that Lili was still a young woman at heart, and a woman of her time. She needed to be courted, and to court in return, in the way gentlewomen of her time did.

That made Nick wonder about himself. How the hell had he missed that about Lili? That part of her unwillingness to leave the house was more than being a vampire. It was fear of the outside world, which was foreign to anything she knew. Sure, this house and her computers were not of her time, but this place was her haven. It was *hers* in a way that it wasn't even Nick's.

Abe had courted Lili, and she'd responded. It had nothing to do with his size or how well he could shoot—which was damn good—but it was his kindness *and* his intellect, which matched her own when it came to computerized security or communication.

Nick's only puzzlement was why they'd bothered to conceal it. Why would he care, much less object? Abe was a good, responsible man, who obviously cared for Lili. And it was about time she had some love in her life. Since arriving in North America with him so long ago, she'd devoted herself to the smooth running of his household, and then his business. It was long past time for her to find some happiness of her own.

"Fuck," Damian complained still staring down the hallway where Lili and Abe had disappeared. "I feel like I'm living in a parallel world, where everyone knows everyone else's secrets except me."

"That's okay, big guy," Casey said, patting his arm in sympathy. "I didn't know about Antonia and Sotiris, either."

"Oh. Wait! So, you *did* know about Lili and Abe? Why didn't you tell me?"

"Well, I wasn't sure, and you being a god of war and all, I just figured you'd already noticed the same things I did." She gave him a toothy, and terribly insincere, smile.

"Nice. My own woman holding out on me," he grumbled. "Come on, I'm hungry. You can at least do your wifely duty and fix me a sandwich."

Nick watched in bemusement as the couple headed for the big kitchen.

"You've made a family here," Antonia said quietly, leaning into his side and wrapping her arm around his waist.

Yeah, he had. Or *they* had. It had taken all of them to make it happen. "You're right," he said thoughtfully, then hugged her close. "And now, you're the most important part of it."

"If anyone holds that position, it's you. You're the reason we're all here. Your warriors would never have met, much less joined together as brothers, if you hadn't called them from lives they hated and given them something to fight for. They never fought for the freedom of people they'd never met, or not solely for that reason, anyway. Not even primarily. They fought for you and for each other. It's been proven time after time that when it comes right down to it, in the heat of battle, when a soldier has to choose whether or not to risk his life, he does it for the guy next to him. You and your four saved a lot of defenseless people, gave them a chance to build new lives, better lives. But they were never more than an abstract when you stood on that line together and faced your enemy.

"Admit it," she added, digging a finger into his abdomen. "The thrill of battle and all that. You all loved to fight together."

He grabbed her finger. "It's not that simple. I'll admit that the adrenaline rush is damn intense, and it feels incredible when I'm seconds away from fighting for my life. And yeah, that includes the lives of my brother warriors. But that adrenaline rush is also what keeps me alive. It heightens my awareness, speeds up my reaction time. Without it, I'm a walking corpse waiting to be killed." He shrugged. "Do I love war? I'm sure as hell looking forward to beating Sotiris to death once and for all. But does that mean I love *all* war? I don't think so."

She studied him thoughtfully, hands to either side of his waist, head tilted back to better see his face, her dark eyes solemn. "I never thought of it like that. The closest I've ever been to war is on a high hill overlooking the battlefield. The fighters are faceless figures, then, and all you can see is the blood and death."

"Did you root for Sotiris to win?"

"At first I did. As I said, I was thrilled to have him for a teacher, and was proud to be his daughter. But that didn't last long. I used to hide in a closet next to the room where he met his generals, because I wanted to know what they said, how they put together a strategy. The closet didn't open to his conference room, but the wall was thinner there, and I gouged a small hole, so I could hear better. I heard the way he spoke not only of the people he fought, but of his own soldiers. They were *nothing* to him. Weapons to be used and discarded in service of his ambition, which was to rule."

"To rule not only his territory, but everyone else's, too."

"Yes! He wanted to rule our *world* and everyone in it. And he still does. He has this irrational idea that with you gone, he'll possess enough power to rule this *planet*. Or at least the more interesting parts. I think he's more than a little mad, to be honest."

"He talked about this with you?"

"Oh, yes. The last year or so, once he saw that my magic was definitely getting stronger again, he decided I was supposed to join him, to use my magic to help him win at last."

"He honestly thought you'd go along with that?"

"I *was* isolated here for a long time, alone and frequently confused, especially earlier. And for a long time, I didn't know anyone but him, so I clung to that, to him. He was the only part of my life that was real. The only part that remained the same from day to day, or week to week. But as the years went on, my memories of *this* world began to stabilize. I still didn't know how I'd gotten here, but he had an explanation for everything, and I believed him. He was my father. He told me that much, and I knew what a father was, and what he was *supposed* to be to me, as his child. So I trusted him.

"Then, as I told you, the reality he'd planted in my memories as part of the curse that brought me here, began to fray. I pretended for quite a while in order to gather information, and later on, to get some idea of who his allies were." She grimaced. "I learned a lot. But before I could discover his endgame, he asked me for help designing a devastating weapon. It was a magical bomb that would kill thousands if planted in a public place, like a big stadium, or I don't know, a government building. And even if the authorities were warned, they wouldn't know what to look for, and wouldn't possess the sorcery necessary to detect it."

Nick jerked in reaction. "I know that device. He planted it in a stadium nearby, and you're right. It would have killed *tens* of thousands if it had gone off."

"Why?" she whispered. "Why'd he do it?"

"Like the Talisman, he was demonstrating its lethal potential to future buyers. But then he discovered that I had the *hexagon*, and he decided to kill two birds with one stone. He tried to distract me with the threat, so he could invade my home and steal it back. If I didn't manage to disable the device before it went off, it would still be a great demonstration, and he could make a fortune selling it. Plus, as a bonus, if I and my people were still in the stadium trying to find or disable it, we'd be killed, too."

"He's almost as obsessed with money, as he is with power. They're linked for him. He used to tell me all the time, back in our world, that if he was to be king, then he had to live like one."

"Yeah, well, apparently, he's a well-known vendor in the criminal world."

"Wait," she said, holding up a hand, palm out. "Did you say you had the hexagon? Do you still have it?"

He grinned smugly. "I do."

She sputtered, unable to form words, then finally asked, "How?"

"It's a long story. We should sit somewhere. Are you tired? Do you want to rest before dinner?"

"Are you kidding me? You say you have the hexagon, and you want to know if I'd like to *rest*? Then, to use what seems to be a favorite word around here, *fuck* no!"

Nick had to laugh, and he wondered how long she'd have to hang around his people before she started cursing like the rest of them. "Can we at least sit?"

"As long as it's somewhere you'll start talking, and preferably where I can see the hexagon, too."

"Your wish is my command, my lady. Come this way."

ANTONIA LOOPED her arm in his, and they walked down a long hall, past a room where Lili was talking and typing at the same time, the energy positively radiating off her. At the end of the hall was a closed door, wider than usual. Nico reached out with one hand, turned the knob and pushed the door open with the same motion, then stood back and gestured for her to enter ahead of him.

She patted his chest as she walked by, and was about to tease him about his manners, when she was struck breathless by the sheer beauty of the office. No, not the office, which she barely saw, but the light and the view through a wall of windows. Stunned speechless, she crossed to those windows as if in a dream. Sunlight streamed in, warming her face and arms, despite the cool air blowing from somewhere near the ceiling. It was late afternoon, and the sun was behind them, but even so, there was a pristine quality to the light that she supposed came from being so much closer to the equator. She wanted to walk out onto one of the high balconies she'd seen on the house when they drove up, just so she could watch the sun set. It would be gorgeous. And maybe while they were in Florida, Nick would drive down with her to Key West, so she could see the famous green flash.

After they dealt with Sotiris, she reminded herself. Nico and the rest were all focused on one goal, and it wasn't indulging her need to play tourist.

"I'm sorry," she said, turning to face him. "This is just so lovely. Is this Pompano Beach? It didn't look like this on the map I studied on the plane."

"This is Lighthouse Point, hence the lighthouse you can see out there."

She turned back to the view. "It's beautiful. Is it real?"

"It's very real, and thanks to a very expensive renovation, fully modernized and functioning."

"Nico, this house, these *houses* . . ." She gave him a worried look.

"No, I haven't taken up a life of crime, my love. I've had hundreds of years to see my ventures pay off, and it turns out, I'm rather good at picking investments."

"You're not using your *other* skills, are you?"

"I'm insulted that you think so little of my honor, *and* my intellect. No, I brought what I considered a reasonable amount of gold coin with me on my first transition out of our world, and into this one. I discovered that what we considered a reasonable amount, was a hell of a lot more here. Or rather there, since as I told you, I landed in Paris." He shrugged. "And I built from there."

"Well, you chose well. This place is just stunning."

"Think you'd enjoy living here with me?" he asked with what anyone else would take as casual interest. But she knew him better.

She crossed to stand in front of him. "I'd live with you anywhere on earth, Nicodemus Katsaros. I don't care if it's in a gorgeous estate like this, or in an ordinary house in a Chicago suburb. I'll take you any way I can get you."

He pulled her against his chest and spoke against her hair. "That's good, because I'm not letting you go."

They stood that way until the light dimmed enough that the automatic timers clicked on the landscape lights just outside the window, and the room began to cool enough that the air-conditioning ceased its persistent blowing. Nico apparently liked his rooms *cold*. It had never come up in their home world, for obvious reasons. But if they were going to share a bedroom, adjustments would need to be made. If not to the thermostat, then to the blankets on her half of the bed.

"I want to show you something," he said, kissing the top of her head. "I think you'll like it."

With that enigmatic statement, he went over to a wall of built-in bookshelves, slid his hand to the back of one shelf, above the books sitting there, and pushed. Antonia didn't understand what he was doing until the wall popped open enough to reveal a complicated lock that looked like something she'd seen in a movie. When he pressed his thumb to what was apparently a scanner, a second bookcase swung open to reveal a door. "A hidden room?" she whispered, delighted by it.

Nico pushed the just revealed door open all the way and stepped into a room that, when she followed, Antonia knew had its own ventilation, completely apart from the rest of the house. The air was drier and, she inhaled, cleaner. No, it was more than clean. It was *too* dry, and somehow thin. This air had been purified to extract anything that might damage . . . . What? She spun and took in the room around her.

"Oh," she breathed in awe, and wondered when the surprises would stop. How many more secrets was Nico concealing from the world? "Where did you find all of this?"

The room was filled with glass shelves and cases of magic devices of every sort and age, some of them so deadly that they'd been kept secret even in their world, remaining hidden in closely guarded stone vaults in the basement of every sorcerer's tower, including Sotiris's . . . and Nico's.

Not everything in this vault was deadly, though. Some were merely dangerous, and others even less than that. But regardless of lethality, in every class of device there was plain and there was beautiful. Jewels sparkled next to ordinary tin. Diamond encrusted knives were sheathed in tooled leather, with no casual observer realizing that the danger was in the sheath, not the blade.

Nico walked by all of these without pausing, going instead to a softly lit shelf set into an alcove all by itself. And on that shelf were four . . . piles of sand. Intrigued, and knowing he wouldn't have created this shrine—for that's what it was—for no reason, Antonia walked over, studying every detail through the filter of her magic.

The shelf was simply a shelf, the lighting just a light, but the sand . . . now that was definitely not ordinary. Studying it some more she finally said slowly, "The sand . . . all of it's been ensorcelled, but . . . ." She studied it some more. "Each pile is . . . *almost* the same, but not quite." She gasped. "Oh! Four different curses by the same sorcerer, using the same elements." She turned to Nico. "What are these?"

"Four piles of sand, four curses, similar but different."

She made an impatient noise, and then it hit her. "Four statues, four piles of sand, but how . . .? Where did they come from? Did you some-how—?"

"Not me. Sotiris. He left them, the statues—the copies of the real statues—as a gift when I arrived in Paris. He, of course, was long gone. I'd defeated him in our last battle at home. He wasn't going to test me so soon afterwards. Not in this world where there's so little magic."

She stared at him. "And as your warriors were freed, the statues crumbled."

"Yes."

She closed her eyes for a moment, feeling as if their shared blood somehow made her responsible for Sotiris's evil. When she opened them, she said, "I doubt he ever expected this—" she gestured at the sand, "—to happen. So they were only created to torture you."

"I'm sure you're right. I take great pleasure in knowing how pissed off he must be."

She sighed. "I'm—"

"Don't say it," he demanded, closing in to put a careful two fingers over her lips. "You're no more responsible for him than your mother is because she married the bastard."

"She'd agree with you on that. But she doesn't share the magic in his blood. I do."

"And if *you'd* come first and passed that magic to him, I'd blame you. But it's the other way around, so I don't. And neither will anyone else. You created the hexagon, and intended it to be used against him. Neither of us could have anticipated what he'd do, how far he'd go to win. Well, he hasn't won yet, and when we're finished with him, he never will."

"Where do you get your confidence?"

He grinned. "It's in the blood, love, mixed in with the magic, which has been shown multiple times to be superior to . . . well, let's face it, superior to everyone else."

"No, darling," she said pleasantly. "That's ego, not confidence. Although, since you have the hexagon, both might be justified. How did you get it? I can't believe Sotiris didn't take it with him when he fled."

"I don't get any credit for that one. Dragan and Maeve brought it with them from New York. Did you know Sotiris had a house there? In the Finger Lakes, not the penthouse in Manhattan."

"I knew about the penthouse, but not the one upstate. That's interesting, because I know of several others, including some he considers his last resort hideouts. Whatever was in that house must have been either very important or very secret for him to have kept it from me. Either that or he acquired it after our relationship soured, and he lost any illusions that I would become an obedient daughter and devoted co-conspirator."

"It was older than that, and I'd say it was both important *and* secret, since it wasn't only the hexagon he kept there." Nico's voice hardened in a way that had her studying him in alarm.

"What was there? What could be more important to him than the hexagon?"

"Dragan."

She frowned in confusion. "He was holding Dragan prisoner?"

"He'd been searching as long as I had for the statues. But where I wanted them so I could free my warriors, he wanted to ensure that they were never set free. They'd already suffered a thousand or more years, buried in caves, left in abandoned dwellings, with no hope of discovery, much less freedom. Sotiris failed in locating the others, but Dragan, he found in Europe, in the basement of a derelict and abandoned house. It was around 1920, as near as I can figure. He went so far as to transport the statue by ship to this country. I don't know if he'd already bought the house, or if his finding Dragan had been the impetus for the acquisition, but Dragan sat in that bastard's gallery of statues for decades.

"Mind you, any house would have been better than the one Dragan was in, but his prospects for being found were worse. He was aware, as were all the others, of what was happening around him. He knew that Sotiris had captured him, and had all but given up hope of ever finding freedom. Until Sotiris made the mistake of hiring Maeve."

"Dragan's pregnant wife."

"Yes. They should be here very soon."

"How did she know he wasn't an ordinary statue?"

"To hear her tell it, her suspicions were aroused because Dragan didn't fit with any of the other statues in the gallery. She's an antiquities specialist, and his presence jarred her sensibilities. But more than that, something drew her to him. So much so that she started sitting with him and talking, as if he could hear, even though Sotiris had forbidden her from being in the gallery. Anyway, events happened and by chance, she said and did the right things, and he was freed."

"And she ran away with him? Why? I'd have been more terrified than in love."

"No, you wouldn't. You'd have been curious as hell, and insisted on hearing his life's story."

She shrugged. "True. But I have enough power to protect myself. What does Maeve have?"

"A heart as big as her brain. They knew that they had to get as far away from the house as possible, as fast as possible, because Sotiris would know the curse had been broken. So they grabbed what they could and ran. But one of the things Maeve grabbed was the hexagon, just because it intrigued her."

"Thank the goddess for smart, curious women, I guess, huh?"

He pulled her close and gave her a smacking kiss. "Hell, yes. So . . . you want to see it?"

"It's here?" She looked around. "In this room? I should be able to—"

"Not exactly in this room, but close. Come on."

Taking her hand, he drew her over to what appeared to be a blank wall, and touched his finger to it while murmuring under his breath. Antonia knew it was a spell of some kind, but couldn't catch the words. Besides, she thought when a small door suddenly appeared on the previously empty wall, the magical veil that had been concealing the door would require more than just the right words to reveal what it was hiding. It would probably respond only to Nico's voice and/or magic. He was more than powerful enough to sustain such a spell, and the hexagon was worth whatever was necessary to keep it hidden and secure.

He murmured another spell and pressed his entire hand against the door, which popped open to reveal a safe-like interior containing a single wooden box. Antonia knew this was the hexagon the minute the door opened. It was *her* blood that had activated the damn thing, and it sang to her like a long-lost relative. For her part, it was a relative she wasn't eager to see, but she still recognized its usefulness.

"Shall I open it?" Nico asked, leaving the box where it was.

"No," she said softly. "It's the hexagon."

"You used your own blood to activate it," he said, his tone telling her that she'd just confirmed what he'd long suspected.

"Yes."

"What if it had backfired, and you'd lost your power instead?"

His voice was hard again, she noticed. "I was almost positive it would work against him. Or at least against *both* of us, which would have served just as well."

"And if it hadn't? If we'd been in the middle of a battle, and suddenly your power was gone?"

"I've never been in the middle of a battle in my entire life," she snapped. "And you would hardly be depending on me if I were. My strength is *not* for fighting, on or off the battlefield. I can *design* a battle weapon, but I don't have enough or the right *kind* of power to make it work in a war. You know that."

He gave her a narrow stare, then conceded, "I do know that. But I still don't like that you put yourself at risk."

"It's that penis of yours. It keeps getting in the way of rational thought."

His look turned disbelieving. "You didn't say that on the plane here, when you were screaming loud enough that the pilot buzzed me, worried something had happened."

"He did not!"

"He did."

"You are terrible sometimes," she gasped, when he started laughing.

"If it's only sometimes, I'm ahead of the game. Some people would say 'always.'"

"Who are they? We'd probably get along very well."

He pulled her into his arms. "Don't be like that. You know you love me just the way I am."

"I love you," she admitted grudgingly. "But I'm not sure about the 'just the way' part."

He laughed some more, clearly *devastated* by her pronouncement, she thought.

"You sure you don't want to take a look?" he asked, when he'd finally stopped laughing, and yeah, kissed her bad mood away. The sneak.

"I'm sure. Lock it back up, sorcerer."

Nico did so quickly, then asked, "Anything else you want to see in here?"

"Not right now." She lifted her arms into a stretch over her head. "What I'd really like is a hot shower. Is there time before we have to meet the others for the video conference?"

"Hey, I'm the boss here. If I say there's time, there's time."

"Fortunately for your friends, I'm more considerate. But I still want that shower. Let's go."

Chapter Six

NICK LED ANTONIA down the long hallway, noting in passing that Lili was still hard at work. But since she didn't call out to him, he knew he wasn't needed. There was no sneaking past Lili's office. She always knew. He figured it probably had something to do with her being a vampire, but had never asked. That was still a sensitive topic for her.

The big house was mostly empty, although he could hear his private chef in the kitchen, directing her assistants, along with the clatter of cupboards and utensils. She came in at least once a week to prepare easily prepped meals for whoever happened to be around. And when there was a special occasion, like tonight, she was always available to him, no matter who else was on her calendar. He was her main client, and any others who contracted with her for an event knew that while she would oversee the menu and discuss every detail with them, one of her sous chefs would be supervising the actual dinner, or whatever the occasion called for, if Nick needed her.

Other than the distant kitchen noise, however, they encountered no sign of anyone as he pulled her up the stairs to his second-floor suite. The double doors were shut, and as usual, secured by a spell which triggered any time they were closed. Lili had a key that could counter the spell for when the housekeeper came, or in an emergency, but other than that, his suite was always secured.

He waved a casual hand and the doors opened to reveal what, he had to admit, was a pretty damn fantastic room. It was a corner suite, and the two outside walls were mostly window. With the twelve-foot ceilings, that was a lot of light coming in. The windows were triple-paned to keep out the heat, naturally. They were also shielded from the outside to prevent anyone seeing in, though there were also black-out shades that he dropped whenever he wanted to sleep, regardless of the time.

"Goddess, Nico. This is as big as my whole house."

"Maybe," he admitted. "If you include the bathroom and the closets."

"Oh well, let's not forget those," she said absently.

He looked around, trying to see it through her eyes. It was big. He wanted it that way. The main room was mostly devoted to a huge bed, which had a mahogany footboard and rails, and a headboard of the same wood, but with ebony inlays in a one-of-a-kind design. The four posts were likewise mahogany, but there was no canopy or drapes, since he had that penis she'd made note of, and besides, they were nothing but dust catchers. It always made him sneeze just looking at those things. There were two matching side tables with ebony inlays in the drawers, and on the wall above the tables were sconces, which had three independent settings and were wirelessly connected to switches on either side of the bed. The bedding itself varied by season, but since this was Florida, it was never much. He liked to sleep in a cold room.

"It's freezing in here," Antonia said at that moment.

So much for sleeping in a cold room, he thought.

"That bed is beautiful. It has to be custom."

"It is," he admitted. "I saw something else, not a bed, but with ebony inlays, and knew that's what I wanted."

She turned to see the rest of the room and, eyeing the adjacent seating area, said doubtfully, "A fireplace? Do you ever use it?"

He nodded. "I read up here sometimes. That couch is long enough to stretch out, and super comfortable. The fireplace is mostly for mood. It's gas, so no smoke or wood mess to deal with."

While she brushed her hand over the fabric, smiling at the soft feel of it, he crossed to the opposite wall and opened the door to the "his and hers" dressing rooms. He'd argued against the "her" version during the renovation, since he'd had no intent of ever acquiring a permanent "her," and he never invited anyone to stay with him in this house. But the architect and designer had both talked about extra space that could be used for anything, and the good old resale value, so he'd caved.

Going back to the pile of suitcases near the door—courtesy of Abe, and Lili's key—he started moving them to the second dressing room, which was still empty, since he had plenty of other places to store things. Antonia turned to see what he was doing and hurried over to help, stopping in her tracks when she saw the large, empty dressing room, with built-in shelves, shoe racks, closets and drawers. And a wide mirror at the far end.

"There's also a private safe for valuables," he added.

She slanted a look at him. "I don't have anything that valuable."

"You will," he said, and left to bring in the remaining cases.

She was still standing in the same place when he returned.

"Nico, this is all too much. I don't need this much room, and—"

"And what? You're planning to stay, aren't you?"

Something in his voice . . . . Oh hell, he knew what the "something" was. It was ninety percent worry, and ten percent challenge, and it had her coming over to put a hand on his cheek and her lips on his mouth. She kissed him firmly, thoroughly, as if to say, "*Stop worrying, you idiot. Of course, I love you.*"

She finished the kiss with swipe of her tongue over his lips and said, "I'm staying."

And though she'd left off the "idiot," he still heard it.

"Well then, this is your closet. Do with it what you will. Bring a chair in. Hell, bring in a widescreen and you can sit in here and watch whatever awful show you want. We'll remodel it to your preference."

"Why can't I watch my awful shows out there, by the fireplace?" she demanded.

He rolled his eyes. "I was teasing. You can watch any damn show you want, in any *room* you want. Just don't expect me to watch it with you."

"Never?"

"Sometimes. Maybe."

She laughed and hugged him. "This is all so wonderful. I keep waiting to wake up and find it was all a dream, like some magical fairy tale."

"It's real, but unfortunately, I'm no prince." He thought about that for a moment. "Actually, I *am* a prince. Huh. Your dream has come true."

"Go away. I want to unpack."

"Can we shower first?"

"We?"

He scoffed. "Of course. Wait 'til you see the shower."

The shower was everything he implied and more, since it was big enough for four, and had so many jets that it had taken Nico a few months to figure out which shower heads he liked best, at what temperature and for how long. He'd quite enjoyed the novelty, actually. But showing it to Antonia was even more fun, especially when he demonstrated the best use of the tiled ledge which just happened to sit at the perfect height for him to lift her onto it, spread her sweet legs, and fuck her to a screaming orgasm, until his body surrendered and shot his own climax deep inside her.

She clung to him in the aftermath, limp and breathless, while steam continued to fill the enclosure and hot water pounded his back. "Did we shower yet?" she asked weakly.

Scooping her off the ledge, he laughed softly. "Not yet. You want your hair washed first, or your body soaped?"

"Oh, no," she insisted. "You can wash my hair, but you are *not* doing the rest. I know you, and I won't be able to stand, much less speak coherently when you're finished *soaping*."

He grinned smugly, even though she couldn't see it. "How about *you* wash your hair, and I'll do the rest?" he suggested reasonably.

She looked up at him. "Did you not hear me? You're not touching the rest of my body. I'll end up a limp rag with prune-like skin, and *maybe* clean hair. I have to meet the rest of your people, *and* sound reasonably intelligent during a very important meeting. And neither of those will be possible—unless you *want* me to sound like I spent the afternoon drinking—"

"No," he protested. "They wouldn't think you'd been drinking. They'd probably just figure we'd been fucking."

She tsked and stared at him in open-mouthed astonishment. "Is that supposed to be reassuring?"

"*I'd* be reassured."

"That's it. No hair, no body, no nothing. This stupid shower *room* is big enough for you to use the other end. Go."

She pointed dramatically, which only made him laugh. But he went, because she was right about the upcoming meeting. They would need her to be able to tell them everything she knew about Sotiris, his allies, and his whereabouts.

Besides, he'd have the whole night after the meeting to leave her . . . how had she put it? A limp rag, with skin like a prune. That shouldn't have appealed to him, but damn if it didn't. He laughed again, keeping it to himself, and moved to the opposite end of the enclosure to finish his shower.

NICK WAS PULLING on his boots when Antonia wandered out of her dressing room and into his, bringing with her the soft sweetness of her scent. She wore a very modern perfume, but a woman's scent was a mix of her unique chemistry combined with whatever perfume or oil she chose to wear. And he'd have known Antonia's scent anywhere.

She used his mirror to check something about her earrings or hair, then turned and frowned when he laced up his combat-style boots. "I know you said casual, but—" she pointed at the boots, "—are we participating in combat drills tonight?"

He finished one boot and started on the other. "These are comfortable. We all wear them a lot of the time, including Casey."

"Not Lili or Maeve?"

"Definitely not Lili. Maeve has a pair, though I haven't seen her wear them since our last battle with Sotiris. I'm sure she won't be wearing them this time, since she's pregnant. Dragan will want her on the sidelines, preferably far away from any conflict."

"Does Dragan still have his wings?"

"He does. Why do you ask?"

"Wings."

Her smile was almost dreamy, which almost pissed him off. What was so great about wings?

"To be able to fly," she said wistfully, answering his unspoken question. "It must be wonderful."

"Don't say that around Maeve. Dragan's wings are usually invisible. When he flies, they rip through the skin of his back, and leave him bloody. Maeve cries every time it happens, though she hides it. So don't tell her I know."

"Why does she hide it?"

"Because Dragan loves to fly. They live in the Appalachian Mountains of Tennessee now, and he flies for the sheer pleasure of it. She'd never take that away from him."

"Oh," she breathed. "That's sad and romantic at the same time. Is there a chance their child will have wings? Is it genetic?"

"We're not sure. His wings are a so-called gift from the goddess of the island where he was born. That was a different world from this one, and thousands of years ago as we now count time. History would have dictated that his brother, who was next in line to be king, would have produced his own second son who then inherited the goddess's gift of wings. But if genetics come into play in *this* world . . . who knows? He can hardly go to a geneticist and ask about his wings, can he? They're hoping for a girl, so it won't be a factor."

"Except for the modern genetics question."

"Well, yeah, but it's definitely sex-linked, so a girl should be safe."

"Any other social landmines I need to avoid? *Unexpected* pregnancies or surprise visits from the mother-in-law, stuff like that?"

"Not that I know of. Grace and Kato have a little girl, so Grace will play a non-combat role. She can shoot a gun, but we're not going to be short on fighters with guns, not in this battle."

"So much has happened. So many battles fought," she murmured. "I feel as though I've slept through it all, like a cursed Snow White."

"Snow White *was* cursed—or rather, poisoned. But since we've already established that I'm a prince, I promise to kiss you awake every morning." He stood, kissed her, and said, "Just don't eat any strange apples."

"Ha ha."

"I thought so." The intercom chirped Lili's signal. "Hey, Lili," he said, activating his end.

"Dragan and Maeve are here," she said happily. Lili and Maeve had become good friends, since they were both total nerds and loved their computers, inside and out.

Nick stomped his booted feet to settle the fit. "We're on our way. Big man out."

Antonia eyed him. "Do you have to say that every time?"

"Nope, I did it just for you. Are you ready for the feast, my princess?"

"I'm ready, but if you call me that even once, I will turn you into a toad."

"I don't believe that's in your skill-set, babe."

"That goes double for calling me 'babe.' And *you* have no idea what's in my skill-set anymore."

THE FIRST THING Antonia heard when they walked down the stairs was the happy sound of lots of people talking at once that only occurred among good friends, and sometimes family. Since Nico's group was both, she wasn't surprised to hear it coming from the dining room. And having met some of Nico's friends, she was no longer nervous at getting to know the rest. If anything, she wondered why she'd ever been worried. After all, Nico hadn't changed, so why would his choice of friends be any different?

Lili and Abe had arrived a few minutes before them, and were just finding seats at the dining room table, which was set in an even bigger room. Nico had grown up in a huge castle, and had built one for himself once he came into his full power and achieved total independence, so she supposed it made sense that when he built a home in this new world, he'd look for wide-open spaces. Besides which, he and his warriors— and Abe too, for that matter—were such big men, that if you put them all together in a smaller room, with a smaller table, there wouldn't be space for them, much less the women.

Lili waved from across the table, while Abe held her chair back, then slid it in beneath her. The gentlemanly gesture had the tiny vampire woman blushing like a school girl, which Antonia thought was wonderful, given the hard nature of her early life.

Nico's hand on her lower back guided her to the left, where the head of the table sat empty, and she shot a quick glance to the right, hoping the plan wasn't to put him at one end and her at the other. The arrangement would have been all but mandatory in the world she'd grown up in, but a nightmare for her on this night. She'd barely socialized before Nico's arrival had broken the curse, and while she could have faked it, she would enjoy the dinner much more with him next to her.

She bit back a smile when he seated her to his left. She should have known better. Nico was far too possessive to ever let her sit that far away from him. She was happy to see Damian to her left and Casey next to him. At least she'd have someone she knew to begin the evening's conversation with.

She'd no sooner sat, however, than Damian shouted down to the other end of the table, where another huge man was getting settled. "Dragan, Maeve! This is Antonia."

Dragan's head came up and his gaze locked on her with the piercing focus of a hardened warrior. *Or a dragon*, she thought as she stared back at him, unwilling to break the contact, though whether to establish equal dominance or to keep an eye on the dangerous predator, she didn't know.

But then he smiled, and it was such a sweet, gentle smile that her heart melted. She remembered what his life had been like even before he'd joined Nico, much less in the centuries or more that he'd spent trapped in stone. Nico had told her that Dragan's stone prison had been particularly cruel since his wings had been lifted in preparation for flight, and he'd been stuck that way for the entire duration of his imprisonment.

"Antonia." Dragan spoke quietly, but she had no trouble hearing him. "I'm very happy to meet you at last. And especially happy that you and Nico are finally reunited." He waited a beat, then said, "This is my wife, Maeve."

A pretty dark-haired woman who'd been talking to Lili looked up at the sound of her name. Her complexion—which was almost certainly extremely pale by nature—seemed just a shade paler, but her face glowed with happiness, and her gaze when it touched on Dragan was filled with love. She started to rise, but Dragan touched her hand to stop her, so she limited her greeting to a smiling wave, and an expressive look at her solicitous husband.

Antonia realized that these men—all of them, except for Abe—were from *her* world. *Their* world, too. She could have told their women— whether mates or wives—that these men would always have been over-protective and sometimes controlling. But never with malicious intent. They were warriors. Protectiveness was in their blood. It was who they were, who they'd been trained to be from the moment they could walk.

A young woman came around and poured wine for her and Nico, who immediately stood and raised his glass. "To friends and lovers reunited," he said, and everybody drank, even Maeve, though with water in her wine glass. Once the glasses were down again, Nico raised his glass again and said, "I'm more accustomed to sharing this toast with warriors, which means mostly men. But everyone in this room tonight has a stake in the coming battle. Everyone has not only a part to play, but a score to settle. So, my friends—" he glanced at Antonia, "—my *family,* I raise a toast now . . . to victory!"

The room resounded with deep, male voices shouting the word, "Victory!" But though the men drowned out the women, that didn't mean they were the only ones shouting. And when it came time to drink, everyone drained their glasses, as if to emphasize their intent. They would find both victory and revenge once and for all in the coming battle. Or they would die trying.

Antonia set her glass down with a solid thud, knowing she sure as hell felt the same.

That done, however, everyone was hungry, and the serving staff was ready. The soup came out first, a cool gazpacho which fit the warm Florida weather. Antonia might have welcomed something hot to offset the air-conditioned chill of the room, but she was glad she'd taken Nico's advice and worn one of the sweaters she'd brought along. She could tell already that living with him, she was going to need them. The gazpacho *was* delicious, however, so well worth the chilly room.

She actually read once that Chicago had more authentic Mexican restaurants than any city in the U.S. She still had trouble believing that, and couldn't help wondering how they defined "authentic." Her reality was that despite living in a Chicago suburb, she'd never even tasted it. Not that her experience was in any way representative of the average person's, since she'd never left her own neighborhood. Regardless of the reasons, however, she loved the opportunity to try something new, and she loved the gazpacho, too.

The serving staff whisked away her bowl as soon as she'd placed her empty spoon on the underplate, and moments later, the salads were delivered. Again, this being sunny Florida, everything, from the greens to the bits of fruit, was super fresh, and the dressing was light and refreshing. She decided right then that she could get used to living in Florida, and then wondered why she hadn't prepared more interesting meals for herself all these years.

"You okay?" Nico's warm voice in her ear had her smiling.

She looked up at him. "Better than okay. I'd say I'm happy, but I don't want to tempt the fates."

He chuckled. "A woman after my own heart. I'm constantly berating those bitches."

"I think you might have missed the logical order of things when it comes to temptation, my love."

"Yeah, well. I was never much of a believer. I just did a lot of cursing."

She laughed. "I remember that." She leaned her head briefly against his shoulder. "I'm so glad to be here with you. With them," she added, lifting her chin at the lively group.

Nico didn't say anything, just put his arm around her shoulders and buried his face in her hair.

"Hey! No necking at the table!" someone shouted. She couldn't have said who, but it didn't matter, because everyone cheered or jeered, and the moment passed into the next topic of conversation. *Just as it should be,* she thought.

By the time the main course had been served and eaten, Antonia was so full of delicious food, she thought she would burst. She was also thankful that the chef, or whoever was making the decisions, was giving them a few minutes before dessert. Maeve had immediately left for the bathroom, with Lili along for company. And the guys had shifted seats, to sit next to each other and confer in low voices—no doubt discussing manly things, whatever those were, though the subject of war and weapons likely played a part.

Nico and Damian were doing the same, rattling off what sounded like an inventory of weapons suitable for a medium-sized country, or maybe something bigger, since she doubted any country in this world included ensorcelled blades or other weapons in their arsenal.

Antonia listened with half an ear, answering the occasional question regarding magic and spells, but otherwise, drinking in the lovely and loving ambience, and hoping with a tiny part of her heart—so tiny that the fates wouldn't notice—that when the coming war was over, they'd all gather again in this room, even Gabriel and Kato and their mates from California, and raise a toast to a better future for all of them.

The scent of herbs and warmth coming too close had her turning to see a pretty human woman, with her long dark hair tied back, leaning over to wrap an arm around Nico's shoulders and exchange double cheek kisses in the style that was common in Europe, but not so much in the U.S. She and Nico greeted each other, speaking in rapid French, which had Antonia switching languages in her head to keep up.

"Nicholas, *mon cheri*. You are more handsome than ever. It's been too long since I've seen you."

"That can't be true. I've been eating your food. I can't be wrong about that."

"That's because I cook for you, but you're never here. I can only imagine the horror of how you re-heat my food."

"Ah, apologies, *ma chérie*. But I think of you all the time while I'm eating."

She slapped his shoulder. "Liar. But I love you, so . . ." She kissed his cheek.

Nico reached out and took Antonia's hand, pulling her into the conversation, and drawing the chef's attention in her direction. "Antonia, this is Viviane Géroux, the finest chef in the Southeast."

Viviane turned a bright smile at Antonia and held out a hand. "Vivi," she corrected. "And he exaggerates."

Antonia took her hand. "Having tasted your food, I don't think he gives you enough credit. It was wonderful."

"Ah, you must keep her around, Nicholas. *She* will eat my food."

"I eat your food," he complained. "But don't worry, Antonia will be living with me from now on."

"*Mon dieu*," Vivi said, eyes wide, "Finally, you are becoming a man." She put a hand to her chest. "I'm as proud as if I were your own mother."

Nico rolled his eyes and muttered, "Prouder, I'm sure."

Someone swung open the kitchen door and signaled silently, but it was enough to draw Vivi's attention. She made a tsking noise and said, "I must go. They are helpless without me."

She kissed Nico, then kissed Antonia on both cheeks, and said, "Good luck with that one." Before leaving, she paused to study Nico a moment. "But he's good-looking, so . . ." Laughing, she tilted her hand from side to side, then hurried to the kitchen where, before the door closed completely, she could be heard speaking very rapid French to some poor soul.

"She's a life force. French?"

"French Canadian, but trained in France."

"Did you . . . date?"

"Fuck, no. Vivi uses twice as much energy as the rest of us just walking from one place to the next. I love her, but she'd drive me crazy in a day."

Antonia looked back at him. "Really?" she said again. "And I'm what? Peaceful?"

"Hardly," he scoffed. "But you're no Tasmanian devil, either."

She laughed at that, having been very fond of Saturday morning cartoons a while back.

"Besides, she has *four* kids, and a retired Navy SEAL husband who's now a vicious corporate attorney. My attorney, actually."

"I wouldn't care if you *had* dated."

"Of course, you would. You're an intelligent woman. Just as I hate the lawyer from *your* past."

"Who's almost ninety now," she commented..

"There is that." He grinned.

Lili and Maeve returned then, passing behind them while Lili was assuring the pregnant woman that the morning sickness would pass soon.

"That's what they all say," Maeve replied. "Until some poor woman's sick for nine months, and then they're all, 'Oh no, it's not just morning, and it's not just three months,'" she said in a chiding falsetto.

Lili stifled a laugh as they reached their seats, where Dragan stood and hooked a careful arm around Maeve's neck, pulling her in and kissing the top of her head. "I'm sorry," he said.

She lifted her face and kissed him back. "Well, I'm not. You're worth that and more. I wouldn't trade this"—she patted her belly,—"or *you* for anything or *anyone in* the world."

He dipped his head, and Antonia would swear the big warrior was blushing. But where the others might have teased Damian or even Nico, they only smiled at Dragan and Maeve.

Their restraint told Antonia that Maeve's reassurance was more important to Dragan and to the others than any joke at his expense. And it made her wonder about his history before he'd joined Nico.

Dessert appeared before she could ask, along with coffee, tea, and more wine for those who wanted it. Though most didn't, because the video conference was coming up, and every one of them wanted to be clearheaded when it came to getting ready for the battle that they all knew was coming.

Chapter Seven

THE CALL TOOK PLACE in the conference room, which was about the same size as the dining room, but with a longer table so people could spread out devices and papers as necessary. It was also a completely interior room, which made it more secure from electronic snooping—on top of various safeguards installed in and around the room itself. The Florida contingent was ready and waiting at the appointed time. Everyone had agreed that the call would be initiated by the California group, since the vampires had specific requirements related to the time of day.

As planned, Kato and Grace had driven to Raphael's estate for the meeting and were in the room, along with Gabriel and his mate Hana, when they came on-line on the large HD screen on the Florida conference room wall. Nick and the four warriors all exchanged cheerful and profanity-laced greetings. The women joined in with somewhat less profanity, mostly. Once the initial exchanges were over, the "meeting" devolved into a verbal cacophony as several conversations filled the room, with no one complaining that they couldn't hear, until Nick finally used his battlefield voice to rise above the others and shout, "Can I have a minute here?"

"Our California colleagues," he said into the ensuing silence, "don't know everyone at this table."

The California group seemed puzzled as they searched the faces in the Florida conference room. But then several mouths opened in silent "ahs" and they smiled, waiting. Nick had no doubt that they knew who was sitting next to him, but Antonia deserved a formal introduction, not merely an unspoken, "Oh, yeah, that's her."

Placing an arm around her, knowing she'd be embarrassed by the attention, he said, "This beautiful woman is Antonia Dellakos. *My* Antonia."

She slanted him a scowling look, but didn't say anything, not in front of these people she barely knew. No, she'd wait until they were in bed later. The knowledge that he could count on them being in bed together at the end of the night made him smile. It was a luxury and a privilege that he'd all but given up on so many times. He tightened his arm around her, and she patted his thigh under the table.

"Gabriel, Kato," she said meeting their eyes over the internet connection. "I'm so happy to finally meet you. I heard so much about both of you back then, and I'm still hearing it now. All good things, of course. I only wish the circumstances were better."

"Lady Antonia," Gabriel said, his resonant voice seeming to vibrate over the connection. "Everyone here"—he glanced around the room to include the others—"was delighted to hear you'd been found. Especially when we learned that your memories had returned along with your magic."

"When the fuck did you become so eloquent?" Damian demanded.

"Hana probably wrote it for him," Dragan said quietly.

Damian laughed. "You're right. I bet she did. Did you practice that, you vamp fucker?"

Hana pounded a hand on the table in protest, but Gabriel covered her hand with his and with a pitying look, said, "Ignore them, *älskling*. They've been in Florida too long. It's sad, but . . . the humidity, it rots the brain."

"Fuck you," came from too many throats for Nick to identify. The whole exchange made him laugh, though, and broke any awkwardness that might have followed Antonia's appearance. They all knew his story—at least the rough outlines—so they knew he'd been searching for her for as long as he'd been looking for them. They might even have suspected that as genuinely overjoyed as he'd been when the four warriors had been freed, he'd begun to despair of ever finding Antonia. He hadn't even known if she was still alive, or if Sotiris had cursed her to a completely different time period, or even a different world.

Fortunately, a bigger and far more annoying distraction entered the California conference room at that moment. Which only made sense, since it was *his* conference room.

"Is that the fucking vampire?" Antonia whispered against his ear.

"Yeah," he growled back.

"Then that must be Cyn with him. Oh my, you said she was beautiful, but Nico, she's stunning."

"I told you—"

"That you never loved her. I know. I'm not worried. But you have to admit . . . they make a gorgeous couple."

"Yeah, I— What? What do you mean?"

"Well, he's as beautiful as she is, don't you think?"

He stared at her. "No. I don't think. What the hell are you talking about?"

Leaning across Damian, Casey whispered, "Think of the children those two could produce."

It was Damian's turn to scowl. "There will be no children," he whispered in turn. "He's a *fucking* vampire."

"I *know* that," Casey said, trying to control her grin. "But they would be gorgeous."

The two men exchanged "what the fuck" looks while the women shared a laugh at their expense.

"Great," Nick muttered, then louder, he said dryly, "Nice of you to join us, *my lord.*" He was disappointed when Raphael did no more than glance at the screen, then leaned over to whisper something to Cyn when she sat on the chair he'd pulled out for her.

When Cyn glanced up with a smile, Nick called, "Good evening, Cyn darling."

She rolled her eyes, familiar with the routine, but then focused on Antonia and asked, "Is that—?"

"Antonia, yes," he interrupted.

"Oh Nick, we heard. I'm so happy for you!" Her smile was huge and genuine, but he'd never doubted it would be. She touched Raphael's arm and said, "Raphael, that's—"

"Antonia Dellakos, yes. A pleasure, Miss Dellakos."

"Antonia, please," she replied, her blush a little high for Nick's taste. Although, he *had* greeted Cynthia with his usual exaggerated endearment.

Raphael looked around his conference room, then the one on the screen and said, "My apologies for being late."

Though he didn't offer an excuse, Nick noted . . . but only to himself since he *knew* it was an asshole observation.

"Shall we begin?" Raphael asked.

Malibu, California

WHEN NO ONE objected, Raphael looked up at the screen and focused on the woman he'd been told was Nick's long-lost love. While he might wonder if she'd have preferred to *remain* long lost, he understood that love was not just blind, but often completely unfathomable. He also understood that he was far from unbiased when it came to Nick Katsaros.

"Miss Dellakos, I understand you are likely to have the greatest insight into our mutual enemy. I'm uncertain of your relationship to Sotiris, but I, and I'm sure others, would be very interested in anything you can tell us that would help in the coming battle. I don't believe anyone among us doubts that there *will* be a battle, and soon."

"Thank you, Lord Raphael. And please call me, 'Antonia.' There's no need for such formality among . . . allies."

She'd probably been about to say, "friends," Raphael thought, but didn't want to offend the fragile ego of her lover. Nodding in acknowledgement of her courtesy, he replied, "Thank you, and I am 'Raphael.'"

"Raphael, then," she said, smiling. "A bit of background first. After I was cursed by Sotiris—much as Nico's warriors were, although my own punishment was far less dire—I was initially unaware of anything about my own identity or past. Sotiris was the only person familiar to me, since he traveled with me when I was thrown into the maelstrom of time and space. More accurately, I traveled with *him*. I know now that he'd just lost that final battle with Nico's armies, though I didn't then. I was sitting in the kitchen garden on Nico's estate, when Sotiris suddenly appeared and simply *took* me. I don't remember anything before arriving on this continent, though I'm certain that this wasn't the first place we went. And I didn't remember even *that* much until about two or three years ago, when the effects of his curse began to weaken more rapidly.

"But it *did* begin to weaken, which is the critical point. And as it did, both my memories and my magic began to return. It was a steady progression, though frustratingly slow, and the more I learned, the more I knew I was missing. Sotiris visited on occasion, checking to see how much I recalled, I'm sure. But eventually the visits became less frequent, while I did everything I could to prevent him from realizing that I was recovering from the restrictions of the curse. His confidence, or more accurately his ego, was his undoing, because he believed me."

"Did you have any warning of when he would visit?"

"No. Though as my own magic returned, I had a steadily increasing interval of warning, since I was able to sense him coming."

"That must have been so stressful," a woman from the Florida group gasped, one hand to her lips.

"Maeve," Cyn identified in a voice low enough that no one but Raphael would hear it. "She worked directly for Sotiris until she freed Dragan. They're married now, the guy to her left. He's the one—"

"Who flies," Raphael interrupted, using telepathy since her hearing lacked the acuity of his own. "I'm not totally uninformed, my Cyn," he added, flavoring the comment with humor.

"It was stressful," Antonia admitted, unaware of the private conversation. "But the same ego that let him believe I was still fully under his curse was of great benefit to me, when I decided to pursue some manipulation of my own. I have a significant magical talent. I'm not a sorcerer—" She held up a forestalling hand when Nick seemed about to interrupt. "I'm not," she told him, before continuing. "My power is of a different nature. But I *do* excel in the design of spells and devices. I can power most of my own spells, although not battle spells. And with most devices, it depends on the complexity of the design. In this instance, however, my plan didn't require anything complex *or* violent. My plan was to spy on Sotiris, and discover anything and everything I could, because by then, I believed that one day I'd be strong enough to escape him altogether.

"I should mention that even as my magic returned, I still had no memory of Nico or the others, until the moment he walked through my front door just over a week ago now. That part of the curse was in full effect. So my escape plan was based solely on a desire to get away from a domineering parent."

Raphael looked around the table as some of those in his Malibu conference room were registering startled surprise. Kato finally broke the moment to demand, "Wait, what?"

"Oh yeah," Damian chimed in. "I probably should have given you the heads-up on that."

"Sotiris is your father? Did you know?" Kato demanded, looking at Gabriel and then the group on the screen.

Gabriel was shaking his head, while Damian said, "We just found out, too."

"We all thought they were married," Gabriel telepathed to Raphael, who kept his expression impassive while sharing that detail with Cyn.

"I don't know where you all got the idea that we were married," Antonia snapped. "Did you think I was cheating on him with Nico?"

"Yeah," they answered in unison, and then all laughed.

"Shall we continue?" Raphael said, finding Antonia's marital fidelity, or not, unimportant, since either way, it had taken place before even *he* was born, and in another fucking world.

"Yes, please," Antonia agreed. "Where was I?"

"Your memory and power began to return, though you still had no memory of me or us," Nick provided.

"Right," she agreed, smiling at him happily.

As if she was delighted to discover he'd been listening, Raphael considered. Maybe she really did like the fucker.

"Anyway, at some point I either slipped up, or the increase in my magical power became so significant that Sotiris detected it on his own. He asked me about it, and there was no point in lying, since he knew already, so I admitted it. But I did so in a way that let me conceal the fact that my memory had returned, as well. His immediate response was to tell me I would be leaving Chicago and going home to live with him.

"When I balked at the command, and asked where 'home' was, he refused to tell me. So, I refused to go. I knew he'd keep pushing for the move, not because of any affection for me, but because he either needed, or simply wanted, my particular skills. Over the years that I'd served as his student, and then his assistant, I'd designed and written many of the spells he'd used. It wasn't that he couldn't do it himself. He just didn't want to take the time. So he'd tell me what he wanted, and I'd create it. It was the same with the hexagon—"

"The hexagon?" Raphael asked.

"One of my best creations, and now, Sotiris's biggest nightmare, and his most serious weakness."

"What is it? And if you have possession of it, why did he not take it from you by force?"

"Antonia doesn't have possession. I do," Nick said. "And yes, the bastard *did* try to take it from me, in Florida, a few months ago. He went to a lot of effort, even putting several thousand human lives at stake simply as a distraction. While all four of my men, plus Casey and Hana, were with me trying to save those lives, Sotiris attacked the house, going after the damn thing. Fortunately, my people at the house got word to us about the attack in time to get some of us back there, and for Kato and Grace to escape with the hexagon, while the others fought him off. They injured him badly enough that once I reached the house, he was forced to retreat."

Raphael nodded. "Yes. Gabriel and Hana briefed me when they returned here. I knew you'd fought, and that Sotiris had been after some magical device. I didn't know it was referred to as the hexagon."

Antonia waved her hand dismissively. "That's what I called it, instead of just the 'rock,' which it really is. A big rock that's roughly hexagonal in shape, that I used as the medium to hold a spell I'd written."

"What does it do, if you don't mind my asking?"

She gave him a smile that was both beautiful and smug at the same time. "It reduces a sorcerer's power by half. But it can only be primed, or targeted, at a single sorcerer. *Sotiris* intended it to be used against Nico, who was his only enemy who'd ever posed a real threat. He assumed that Nico would automatically be *my* enemy, too. Which goes to show how utterly blind he was to my true feelings about him by then. Anyway, once I realized Sotiris's intent, I visited Nico, whom I'd never met before. I wanted to evaluate him personally before deciding what to do. He had a reputation for being a more benevolent ruler than Sotiris, which wouldn't have required much, but also for being more loyal to his people, and they to him. I wanted to judge for myself."

"And upon *meeting* me," Nick interrupted, "she was completely dazzled and within moments, half in love. She saw at once that my reputation was a shadow compared to the truth."

"Uh huh," she said in a monotone. "That's one version. But I *did* know after that first meeting that I couldn't turn the hexagon over to Sotiris."

"And you still have this weapon?" Raphael asked Nick.

"Yes, and it gets better. She—"

"I primed it against Sotiris," Antonia said, before Nick could steal the moment. "He knows it, too, which is what made him decide to curse me the way he did. He already had a plan to curse Nico's warriors before the battle started, and believed that, between the hexagon and the loss of his warriors, Nico would be so weakened that Sotiris would easily kill him during the fighting. As the most powerful sorcerer left alive, Sotiris would then have ruled our world. What he hadn't counted on was that I would betray him."

She shrugged. "He found out before the battle started, but I think he waited to curse me, hoping Nico would sense my fear and sudden disappearance, and be distracted, or weakened even further. But despite everything he'd done, Sotiris lost that battle. And so, he fled, taking me with him."

Raphael studied her for a long moment. "You used your own blood to prime the device?" he asked, knowing he was right. "Did you worry that it might not work? He's your father, but his blood would have been diluted in you."

"I *was* worried, so I modified the spell to widen the blood parameters just enough to make my blood work."

"Can this hexagon be used more than once?"

Antonia paused, and appeared to consider her answer, which surprised Raphael. She'd crafted the spell herself. Surely, she'd have included the device's life expectancy in her parameters.

"The original spell," she said finally, "was designed for a single use every time it was primed, and after each use, it could be primed against someone else. I estimated the rock could absorb no more than five uses, before the spell's magic destroyed the structure of the rock itself. At that point, it would have self-destructed, and become a pile of gravel and dust. But when I altered the spell to use my own blood, it also became less precise. I didn't have time for anything else."

"Which means what?" Cyn asked, trying to conceal her impatience at the lengthy explanation.

Antonia switched her gaze to Cyn, and Raphael saw a flash of something like resentment. Apparently, she knew about Nick and Cyn's past, and didn't like it any more than he did. But Raphael had no doubts about Cyn's love for him, and while he'd reconciled the fact of Nick's sexual relationship with her, he knew that she and the sorcerer had never been more than friends. He still didn't like Nick Katsaros, but he knew the affair hadn't been important to Cyn. Antonia, on the other hand, didn't have his vampire-enhanced ability to know the absolute truth, and it would seem that she wasn't yet reconciled to the relationship between Cyn and her lover.

"It means," Antonia said finally, "that I suspect the hexagon will self-destruct after a single use. And even if it doesn't, its internal structure will be sufficiently degraded that it will become useless."

Cyn turned her attention to Raphael. "Then we need to be absolutely sure before we use it."

He nodded and turned to Antonia again. "You mentioned some subterfuge that you undertook to spy on Sotiris. Do you mind telling us what you learned?"

"No, that's why I'm here. I can probably tell you where he's living—or more accurately, hiding—right now. And also the identities of the people who have been coming to see him, while they plan their next attack."

"Attack on whom?"

"On you."

Raphael concealed his surprise, only smiling slightly. "Do you mean me, specifically? Or this alliance in general?"

"No, he has a broader plan, but the first step is to eliminate *you*, and replace you with the vampire he thinks will kill you. That's how it works, right? That whoever kills you takes over your territory? At least, that's what I've deduced from their conversations about it."

Nick was staring at her in stunned silence, so Raphael said, "I would be most interested in learning which vampire Sotiris believes is capable of such a thing. But apart from that, I would also be interested to know *how* you heard it. And how you know where Sotiris is. It was my understanding that you never left Chicago until very recently."

"That's true, but as I said, Sotiris continued to visit until about a year ago, when we argued over my refusal to help him. By that time, my surveillance spells were so well set that I could lose a few and still keep track. As for where he himself is at any time . . . Sotiris is immensely powerful. That much power leaves a mark in a world like this one, with so little free magic available to draw upon, or to inadvertently camouflage his location. It's the same with Nico," she added, giving her lover a puzzled glance. "Sotiris can locate him just as easily, unless Nico's actively concealing himself."

"Yeah, but Sotiris has been concealing himself all along. He knows we're looking for him," Kato asked.

Raphael was reminded that Kato had magic of his own. It was different from that possessed by the two sorcerers and, apparently, Antonia, too, since she'd mentioned the lack of available magic in this world. Kato's magic, like Raphael's, came from an entirely different source, though they were both rooted in blood. Kato's was inherited from his mother, though she'd never intended him to be an independent power. Raphael's was derived from no one's blood but his own, courtesy of the vampire symbiote.

"Yes, Sotiris *is* concealing his power, but I share his blood. I inherited my magic from him. He cannot hide from me."

"But then logically, you can't hide from him either."

"That's true. Unless a sorcerer who's powerful enough, more powerful than Sotiris"—she patted Nick's forearm where it lay on the table, —"shields me from detection."

"Which I assume you're doing?" Raphael asked Nick.

"Not yet," Nick replied. "He knows she's left Chicago. That was inevitable. And he knows she's with me in Florida. Also inevitable, since only my finding her could have broken her curse. Where we go from here is the question."

"Antonia, can he spy on *you*, the same way you can on him?" Raphael asked.

"In my house in Chicago, I'm sure he could. But here in Nico's home, with all the protection he has on this property and its residents?" She shook her head. "No, I'm sure he cannot."

"I reinforced everything as soon as we arrived," Nick added. "And my security chief, Abe Putin"—he nodded at a man sitting down the table, —"did the same to our physical protections and presence."

"If Antonia transmits everything she knows about this vampire ally of Sotiris's, as well as his current location . . ." He frowned and added, "which is where, Antonia?"

She grinned. "In your backyard, Lord Raphael. He's plopped himself down in a place called Bel Air. Very pricey real estate. I guess he figured if he hid out among the richest of the rich, no one would dare disturb the peace by coming to look for him."

Next to Raphael, Cyn laughed. "Hey, we took on another private haven of the very rich and famous in Santa Barbara, and walked away free and clear. What's a few more wealthy assholes?"

Raphael raised an eyebrow at her description of Bel Air's wealthy residents, considering her own grandparents had lived there until her grandmother's recent death. Her grandfather still did, but he *was* an asshole, so . . .

"My Cyn is correct. I'm very confident that between us, we can keep any noise to a minimum, whether we end up fighting in Bel Air or anyplace else. But my question had to do with whether between us we have a secure means of transmitting information."

"Absolutely," said the tiny blond who was Nick's assistant—Lili, he recalled. "I'm assuming your server is secure, as well?"

"I'm told it is, but I'll have my people contact you. Or should they reach out to Abe?"

"I'll text our secure line to Gabriel, since I have his cell number. And I can bring Abe into my office, whenever they call, no problem there."

"Excellent. Thank you. Then I have no other questions at this time. I'd like to review everything you've learned, including this plan to assassinate me and take over my territory. I shall be most curious to learn more about that. But once we've reviewed everything here, then we can meet again to discuss our response in detail." He paused and met Nick's gaze, and though it was over a video link, there was no question that they were looking at each other. "I assume that you will accept my participation in these hostilities, especially now that it appears your fellow sorcerer has chosen to involve me directly."

Pompano Beach, Florida

NICK HESITATED. He wanted to tell the fucking vampire that his *participation* wasn't required. But he did have a point about Sotiris involving him, and the fucker *was* damn good in a fight. Plus, there was Gabriel. And Nick didn't want to come across as petty enough to hurt *himself*, just to spite the damn vampire. Argh.

"It seems we're both involved this time, and the more the merrier when it comes to Sotiris, so . . . yeah, sure."

It wasn't the most gracious acceptance, but it did the trick, because on the screen, Raphael was checking to see if his people had any questions, before he said, "We'll talk later, then. For now, it's your meeting."

NICK WANTED TO growl and say it always *had* been his meeting, but since he figured the fucking vampire would only get a jolt of smug satisfaction from the comment, he merely smiled, looked around at his own people and said, "Anyone?"

When no one responded, he looked at the vampire. "Shall we convene again tomorrow night, once we've all had a chance to review everything?"

Raphael nodded once. "Same time?"

"That'll work. Until we meet again, then," Nick finished, and had the satisfaction of disconnecting first.

They all stood at the same time, everyone eager to stretch their legs and get out of the conference room. Or maybe they just wanted to escape the meeting room that seemed far too corporate for anyone there to enjoy.

"We'll be staying here until whatever happens next," Damian announced, slinging a loose arm around Casey's neck. "If Sotiris knows Antonia is free, there's no telling what he'll do. And we know he'll work with hired guns when he can't be there personally."

"Agreed," Nick said forcefully. "We should all remain together until Sotiris is dead. The threat he represents won't end until that happens."

"I'll brief my people on the situation," Abe added. "We're already on high alert, but they need to know the latest info we have."

"I trust everyone here," Nick said loudly enough that everyone stopped talking and looked at him. He glanced around the room, his gaze touching on each of them. "But that's as far as it goes. Nothing discussed in this room tonight, or before or after tonight, leaves this room, or the people in it."

"What about Raphael and the others?" Lili asked. "We agreed to exchange information."

Nick grimaced. "Them, too, of course. As much as it pains me to say it, we and they are all on the same team . . . for now."

"Forever, Nico," Antonia said quietly. "Family isn't blood. It's the people you love," she reminded him. "Gabriel and Kato are your brothers. You've said the same to me more than once, in our world and in this one. They and their women, and everyone in this room is family."

"Well, yeah, but—"

"And if Raphael and Cyn are willing to put their lives and people on the line to defeat Sotiris, then you should be willing to set aside whatever grievance you have against him, or vampires in general, and get over it."

Damian was the first to react, with a swallowed snort of amusement, but everyone else was grinning. Except for Nick, who watched them all with eyes narrowed in irritation. "This meeting was over ten minutes ago," he snarled. "So get the fuck out of here, all of you."

"DID YOU MEAN what you said up there?" Nick asked Antonia sometime later, when she was already in bed, half asleep. Her life in Chicago had been less hectic, and *far* less demanding. Plotting the death of one's father, regardless of how much he was hated, was a stressful thing, he supposed.

"I did," she said, rolling to face him, where he stood next to the bed. "We talked about it before."

"You didn't include Raphael and Cyn before."

"They're allies."

"Uh huh. But most allies don't become lifelong family. Especially not when a significant number of the family members might live a long fucking time."

"I suppose that's true." She yawned. "But they live in California, so it's not like they'll be dropping in for dinner every weekend."

"That's good, since *his* dinner might be one of us. Well, unless Cyn's with him. She's probably his sole source by now."

Antonia sighed and sat up. "I knew that's where you were going with this. What do you want to know?"

He sat on the side of the bed. "What did you think of Cyn?"

She shrugged. "She's confident, and appears extremely fit. She was also armed, even though there were at least three very dangerous people in that room, any one of whom would probably have jumped to her defense if an assassin came through the door."

"Raphael's estate is filled with dangerous people who would die for him in an instant. Besides, Cyn's pretty damn dangerous herself."

"I'm sure she is. I did my research on her. Not public sources, those are useless. Gossip is far more revealing. I also spent some time with Maeve and Lili, both of whom filled me in on the legend of Cyn."

"I got the impression you weren't sure about her."

"Sure about what? I'm totally convinced that she's good in a fight, and glad to have her on our side."

"Uh huh. And the rest?"

"Damn it, Nico," she snapped, punching the pillow next to her. "Do you want to know if I'm happy that you and that beautiful woman were . . . fuck buddies? Yes, I know the term," she insisted, at his look of surprise. "No, I'm not. Okay? But she's been with Raphael for several years, and anyone could see, after watching them together for even a few minutes, that those two are solid as a rock. He adores her, and she can't take her hands off of him. They're always touching, did you notice that? And she was armed to protect *him*, not herself. Because she knows he'll be there for her, too."

"I didn't mean—"

"Yes, you did. There's just enough frat boy in you that you'd like me to be jealous. Well, I'm not, and you want to know why? I'll tell you," she continued, without waiting for his reply. "Because as strong as the love is between those two . . . what *we* have is stronger. You and I have been through hell and back, and against all odds, and some powerful forces working against us, we found each other. And that struggle only made our bond stronger. I love you, Nicodemus. I will love you until I take my last breath. And—"

Nick covered her mouth with his, swallowing her words and kissing her with all the love he possessed. "We will take our last breaths *together*, my love. I swear it."

"I know," she whispered.

THE NEXT MORNING, Antonia was up early, eager to compile the latest data from the tracking devices and spells she had on Sotiris. Most were magical in one form or another, but oddly enough, some of her most useful information had come from a few very sophisticated but low-tech bugs she'd managed to smuggle in to Sotiris's home and office, though she'd never been to either place. He would have been astounded if he knew just how compromised his security was. The majority of the bugs were digital and had been inserted into his various computers via emails sent to him or his assistants. Not even Sotiris could run a criminal enterprise on his own. He required personal assistants and lawyers and lesser magic-users to do the grunt work. Just as she'd once done. And while people were constantly warned about email from unknown senders, *she* wasn't unknown. She was in Sotiris's address book, at least. And by now, in the address books of others who worked for him, as well.

Antonia was no hacker wizard like Lili or Maeve, but she was intelligent enough to follow directions. And instructions for how to snoop on someone else's computer, or more, were easily found on the internet. Especially if you were willing to venture into its less savory parts.

As for the mechanical bugs, Sotiris himself had carried both spells and a few of the very lowest-tech bugs. She'd attached them to his person during visits when he'd been too busy shouting at her to notice. She only hoped he lived long enough to realize that he'd contributed to his defeat.

She was coming out of her dressing room—which, she now admitted, she loved—freshly showered and dressed, when Nico stretched a strong, tanned arm out from under the sheet and muttered, "Come back to bed."

She smiled. "I've work to do, but you were up late. Go back to sleep."

"I'd sleep better if you were with me."

She snorted. "No, you wouldn't." She blew him a kiss, rather than risk being pulled back into bed. Nico's idea of waking early was noon, but her brain was at its best in the morning, and the work waiting for her today demanded her best.

She didn't bother telling Nico again to go back to sleep. He was gone before she closed the door.

Chapter Eight

LILI WAS ALREADY hard at work when Antonia walked into her office, carrying a canvas satchel over her shoulder. Her laptop computer was in there, along with a few of the journals she'd kept during her years in Chicago. She'd begun keeping a record of her days when she'd first become aware of herself after Sotiris's curse. It was an odd way to describe it, she supposed, but it was also the most accurate.

She had no memories of her very earliest days. She'd woken up in a place she didn't recognize, but knew she belonged, with no memory of the previous day or week, much less a detailed history of her life. Food had been delivered weekly—simple basics that she could prepare easily and had somehow recalled from, she supposed, her earlier life. She'd never even thought about bills, like the mortgage or utilities, or who paid them. She'd existed in that nothingness for the first few months, she thought, though couldn't be sure of how much time had passed. But then the fog cleared enough for her to recall not what she'd done the day before, but knowing that she *had done something*, that she had *existed*. And so, she'd begun writing detailed records of her days. She'd done it faithfully every night before going to sleep, and checked it every morning as soon as she woke, to remind herself of what she'd done all the days before.

Slowly over time, her memory improved, although without the diary, she wouldn't have recalled more than the prior week at best. Her entries became more detailed then, and began to include speculation as to who she was, and how she'd come to be in what was a nice home in a Chicago neighborhood. When Sotiris visited her for the first time, and presented himself as her father, she'd been delighted, convinced that this man would have all the answers.

But when he brushed off the more serious questions, anything that went too deep, or back too far, she began to include *him* in her speculation about the origins of her situation. He'd continued to pay all the bills as usual, and the groceries were still delivered, though she'd known enough by then to leave a list with the delivery boy, including extras she wanted, or the deletion of anything she didn't.

Sotiris had always made an effort to be pleasant, sometimes friendly even. But he'd been too intrusive, going through her cupboards and drawers in the kitchen, shuffling through the papers on and in her small desk, studying every utility bill, every newspaper she left around, as if looking for anything she'd marked in some way. Even his questions about her well-being were disturbing and insensitive, and his eyes when he asked were always penetrating, as if she were being studied, rather than cared for.

The unavoidable truth was that she'd suffered an injury or some other sort of memory damage, but she was still intelligent, still human enough to have and sense emotion. And her "father," if he even was that, appeared to have no real emotions at all. He was so cold, that she sometimes wanted to touch his hand or face, just to see if his body was as frigid as his soul seemed to be.

She began hiding her journals after that, leaving one diary "hidden" in her desk, where he would be sure to find it. It contained nothing but detailed notes about routine daily activities, and the general memory exercises she'd begun to work on. But she was careful to conceal how much her memory had improved, celebrating in her notes how she'd managed to remember a single event of the prior week, or occasionally most of the previous day. But increasingly, the diary became about her gardens—what she had planted, what food or other treatments she'd used, how different plants had survived the winter, and so on.

Sotiris had begun leaving sums of cash for her to use, as if expecting her to leave the house and shop for herself. But since she'd never stopped the grocery deliveries, and the utilities and mortgage were still paid, she'd just buried the cash in a box in her backyard, and continued her routine.

Her father stopped reading even the diaries after a while, although she continued to maintain detailed records of her beloved gardens. They became a refuge—the one place he would never intrude, because he didn't care enough to visit or ask about them. But she didn't stop hiding the other journals. And those were the ones that she planned to consult now.

"I'm sorry to interrupt, but I need a place to work," she told Lili, wincing at the request and hoping she wasn't intruding. "Nico offered his office, but honestly the view is too distracting, and so are the books. And he has some gorgeous pieces of art in there that I know must be valuable. But I'm working with magic. I need a place I can stretch out and even make a mess, if necessary. Doesn't he have a shielded work-room, or at least a stillroom?"

Lili stood with a friendly smile. "You're not interrupting and there's no need to be sorry, ever. This is your home now, too. Any room can be yours. Still, if it's magic you'll be doing, I think your idea of a shielded room would be best. Come with me." She walked out of her office and started back toward the living area, but when they passed the kitchen, she paused. "You want some coffee? Breakfast? Snacks to take with you? I know what it's like when you're deep in a project and don't want to stop long enough to run to the kitchen, even though you're hungry."

"I had coffee already, and some breakfast, too. But now that you mention it, I'd love a travel mug of coffee to go, and some sugar to keep my energy up. Cookies or candy. At home . . . I mean, back in Chicago, I always kept a stash of Snickers handy. I don't suppose—"

Lili turned into the kitchen and grinning broadly, opened a long, pantry-style cupboard, to reveal a virtual candy store of snacks. "You're not the only one around here with a sweet tooth."

"Goddess, I guess not."

"Help yourself. We even have handy little canvas bags there—we're environmentally friendly in this house—to carry your supply in. And while you do that, I'll get you a big travel mug for your coffee. Cream and sugar?"

"Sugar, please. Thanks. This is great," she said over her shoulder as she began to fill her bag, feeling like the proverbial kid in a candy store.

With the candy stuffed in her satchel, and the giant tumbler of coffee in her hand, she and Lili started down the hall again. When they reached the big living area near the front, Lili pointed to a closed door inside the tiled foyer. "We're going to the basement, which will be colder than up here. Will that sweater you're wearing be enough? If not, there's a closet full of jackets and coats. I don't know who half of them belong to, so help yourself. No one will care."

Antonia's sweater was warm, and she was wearing long sleeves beneath it, but just in case, she opened the closet and took out a fleece jacket that smelled like Nico, then rejoined Lili. "I'm ready."

"There are stairs or an elevator. Preference?"

"Stairs. With all this candy, I'm going to need the exercise."

DOWNSTAIRS, LILI used a key to open a thick metal door, then handed the key to Antonia before entering the room. "I don't want to forget to give you that."

Antonia didn't need to step inside before she knew what the room was. The scent of herbs surrounded her like a warm hug, nearly bringing tears to her eyes. She missed her gardens, but more than anything, she missed her greenhouse. It had been built to her specifications some twenty years earlier—Sotiris had paid for it, for some reason, probably because he thought it was keeping her from thinking about anything else—but she'd updated it just five years ago, and had continued to improve it as technology provided new and better ways of growing plants through a Chicago winter.

It had smelled just like this. The deep, dark aroma of enriched soil lingered beneath the multitude of scents that were the various plants and herbs. Mostly herbs, she saw, since this was a working greenhouse, whereas her own had been as much for pleasure as utility. She'd ask Nico if she could add to this one, or have another built for her own. She had the money Sotiris had given her over she didn't know how many years, and she'd saved all but a small amount. Eventually he'd just given her a credit card, so she hadn't used any of the hidden cash at all, except for the mechanical bugs she'd bought. She could probably have bought those from an online store that was generic enough that the specific item wouldn't have shown on the credit card, but hadn't wanted to risk it.

As soon as she'd refused to help him, he'd taken the card, of course, though either from neglect or a desire to make her dependent on him, he'd never stopped paying the other bills. And that meant she still had most of the cash, and could pay for a new greenhouse here in Florida herself. Although she knew Nico would never let her. Still, she needed to make the offer. And she had to start thinking about a way to earn her own money, she thought. But not today—not until Sotiris was dead.

"And through here . . ."

Antonia jumped at the sound of Lili's voice. She'd become so lost in the joy of once more being surrounded by the familiar scents of a greenhouse that she'd almost forgotten where she was. She turned to see Lili entering a complex digital code on a keypad against the far wall, and frowned. It was just a keypad. No door, so . . . . She gasped when the "wall" moved, and another of Nico's secret doors revealed itself.

"Yeah, I know," Lili said. "He's like a kid with his toys. And he *loves* hidden rooms." She entered another code, and placed her hand on the biometric scanner. The door, which reminded Antonia of the vault door upstairs, popped open a few inches, and Lili shoved it open farther.

"Here you go," she said, holding out one arm like one of those prize women on the game shows. "One magically, environmentally, and every other kind of 'ly' shielded workroom."

Antonia stepped into the open doorway, but didn't enter. It was recognizable as a shielded workroom, but magnitudes more sophisticated than anything she'd ever used before. For one thing, she hadn't needed or used a shielded room in this world at all. What magic she'd used had been for her garden and plants, except for the few listening spells she'd attached to Sotiris. And all of them had used only her earth magic. So even if Sotiris had noticed the use of magic, he'd have thought nothing of it.

But this . . . this was a modern, sophisticated shield room. It still was primarily shielded with magic, since technology and magical spells did *not* get along. Even *she* knew that. But the building materials and the construction were so much stronger and sturdier than anything she could have imagined. There were shelves on or around the walls, and a single wooden table sat in the center of the room, with nothing on it. It was assumed that the magic-user would bring every element he or she required into the room with them, and cast a cleansing spell when they left. Based on its location in the basement, and since Nico had designed it, she knew there would be clean soil for several feet all around, and nothing but natural products would have been used for the walls. Of course, "natural" took on a new meaning in this modern age. Wood and metal could be manipulated in ways that added nothing foreign, but still made it stronger.

"Is this Nico's?" Antonia asked. "I don't want—"

"No, this is a *guest* workroom, I guess. Kato's used it a few times. But Nick has his own under the weapons room out back. In an attack, he figures all of his weapons will be reachable at the same time."

"That's not necessarily a good thing," Antonia said absently, but still didn't step inside. Call her paranoid, but she wasn't walking into any room she couldn't get out of. Gesturing at the biometric scanner, she asked, "Do you need to enter my data into that?"

Lili's eyes went wide. "Oh my gosh, of course. Nobody new has used this in forever. Kato's the only one with the right kind of magic, and like I said, he's already in there. Damian *is* magic, so he doesn't use any of this. Here."

She back-stepped out of the room, closed the vault door, and then the secret door in the wall. Then, entering a different code, instructed Antonia to place her hand on the scanner, all five fingers and palm. She gave Antonia both codes, one for the wall and a separate one for the vault door.

"Do you need to write those down? I'd rather you didn't, but—"

"No. I was raised in a time where histories were more likely to be spoken than written. We learned to remember things. Besides, I can always ask Nico."

"Not if you're stuck inside there. And your phone won't work, either."

"Huh. I guess I better remember, or at least be sure someone knows I'm in there."

Lili studied her with serious eyes that were completely at odds with her usual friendly personality. "You're sure about this?"

"Yes. I'm sorry. I shouldn't joke. My memory is excellent. There's no need to write it down."

"Okay. Well, I'm going to check in a bit later to be sure you're okay. And Nick will be awake eventually. I'll make sure he knows, too."

Antonia could have told her that Nico *always* knew where she was, but the woman was already freaked out enough at the possibility of her getting stuck inside. "I appreciate that. And if I need anything else, I'll step outside and call. I'll be fine, Lili. Honest. I have my candy and my coffee. Everything else I need is right here." She patted the satchel with her journals.

Once Lili had been sufficiently persuaded enough that she'd left and gone back upstairs, Antonia closed the vault door and slid the concealing wall back into place. Before she could do any work with magic—whether to tap into the spells or devices already in place with Sotiris, or to devise new ones—she had to refresh her knowledge of them. Even though each of the ones she'd be working with were her own designs and castings, she needed to be absolutely confident before activating them enough to "download" their data. Use of the technical term wasn't precisely accurate, but it was an excellent description of what she did.

Drawing a deep, purifying breath of the herb-scented air, she settled on a padded stool in the greenhouse, placed her coffee and candy within reach, and opened the journal holding the notes of when she'd first begun working on the design of a spell that could be used to spy on Sotiris.

NICK GRABBED A towel and stepped out of the shower. He'd spent two hours in the weapons room with Damian, Casey, and Dragan. They each had their preferred weapons, but to say that Nick's personal armory was overstocked was an understatement. If an ordinary human had his stockpile, they'd be arrested. The variety of guns might not be unusual enough in some states, but the RPGs and explosives, along with all the supplies necessary to use them, were an insurrectionist's dream.

There was also a large and varied collection of edged weapons, from the tiniest pocket knife, to an ancient broadsword that required a man of Damian's strength to wield. Not that the former god of war would be using a broadsword, except as a backup. Damian had fallen completely and utterly in love with modern weapons, and considered sub-machine guns to be a miracle of invention. That didn't mean he'd be going into battle with no blade at all, only that the HK MP5—which he'd modified, using his godly knowledge and modern techniques, to better suit his unusual strength and speed—would be his weapon of first choice. It was almost guaranteed, however, that the sword would be drawn before he was finished, when the ancient warrior he'd been born to be came out to play.

Kato's main weapon was his magic. Dark, deadly, and unforgiving, the magic he'd inherited from the infamous Dark Witch who'd been his mother was unforgiving and always inside him. But he also carried an MP5, for when the enemy came in too great a number and demanded an immediate death.

Dragan used a blade, pure and simple. His wings dictated the placement of his weapons, and he'd been trained to fight with wings nearly from birth. Rather than an encumbrance he had to work around, they were themselves a lethal and intimidating weapon. Sharp and taloned like a dragon's, he could gut or even decapitate a man with the single swipe of a wing as he flew past, on his way to battle someone else. He was deadly in the air or on the ground, but always used a blade.

Gabriel was a vampire, and bound to Raphael, so he'd be joining the battle with the vampire lord's fighters. Raphael wasn't an ordinary vampire, however. He was very possibly the most powerful vampire alive, and as such, could share his enormous power and strength with the vampires going into battle with him. He also had the advantage of telepathic communication with them, so that coordination during the fighting was fast and accurate. Nick had hated to lose Gabriel to the fucking vampire, which was how he saw it. But he had to admit that his brother warrior was healthier and happier since he'd pledged fealty to the vampire lord. Apparently, the connection between lord and vampire was essential to a vampire's well-being. Nick hadn't known that when he'd "healed" Gabriel, but then, the vampires of their world had been very different than those of this one.

Casey and Cyn, of course, would both be in the thick of the battle. It would have been impossible to stop them, no matter who tried. They were both highly trained and experienced fighters, equally skilled with gun and blade, which, in their case, meant a variety of knives. Casey had tried a sword to please Damian, but had found a long knife worked better with her strength and reach.

The other women, Antonia included, were to be in secure locations, manning the extensive network of computer and other electronic data gathering. Antonia was already working to access her magically-obtained surveillance data, which should grant them a tremendous advantage, and one that Sotiris wouldn't know to look for, until it was too late, if then. There was no reason for—and every reason against—Antonia to be on the battlefield itself. It was not only unnecessary for the retrieval of her data, but might actually work against her. By her own admission, she'd never been on a battlefield, much less in an actual fight. Her concentration would be shattered. Far better for her to remain on Raphael's estate, where he almost certainly had his own equivalent of a shielded room. Vampires might not use magic the way a sorcerer did, and frankly Nick wasn't sure about all of them, but they *did* use magic. There had to be times when they required a magically *quiet* room.

Of course, Nick hadn't yet told Antonia what her tactical position would be. When he did, he knew she'd argue about it, but even during the years when she'd still been helping Sotiris design weapons for the battlefield, she'd never used or even tested any of them.

But then, Sotiris had rarely stood on a battlefield either. His only guaranteed appearances had been when he and Nick had faced each other directly, which was usually separate from the rest of the fighting.

Thoughts of Antonia had him automatically searching for her on the magical plane, as he'd done at regular intervals through the afternoon. He didn't find her, not her physical presence anyway. But he knew from Lili that she'd started working in the still room that morning, and intended to use the shielded room as well. And after their conversations yesterday, he wasn't surprised. Though she rarely spoke of it directly, her need to destroy Sotiris was probably stronger than any of theirs. She might have felt some need to stamp out the stain on her blood lineage, but her desire for revenge came mostly from the fact that the bastard had stolen her *life* for so many years—most of which she still had no memory of. She didn't know what he might have had her do in that time. Nick *knew* Antonia. He'd known her before Sotiris had cursed her, and saw the heart of that same woman in her still. She grew into herself more and more with every day, since they'd been reunited. She was strong and independent enough to have primed the hexagon with her own blood in order to stop Sotiris, and then to have stolen and delivered it to *him*, knowing that Sotriris would kill her. She'd been willing to *die* to stop him.

But he'd done worse than kill her—he'd stolen everything she was. Her magic, her strength, her will, the freedom to govern what her body did. Oh, Nick didn't doubt that Antonia wanted Sotiris dead. He just wanted to be sure she didn't die making it happen.

Feeling the sudden, urgent need to see her, to reassure himself that she was alive, and that their reunion had been real, he finished drying off from the shower with a few quick swipes of the big towel, pulled on a clean T-shirt and jeans, shoved his feet into socks and boots, and went in search of her.

Taking the stairs a few at a time, he used his key to open the still room door and tried not to sneeze as the scent of herbs and dirt struck his sinuses. He rarely worked in the still room, preferring his office upstairs. And with his own shielded workroom, he rarely had to even pass through this place. He'd show the workroom to Antonia once this mess with Sotiris was over, although he knew she'd prefer to use this one, because of the still room, and also because she wouldn't want her work affected by his much more powerful and more violent magic. Workrooms were shielded to prevent magic from leaking outward and wreaking havoc, but there was no way to shield against the room itself absorbing at least some of the magic used within, especially when that magic was Nick's.

Leaving the still room door open enough to admit some fresh air— which Antonia would scold him for—he saw that the vault door was closed, which meant she was still working inside. He had a choice then— he could either sit among the herbs and wait for her, or interrupt what she was doing and let her know he was there. Opening the vault door without warning was risky. Theoretically, he could be injured when whatever magic she was using broke free, but his power would protect him. He wasn't worried about himself, however. Antonia would be at much greater risk, since her magic would abruptly whip out of control when the shielding was broken by the opened door.

He decided on a quiet telepathic hail instead, dampening his mental voice as much as he could while still being assured of penetrating the vault. *"Antonia,"* he sent, intentionally flavoring her name with his deep love for her. He waited patiently after that. If she was in the middle of something, she'd want to finish.

When she responded, it was by opening the vault door. "You called?"

"Did I interrupt you?" he asked.

"Not at all," she said smiling. "I was just finishing up anyway." Walking into the still room, she went directly to the hallway door he'd left open, and with the expected chiding glance in his direction, shut it completely. "The air in here is warm and moist for a reason, oh great one."

He shrugged. "I don't like it."

She laughed. "I'm guessing *your* workroom does *not* include a still room."

"You've got that right. I don't use herbs often in my work." He pulled her between his legs, where he sat on the stool, and wrapped her in a tight embrace. He needed to *feel* the warmth of her body and the softness of her curves, and to inhale the sweet scent of her hair. "You smell good."

"It's the magic that your sorcerer nose is picking up."

"Nope. It's just you." He kissed the top of her head.

She pulled back enough to see his face. "Is everything okay?"

He kissed her gently. "It is now." Nodding at the closed workroom door, he said, "You've been working a long time."

"I took breaks for snacks and water, and to check my notes, too. But I finished everything I'd hoped to. I'm not ready for battle yet, but I am ready to brief you and Raphael, and the others, on where Sotiris is, and some of what he's planning. Or at least, who he's planning it with, including the name of the vampire he thinks will take Raphael down."

"Really? Does the guy have a death wish or something?"

"Didn't sound like it. Maybe he knows something, or maybe Sotiris is going to help him out?"

"Well, shit. I can't ask for anything more than that. All I did was play cops and robbers with everyone."

"You're joking."

"I mean, we didn't run around the neighborhood shooting finger guns and arresting each other, but we did fire a hell of a lot of ammo at a bunch of human-shaped targets, and compete to see who won."

She tilted her head in bemusement. "Who did?"

"Fucking Damian. He always wins."

"He was worshipped as a god of war," she reminded him unnec-

319

essarily. "And I don't have to tell you that sort of adoration has a power of its own."

"So he constantly tells me. You want to give me an overview? Ask any questions? Or do you want to save it all for the bi-coastal meeting of minds tonight?"

"I'd rather save it, so I can get everyone's input at the same time."

"You know, I'm a little surprised that Sotiris would ally with a *vampire*. He never had much use for them."

"He didn't have any use for *our* vampires. I think these vampires are a whole different kettle of fish."

"Kettle of fish?"

She shrugged. "My longest-running neighbor used to say it all the time. I picked it up, I guess."

"I'm curious to see what Raphael's reaction is when you tell him who the vampire is. We're not buds or anything, but I do know that others have tried and failed."

"You said you helped save his life once. Was that—?"

"Yeah. Although what I really did was help *Cyn* save his life. She did all the heavy lifting. All I did was hand her a key."

"That sounds interesting."

He grimaced. "Let's just say, it's a story for another day."

"Is it? Now I'm even more intrigued. Fortunately for you, I'm also tired and hungry. I want a shower and hopefully a nap before dinner."

"That's something I can help you with."

"I'm not sure I *need* your kind of help."

"I'm wounded."

"As long as I get at least an hour's sleep before dinner. Okay?"

"Sure."

"LIAR," ANTONIA said two hours later, as they finished dressing for dinner.

"Whatever it is, I'm innocent," he complained, pulling a clean, long-sleeved shirt over his head.

"You haven't been innocent since you were ten. No, make that three."

He laughed. "You didn't exactly object, babe."

"Don't call me that. And I couldn't object—you kept my mouth busy."

He tugged her into his arms and kissed her. "I did, and you were amazing."

"I'm sleeping in the other room tonight."

"There is no other room, and besides, no, you're not. If you tried, I'd just fetch you back to where you belong. Come on," he said pulling her back, when she tried to escape. "You loved it. Admit it." He kissed her neck and she laughed.

"I'm not going to admit anything. You're too cocky as it is."

He waggled his eyebrows in response, which only made her laugh harder.

"Goddess, you're impossible. Now, let's go downstairs. If you're not going to let me sleep, you at least have to feed me."

"That I can arrange. Or I can arrange for someone else to arrange it, which I've already done. Would you like me to carry you down the stairs? Since you're so tired, I mean."

"No. Now behave and get me some food."

Malibu, California

RAPHAEL LISTENED with less than perfect attention while Antonia detailed the methods and limitations of her surveillance efforts, most of which involved various spells she'd managed to attach to Sotiris during his regular visits to her home in Chicago. His own magic wasn't dependent on spells or ingredients of any kind, other than his own blood, which for obvious reasons, was always with him. So he used the time to study the body language of the people on the other end of this video conference. He'd arranged for the call to go through before everyone was assembled in Florida, not to compensate for his tardiness on the first call—which might be assumed by some, though not by anyone who knew him—but to give him the opportunity to observe the Florida half of their group in the less structured minutes before the meeting began. And after offering the appropriate greetings, he'd continued those observations during Antonia's initial comments.

Juro and Jared had both joined the original group in the Malibu conference room, since he'd assumed details of the coming conflict would be discussed during this meeting. They'd both watched video of the previous call and were up to date on what was already known. And he could count on them to remember everything that was happening while he wasn't listening. In the hours between that meeting and this one, his people had been working as hard as Antonia to generate information on their mutual enemy. Ever since the fight to rescue Gabriel's mate, Hana, from Sotiris's clutches just over a year ago,

Raphael's security team had been collecting whatever data they could find on the sorcerer's movements, property, and wealth. In Raphael's experience, one of the best ways to nullify an enemy was to cut off his funding. In Sotiris's case, that was less effective, since he was old and crafty. Raphael's people estimated that for every bank account or property record they managed to steal, transfer, or delete, Sotiris had two more he could access. One could hide a lot of wealth over several centuries of living. No one knew that better than he did.

Next to him, Cyn hid her sigh of boredom behind a cough. His mate had an excellent mind and could, when motivated, apply it to the task at hand. But like him, she was waiting for what she called the "meat" of the matter, not interested in the appetizer, which was apparently Antonia's methodology explanation. He hid a smile of his own and stroked a comforting hand up her thigh.

"Raphael, the most critical thing I discovered involves your people the most."

Antonia's comment drew his immediate attention. "The vampire ally. There are a few I'm aware of who might think to try, but my own people have verified their recent activities and found nothing suspicious. Did you, by chance, get a name?"

"I did," Antonia said with a note of satisfaction. "I don't know if it's a first or last name, but Sotiris called him 'Reinhart.'"

Raphael frowned, then glanced at Juro and Jared who both shook their heads, indicating they too were unaware of a vampire by that name, much less one who was strong enough to contemplate taking on Raphael.

"Is it possible that Sotiris is planning to assist this Reinhart through magical means? Challenging me is not without risk," he said, in a massive understatement.

"I can't say with certainty. But Sotiris did make vague references to something or someone who would be waiting for Reinhart upon his arrival in California."

Now *that* was interesting. "So he's not in California yet?"

"No. I'm quite certain of that. If I were to guess, or interpret what was said, I would think he's been moving around almost constantly the past few years. Something happened in Chicago, I think, but definitely the Midwest, that caused Reinhart to go on the run." She made a face. "That sounds silly, but it's essentially accurate, I think. Maybe 'fugitive' is a better word. None of it made sense to me, but I thought you might have a better understanding." She looked up from her notes to peer at Raphael. "Do you?" she asked curiously.

Cyn inhaled sharply, digging her fingers into his arm at the mention of Chicago, whose previous and now dead, vampire lord had tried to assassinate Raphael. Slipping his hand over hers, he soothed silently and answered Antonia. "I do, thank you. I will locate this Reinhart and deal with him myself. He won't be a consideration by the time we confront Sotiris."

"If you're sure? I can try to get more."

"That won't be necessary. I probably have better sources for this hunt."

"If I overhear anything more from the surveillance bugs, I'll let you know."

"I would appreciate that."

"All right, now about the rest of Sotiris's planning . . ."

Raphael tuned out again, confident the others would pick up anything he needed to know. His mind was racing. Klemens was the former Lord of the Midwest who'd tried to kill Raphael, but he was long dead. If this Reinhart was powerful enough that he thought to defeat Raphael, even with Sotiris's help, he had to have been someone high up in Klemens's organization. Fortunately, the current Midwestern Lord, Aden, was part of the new North American alliance, which included every vampire lord on the continent. As Klemens's successor, Aden would either know of Reinhart, or be able to find out about him.

Sotiris magical assistance *might* be a complication, but because it was completely different than Raphael's own magic—which was considerable—his should be capable of overwhelming the sorcerer's so-called assistance for this Reinhart, whoever he was. His first task would be to find the would-be challenger, and for that, he'd need to call Aden. Impatient to begin eliminating this enemy, he had to force himself to remain seated, to give at least the appearance of listening to the rest of Antonia's briefing, until finally the words he'd be waiting for were said.

Pompano Beach, Florida

"THAT'S EVERYTHING I have for now," Antonia finished. She looked up to find Raphael watching her intently. "Unless you have questions, Raphael?"

He stared a moment longer, then blinked. "No. We'll pursue the Reinhart matter, and deal with it. Thank you, Antonia. You've accomplished more than we could have hoped."

"Thank you." Pleasure tried to heat her skin, but Antonia fought it back with a bit of magic. She'd been away from most people for so long, that even simple courtesy had the power to embarrass her. Especially when it came from a man as inherently charismatic as Raphael. Or Nico. She wondered if the two men realized how much alike they were. She imagined Nico's probable reaction, and decided not to mention it.

"If that's all, Katsaros?" Raphael asked.

Nick stirred next to her. "That's all for us. We have time to do this right, I think. I'll advise you immediately if there's any indication Sotiris is trying to move up the timeline."

"Good. Goodnight."

The screen blanked out and she looked at Nick. "Was it me, or did he stop listening at some point?"

"It wasn't you. He definitely checked out, but his people were as alert as ever. He'll count on them to fill him in."

"Was I boring, or—?"

"Hell, no. But once you gave a name to Sotiris's vampire ally, old Raphael there was working a mile a minute, figuring out how to find him."

"Oh, okay. That makes sense. How about you?"

"I'll leave the vampire to him."

"I know *that.*" She gave him an exasperated look. "I meant about the rest of it."

"The rest is for us, and thanks to you, we've got plenty to work with." He raised his voice to include the others. "We're meeting here tomorrow at noon. I want ideas, suggestions, information, including blueprints if you can get them, Lili. But basically, bring anything you can find or think might be relevant to an assault on Sotiris's latest hiding place."

Chapter Nine

Malibu, California

RAPHAEL WAITED until Juro confirmed that the connection was terminated between them and Florida, then pushed away from the table. Stretching his legs, he looked at the others in the room with him, including Gabriel and Hana. "Suggestions?"

"Find that fucking Reinhart," Cyn muttered.

He smiled and tugged her chair back next to his. "Agreed. Any suggestions on *how* to do that?"

She sighed and droned, "Networks."

Raphael laughed. "Such enthusiasm warms my heart. But I think Aden's network will be the most useful. I'll call and ask what he knows, and what he can find out discreetly. I don't want this fool getting word and disappearing before we can catch up to him.

"Gabriel," he added, "I'd like it if you could check with the guards here—vampires only—and see if any remember a vampire by that name. A lot of Klemens's people migrated here before he died. Don't tell them why. Most won't ask, but if they do, make something up. But be consistent."

"I could say I have a friend who's asking, that Reinhart's trying to set himself up in a smaller city in the Midwest or close by?"

"Keep it vague, and if anyone pushes too hard for details, let me know."

"Yes, Sire."

"All right. There's still time to call Aden tonight, so that's it."

Raphael left for his office, which was just down the hall. Cyn went with him, but on the way, she said, "You know it might be worthwhile to call Kate Hunter. Her FBI contacts might turn up this Reinhart guy, too."

Raphael winced. Lucas was Raphael's oldest vampire child and Lord of the Plains territory, which abutted Raphael's own. He was devoted to Raphael, and at the first sign of a threat would jump in to protect him, which was neither necessary nor wanted, at this point. He was also bloodthirsty and would add himself to the Sotiris battle, just for the thrill of it. And unfortunately, in this case, Kate Hunter was Lucas's mate.

"Only if Kate can keep it to herself," Raphael said, "If Lucas finds out, he'll start hunting the bastard himself and then he'll want in on the fight with Sotiris, which is one vampire lord too many. This is Nick's battle, not ours. We're just the support staff on this one."

Cyn grinned, then kissed him good-bye and went off to call Kate, while Raphael continued on his way to his office. Sitting at his desk, and using the phone dedicated to calls between the North American lords, he tapped Aden's number.

He answered almost at once, with a brisk, "Lord Raphael."

"Good evening, Aden. Is everything well with you and Sidonie?"

"We're both well. Sid is busy adopting every homeless animal she can find, but we have room and she gets great pleasure from it."

Raphael paused long enough to be grateful that, thus far, the only thing his Cyn collected was weapons, before getting to the heart of his call. "Aden, I'm trying to find a vampire who I think might have worked for Klemens. I believe he's left the territory by now, but I thought you might remember him."

"Sure. What's his name? And is he powerful?"

"Powerful enough to think he can challenge *me*, with a bit of sorcerous assistance. The name's Reinhart."

"Well, fuck. *He* can't take you. I don't care how much assistance he has. He's nothing but a world-class ass-kisser, which is probably why Klemens liked him. He ruled Ohio, which is a big state, but peaceful for the most part. Not too many troublemakers. He fled as soon I told him I had no further need for his services."

"Do you know where he went?"

"We tracked him as far as we could. Near as we could figure, he took a straight line out of my territory, skirted DC, then eventually disappeared. Probably flew from there."

"If he flew to Mexico," Raphael said slowly. "He could remain hidden for a long time. It's a lot of territory, with plenty of empty places to hole up, especially if he kept his head down."

"And if he was hiding in Mexico, California's right across the border."

Raphael considered that. "I'd have sensed him, and so would my people in San Diego, especially if he stayed. If he's smart, he'll remain in Mexico until it's time for him to move."

"How's he going to make it to Malibu without you knowing about it?"

"That's where the sorcerer ally comes in, I suspect."

"Sorcerer?" Aden asked. "I thought those fuckers were scarce these days."

"They are," Raphael agreed. "Unfortunately for us, the only two truly powerful ones still alive are both in North America. Deadly enemies, of course."

"Oh, of course. What's that got to do with us?"

"You know Gabriel? He's on my security staff," Raphael said.

"Yes. He's deadly with a blade," Aden said.

"He has a complicated history that includes Nicholas Katsaros— also a sorcerer—having saved his life at one point, long before he came to me. Gabriel's mate was kidnapped by Sotiris last year. She possesses a very desirable magical ability which Sotiris decided he wanted for himself, and so he planned to keep her prisoner . . . permanently. Katsaros and I worked together to locate and free her. He and Sotiris ultimately fought, and Sotiris escaped. But now he's back."

"What the hell does he want?"

"Actually, it's what *we* want, which is to be rid of him."

"Pre-emptive strike," Aden said approvingly.

"Something like that. Sotiris has the same idea, and part of *his* plan is for this Reinhart to challenge, and presumably defeat, me."

"Yeah," Aden scoffed. "Like I said, that's not happening."

"I think they would disagree. We have reason to believe that Sotiris has provided Reinhart with a device or spell that will make me vulnerable long enough for him to kill me."

"Yeah, right," Aden scoffed. "For any device to work, it would have to take out you and your entire estate full of vampires before he ever got there." He chuckled. "And when that failed, he'd have to deal with Cyn, who'd hunt him down and butcher him slowly just for trying."

"I don't intend for it to get that far. My part of the pre-emptive strike is to locate and challenge Reinhart before he's ready."

"Throw out the trash, before it stinks," Aden agreed.

"Yes. Once I take out Reinhart, most of the action will be between sorcerers. I'll be providing backup at that point."

"How much time do I have?" Aden asked, reverting to his serious self.

"As soon as possible."

"I'm intrigued. I'll get started this morning, if there's nothing else?"

"No. I don't have to tell you to be discreet. You might want to bring Vincent in, if necessary. But no one else."

"I understand."

"Thank you, Aden."

"Any time, my lord. But bear in mind, if you require an ally, I'm always willing to engage in whatever bloodshed is necessary."

Raphael chuckled. "I shall do so."

They both disconnected at the same time.

IT TOOK NO TIME at all for Aden to learn that Reinhart was indeed in Mexico, and that he'd made a name for himself consistent with his disreputable history. When the sun rose in Chicago, he turned the hunt over to Vincent, who was Lord of Mexico.

Vincent learned that Reinhart was holed up so close to the California border that he was in more danger from US Border Patrol than anyone else. He was, however, still in Mexico, which was why none of Raphael's people had picked up any attempt to enter Raphael's territory.

By the time his specific location was confirmed, however, the sun had risen on the West Coast, and so it was Vincent's mate Lana who called Raphael's estate, and Cyn who answered.

"Hey Lana," Cyn said. "What's the news?"

"I hear you're looking for Reinhart."

"Yeah, you know where he is?"

"I can tell you where he's been living for the past week, and that he was still there as of last night."

"Great. Where?"

"Just this side of the border, east of the Otay Mesa Port of Entry. There's kind of an industrial park there. He's holed up in one of the empty offices, waiting, it seems like. Though I don't know what for."

"As long as he's there, it doesn't matter what he's waiting for. He'll soon be too dead to get it."

"You're not heading over there by yourself."

Cyn sighed. "I'd love to, and you know damn well you'd love to join me. But Raphael would *not* be happy. So, I'll be a good little human, make the calls, and get everything set up, so we can fly down there *together*, where it will take him three minutes to stomp on this irritating insect. After which, we'll be home in time for cocktails."

"Huh."

"No, really, Lana. I'm making light of it, but this one is important and has to be Raphael's. You guys and Aden worked at lightspeed to find this asshole, and we really appreciate it. I know Raphael will call Vincent when it's over and tell him what's going on."

"And Vincent will tell me, and so the world turns once more."

Cyn laughed. "So I've heard. I have to start making those calls I mentioned. Thanks again, Lana. Hope to see you soon. Your place or ours! Bye."

WHEN RAPHAEL woke that evening, Cyn was next to him, as always. But instead of a naked Cyn who rolled into his arms, he found a combat-ready Cyn, minus only her weapons and boots, sitting cross-legged and obviously waiting for his eyes to open.

"What is it?" he growled, sitting up enough to pull her down for a kiss, despite the belts and, Christ, the knife hilt digging into his side.

"We have Reinhart."

THEY WERE ON their way to the Mexican border forty-two minutes later. Vampires could move damn fast when they wanted to, and they *really* wanted to this time. Cyn had already arranged for the helicopter to be waiting on the green inside Raphael's estate, so getting ready had been mostly a matter of waking the necessary vampires. Raphael was old enough and powerful enough that he was always the first vampire to wake, so while he dressed, he sent telepathic wake-up summonses to Jared and Juro, along with Gabriel and Juro's twin brother Ken'ichi.

As Raphael's lieutenant, Jared would be remaining on the estate, overseeing its protection in the event someone thought to take advantage of Raphael's absence. Juro and Ken'ichi were both mountain-sized vampires who'd been with Raphael for well over a hundred years. Juro was his security chief, and Ken'ichi had accompanied and protected Cyn when she'd rescued Raphael from a close call with death at the combined hands of several European vampire lords not long ago. Along with Gabriel, these were the vampires that Raphael trusted unconditionally to have his back.

Vincent had called as they were boarding the helicopter, but only to ask if Raphael wanted him to meet him at the border in case Reinhart tried to claim some false jurisdictional protection.

Raphael had laughed and said he didn't expect to be in Mexico long enough for the matter to come up.

Vincent had offered Raphael a tongue-in-cheek—but still valid—

invitation to visit Mexico that evening. They'd both been laughing when they hung up.

And now, with the human government's permission also acquired, the helicopter made its way across the border into Mexico. They were only minutes from landing, and Raphael reminded his people that they still didn't know what assistance Sotiris might have rendered, and to be prepared for a magical attack or weapon. With the exception of Cyn, they were all powerful enough to have some magic available to protect themselves, but if it came down to that, it would be Raphael who protected them all.

The helicopter landed in an empty parking lot, one building over from where Reinhart was holed up. They ran from that point, taking great pains to stick close to the shadows, just in case Reinhart was smart enough to be keeping watch.

He wasn't. But it wouldn't have mattered, if he had been.

REINHART LOOKED up when the door opened and was on his feet by the time Raphael entered. He remained that way while he watched Juro, then Gabriel, and finally Cyn and Ken'ichi enter the building, not speaking at all until the door was shut.

"Forgive the surroundings," Reinhart said, gesturing at the dirty cement floor and open-studded walls. "This wasn't my choice of meeting place."

Raphael studied him curiously, wondering at his lack of fear or even defiance, while searching for any indication of power or physical device that could be at the root of the vampire's attitude. It was possible that Sotiris had shoved some nasty piece of magic *into* the vampire without his knowledge. The sorcerer didn't need *Reinhart* to survive. He wasn't strong enough to be a power in battle, and he wouldn't survive long enough to rule *any* territory, much less Raphael's.

"Juro, it occurs to me that my . . . challenger," he said dismissively, "might be an unaware Trojan horse of sorts? Perhaps you and others should wait outside."

Cyn's reaction was immediately, profane, and decidedly negative. While Juro said only, "If that's true, Sire, then perhaps you should let *me* remain, while *you* take the others outside."

Sometimes loyalty is a pain in the ass, Raphael thought. "Fine, but if we're threatened, just shoot him. I'm sure my Cyn has an extra weapon to loan you."

"No need, Sire. I brought my own, just in case we met up with some humans."

"It's all fun and games," Cyn hissed, "until you both *die*."

Raphael turned to caress her cheek, and spoke telepathically. "*I am not going to die, my Cyn. I am not finished with you yet.*"

"*You better not be,*" she telepathed back at him, making him smile. That was twice in a short period of time that she'd used mind speech with him.

Raphael walked up to Reinhart. "Here I am. I understand you intend to challenge me?"

The vampire lifted his chin in a show of defiance, and said, "I do. Shall we discuss terms?"

"We're vampires, Reinhart," he snapped. "There are no terms. You can't possibly have risen as far as you did under Klemens without knowing that."

"Yes, of course," Reinhart replied quickly. "But we agreed on the time and location at least."

"Ah, you're hoping to delay until your allies arrive."

"Allies?"

Raphael sighed. "This grows tiresome."

"What do you want?" Reinhart demanded.

"This is *your* challenge. But you should know that I am aware of your partnership with Sotiris, and whatever assistance he promised you will not be arriving. In the spirit of fairness, on my part at least, you may now surrender and beg for a merciful death. Or we can proceed, and your death will be far from merciful."

"I *need* no allies. I have *this*. Reinhart produced a dagger, seemingly from the air itself. Before he could turn his wrist to aim the weapon, Raphael reached out with blinding speed and caught Reinhart's wrist, stopping it in midair as the vampire fought to free himself, muscles bulging and his face set in a grimace of effort.

As Reinhart struggled, Raphael stood almost casually, holding on to the would-be assassin's wrist and studying the dagger. "Did Sotiris give you this? Was this his *assistance*?"

"It's all I *need*. Which you'll know soon enough. Its magic will turn you to ash faster than the sun itself."

"Really. Let's see, shall we?" While the vampire stared in terrified disbelief, Raphael turned the dagger, still clutched in the challenger's bloodless hand, and plunged it into Reinhart's own chest.

The vampire's body filled with a sudden and brilliant light, as if a torch had flamed to life inside him. White flames seared through his skin and he stared at Raphael knowing that death was at hand. Not Raphael's, but his own. His mouth opened, as if to scream, but no sound came out, as his chest exploded in a burst of white light, and Reinhart, the vampire who thought to become lord, was nothing but dust on the dirty concrete floor.

Chapter Ten

Pompano Beach, FL

NICK WAS SURPRISED when the phone rang late that night, as they were all loading up for a trip to the airport. The surprise was that the caller was identified as Raphael. Usually it was Cyn who called, but these weren't usual times.

Putting it on speaker, he said, "Nick Katsaros."

"Reinhart is no longer a threat," Raphael said simply, his smooth, deep voice recognizable, even to Nick.

He waited for details, but when none came, Nick said, "May I assume that 'no longer a threat' means he's dead?"

"Very."

"Very," Nick repeated. "Anything more you'd like to say? Any strategic clues you might have acquired during the confrontation?"

"Confrontation is too strong a word for what happened."

"Give me that," Cyn said in the background, then added, "He had an ensorcelled blade. I don't know if that's technically correct, but that's what it acted like. And he said Sotiris gave it to him."

"What did it do?" Antonia had been about to leave his office, but now came close enough to be heard.

"Raphael turned the blade on him, instead, and Reinhart lit up like he'd swallowed a really big light bulb." She chuckled. "And then he exploded, and . . . poof. Nothing but dust."

"Was anyone with him?"

"Nope. He was hanging close to the Mexican border, so maybe he was supposed to be picked up by someone, but . . . no more."

Nick shrugged. "I'm not shedding any tears over him."

"Me either," Antonia agreed. "Can I just add that based on Cyn's description, the blade Reinhart had wasn't really a blade at all, just a blade-shaped device that he told Reinhart to stab Raphael with. It wouldn't have mattered where he'd stabbed him—the arm would have worked as well as the chest. It was the act of penetration that triggered a spell that was the truly fatal weapon. Fortunately, Reinhart failed, making him the only fatality. I *can* tell you that Sotiris will be furious when he hears. And my guess is that he heard about it almost immediately. He had to have had at least one agent keeping an eye on Reinhart. He would never have trusted him on his own."

"Good. I want him to know," Nick said, then raised his voice and asked, "What about Sotiris, Raphael? Are you still with us on that?"

There was a tiny click as someone switched the phone to speaker in Malibu, then Raphael said, "Gabriel and Hana will be there, and so will the rest of us."

"Good. Listen, we're heading for the airport, and will be there by early morning. Maeve and Lili took advantage of Antonia's infiltration of Sotiris's email, and went full hacker on the asshole. They have eyes on his Bel Air property everywhere he does. They also scoured his personal computer and communications, so we know how deeply he's dug in. Which is deep."

"Send us what you can, so we can review it before you get here," Raphael requested.

"Absolutely. We have blueprints of the house, both before and after a renovation by the owner who leased it to Sotiris. The lease was a surprise—he usually purchases—but maybe he thought it would make it more difficult to find him. Or maybe it's in some flunky's name. Either way, it doesn't really matter for our purposes."

"Excellent. I know a helicopter pilot who will be glad to help. I'll have him do a few passes. Is there any way you can determine how much and where magic is being used in the house?"

"Absolutely. Any way I could go up with him?"

"I'm sure it can be arranged. Also, you're welcome to stay here, on my estate, when you arrive. We have plenty of room," Raphael said.

"That's kind of you." Nick tried to keep the surprise from his voice, and wasn't sure he succeeded. He'd been surprised enough when Raphael had offered the helicopter, but now this? Geez. Were they becoming *friendly* or something? Fuck.

"We'll need a list of how many, and who sleeps with whom," Cyn called. "So the rooms will be ready."

Nick nodded, though no one saw except Antonia. "I'll have Lili email the list to you as soon as we finish this call. You're sure you don't mind."

"I wouldn't have asked otherwise," Raphael said smoothly. "Having all of us in one place will facilitate our planning."

"All right. We'll see you . . . . Hell, we'll see some of you in the morning. If you and yours can review everything we send, we should be able to meet up as soon as tomorrow night, and if it looks good, we can hit him late, when he won't expect it."

"Will you need transport from the airport?" Cyn asked.

"I can arrange that from here. I have a guy."

"A guy?"

"Someone who makes that kind of arrangements for me when I travel." He almost added, "You know me and cars, Cyn," but caught himself in time. Instead, he just said, "Not everywhere I go has a rental car counter in baggage claim."

"Okay. Anything else? Raphael? No? See you in the morning, then."

"I'll call when we're on the ground," Nick said and disconnected.

MAEVE HAD INSISTED on going out to California with the others, despite Dragan's worries about the baby's first flight. She'd assured him that their child was in no danger, that it wasn't until much closer to her due date that she'd need to be careful. That hadn't stopped him from watching her like a hawk the entire flight, even when she slept. Or so she assumed, since he was always wide awake and studying her when she woke. Across the aisle of Nick's spacious private jet, Casey and Damian had pushed their seats back soon after boarding and slept peacefully, holding hands. The sight made her smile. She wished she could persuade Dragan to do the same. He'd be deep in the fighting the next night, and almost certainly flying, which consumed a huge amount of energy and calories. He should be downing tons of carbs and sleeping to get ready. Thus far, she'd been unsuccessful in convincing him of that.

Maybe after they arrived in Malibu, she and the baby would finally be safe enough for him to sleep. After all, she'd be inside Raphael's walls and protected by his security the entire time. She and Lili would be working hard tomorrow. They'd already poked into every corner of Sotiris's private network and estate, but now were digging through every site they could find—government and private—to uncover information on the neighborhood, especially the roads and traffic patterns. The house was behind the gates of Bel Air, which was less of a problem now that Raphael and his vampires were involved. According to Gabriel, the vamps could "persuade" the gate guards to let them through using a sort of hypnosis or something. Some kind of mind trick, anyway. Lili had remained in Florida with Abe, just in case Sotiris had hired people to attack the compound while Nick and the others were gone. Hell, he'd done it before. But distance was no barrier when two computer nerds with excellent hacking skills got to work.

She finally took Dragan's hand and said, "I'm tired. I think I'll take Nick up on his offer to use the bed in the back. Will you keep me company?"

Dragan moved so fast, she didn't even see him remove his own seatbelt, before he was in the aisle and reaching for hers. Sliding forward, she let him help her to her feet, then preceded him down the aisle, while his hands rested on her hips (just in case). Nick looked up when they passed, and gave her a knowing smile, but only wished them a good rest and went back to his reading. Antonia reclined on the seat next to him, appearing to be sound asleep.

Once they were inside the bedroom, with the door closed, Dragan said, "I'm glad you decided to rest in here. It's better." He glanced around. "Much better. Come on, I'll help you onto the bed."

Maeve could have told him she'd been getting herself into bed since she was about two years old, but she loved him, so she let him "help" and gave an appreciative sigh of contentment when he lay down next to her. With her head on his shoulder, and his arm holding her close, he finally slept, and so did she.

Malibu, California

BY THE TIME darkness fell over Malibu the next night, Maeve and Lili, with the help of Raphael's excellent and well-equipped daytime tech staff, had worked through the day, doing everything they could to ensure the fighters would have all the information available on Sotiris's base, so that when the fight was over, they could all go home alive and whole.

They'd downloaded the blueprints of Sotiris's mansion, which as Nick had told Raphael, included both the original builder's blueprints, and a later set, which had been submitted by the contractor who'd performed recent renovations. They'd joked then that they hoped the owner had good insurance, because he wasn't going to get his house back in the same condition as when he'd leased it to the sorcerer.

They'd also obtained live images of the mansion, courtesy of a human helicopter pilot who was mated to a local vampire, and so was happy to help out Lord Raphael and his friends. Nick had gone up with him to see if he could scan for magical use, which he had. And that had been tremendously helpful. But they'd also done several additional passes, including one using infrared technology, which provided a rough idea of how many human mercenaries Sotiris had concealed around the property. Vampires were another matter, however. If there were any, they'd probably be concealed underground. But even if they were in sealed rooms above-ground, vampire body temperatures were distinctly cooler than the human norm. If the room they were sleeping in was kept cool enough, they wouldn't show on the scans, since infra-red detected temperature differences. The humans showed up clearly enough, however.

But while they were interested in the number of troops Sotiris had on-site, they were mostly concerned about detecting any structural changes to the property that the owner, or more likely Sotiris, had performed. They were looking for newly installed escape tunnels, or doors in unusual places, all of which were provided by a combination of the blueprints and any records they could find in Sotiris's network of workmen being called to the property. Everything they found would be downloaded to the cell phone of every fighter, although it was made clear to them that these were to be used only in extreme circumstances.

As for communications, Maeve again worked with Raphael's amazing tech people to link up a Bluetooth comm network. Every fighter was assigned to a small troop, and every member of that troop received an identical call frequency. In addition, there was a general frequency for everyone's use, and of course, a command frequency for Nico and Raphael, Nico's four warriors, and Juro, Raphael's head of security.

Grace and Kato showed up late afternoon with their adorable baby girl, who was crawling like a racer, and according to Grace, would soon be walking. Kato and Dragan went off to do warrior-like things, probably checking the weapons brought in from Florida and checking *out* those in what Kato described as Raphael's massive weapons collection. Grace left at the same time, a little nervous at having the baby around all that equipment, although she said it was for the baby to get some sunshine. Maeve could have told her it was cloudy as hell outside, and that she didn't need an excuse to take her daughter to a room more kid-friendly, but instead, she just kissed them both, and promised to have more time later to catch up.

About an hour after sunset, they all headed to the briefing with Nico and Raphael, which would include everyone involved in the night's battle. Despite the pressure and the pace involved in getting everything done and distributed on time, they were ready when the briefing began.

NICK STOOD WITH Raphael in the front of a large, underground conference room. Not every fighter was in the briefing, since each commander would brief his or her own people en route, but there were enough to fill the chairs and tables that had been set up for tonight's purpose. Nick's four warriors sat at the table closest to the front, with their wives or mates. Cyn and Antonia sat at the table across the aisle, along with Juro, Jared, and Ken'ichi, who together would be leading three teams of Raphael's vampires during the battle. Raphael himself would lead the fourth, and it was understood that Cyn would be fighting alongside him. Nick had no more problem with that than he did with Casey going in with Damian.

Nick glanced at Raphael, who indicated he should go ahead and begin.

"All right," Nick said loudly, then waited until the room settled. "I'll make this sweet and simple. Sotiris—" He paused for a few boos and hisses to die down, then continued. "Sotiris is hunkered down in a big house in Bel Air. Those of you from this area know just how big I mean, but all of you should have a blueprint of the house on your cell phone or other device. When I say hunkered, I mean he's ready for us. He didn't try very hard to hide, because he wants this confrontation, and thinks he can win.

"Now to begin with, he got a rude surprise when Raphael took out the assassin he'd sent—we can't really call him a challenger, for fuck's sake, can we? Anyway, he sent this asshole with a fairly strong magical device that might have worked in better hands. But it didn't, and I, for one, am grateful. So we have our vampire allies, including Raphael, with us tonight. And that's something Sotiris could *not* have planned for. He'll have tried to compensate, but it's a weak point for him.

"You all know he's a sorcerer, and that's his strength. He's made full use of the time he's had to magically enhance his defenses, and from what we can tell, he's got the whole house booby-trapped with magical spells and devices. The bad news is that forces us to proceed with caution, and to limit penetration of the structure itself to those with the power to offset whatever traps they encounter. The good news is that it also has Sotiris securing himself in one room at the very center of the building. He assumes we'll be unable to break through the traps and all the protective spells surrounding him. And we have to assume he has a way out, in the event his defenses don't work. We haven't found any evidence of a tunnel, so I'm guessing he'll fall back on his favorite escape route, which is a sorcerous worm hole, for lack of a better term. For those who don't know, a worm hole is a theoretical passage through time and space. Except that in sorcery, it isn't theoretical. It is, however, highly unstable and requires a great deal of power and knowledge—both of which Sotiris has—to use successfully. Luckily, so do I." He turned to the vampire beside him. "Want to take it from here?"

"Yes," the vampire said. "We'll start from the outside perimeter and move inward. The attack will unfold from four directions at once. My vampires will go in first, taking out most, if not all, of the human mercenaries Sotiris has protecting the grounds around the house. As far as we can determine, he hasn't laid any magical spells or traps in that perimeter, probably to prevent the mercenaries from tripping them accidentally and saving us the trouble of killing them.

"Once we have cleared the field enough to avoid unnecessary casualties, Nick and his team will filter through the vampire detachment, and enter the building. At that point, I and my vampires will tighten the noose around the building so that none of Sotiris's allies may enter, and none of his magic users, and possibly not even him, can leave. Nick?"

Nick grinned when he took control of the conversation again. He had to admit he liked the brevity with which the vampire lord had described the initial phase of the assault. Obviously, his vampires were accustomed to working with him, and just as obviously they weren't concerned with human casualties on the enemy side. They also didn't worry overmuch about their own casualties, since vampires could heal or be healed from horrific wounds. And then there was the fact that they would be in telepathic communication at all times.

But now it was his turn, and this part of the conversation had to be handled somewhat more delicately.

"Yep," he said. "Each of my warriors"—he nodded to the four sitting up front, though by now everyone knew who they were—"will take a side. I'll go in with Dragan, to clear the house. Once I'm in, he can provide an overwatch, flying wherever he's needed. Casey, you're going in with Damian—"

"Like you could stop me," she muttered.

"Hana, I don't want you inside the house. There's too much risk that Sotiris will be able to feed off of you, and that's the last thing we want." He waited for her reaction. While he'd discussed this with Gabriel, who'd agreed, he hadn't yet broached it with Hana. There was no reason for her to go inside, since other than her ability to amplify someone else's magic, she had no magic of her own. And as a vampire, Gabriel could draw from Raphael's magic, which was different than a sorcerer's and did not react to Hana's ability.

But maybe Gabriel had discussed this with her, because she simply nodded her acceptance. "I'll work with the rest of the fighters. I'm better trained than any mercenary."

"Thank you. Now, Antonia—" He mentally steeled himself for her response, especially since Casey and Cyn would both be fighting. His only hope was that she'd hold back, given the size of the audience. "—you'll remain in the SUV."

"What?!" Antonia demanded.

So much for that theory. "Hear me out," he said patiently. "Sotiris is going to be looking for you, since, in his mind, you've betrayed him and he'll want to punish you for that. If you stay in the SUV, with the hexagon, then if he succeeds in finding you, you'll at least be facing him with only half his power, which gives you a chance to escape."

"I don't plan to *escape*," she snapped back at him. "You're right about me carrying the hexagon, but everything else is wrong. I have the best chance of getting close enough to take him out, even if I do nothing but shoot to disable him, so you can come in and finish him off. I created the hexagon and understand it better than anyone. I primed it against Sotiris using my own blood, which means I can still control it. If anything goes wrong, if it starts acting wonky, or whatever, I have a good chance of saving anyone who's in danger because of it."

Nick had been staring at her the entire time, wondering why she was suddenly telling *him* how the battle was going to be fought. As if all *he* had to do was send her into the belly of the beast on her own. Like that was *ever* going to happen.

"That's not happening," he said, repeating the thought out loud. "There's no way in hell I'm letting you be the spear point of this attack. If we're going to defeat Sotiris, I need to confront him one on one, his power against mine. It's the only way this works. And it needs to be done with *sorcery*, not a gun."

Antonia stared at him defiantly for a moment. "Fine. We'll do it your way."

He didn't trust her agreement—it had come too easily. It wouldn't matter, however. Not once the battle got started. He'd been trained to fight all his life. He'd been in the middle of more battles than she'd even read about. He'd led armies, while by her own admission, she'd stood on a distant hillside and kept notes. Antonia wasn't a warrior. She had no idea what it was like to be surrounded by the screams of people you knew, to ignore those screams and keep fighting to stay alive lest you become one of those who screamed. She'd never inhaled the spilled-gut smell of a battlefield with every breath, never choked on a stench that could make grown men puke with fear. Antonia had never so much as set foot in the blood and shit, whose scent would fill your nostrils for days after, no matter how much you drank to get rid of it.

There was no way in *hell* he would send her into *that,* much less expect her to face down her own father and kill him. She might think she hated the other sorcerer—and maybe a part of her really did—but could she look him in the eye and end his life? Nick didn't think so. His Antonia was strong and courageous . . . but he just didn't think she could strike the blow that killed Sotiris.

Besides, as he'd told her, he needed to do the killing, to put his power against Sotiris's and destroy him. It was a matter of honor and principle. He'd defeated Sotiris time after time, but had never ended his life. He needed to prove to himself that he could do it. If it ended any other way, he'd always wonder. And it would destroy *his* life, instead of Sotiris's.

He studied the stubborn set of her jaw distrustfully, but said only, "Good. Then, I think it's time"—he glanced at Raphael who nodded once,—"to load up."

Chapter Eleven

ANTONIA SAT IN the middle seat of one of the biggest SUVs she'd ever seen. It was black everywhere with shiny black exterior paint, black tires and wheels, and blackened windows. Even the chrome was black. Maybe Raphael simply liked black, she considered, since most of the vehicles they were using belonged to him. A few of the smaller vehicles—and she used the word "smaller" loosely—were owned by various vampires in Raphael's household, most of whom were part of tonight's army.

Nico sat to her right, and Hana to her left. Two vampires she didn't know rode in the third-row seat behind them, while Kato was up front, riding shotgun and playing navigator to another vampire she didn't know, although the nav system appeared to be doing most of the work. Kato's job mostly consisted of fielding questions coming from vehicles which had taken different routes. Their group consisted of too many people and vehicles to drive through Malibu and inland to Bel Air without drawing attention. She'd checked the map herself before leaving, but wasn't familiar enough with Los Angeles to say where anything was or how long it would take to get there.

Nico and Raphael had decided for practical and strategic reasons to split the motorcade into four segments as they left the estate. That made sense to her, given the four-front attack strategy. Raphael's team would surround the house quietly, and then attack on all four sides at the same time. Juro would command the rear, his twin Ken'ichi, the left, and Jared the right, while Raphael would remain in front with Cyn, but essentially command all the vampires. Most of the fighters were Raphael's people by necessity, which meant they were also vampires, although there were one or two human fighters on Raphael's team.

Nico and the warriors had chosen their respective entry points, based on . . . what? She didn't know. It didn't matter, since while they knew the house had been magically trapped and spelled against entry, they didn't know whether one side was worse than any other. And since Sotiris was in the middle, the sides were up for grabs.

As they zoomed down Pacific Coast Highway, passing houses at what Antonia thought was an alarming speed, she became aware of her power bubbling over inside her. Her magic was always there, always at a consistent level with which she was very familiar. But she'd never sensed anything like this. It was as if someone had turned a switch she'd never known was there, and her power had begun to grow.

Turning, she regarded the woman next to her. Hana appeared completely human to both her eyes and her senses. But she wasn't, was she? Nico had told her about Hana's ability to amplify another's magic, but she'd assumed it was something the truly lovely young woman could turn on and off at will. But what if it wasn't? What if it was simply a part of Hana, like her black hair, or beautiful skin? That would mean . . .

"Goddess," she breathed softly, causing Hana to turn and meet her stare. "It's you."

Hana's brow furrowed briefly, then cleared. "Oh, right. You have magic. Sorry about that."

"Don't be sorry," Antonia said in wonder. "I should be thanking you. I've never felt like this before. It must be what it's like for them all the time."

"Who?"

"Nico and Raphael, and Sotiris, too. How do they stand it, I wonder?"

"Some people would wonder the same about you and your magic. The answer, of course, is that you and they were born with it, so it's all you've ever known."

"Not Raphael."

Hana smiled slightly. "Raphael may not have been born with power, but he was sure as hell born to wield it. Besides, he's something like five hundred years old. He's had a lot of time to get used to it."

She nodded. "I suppose you're right. Well, thank you anyway. It feels great, and I'm glad to have it tonight."

They slowed to stop at an arched gate, where a uniformed man stepped out of a white booth to check their identity and verify their permission to enter. They had neither, but as planned, the vampire driver said a few words, the guard smiled and stepped back, and a moment later, the gate slid open before them.

"Handy trick," Antonia commented.

Hana laughed a little. "You get used to it. Every vampire driver on Raphael's estate can do it. It's a required skill."

Once through the gate, the road wound up and around, passing an amazing collection of estates. Some of the houses were big, and certainly beautiful, built on enough land that they were able to sit well back from the road, behind gates of their own. But the farther they traveled into Bel Air, the bigger the houses and larger the estates. Many of the homes couldn't be seen, because the privacy walls were so tall, and acreage was so large, that the houses were invisible from the road. Antonia couldn't even guess how big those estates had to be, or who lived on them.

The road traveled upward for some distance before they finally slowed and pulled to a smooth stop in the shadows beneath a row of overhanging trees. No one moved for a minute, while the vehicles behind them did the same, and then the driver turned off the engine.

"Raphael, Jared, and Ken'ichi are in place," Nico reported softly. "We're just waiting on Juro. He had the longest route."

Antonia had to concentrate to avoid holding her breath, because Nico was right. She'd watched a lot of battles from afar. But she'd never been *in* one.

Finally, Nico said, "Juro's set." He paused, listening, then . . . "Let's go."

Everyone moved swiftly, but quietly. Vehicle doors were opened with care, and closed with more. No one spoke once they stood outside. They simply gathered in the shadows and watched Nico, waiting for orders. Antonia did the same, wondering how the orders would be given, since he could hardly call them out to everyone. But then she remembered the comm system and cursed her own inexperience. She'd bet none of the others had forgotten.

She knew her assignment, which was to sit in the SUV with Hana, as humiliating as that was.

She took some small comfort in the knowledge that she was also tasked with keeping the hexagon handy, just in case. Yeah, right. Nico didn't want her in the house, hexagon or not. And he didn't want the hexagon in the house with or without *her*. He wanted her safe, and he wanted to fight Sotiris at the peak of his power, not weakened by the hexagon.

So while she stood with the others, who were waiting to move out, she made a decision for herself. She could study a blueprint as well as anyone, so she knew where Sotiris was holed up. And since she was his daughter, and they shared blood, she could create a tracing spell and track him, every bit as well as Nico could with his power alone.

Hana sidled closer and muttered, "What's the plan?"

Antonia faked confusion. "I thought everyone had their assignments already?" she whispered, glancing around to see if anyone—especially

Nico—noticed they were talking.

Hana gave her a knowing look. "Like you're going to just sit in the SUV. Look, I hate him as much as you do. So what's the plan?"

She wasn't sure how to respond. Admit she was going against orders, and maybe blow her only chance? Or trust Hana, whom she barely knew, but who'd been captured by Sotiris and had good reason to want in on the kill.

"All right," she said quietly. "Just follow me. We're going inside."

Hana winked. "Fucking A."

RAPHAEL DIDN'T need to speak to command his vampires. Every one of them had been sworn to him for years, and most were his own children. His communication was telepathic, fast, and indetectable. And because they were vampires, they moved with a speed that no human could match, and in perfect silence, they made their approach to Sotiris's residence unnoticed. This, despite the number of guards posted in what they probably thought was impenetrable darkness, except that the dark was no impediment to a vampire's sight. They really were the perfect soldiers, but chose to serve only their own.

Raphael was aware of his people moving in on either side of him, and could also sense the sorcerer and his warriors, poised behind them. They'd discussed having Nick or Antonia cast a spell to silence whatever small noise Nick's second wave might make, but with Sotiris employing magic-users of his own, there was concern that the spell itself would be noticed and give them away. And since they had such small teams, it made sense to walk quietly, especially as they were all warriors and accustomed to covert movements.

The go command, when it came, was a single word spoken by Nick, since his people were the last ones to get into position. "Go."

Raphael grinned in anticipation, and ordered his vampires to, "*Go.*" He heard his three commanders repeat the order, and sensed their bloodlust matching his. Vampires could appear sophisticated and modern when they wanted, but nothing could change the drive in their blood to kill and conquer. Nights like this, when they were set free, was a rush like no other.

Next to him, Cyn's grin reflected his own. She was his perfect match in every way. Yanking her close, he kissed her hard and fast, then ordered, "Don't get hurt."

She snorted. "I won't, if you don't. Now let's do this, fang boy."

ANTONIA WAS READY when Nick gave the silent signal to move out. Waiting until he was out of sight, she grabbed Hana's hand, and felt power simply *blast* through her. *Goddess,* she thought. She'd thought it was incredible before, but when Hana touched her . . . . This . . . was *this* what Nico lived with day in and day out?

Casting a particularly effective concealment spell—something which would work even on any magic-users Sotiris had in or around the house, given the double whammy of magic she'd used to drive it, courtesy of Hana—she pulled the other woman toward a garden door she'd seen on the blueprints. It was shorter and narrower than was common these days, and she assumed it was left over from the original 1940s construction. When they reached it, she discovered it was so covered in vines and overhanging bushes as to be invisible, which was perfect. She took a minute to study it, deciding whether they should go over and cut their way through. She had a knife, and she assumed Hana did also, since she, unlike Antonia, was a trained fighter. But that would be slow and messy, and since she had all this power at her command, why not use it? Drawing a roughly blade-shaped image in front of her using nothing but magic, she took hold of it and sliced the gate free as if the vines were made of butter. Hana watched in bemused silence, but stopped Antonia when she would have reached for the gate.

"Too noisy," Hana whispered, pointing at the rusted hinges. Antonia grimaced, then followed Hana's nimble climb over the gate, with grace if not the same level of nimbleness. She then led the way to the edge of the shrubs which blocked the house from the street on this side, and pointed at a large window, which was situated almost exactly in between two sides of the house, and behind an out-of-control oleander bush. Sotiris's gardener was doing a crap job on several fronts. She hadn't known about the bush, but had figured that since the "big boy" teams were entering through doors, she'd try a window. And this was the closest one to the tiny gate.

Hana studied it for a minute, then looked both ways. "We should wait until the vampires start their attack," she said, barely speaking loud enough to be heard. "They'll hear us if we go now."

"Oh," Antonia mouthed silently, and they both settled down to wait. But not for long. The vampires attacked with shocking speed and silence, until they encountered the first of Sotiris's mercenaries. And then the screams began.

Exchanging a quick glance, the two women took off running. Hana reached the window a half-step sooner, and without pausing, smashed her gun butt into the glass, then reached in, unlatched the old-fashioned frame, and raised the window enough for them to slip in. An alarm blared at the intrusion, but there was so much other noise that Antonia figured it wouldn't even be noticed.

Once they were both inside, she dropped the concealment spell, since Sotiris would sense it no matter how much power had gone into it. Actually, he might sense it easier, *because* of the power.

Regardless, he'd know she was coming before she reached him, for the same reason that she could easily find him. He was her father. But hell, she hadn't come here to slide a knife between his ribs from the shadows—she *wanted* him to know she was there. Wanted to face him down with the hexagon in her hands, so he'd know who'd killed him.

Tiptoeing—which made no sense—to the door, she listened first, and then opened it. She could sense magic traps up and down the hall, but apparently Nick and the warriors hadn't entered the house yet. She glanced back at Hana, who nodded, then walked down the hall, avoiding the traps she could and disabling the ones she couldn't. *Boy, all this power was great!* They turned left down an interior hallway, then right on another, and stood outside a room where her father waited inside.

Antonia had to pause then, to breathe, and to steel the strength that Nico insisted, and she *knew*, she possessed. She'd survived everything this man could throw at her—his cruelty, his contempt, his utter disregard for the fact that she was his daughter. And finally, she'd lost centuries of life because of him. He needed to die, and she needed to be the one to end him.

With a final glance at Hana, she opened the door, saw a man sitting at the desk, and said, "Hello, Father."

NICK FELT AS though he was back in his own world, surrounded by the sounds of battle, the screams of the wounded, the unexpected and *eerie* sound of vampires howling with sheer joy as they fought their way through Sotiris's mercenaries and the few magic-users unlucky enough to have been assigned to the outside of Sotiris's house. There were far more mercenaries than vampires, and they managed to rally themselves into a counterattack, coming in behind the vampires who were occupied with those trying to use magic. But while it forced some of the vampires to turn and face the mercenaries, it didn't help the magic-users. Nick gave them credit for doing their best against overwhelming odds, but Sotiris had kept his strongest people for inside the house. These were little better than apprentices, none with any real power, and they went down quickly, one after another.

Nick made his move with Dragan by his side, the warrior's sword flashing so fast and with such deadly grace that those who died didn't know what hit them, until they looked down and found their torso had been split in two. Nick fought side-to-side and back-to-back with his warrior, whatever worked best as they focused not on killing the enemy, but on getting through to the house. The vampires saw them coming, and did their best to clear the way, before taking up positions facing away from the residence to make sure no one followed them in.

Once he had the door open to the house, he paused to grip Dragan's hand, then watched as the warrior leaped from the ground to the top of an arched doorway, then cleared the ground enough that he could leap into the air and spread those deadly wings.

Nick couldn't wait to see Dragan begin taking down enemies, although it had always been a glorious sight. But instead, he entered the house, closed and sealed the door behind to make it harder for anyone else to enter, then after giving the agreed upon signal to Raphael, took his bearings and strode toward his rendezvous with Sotiris.

RAPHAEL HEARD the barely audible click of the command frequency and knew what was coming before he heard Nick utter what he con-sidered a pathetic go command. "It's time."

Rolling his eyes, he nonetheless replied, "Ten four," then sent a far superior and wordless telepathic message to his vampires all around the house, letting them know that the battle was about to enter its next phase. Looking around for Cyn, he strode over to where she was gleefully shooting and reloading, thankfully having enough sense to shelter behind a massive stone sculpture of the modern variety that required more time than he had to decipher. Calling her name via their mating bond's mind link, he waited until she could safely disengage enough to look at him, and held out his hand. He didn't *need* her to be standing next to him when he took the next step, but he *wanted* her there, since once he exerted his power, he would be separated from the others to a large extent, and wanted to be sure she was with *him*.

He'd warned her in advance what he was going to do, and although she'd complained that he was spoiling her fun, she now took his hand, and held on tight when he squeezed her fingers.

Then, diving deep into the heart of all that he was, deeper than he'd gone since the time he'd used everything he had to save his Cyn's life, he gathered every trace of magic that his vampire blood granted him, and created a huge magic force that roared around the house in a controlled wave, remaining close to the building to block defenders from escaping within the house, while sliding inside through doors and windows, to kill anyone trying to escape.

Raphael's undertaking was such that it took every shred of his attention, but he still felt Cyn squeeze his hand that little bit harder that told him his gambit was succeeding, and gave him the strength to continue.

NICK HAD TO LAUGH in reluctant admiration for the fucking vampire who'd accomplished something that even he wouldn't have been able to sustain long enough to work. Though if asked, he'd never damn admit it. So far, he'd encountered more than a few of Sotiris's magical flunkies—some with a respectable amount of power, though none who could defeat him. He disarmed the traps and spells with a wave of his hand, until he reached the hallway that was one away from Sotiris's office. There he met surprising resistance, as if Sotiris had pulled back everyone worthy of the title of sorcerer—no matter their relative strength—to defend this one hallway.

Ducking back around the corner, Nick listened to the reports of his warriors as one by one, they progressed through the house. He knew Kato was making rapid progress, because he'd sensed the dark power of the warrior's magic as it rose to kill. Sotiris's people didn't have a chance against the Dark Witch's son. They'd probably never even encountered such deadly black magic before.

He listened for Damian next, though with Casey by his side, the big warrior would be warned long before any magical attack manifested close enough to do harm. And though Damian was very much human, he was also the creation of Nick's magic. He'd deserved to be worshipped as a god of war, and was a one-man army once he got riled up. And it certainly sounded as if he was riled now. *Oh shit*, Nick thought. Apparently, Casey had been wounded. Damian would destroy his way through the house now. He wasn't an army anymore, he was a supernatural, fucking tank, plowing his way forward through friend or foe. Good thing there weren't any friends in his path until he met up with Nick, and hopefully recognized him.

It was Gabriel that Nick was most concerned about. He was a vampire and was feeding off Raphael's magic, effectively turning him into a

Raphael duplicate in terms of power. He had centuries of experience on battlefields in his own world, both before and after meeting Nick. And if that wasn't enough, he'd defeated every one of Raphael's vampires who'd challenged him with a blade since he'd arrived in Malibu, as well as a certain visiting vampire lord who would remain anonymous. Gabriel wasn't counting solely on magic, however. He was carrying one of Damian's specially modified HK's, along with enough spare magazines to start, or win, a war.

Nick hadn't heard from Gabriel yet, other than the expected sounds of men screaming or pleading, sometimes both, magic spells being shouted, and guns firing, which gave Nick hope that his warrior was still alive and the one firing.

While waiting to hear from Gabriel, Kato came over the comm saying Nick's name, which was the agreed upon code meaning he needed Nick's attention. The others heard and tuned down, but not off, their own comms, so that Nick could hear what Kato had to say.

"I've reached the final hallway, though not before meeting serious resistance in the one before this. I don't see you yet."

"That's because I've hit the same kind of resistance. Are you injured?"

"Negative."

"What's the final turn like?"

"Empty. Which is just fucking weird. There has to be a catch."

"Agreed. Hold there, until I hear from the others."

Since the others were listening, they turned their comms up slightly, but not as loud as they had been, so that everyone could listen without anyone being drowned out. Damian was next to report, though there was no need to say Nick's name first.

"We hit the same kind of resistance Kato did," Damian reported. "But those bastards made the mistake of shooting Casey, so they're all dead now."

"What's her status?" Nick asked.

Casey who was on the same comm line as the others answered for herself, saying, "She's fine. There was no need for the big guy to go crazy, but what the hell, it worked."

"And the injury?" Nick inquired.

"Nothing. It went right through, upper arm, no bone involved, and not the arm I shoot with. I see Kato. We're walking toward him, and now I'm waving."

Nick would have smiled, but he still hadn't heard from Gabriel. As with Kato and Damian, he and Gabriel would see each other once they reached this hallway, since Sotiris's office corridor was like the bar on an "H." Kato and Damian were meeting on one leg, and he and Gabriel on the other. But in addition to the serious resistance which the others had met and defeated, Nick still had no sight of . . .

"Nick."

Gabriel's call interrupted Nick's concerned musings, and he breathed a sigh of relief before answering. "Gabriel, good to hear from you."

"Yeah, the *people* in my way were easy enough to take down, but I had to work a little harder on the traps and spells. They don't like my kind of magic."

"But you got through safely, right? No injuries?"

"Nothing as bad as Casey's anyway."

"Ha ha," Casey droned.

"How would you like to take our last hallway, Nico?" Gabriel asked.

"I doubt they're expecting both of us, so why don't I go first—since their traps and spells *do* like my kind of magic—then we take down the people and meet in the middle."

"Ready when you are."

Surrounding himself with the strongest protective shield he could conjure quickly, Nico stepped into the open. Spells fired at him bounced off his shield, while Gabriel took out a couple gunners, until Nico sent a spell of his own thundering down the hallway in a destructive wave. It took out every magical device and spell it came near, making Sotiris's people scream when spells they'd held waiting in their hands, were destroyed. They were still screaming when they died, as Nick and Gabriel stepped out in unison, with Gabriel shooting and Nick blasting magic, until they met in the silent middle.

And looked down the crossbar of the H, to see Kato and Damian looking back at them from the other end of the hallway.

"See what I mean," Kato called. "No resistance once you get *here*. Weird."

Nick was about to reply, when he sensed something . . . no, some*one* who shouldn't have been there.

Damn.

ANTONIA STOOD IN front of her father, holding the hexagon like a shield, watching him grow weaker by the minute, and wondering why he hadn't done anything other than throw the occasional taunt her way, *daring* her to kill him. And when she didn't, he'd mocked her, saying she was too weak, that she couldn't kill her own father, and laughing at the tears that inexplicably filled her eyes.

Her arms felt as if she'd been standing that way for hours, though she knew it couldn't have been long. She could still hear the battle raging outside, and more recently screams and gunfire from much closer, which told her that Nico and his warriors were closing in. If she didn't kill Sotiris soon, she wouldn't get the chance, because Nico would do it for her.

She *hated* Sotiris with every ounce of her being, so why couldn't she do it? Was Sotiris right? Was she so weak that she couldn't kill this monster who'd killed so many others, and who'd tormented her unbearably?

"Your lover's outside," Sotiris crooned. "He won't be happy with you, will he?" He laughed. "What's it going to be? Will you *finally* prove yourself worthy of being my daughter, or will you let the big, bad sorcerer do it for you?"

She stared at him, more puzzled now than angry. He had something planned. Something more than just an escape, although he certainly had that ready to go to. Why did he want *her* to kill him? Did he plan to kill her first? Was she to be some sort of sacrifice to whatever dark magic he had planned to defeat Nico? But then, why not just kill her?

She was still trying to figure that out, when the door burst open behind her.

NICK DREW CLOSER to Sotiris's office, and his senses confirmed his suspicion. Antonia was definitely in there. Why? Signaling his warriors to remain on watch, he shoved open the door, and found Antonia holding the hexagon in front her like a shield, while facing down Sotiris. The sorcerer was snarling something at Antonia, his voice too low for Nick to overhear. But it was obvious that the only thing holding him back was the hexagon. And it was just as obvious that Antonia's arms were weakening under the constant weight of the heavy stone, which made Nick wonder just how long she'd been standing there.

"Nick."

His whispered name had him turning to see Hana standing on one side of the door, a miserable look on her face. And he finally understood that it wasn't just the rock keeping Sotiris at bay. It was the rock's power, boosted by Hana, who had probably boosted Antonia's magic to get them this far. *Fantastic.*

As furious as he was to find them in this office, he was more worried that anything he did might upset the fragile balance existing between father and daughter, and kill Antonia. It might kill Sotiris, too, but he didn't give a fuck about that bastard.

While he studied the flow of power between them, he saw for the first time the trembling of her muscles, the slight sheen of sweat on her face and neck, and he knew that Antonia's *physical* strength might well collapse before the hexagon did anything at all. And if that happened, there would be little he could do to help her.

Several painstaking minutes later—every one of which felt like an hour—he'd managed to examine the threads of magic stretching from Antonia to Sotiris, and the much more dangerous, barbed spikes of power coming from Sotiris himself, the bastard. He turned to study the third magic source in the room, which was Hana sharing her unusual magic with Antonia. It flowed between the two women in gently rolling waves, boosting Antonia's power without making her work for it, or disturbing her concentration in any way. The sight of that sharing stunned him so thoroughly that he stared for a fraction of a second before jerking himself back to the task at hand.

Brief as it had been, his examination of the balance between Antonia and Sotiris had shown him its weakness. It was in constant flux, as Sotiris fought back against Antonia's power, only to have Hana's boost cause Antonia's strength to surge and push him away once more. The trick then would be for Nick to interrupt the flux at the peak of Antonia's magical strength, so that he could replace her power with his own, forcing Sotiris to confront *him* without ever having a chance to strike at Antonia.

Nick knew he could take advantage of the hexagon's proximity to destroy his ancient enemy in that moment, when Sotiris's power was diminished, while his own was as strong as ever. But as he told Antonia before, he didn't want to defeat a weakened Sotiris. He wanted his dishonorable and cowardly foe to be forced to face him in a fight to the death, not flee as he'd done every other time they'd met, both in this world and their own.

Nick wished he could have warned Antonia of what he was about to do. Unless he was very careful, the backlash when the flow of her power was severed, however briefly, could hit her physical body a blow like that of a boulder slamming into her chest. He'd seen this kind of disruption stop a sorcerer's heart. It would be only a matter of seconds, but it would feel like dying.

He would have liked to warn her, but he couldn't, because Sotiris might overhear, and use those few seconds to kill her.

So Nick waited until he felt Hana's magic strengthen next to him, until he saw Antonia's magic surge . . . and then ruthlessly sliced her magic in two, and shoved his own power into the miniscule period of vacuum the disruption created. He couldn't even look back to see if Antonia was all right. He knew she lived, and that her magic would survive, but he couldn't know how badly she, or Hana for that matter, had been injured.

All he could do was order her in a roar to, "Get out of here and take that damn rock with you!" And then he was facing a Sotiris who was now returned to the entirety of his full power.

"Run, bitch. You'll be next!" Sotiris screamed after Antonia, and immediately staggered under the strength of Nick's first blow.

"Worry about yourself, fool. Or don't. Either way, you won't survive long enough to touch her ever again," he snarled and shaped a massive blade of shining silver magic and shoved it with massive force at Sotiris who hadn't yet recovered from the double hit of Nick's first strike on top of the shocking appearance of his most deadly enemy.

But Sotiris hadn't survived so long by being taken that easily. Shaping his own magic into a hammer blow of sheer power, he sent it hurtling at Nick's head, forcing him to duck to avoid it rather than use the energy it would take to repel it instead.

Instead of standing after the duck, however, Nick rolled, coming up several feet away from his previous position, and putting himself to one side of Sotiris, who was still focused on where he'd been. Forming a whip this time, and barbing it with fiery energy just as Sotiris might have done, he snapped it forward to circle his enemy's neck, where it dug deep with both fire and magic, threatening to decapitate the sorcerer regardless of how he moved or what he tried to do.

Compelled to use his magic to deal with the unnatural garrot around his neck before it killed him, Sotiris shrank his defensive power as far as he dared before using every remaining trace of his magic to forge a blade capable of severing the incredible strength Nick had vested in his weapon.

Before Sotiris could achieve his release, and bring his power to bear once more on his own defense, Nick had launched yet another attack. A lightning strike of power swept in and exploded in bolt after bolt of brilliant gold energy, blinding Sotiris, even as it crippled him with shocks of electricity so strong that a single one could have traveled far enough, and over enough ground to kill a hundred humans, no matter the distance between them.

Nick saw knowledge of his predicament in Sotiris's eyes, and *knew* what the coward would do next. It was what he'd always done when faced with the possibility of his own death. He would run. But not this time.

He sensed the wormhole beginning to form, and smiled. It had worked for Sotiris so many times. His mastery of that bit of sorcery had saved his ass, time after time. But Nick had been studying, experimenting, practicing over and over, for all the years he'd searched for Antonia. Long after he'd all but given up hope of finding her, he'd known that he would face Sotiris again someday, and that the coward would try to run again.

But despite all his preparation, he hadn't been ready when the time had come. Four times he'd battled Sotiris in the last few years. Every time one of his warriors had broken free, Sotiris had come for him, and every time he'd failed to stop the monster from slinking away down his hole.

Not this time, he swore to himself. He would *not* permit Sotiris to live long enough to threaten Antonia ever again. Creating a cocoon of protection that surrounded and clung to his body, he stepped between Sotiris and the opening tunnel, crashing the wormhole around himself. A tremendous amount of energy pulsed against his shields, but the cocoon held.

Sotiris screamed his fury and threw bolt after bolt of energy, striking Nick where he stood between the coward and what he'd thought would be his escape. When Nick shrugged off the powerful blows, Sotiris's gaze sharpened with cunning. He turned and ran for the closed office door, behind which Antonia had escaped. But when he yanked the door open, another kind of nightmare waited for him.

All four of Nick's warriors stood in a semi-circle facing the exit, each one surrounded by the nimbus of his power—Damian, gold, and bright enough to make your eyes tear, even as you fought to gaze longer upon the sheer beauty of his godhood. Gabriel, surrounded by the silver gleam of a starlit sky, as he channeled the incredible power of his Sire, which was now a part of him. Dragan, whose magic had been unwanted for most of his life, and who'd once cursed the goddess who now defended her child with the red-tinted fury of a dragon's eye against the evil that would destroy him. And Kato, who gazed at his enemy with the full power of the Dark Witch, while shards of black lightning flashed over his shoulders.

Sotiris backed away, drawing every bit of his power to create a buffer between himself and the warriors he'd cursed into a tortuous existence that he'd hoped would last for eternity. Turning, he fought frantically to create a second wormhole. Weaker than the first one that Nick had destroyed, it would still have worked well enough in the hands of one as experienced as Sotiris. But in his desperation to escape, he forgot about Nick.

Nick laughed as he exited the wormhole, and shed the shell that had once again protected him while he followed Sotiris, but without touching the bulk of his power, other than the small amount necessary to sustain the shell itself. Unlike Sotiris, who stood staring in disbelief that Nicodemus, who'd *never* succeeded in following before, now stood before him with his defenses and magic both at full strength.

Nick met his enemy's horrified gaze, watched him try to gather the shreds of his power to defend himself, while he pulled on the full power of his magic to form a ball of energy so fierce that he had to squint or be blinded by his own weapon.

He grinned seeing the same terror on Sotiris's face as he'd seen on so many of the sorcerer's victims.

"I surrender!" Sotiris screamed, still struggling to gather wisps of his power into a defense that might save his useless life. "You'll never see me again, I swear."

Nick knew the bastard was only buying time, hoping to gather just enough magic to escape. But he wouldn't have agreed to a surrender even if Sotiris had been on his knees, blinded and broken, and begging for his life. His enemy was going to die here, now, and by Nicodemus's fucking hand.

He granted himself another moment to enjoy Sotiris's fear, mocking him by pursing his lips and blowing, as if that tiny wind was all it took to send the terrible destruction of his sparkling ball of magical death smashing into the sorcerer's body.

Sotiris screamed. Oh, yes, he screamed in agony, and Nick drank up every note of it like the sweetest nectar the gods had ever envisioned, but even *they* had lacked the power to create.

The door slammed open behind him as Antonia ran in, screaming *his* name, as if afraid that those god-awful shrieks were coming from *his* golden throat. As if.

Holding a hand behind him to stop her, he cast a quick spell to keep her back, knowing that the same magic killing Sotiris could strike *her* if she came too close.

They stood that way until Sotiris was dead. It wasn't fast. Nick hadn't wanted it to be. Sotiris writhed in agony for the better part of an hour, and even that wasn't long enough. Nick had wanted the person he hated above all others to suffer every sliver of agony he'd ever inflicted on those who'd had no chance of escaping.

Antonia, who'd lived several lifetimes under his cruel hand, while he'd played with her like a mindless doll, stealing what few memories she managed to collect, only to shove her into another transition, another empty life. His warriors, the strongest men he'd ever known, who'd had that strength used against them, condemned by their own courage and determination to prisons that would have driven weaker men insane. But his warriors had suffered for centuries, and still somehow survived. And finally, there were all the innocents who'd been in the way of Sotiris's ambition. Those who'd have run and never come back if he'd but given them the chance. But he'd *enjoyed* their terror, their screams of heartbreak and agony, as the people they loved most died, only to leave them so broken that they welcomed their own deaths when it came.

When Sotiris finally died, when he was nothing but a shriveled pile of blackened bones, Nick sent a searing blast of heat to reduce even the bones to ash, despite his conviction that the bastard still hadn't suffered enough. He then collected the ashes into a tiny whirlwind and sent *that* into a quickly conjured urn which he capped and sealed with magic, intending to scatter the ashes into every ocean on earth, insuring that Sotiris's evil would never rise again.

And then, he stood perfectly still for a moment, trying to comprehend the enormity of what had just happened. He'd spent all but fourteen years of his life battling the same monster. And now, finally, that monster was . . . simply gone. Forever.

He heard Antonia crying behind him, not for the man who'd never been a father to her, but for *him*. Because she knew what he was feeling, knew the strange sense of not knowing what to do next, what *happened* next? Because the thing that had driven him for so long was gone.

His power collapsed back into his body, releasing Antonia and allowing her to slam into his back and hug him from behind. She was crying too hard to do anything else, to say . . . anything. He turned and took her in his arms, holding on until she finally gathered herself enough to speak through her tears. "I'm sorry," she sobbed. "I'm so sorry, Nico. I tried, I did. I tried so hard, but I couldn't kill him. Why couldn't I do it?"

"Baby," he said in disbelief. "Of course, you couldn't do it. It's not who you *are*, don't you know that yet? You give life, you don't destroy it. You gather up lives on the edge of death, and bring them back. I know this, because you did it to me. Don't you know that? All I'd done with my life was kill, until I met you. You took my blackened soul, and brought *it* back to life. I love you, Antonia. I love everything about you. Don't ever think I want you to be anything but what you are."

She began to cry even harder, and for a moment, he thought he failed her again. That his clumsy words hadn't been the right ones to show how much she mattered, not only to him, but to a world that had too much death in it.

"I love you, Nico. I love you so much. I was so afraid, so afraid I'd lose you."

"Never, my love. Never again."

WHAT LITTLE RESISTANCE was left faded the instant Sotiris died. Quite literally in some cases, as magic-users and mercenaries alike tried to disappear into the surrounding foliage. No one bothered to chase them. Without Sotiris to make promises of magical or monetary reward, they were no threat to Nick or Raphael or those they loved and protected.

Vampires were sent to drive the vehicles around, since they were the only ones fast enough to do it, while others gathered their wounded, and in one case dead, to be treated by human or vampire healers once they returned to the Malibu estate. Once there, Raphael himself would step in to heal the most seriously injured with his powerful blood.

The rest piled into the vehicles regardless of who was driving, or which vehicle they'd arrived in, eager to leave before the neighbors noticed there were too many vehicles parked on the road, and called the police.

Which was pretty funny, when you thought about it.

Chapter Twelve

Three months later, Yosemite Valley, California

"CAN I LOOK YET?" Antonia asked, gripping Nick's arm with iron fingers as he maneuvered them over the uneven surface on top of the famous Half Dome, despite the rapidly dimming light, as the sunset drew near. It wasn't safe to be up there. It wasn't even legal. But Nick had wanted somewhere spectacular for the surprise he had planned, and nothing was more spectacular than Yosemite's Firefall. He would have waited as long as it took, but luck and the weather was with him, and the phenomenon known as Firefall, which only happened once a year, and then only if conditions were perfect, was happening tonight.

That was why he'd bundled Antonia into his plane on the pretext of visiting their many California friends, and then, promising something special, had flown them via helicopter from LAX to Fresno, then taken a limo to Yosemite Valley. After which, it had required magic to reach the top of Half Dome.

But it was going to be so worth it.

"Now?" she asked pitifully.

"Now," he said, whisking the blindfold away with a wisp of magic.

Antonia blinked, first to let her eyes adapt to the light, then looking around while trying to figure out where they were. "Nick? Where are we?"

"Yosemite Park in California."

"Oh. It's beautiful, but wouldn't it be prettier during the day?" she asked carefully.

He laughed. "Wait a few minutes more. It's almost time."

"Okay," she said agreeably, then leaned into his side and gave a contented sigh when he put his arm around her . . . sigh that made him feel like a legendary hero every time he heard it.

Down below, the gathered people began to stir, as park rangers let them know the time was only seconds away. The observers waited in silence, not wanting to disturb the almost mystical air surrounding the moment.

High above, Nick and Antonia did the same, staring at the fall of water across the valley, heavy with runoff this year from a snowy winter. Nick closed his eyes, afraid to look. What if . . .

"Oh Goddess!" Antonia's cry of wonderment told him he'd been right. Not about the timing, which owed nothing to him, but about how much it would mean to her. "Nico," she sobbed. "It's so beautiful. It's nature's magic in all her glory."

"Marry me, Antonia," he whispered, as the beauty of sunset and the perfect sky joined to create fire from water.

She didn't say anything, didn't even acknowledge she'd heard, until the incredible flow of liquid fire—which lasted for only a few minutes on a very few nights once a year—began to dim for the final time this year. Then, she turned to gaze up at him, eyes shining with tears, and said, "What?"

He laughed and repeated what he'd meant to be a dramatic question. "Marry me, love. Right now, right here, with that still shining in your eyes." He pointed to the rapidly dimming Firefall.

Her mouth opened wide in surprise, as fresh tears drowned her beautiful, dark eyes. "Yes. Is that what I'm supposed to say? Yes?"

"It will do."

"But how?"

"You and I come from a different world than this one. A world where two people don't need a judge, or a priest, or anyone else to decide they could be married. This is between us, for us, and our children, when they come. No one else. So, Antonia, my love, I pledge you my troth from this day until forever."

"Nicodemus Katsaros," she said, fighting to get the name out despite her tears. "I pledge . . ." She had to stop and draw a breath, then started over. "Nicodemus Katsaros, I pledge you my troth, from this day until forever, because I love you so much." And then the tears came in hiccoughing sobs as she buried her face against his chest.

He held her, happier than he'd ever been, until she looked up at him and said, "You remembered."

"Of course, I remembered. Memories of making love to you inside that waterfall were all that stopped me from ending my life all those centuries you were gone."

"Oh, Nico. Don't say that. What would I have done without you?"

"We'll never have to know now, will we?"

She smiled. "This is going to be the best engagement story *ever* for our grandchildren."

Chapter Thirteen

One Month Later, West Tennessee

IT WAS A SMALL wedding on a cool spring night. Dragan's happiness was matched by the pride lighting his eyes as he stood next to Maeve, her delicate beauty only enhanced by the growing swell of her belly. The ceremony had been a simple one—an exchange of vows that hadn't left a dry eye in the house. They'd looked so damned besotted with each other, so much in love, that even Nick's emotions had been pushing to get out.

"You should be proud of all your warriors," Antonia said, coming to stand next to him, hooking her hand over his arm.

"I didn't have anything to do with it," Nick said softly, shaking his head. "They were already great warriors by the time they came to me, willing to fight for what they believed in." He frowned ruefully. "All I did was give them wars to fight, and a nightmare to survive."

"Oh, be quiet," she scolded. "You brought them together, gave them a brotherhood to believe in, to live for."

"You think? I'm not sure."

"Why are you so sad, Nico? It's a wedding, and a new life on the way. This is a celebration."

He smiled and put his arm around her shoulders, pulling her close. "I just . . . I don't want to lose them. With Sotiris dead—"

"Aren't you the one who said that we're all family? You don't lose family, my love. Not when it's this strong and good. Look around, everyone here is family."

Nick's gaze fell on Raphael and Cyn. She was laughing with Maeve's mother, while the vampire stood silently by her side, seeming to listen. He was probably pretending, but Nick could hardly hold that against him. He'd probably have done the same thing. "Well," he muttered, "maybe not everyone."

"Honestly, you're both so stubborn about this. The two of you worked together to take down Sotiris. You even admitted that the magic shield he created to isolate the house was a remarkable feat."

Nick grunted, his gaze fixed on the fucking vampire and Cyn, who now appeared to be heading their way.

"Be nice," Antonia ordered.

"I'm always—"

"Oh, pooh. You're not, and you know it."

"Why the scowl, Nick?" Cyn asked, laughing. "It's a wedding. The blessed couple are gorgeous and happy. What more do you want?"

"Exactly what I was just telling him," Antonia agreed, and the two women shared a laugh.

When the hell did they get so chummy? he wondered.

"Nick."

He looked at Raphael in surprise. He couldn't remember a single time they'd spoken outside of the strategy sessions and briefings for the attack on Sotiris. "Raphael," he replied cautiously.

A small smile flirted around the vampire's lips, as if he found the situation amusing. "I understand congratulations are in order."

Nick barely managed to conceal his surprise. Antonia must have told Cyn about their Firefall mating. "Uh, yeah. Yeah. We did it the old way."

"As it should be. Cyn and I wish you both a long and happy life," Raphael said, and held out his hand.

Nick took the hand, and they shook. "What about you and Cyn?" he asked, feeling lame even as he said it.

Raphael's smile was as small as before, but his eyes, when he glanced over at Cyn, glinted silver with power . . . and possession. "We, too, chose an old way. We're mated in the way of vampires, which is enough for both of us." His gaze shifted to Nick. "But more than that, she is . . . my mate, though it took centuries to find her. You understand this, I think."

"Yeah, I get it."

A raised voice drew their attention, as someone from the bride's side called for a toast. A member of the venue's staff came around with a bottle of champagne and filled their glasses, before moving on.

"To true love," the toaster called, raising his glass. "Wherever it finds us."

And the two men, vampire and sorcerer—each the most powerful of their kind—raised their glasses with everyone else, and silently thanking the fickle whims of fate, drank a toast to love.

Epilogue

THE FEMALE SERVER retreated to the shadows beneath the trees, still holding the champagne bottle and tempted beyond reason to take a quick gulp to calm her nerves. Nerves! She was never nervous. She'd taken down powerful vampires and sorcerers, as well as the odd creature or two, all over the world without so much as a raised pulse. But those two . . . Christ, she'd felt like a paper doll facing down a tornado, when she'd stood in front of them.

The true wonder was that she'd managed to pour the damn champagne without sloshing it all over their six thousand dollar suits. Their power had been that overwhelming. How was it that she was the only one who seemed to feel it? Maybe the others were just so accustomed to being around them that they'd grown numb to the power those two possessed.

She should have been prepared. After all, she'd studied them both before taking on this assignment. Though, in retrospect, she understood that no amount of preparation would have made it possible for her to take down her target. She'd witnessed the battle from the shadows, had seen and *felt* the tremendous forces necessary to penetrate Sotiris's residence, and to kill him.

She wouldn't have had a chance—a fact which had her questioning the wisdom and, more importantly, the honesty of whoever had decided that *she* should be the one to assassinate Sotiris. There was no question the bastard had deserved to die. He'd cheated and killed his way across Europe, before fleeing to North America. But why send her? She had no magic.

She shook away the pointless speculation. There were far more important details to worry about now. She'd need to debrief, which could be handled with a phone call, and then arrange flights to Portugal, where her next assignment already waited.

Antônio Silveira, Vampire Lord of Portugal. Deadly and dangerous, but then all the powerful vampires were. No, what made Lord Antônio worthy of her attention were the black rages that consumed him in battle, or for that matter, any confrontation that threatened his life, or the life of his people. One such confrontation had taken the life of the wrong man. Or at least the *son* of the wrong father. She knew both men. Knew the son wasn't worthy of his father's adoration, much less retribution. The idiot had made a game of challenging every supernatural creature he encountered, as if needing to prove something to himself, or to his daddy.

Whatever he'd planned to prove the day he'd died, however, and whatever skills he'd thought he'd possessed . . . he simply wasn't in the same league as a full-blown vampire lord. Hell, he hadn't been in the same *universe,* much less the same league. He'd tempted death, and it had found him woefully inadequate.

Although Lord Antônio had left plenty of dead humans in his wake over the centuries, he didn't deserve to die for killing that particular asshole . . . who, after all, had been trying to kill *him*. But that decision was well above her pay grade. She had her assignment, and she'd carry it out. Because she was good at it. And because if she didn't, the Society would send someone after *her* next.

Sighing, she dropped the champagne bottle to the ground, then slipped away in the night. Time to fly.

To be continued . . .

Acknowledgements

Well, Brenda Chin, we did it again. We're such a good team, maybe we should work on books together. Oh wait, we already do . . . and it's great. Thank you for all the hard work and creativity you bring to the books. They're so much better for having you on our side.

I also want to thank Debra Dixon, who somehow maintained the business of publishing, while dealing with the terrible personal losses of this past year. And to all the others at BelleBooks/ImaJinn who put so much effort into making all of this work.

Love and thanks to fellow writer Angela Addams for being a voice in the darkness telling me it will all work out. And to Julie Fine, who took time from her already busy life to give Nicodemus's story a read and catch all those words that my flying fingers skipped over. Love also to Eva Kildmaa for the ledge. She's laughing now, because she knows what that means.

And as always, love to my family who keep me strong and moving forward.

xoxo

—*DBR*

About the Author

D. B. REYNOLDS arrived in sunny Southern California at an early age, having made the trek across the country from the Midwest in a station wagon with her parents, her many siblings and the family dog. And while she has many (okay, some) fond memories of Midwestern farm life, she quickly discovered that L.A. was her kind of town and grew up happily sunning on the beaches of the South Bay.

D. B. holds graduate degrees in international relations and history from UCLA (go Bruins!) and was headed for a career in academia, but in a moment of clarity she left behind the politics of the hallowed halls for the better paying politics of Hollywood, where she worked as a sound editor for several years, receiving two Emmy nominations, an MPSE Golden Reel and multiple MPSE nominations for her work in television sound.

Book One of her Vampires in America series, RAPHAEL, launched her career as a writer in 2009, while JABRIL, Vampires in America Book Two, was awarded the RT Reviewers Choice Award for Best Paranormal Romance (Small Press) in 2010. ADEN, Vampires in America Book Seven, was her first release under the new ImaJinn imprint at Belle Books, Inc.

D. B. currently lives in a flammable canyon near the Malibu coast. When she's not writing her own books, she can usually be found reading someone else's. You can visit D. B. at her website www.dbreynolds.com for information on her latest books, contests and giveaways.

CPSIA information can be obtained
at www.ICGtesting.com
Printed in the USA
BVHW082319080621
609009BV00001B/53